HE KNEW THIS WAS A MISTAKE...

She ran her hands up his chest. "I don't want to like you."

"Don't blame you." Her hands created too much warmth. Man, he wanted to be warm. Step back. He really needed to *step back.*

She leaned up and nibbled beneath his chin.

Desire cut through him with a painful sharpness. "We can't," he rasped.

"I know," she whispered, pressing her full breasts against his chest. "Kiss me, just once."

He couldn't say no. So he lowered his mouth, taking hers. Sweetness. So soft and sweet. She made a sound, one he'd never forget, in the back of her throat. Then she kissed him back.

At that point, he was lost.

Completely.

STORM GATHERING

SCORPIUS SYNDROME BOOK 4

REBECCA ZANETTI

COPYRIGHT © 2017 BY REBECCA ZANETTI

* * *

To contact author:

Website: www.RebeccaZanetti.com

Facebook: www.facebook.com/RebeccaZanetti.books

Newsletter: http://rebeccazanetti.com/rebeccas-newsletter/

Twitter: @RebeccaZanetti

Instagram: RebeccaZanetti

DEDICATION

This one's for every girl who daydreamed in geometry class and wondered...what if?

CHAPTER ONE

We're following protocol and keeping written records of life after Scorpius. It's lonely here in the desert, and I fear the world out there is scarier than I can imagine. I hope I stay here indefinitely.
—Maureen Shadow, Notes

ONE MONTH ago
ZAL Labs in the Arizona desert

HE WAS the most striking man Maureen Shadow had ever seen in real life. Defiant black hair to his shoulders, tall and broad, gray and green and even blue in his eyes. Different colors, and all intense.

Danger shrouded him...along with intent.

And he stood between her and the softly closing door of her lab. She didn't speak. Didn't have to. He couldn't be there for a good reason.

"Maureen Shadow?" he asked. Dark and deep...his voice was almost raspy.

Her chin lifted. "No." The meager security for the small part of the facility still working had obviously been blown. Quietly and with absolutely no warning. Not a shot fired. Who was this guy?

He slowly, deliberately, reached into his back pocket and brought out a faded and very wrinkled piece of paper while holding her gaze. The paper crinkled and partly tore when he unfolded it. Without even looking at it, he lifted it up to show a picture of her next to her title from the website of ZAL Labs, where she still worked. "You."

She blinked. Her nerves flashed warnings, but where could she go?

His gaze traveled over her, top to bottom and back up again.

She barely kept from shifting under his perusal. Her jeans had a hole in them, her black sweater had seen better days, and even her white lab coat was threadbare. Life had gone to hell after the Scorpius bacteria had attacked the world nearly five months ago. Though the lab wasn't so bad. "Who are you?" she asked, trying to sound normal and not scared to death.

He finally looked away, his gaze taking in the square room with its solid table in the middle. Lab equipment, some that still worked, lined every counter, while papers covered the table. His scrutiny settled on the wall of refrigerators that held different plant specimens. "That's a hell of a generator you've got there. The rest of the world has gone dark."

She swallowed. Nearly ninety-nine percent of the US population was dead from the Scorpius bacterium. "We're almost out of gas for the generators, and I need to finish my work before that happens." She glanced at the microscopes lining the counter. "We only have about three months of water and food before our stores are depleted." If he'd already checked out the place, he'd know that. "I can't stop you from taking our resources."

"I don't want your food or water."

Her lungs seized. "There's nothing for you here, then."

"You couldn't be more wrong." His gaze was back to her.

A shiver wandered down her back. She craned her neck to listen, but the corridor was silent. Twenty people still worked at ZAL, several brought in from other parts of the country after the world had died. "Who are you?" she whispered again.

"Greyson Storm." He said the name almost absently, glancing at the fridge again. "Are you working on a cure for Scorpius?"

"No. I'm a biotechnical engineer," she said.

"I read that in your bio," he murmured. "Say more."

Commanding, wasn't he? Was help coming or not? Why the hell did he break into her lab? "I have degrees in horticulture, genetics, and plant molecular biology."

He cocked his head to the side. "So you splice and dice plants. Create super crops."

It had been necessary to feed billions...before they'd all died. "Among other things. As you can see, if you're looking for a scientist to cure Scorpius, you've come to the wrong girl." Time was running out, and she had a job to accomplish. "So go away."

He smiled then. Most men, when they smiled, softened. Even a little. Not this man. A promise of danger with an edge lived in his grin. "No."

She'd back up, but there was nowhere to go. "Destroying my lab won't help anything."

"Don't want to destroy your lab. Why the hell are you still working on super crops? We no longer need to feed billions."

She shook her head. "I'm not creating super crops. I'm trying to save the resources we have left."

No expression showed on his face. He obviously didn't care about crops. The way he stood. Just like her brother—another soldier. This guy had definitely been military. He focused entirely on her. "Are you or your lab in touch with the president?"

"Not anymore." At his raised eyebrow, she continued. "President Atherton's last check-in with us was over a month ago. Haven't heard from him since, but we kept working per his directive." Was the president even alive? Was there anything close to a working government? Cell phones were down and useless.

Greyson nodded. "That's what I thought."

She swallowed. "Why did you think that?"

"I've been watching you for three weeks." He gestured around. "In your nice and safe lab in the middle of the Arizona desert. Just waiting for Atherton to send a missionary."

Why would this guy want the president? At least in her desolate part of Arizona—the perfect place for the lab and what it contained. She finally took that step back, her heart pattering wildly. "Why have you been watching us?"

"You," he corrected softly. Very softly. "Just you, Maureen."

She stopped breathing. All right, then. The picture. He had her picture and had been carrying it for some time. Oh God. She'd have to fight him, and he was so damn big. "You survived Scorpius."

"Yeah. You?" His eyes were grayer now in the florescent lights of the lab.

She nodded.

"Did you get enough vitamin B when it happened?" he asked.

"Yes," she whispered. For some reason, the vitamin Bs softened the effects of the bacterial infection—a little. The bacteria attacked the brain, leaving survivors...different. Some turned stronger, some smarter, and some sociopathic. Which in itself didn't always have to be bad. "Did you?" she asked.

"I did."

Yet here he was stalking her. Some sociopaths turned into serial killers—either the wild, crazy kind or the brilliant, strategic kind like Ted Bundy. Greyson Storm had been stalking her, watching her, and had now made a move. "Do you want to put my head in your cooler?" she asked, searching for a weapon. Any weapon.

His eyebrow arched again. "No."

He didn't laugh. So, no humor. She shuffled her feet, trying to remember the self-defense moves her brother had taught her so long ago. Anger started to boil through her blood to mingle with the fear. Was this guy here to kill her or not? "Greyson, this is getting tedious. What do you want?"

He crossed his arms and leaned back against the door in a not-so-subtle reminder that she was trapped. "When was the last time you talked to your brother?"

Her stomach cramped. Oh God. She took a step toward Greyson. "Is it Raze? Did something happen to him?" Panic pricked along her arms.

"No. He's fine. On his way here, actually. Scouts tell me he should arrive in a day or so."

"Oh." She started to relax. Wait a minute. A fellow soldier aligned with Raze wouldn't have watched her—stalked her—for weeks before checking in. "I haven't talked to Raze in seven months. Don't even know if he survived the bacterium."

Greyson's eyes darkened to a greenish gray with barely a hint of blue. "You...are a terrible liar." His upper lip twitched in what had to be amusement. "Just horrible."

So she'd heard. She lifted her chin. "I'm not lying."

"Yeah. That's fine. We're leaving now. Is there anything you need to bring with us?" he asked as if discussing breakfast recipes.

She had a ballpoint pen in her pocket, and she casually inserted her hand. Hadn't she seen a movie once where the heroine stabbed the bad guy in the jugular with a pen? She shoved the cheap cap off. "Where do you want to go?" Was the guy nuts?

"Have you heard of the Mercenaries?" he asked.

Her fingers trembled as she tightened her hold. The Mercs were a band of vigilantes who had taken over the Santa Barbara area by force, death, and blood. "Yes."

"I'm their leader."

A metallic taste filled her mouth. Fear. Adrenaline and dread.

If that were true, he was one of the most dangerous killers left on Earth. If not, he was a delusional psychopath. Either way, she couldn't go anywhere with him. "You're the leader of the Mercs?"

"Yep."

She shook her head. "Why would the leader of the Mercs, if that's what you really are, want me?"

His gaze traveled her again, burning this time. "It's not you I want." His eyes flared. "Not for that reason, anyway. You're much prettier than your picture."

She swayed. "No."

He lifted a hand. "I won't hurt you, and I won't let anybody else hurt you, either. You have my vow."

The vow of a nutjob who led the Mercs. Yeah. That was just great. "I don't understand."

"I know. Here's the deal. Your brother has been working for the government, what's left of it, for a while. Taking out killers, basically. He's in touch or has been in touch with President Atherton, who I can't find right now."

"Why do you want the president?" None of this made sense.

"He has something I want," Greyson said. "Somebody I want to find." His eyes cleared. "Vivienne Wellington. Any chance you know her?"

"No," Maureen whispered. She'd never heard of the woman. "She's your, ah, your..."

"No. She's not mine. But she can get me something I want, and I have to find her. Your brother can locate the president and Vivienne." Greyson motioned her toward him. "We have to go now."

"No." She held firm. If Raze didn't want to be found, he wouldn't be. Made sense Greyson had sought her out instead. "We haven't heard from the president, so it's possible Raze has no clue where he is." In fact, she hadn't heard from her brother in over a month, so he was on mission somewhere. But she had to believe he was safe.

"Then Raze will have to find them. He was the best hunter in the military, and he'll do it." Greyson took a step toward her. "With the right motivation."

Fire lanced through her. "I won't be used to blackmail my brother." Plus, her work was too important. Life or death, really.

"Extort. You will be used to extort what I want. Not blackmail." Greyson moved then, reaching her in several long strides. "I don't want to hurt you, and I'd much prefer if you came along willingly."

She tightened her hold on the pen. "And if I don't?"

He lowered his head closer to hers. "Then you'll come unwillingly."

Her throat clogged. "Did you kill the guards? The other scientists?"

"No. I haven't killed anybody." He lifted back up. "Today, anyway."

Taking a deep breath, she moved and struck with the pen.

He easily, almost casually, grabbed her wrist and stopped her movements cold. Keeping her gaze, he slowly took the pen away and tossed it over his shoulder. "A pen?"

"It's all I had," she whispered, feeling like a rabbit caught in a snare. His hold around her wrist was warm and firm —unbreakable.

"Huh." He jerked her forward.

She stumbled but ended up against him. The guy was built like solid rock.

Heat rolled off him along with the scent of salt and man. "We should probably get a couple of things straight," he murmured.

The spit dried up in her mouth. This close, she could see the triad of colors that made up his odd eyes. She couldn't speak, so she didn't try.

"You're coming with me, your brother will do as I say, and so will you. Don't cross me, blue eyes."

"I can't go into Merc territory," she finally managed to push out.

"You can and you will," he countered, his breath minty on her face.

Everybody knew that there weren't women in Merc territory. God. What would happen to her?

His chin lifted. "You won't be harmed. Ever. Trust me." With that, Greyson Storm, the most handsome and dangerous and quite possibly craziest man she'd ever met, tossed her over his shoulder and too quickly kidnapped her from her very nice and safe lab.

CHAPTER TWO

I'm continuing my hunt to avenge Ferris's death. If you were still alive, you wouldn't be happy with me.
—Greyson Storm, Letters to Miss Julian

GREYSON EYED the sandy landscape while driving bumpily over roads already gone to shit. His second in command, Damon Winter, took point on the passenger side, his gun resting casually on his thigh. A very pissed off Maureen Shadow stewed in the backseat of the two-door jeep, sending him glares every few minutes.

She had pretty eyes. Light blue, nearly translucent. With her curly black hair and stubborn chin, she was everything bright in a crappily dark world.

And she hated his guts.

Couldn't blame her. He'd taken her from a fairly safe location in the middle of nowhere and was forcing her into danger.

He'd meant what he said. Nothing would harm her on his watch.

By her white knuckles from her clasped hands in her lap, she might not believe him. He cleared his throat, watching her in the cracked rearview mirror. "I won't let anybody hurt you, Moe."

The nickname came naturally to him, so he didn't question it.

She glared harder, if that were possible.

Damon stiffened next to him. "Incoming."

They had a truck in the lead, another behind them, with the jeep secured between the two because of the woman. Grey hated being in the middle, but after one minute with Maureen, he had decided to drive the vehicle containing her.

"Use the binoculars," Grey ordered.

Damon reached into the jockey box and took out a pair of Army-issued binoculars they'd found on a base months ago. "One truck, speeding at us, two guys with shotguns in the back. Standing," Damon said. "They're not here for a tea party."

"Shit." Grey scrutinized the sand dunes on either side. There was no cover. He looked at Maureen. "Have you had any trouble out at the lab?"

"No," she whispered, the color leaving her face. "It's too far out for anybody to know about."

Yeah. That's what he'd thought. It had taken him over a month to track her down, and it hadn't been easy. When he'd decided to make a move on Moe, he'd sent Damon back with the jeep to bring enforcements. Somebody had seen them. "Somebody caught wind of the two trucks coming in today."

"Affirmative," Damon said, no inflection in his deep voice.

It hadn't been Damon, but he didn't bother defending himself. The guy had been LAPD and probably saw more shit before Scorpius than afterward. After four months of fighting together, Grey trusted him as much as any soldier he'd ever fought with. "Ideas?"

"Only one thing to do," Damon said.

Yeah. Fuck. He'd only had the woman in his possession for thirty minutes, and he was about to get her into a firefight. Grey brought the walkie-talkie to his face. "All stop. Trucks cover, jeep in back. If they engage, no prisoners."

The four men in the trucks were well trained, and he trusted them as much as anybody these days.

The truck in front of him swerved and blocked the road sideways. Grey jerked the wheel of the jeep and drove off the road, waiting until the second vehicle passed him before pointing the SUV in the opposite direction. He stopped the engine. "Maureen, what kind of protection do you have back at the lab? Anything we didn't see because of the surprise infiltration?"

She didn't bother to answer him.

Damon jumped from the vehicle and started yelling orders for the four other men to take cover and get ready to shoot.

Grey turned and reached for Maureen.

She fought him, struggling, punching out.

The woman had a decent uppercut. She nailed him, and his jaw snapped shut. "Damn it." Manacling her arms, he dragged her over the center console and out of the jeep, all but carrying her around to the front, which faced back the way they'd come. Nothing but sand and dunes met his eyes. He set her on the ground. "Get low and keep your head down."

She bunched to run, her eyes wild.

He grasped her chin, forcing her to meet his gaze. Her skin was incredibly soft. "If you run, they'll shoot you." The woman sucked in air, her chest heaving. He waited several precious moments and tightened his hold until she finally focused and gave a short nod. Good. "Stay behind the jeep, and you'll be covered." Yanking his Glock from the back of his jeans, he strode over to Damon, who was partially ducked down behind one of the trucks. "Status?"

Damon jerked his head toward the oncoming vehicle, which had stopped to face them about fifty yards down the quiet road. Two guys with shotguns leaned the weapons on the top of the cab, pointed at Greyson's group. "They're thinking," Damon muttered.

Grey nodded. They'd need to get closer to shoot. Probably hadn't thought they would meet resistance quite yet.

"Should we go to them?" A guy named Schmidt asked from the far right, his gun pointed around the side of a truck.

Greyson would love a good fight, and he wanted those shotguns, but Moe had to be protected. He'd promised. "No. If they retreat, let them." Might just be decent people wondering if his trucks had been going somewhere safe with food. Like anywhere was safe...or had enough food. "They choose their destinies." Today, anyway.

Damon shrugged. "They see the trucks and the guns. It'd be suicide for them to attack with only a couple of shotguns." He began to lift the binoculars again. "Though they may be desperate enough to do it."

Grey didn't want to have to kill anybody in front of Maureen. Why, he'd figure out later. Only part of his former job as a sniper had been shooting people. Another part was shooting targets to *influence* people. "Hold tight." He slipped his Glock back into place, unzipped the plastic window of the jeep, and lifted out his rifle.

Damon whistled. "That's a pretty one. Thought you Marine Scout Snipers only used the M40."

The rifle had been about to be retired when all hell had broken loose. Not that he didn't have one back at headquarters. "A month ago when you were scouting up north, we raided a couple of houses near LA that had a lot of guns." Grey brought out the Mk.21, holding the sniper rifle with care.

Damon lifted the binoculars and peered through. "Two guys inside the truck. Can't make out faces or weapons." He glanced over. "You going to shoot them?"

"No." Grey moved toward the nearest truck and set the weapon down, crouching to see through the scope. Holding the rifle, a sudden pang hit his gut. God, he missed Ferris. The guy was the best spotter in the world. At the reminder, Greyson settled himself, taking precious moments to calculate distance, light, range, wind speed, and direction. Hell, there wasn't wind. But there was always gravity. He focused and squeezed the trigger, purposefully hitting just to the right of the enemy truck. Sand flew up in every direction, partially covering the front window.

"You missed," Damon said mildly from behind him.

"Nope." Grey straightened and quickly reloaded just in case. "Don't want to leave them helpless in the desert." But hopefully he'd made his point.

Movement showed in the truck, and the two guys in back ducked down.

"They're leaving?" Damon asked. "That was easy."

"What the hell is going on?" Maureen asked, sounding way too close.

Grey looked over his shoulder to see her coming his way, crouching down. "Go back—"

"Shit," Damon muttered.

Grey swiveled back to target. Suddenly, one man stood up in the back of the truck, a grenade launcher over his shoulder.

"Shit. Retreat!" Greyson yelled.

The guy fired.

Grey squeezed the trigger a second later, taking the guy out. The truck to Greyson's right exploded, flipping over in a flash of fire. Heat smashed into him, and only training kept him from ducking. Somebody shrieked in pain and then fell silent. Fuck. He reloaded, hitting the other standing guy center mass. The guy flew back and out of sight.

Damon ran over and dragged Schmidt away from the burning tires, patting out flames along his torso.

The enemy truck started again, and the driver punched the gas, driving straight for them.

Grey settled and shot the driver between the eyes. The guy slumped forward, and the truck slowed. Without missing a step, Grey reloaded and then squeezed the trigger. The passenger died in a second.

Four dead.

The truck finally rolled to a stop.

Greyson stood and turned. Damon stood over a partially burned body. "Status?"

Damon wiped a hand across his sweaty forehead, his deep brown eyes sober. "Two of ours dead." He jerked his head toward the mangled body of another soldier, still burning by the ruined truck. The stench of burned flesh and tires clogged the air.

The soldiers from the right moved Grey's way, their gaze on the fallen guy on the ground.

Pain cut into Grey's gut. He'd lost two. Good soldiers, and men he'd trusted. Failure settled heavily on his shoulders, but he let nothing show. *Never let anything show.* Yeah. He'd learned that lesson multiple times in his life.

Maureen leaned against the back of the jeep, her face whiter than paper and her eyes open wide. In the hazy day, they were a stunning aquamarine.

Grey shoved all emotion away. "Get the guns, rocket launcher, and anything else of value from the other truck. Put our dead in the back of our remaining one, and we'll bury them at base."

Damon started moving around the still burning truck. "The gas tank already exploded," he muttered, not hitching his stride. The other two soldiers went for blankets for the bodies.

Greyson headed for Maureen. She shrank from him, and he slowed his pace. "You okay?" he asked quietly.

She blinked, her pupils expanded.

Keeping his voice firm and low, he gently grasped her arm and pulled her to stand fully upright. "You're in shock, but you're safe. I told you nothing would happen to you, and it won't."

She focused on him, realization filtering into her eyes. "Unless my brother doesn't do what you say."

He straightened.

She pressed forward, color finally filling her face. "What if he doesn't, Greyson? You going to shoot me like you did those men?" Her hair tumbled around her shoulders as she shook with her anger. Or was that terror? "You going to take me out?"

Loss, fury, and desperation ripped through him with claws. It was his fault there were now six dead men nearby. Even the ones who didn't belong to him could've been saved somehow. He stepped into her. "Not for one fucking second do I need a bullet to take care of you." Grasping her elbows, he lifted her right off the ground. The woman weighed less than the chocolate Lab he'd had years ago.

She kicked out, nailing him right below the knee.

The instant pain calmed him, somehow reassuring. She was okay and no longer cowering. Good. Yet he'd sworn at her. Miss Julian would be so pissed at him.

Yet Southern manners were a luxury that no longer existed. Keeping Maureen aloft, he studied her.

She glared right back, her expression projecting her intent.

"Don't kick me again," he said softly, letting the threat show in his eyes.

She paused, thoughts scattering across her face.

On some level, one she'd probably never admit, she must feel somewhat safe with him. If she didn't, she wouldn't be glaring and seriously considering kicking him again. He cocked his head to the side. Why? He'd kidnapped her, and he'd just taken out four men. Yet her internal struggle was real.

He saw the second she decided that spirit was more important than survival and decided to kick again. Going on instinct, he tossed her up, released her arms, and manacled her hips, stepping right into her.

She gasped, pinned to the jeep, her thighs on either side of his hips. "What the—"

"I said not to kick me." The position caused him more pain than it did her, unfortunately. With her thighs spread and her core so close, his dick perked right up. Damn it. He swallowed, keeping his hold firm but not bruising. This close, he could smell her. Woman and...bluebells. The wild kind. "We're having a problem right now, sweetheart."

She swallowed, the fine line of her delicate throat moving. "Let go."

"I'd like to," he lied. "But you keep pushing. Just how far do you intend to take this?"

CHAPTER THREE

All scientists need to keep unemotional records for later study. What a load of crap.
  —Maureen Shadow, Notes

MAUREEN COULDN'T BREATHE. There was just too much happening. Smoke rolled from the fallen truck as fire roared through the interior and smelled like burned rubber. Heat poured off the man holding her against the jeep as if she weighed nothing. Her legs were spread, nearly around him, and warmth filtered into her face. She averted her eyes from the guys lifting bodies into the one remaining truck. "Let me go."

"No," Greyson said softly. How come the softer his voice became, the deadlier he sounded?

She lifted her chin. No matter what happened, she'd never cower. Never. Her heart hammered, and not all of it was from fear. There was just something about him. Even after she'd kicked him as hard as she could, he hadn't lost his temper. Not an inch of him seemed angry. It was as if holding her aloft had just been the most expedient way to keep from being kicked again. Who was he? "Release me," she whispered.

Damon strode toward them with shotguns and some big, black rocket thing over his shoulder, the sun glinting off his sunglasses. He wasn't quite as tall as Greyson, but was wide across the chest and muscled.

She couldn't take both of them down, even if the other two soldiers weren't around.

Damon approached, black eyebrow visibly lifting over the glasses. "This is weird."

If Maureen thought Greyson would get embarrassed or put her down as his buddy approached, she was definitely mistaken.

"We're having a difference of opinion," Grey said quietly, holding her in place, her legs all but wrapped around his waist.

Temper and an uneasy awareness filtered through her. He held her so easily, his strength impressive. She shoved both hands against his chest and pushed as hard as she could.

Nothing happened.

It was a long shot, but maybe Damon could help her. The guy looked like some sort of hero, and he moved with grace. He also seemed to be sticking close as if he wasn't quite sure what to do. "Damon? I don't know you, but this is improper. Could you help me?" She kept Greyson's gaze as she asked.

A flash of humor lit Greyson's intriguing eyes.

Damon shuffled his feet. "Well, now." He shoved his glasses up on his head, showing soft brown eyes barely a shade darker than his skin. With his angled jaw, he looked a little bit like a movie star. Well, what used to be a movie star. Now, everybody was a soldier. "When a lady asks for help, I do like to oblige."

Triumph filled her.

"But," Damon said, "Greyson saved my life, and I don't see you as actually being in danger. What'd she do?"

"Kicked me," Greyson said easily.

"Ah," Damon said. "Well, I guess that's one way to keep from being kicked." He cleared his throat. "Do you guys mind moving this around the jeep a little? I'd like to put this stuff in the back."

"No problem." His hands flexing, Grey easily pivoted and walked around the SUV, pressing her against the plastic door of the driver's side when he got there.

Were these guys joking? Having fun? "I'm about to punch you in the nose," she told him primly.

"Darlin', you never tell somebody before you punch them in the nose," he said, his voice lowering.

She knew that. Everybody knew that.

"So I'm thinking you're not really going to hit me," he said. "Which tells me a couple of things."

Just who was this guy?

He continued. "You're scared, but you're trying real hard to hide it. I get that. You're proud and stubborn, and you want me to know it. I get that, too. Hell, I admire it."

She blinked. All right.

"But here's the rub. I'm telling you a couple of things, too." Pressing her to the jeep, one of his hands released her hip to clasp her nape. His hand was wide enough to hold her whole neck with room to spare.

She couldn't move. Her lungs seized. "What's that?" she asked, shocked as hell when her voice didn't tremble.

He breathed out, his chest way too close to hers. "You can't win, baby."

Her temper rose, and her eyes widened. "Listen—"

"No. You listen." He waited until she snapped her mouth shut before continuing. "You're coming with us. You can't control that."

She kept silent because there wasn't much to argue with.

"You're staying with me until I let you go, and you can't control that."

Her nostrils flared, but she kept silent.

He gave a short nod, his fingers caressing her nape. "What you can control, what you're gonna want really badly to control, is the way you behave once you're in my territory."

The absolute conviction in his tone was terrifying.

Her instant fear moved right into frustration. "Are you threatening me?" she asked, her teeth grinding in the back.

"Yes."

Her hands were still against the thin material covering his chest. Beneath the meager black shirt, his torso was ripped and predatory. Strong. She could curl her nails in and scratch him, but as a defense went, it sucked.

Damon poked his head around the front of the jeep. "I'm sending the remaining truck on before us. You guys, ah, about ready?"

"In a second," Greyson said quietly. "Get in the jeep."

"Sure thing," Damon said cheerfully, disappearing around the front again. There was something watchful about the guy. Something that gave her hope.

She focused on Greyson. "I don't think he'd let you hurt me."

The sun moved behind Grey, casting his rugged face into shadow. "He's ex-LAPD, and you're right about him," he said softly. "But here's the thing." His fingers stopped moving on her neck.

Adrenaline flooded her. "What?"

"I wouldn't let me hurt you, either."

What the hell? "So, we're at a stalemate." This was so damn confusing.

"Not really. The point I'm trying to make—that I'm not making very well—is that your idea of hurt and my idea of hurt might be two vastly different things."

The spit in her mouth dried up. Completely. Panic engulfed her, and she started to struggle. Arms, legs, elbows...she used them all.

He held her, patiently waiting her out.

Frustration shot heated tears to her eyes, and she blinked them back. She punched her fists into his chest, and her knuckles instantly protested. He didn't so much as blink. After a couple of minutes, she halted, her chest heaving. "You are such a dick."

"Yep." He hadn't moved an inch. Was he even breathing? Barely. He was just way stronger than she was.

She subsided. Physically fighting him was a waste of energy. But she had a brain. "I'll survive anything you do to me."

"I know," he said, his expression unreadable.

She couldn't help but punch his chest one more time. "The Mercs are killers."

"We truly are," he agreed.

"No women are Mercs." Her voice cracked.

He paused. "No. All of my soldiers are men. But some do keep women."

Her stomach revolted.

"Willing. All of them are willing." He leaned in then, his nose nearly touching hers. "I don't condone rape or anybody harming women. Forget anything you've heard about the Mercs. We're assholes and killers, but we don't abuse women or kids. Ever." His voice remained sure and steady.

Was he telling the truth?

"I don't want to go with you," she said, her mouth working independently of her brain.

"I know." No give. Just pure, implacable soldier. "I'm sorry."

She shook her head, her nape brushing his strong fingers. Tingles cascaded down her spine. "Then leave me here. I have important work to do, Greyson."

He was silent for several beats. "No. But if your brother does as I ask, I'll bring you safely back here."

She struggled briefly. "You don't understand. Several crops were damaged when Scorpius ruined the world."

He leaned back. "Scorpius infected plants? Crops?"

"No. Research facilities went under, and protocols were lost. Harmful agents have escaped labs." That's all she knew. But it was bad.

"You think? Or you know?"

She paused. "I, ah, know. I definitely know."

"Man, you're a crappy liar. Just terrible." He shook his head. "So you don't know for sure. Either way, sweetheart. You're coming with me."

"Or you'll hurt me because we have a different definition for the word 'hurt,'" she murmured.

He sighed. "I can make life easy for you with great food, nice digs, and a whole lot of space. Or I can make it difficult. It's totally up to you." With that, he somehow swung her around, cradling her, and opened the door to deposit her in the backseat.

"About time," Damon grumbled, wiping sweat off his dark forehead.

"Had a few things to get straight," Greyson returned, his gaze meeting hers in the rearview mirror. "Right, Maureen Shadow?"

Irritation bordering on fear remained, and she couldn't find it within herself to see a way out of the situation. So she crossed her arms and gave him a harsh look, her chin firming, and her back teeth grinding together once more.

He sighed. "Or, maybe not. But we will. That I promise you."

She couldn't meet his gaze any longer, so she turned to stare out the plastic-covered window. Sand spread out in every direction for miles. Within an hour, the sun turned to cloudy sky. By the time they reached the interstate, the sky had turned dark.

"We're having an unusually strong rainy season in California," Grey said congenially as Damon continued to watch out his window.

Maureen didn't even turn her head toward him. She couldn't stop him from kidnapping her, but she didn't have to be nice about it.

Soon hollowed-out vehicles began to dot the area on either side of the road.

She shivered. It had been months since she'd ventured out into the very unsafe world. Instead, she'd worked around the clock to fix what had been broken. Then the lab had lost touch, and the information had stopped coming in. So she'd worked harder. In fact, it had been about twenty-four hours since she'd slept. Her eyes grew gritty.

"Are you hungry?" Greyson asked. "Moe?"

She ignored him and tried to keep her eyes open.

He may have muttered something about stubbornness.

The jeep drove on, the interior warm, the engine a quiet purr. Against her will, her eyelids closed. Just for a moment. Then she'd figure out a way to freedom.

Her dreams were peaceful and full of nothing. For once.

Hours later, it had to be, she awoke with a start. Surrounded by darkness and the feeling of man. She jerked and opened her mouth to instinctively scream.

"You're safe." The voice was low. Commanding. Strong. As were the arms around her and the chest she rested against.

She opened her eyes and looked up to see Greyson's stubborn chin. He easily carried her through what appeared to be a luxurious living area in some type of villa lit by candles. Maybe a lodge. Panic clutched her, and she started to struggle.

"Stop it," he barked.

She instinctively stilled. The last thing she wanted was to be dropped on her butt. "Where, ah, where am I?" she asked.

"Santa Barbara. Merc Headquarters." He walked down a spacious hallway and nudged open a door at the far end. Candles had been lit and placed in strategic areas, softly illuminating a large bedroom complete with a king-size bed in the middle. The sliding door was open, leading out to what appeared to be a dark deck. A sliver of moonlight glinted off the rolling ocean beyond. The smell of salt and brine wafted in.

He set her on the bed and backed away.

Her nails curled into the lush bedspread. Pretty landscapes covered the wall. "I slept all the way to Santa Barbara?" She shoved her curly hair away from her face. How in the hell had she actually fallen asleep?

"Yeah." He leaned back against the door and crossed his arms. "You talk in your sleep."

She blinked. "I do not."

He lifted a shoulder. "Okay."

The door was wide open to the beach. She tried really hard not to look at it.

His lips twitched. In the soft lighting, his face was all dark shadows and hard planes. Those odd eyes seemed to glow through the dusk. "I'd very much like to allow you some freedom here, Maureen."

She lifted her chin, feeling vulnerable on the big bed. The word 'allow' didn't sit well with her, but she couldn't much argue that he was in charge. Of the entire territory apparently. "So?"

"So?" Lines fanned out from his eyes. When was the last time he'd slept? "I can't watch you every minute. This here is a learn by experience situation."

She blew out air. "I'm about as literal as possible, and I'm totally not understanding you." He seemed to be trying to tell her something, and she just wasn't getting it. "Would you please stop speaking in riddles?"

His eyes darkened. "Sure. Do what I tell you to do, behave yourself, and you'll enjoy your time here. Disobey me, and you'll regret it. Profoundly."

Every once in a while, beneath the hard tone and rough words, there was a hint of something cultured with him. "Where did you go to school?" she asked, surprising herself.

His eyebrow lifted. "Do you understand me?"

"Not really." She glanced toward the open doors, unable to help herself this time.

"In this lodge at all times, you're safe. Before dark, you're safe on the deck. Men I know and trust well are guarding this house. If you leave, I can't guarantee your safety." He looked out at the turning ocean. "If you run, and I catch you, I'll make sure you won't think of running again." His voice went low and gritty with the words.

She shivered from the threat. Even so, she wasn't sure what he meant. Would he beat her up? Starve her? Torture her? Something in her, something deep down, didn't think he'd do any of those things. Yeah, he reminded her of her brother. Kind of. But maybe he wasn't anything like Raze. Maybe he *would* do those things.

"I guess if I escape, I should make sure you don't catch me," she said softly.

For a moment, he didn't react. When he did, he took her by surprise. He looked back at her. A slow and intriguing smile curved his lips, but his relaxed body didn't move. "This is gonna be interesting."

CHAPTER FOUR

You'd be really pissed at me these days. Shouldn't have died at eighty years old. I miss you.

　　—Greyson Storm, Letters to Miss Julian

A WEEK after Grey had kidnapped Maureen Shadow, he sat in his home office and read over the reams of paper he had gathered from one of the nearest greenhouses. A lot of formulas and crap filled his gaze, so he looked away and out the window at the rolling Pacific Ocean. Thunder bellowed above, and the wind forced bruised-looking clouds across the already depressing sky, nearly hiding the fact that it was around noon.

Damon turned the corner, a sandwich in his hand. "This is the damnedest spring."

Grey sighed. "The rain is good, and we can't forget it. At some point..."

"We could be out of water." Damon nodded, shoving the rest of the food into his mouth and chewing slowly.

Grey rolled tense neck muscles. "Did the latest scouts check in?"

"Yep. Nobody has seen or heard of Zach Barter at any of the encampments. I'm thinking the guy is dead."

Maybe. But until Greyson had confirmation, he wouldn't stop hunting. Zach Barter was a blight on humanity. A former scientist, he'd purposefully spread the pandemic while killing indiscriminately. Grey had made a promise to hunt him down, and he would. "Barter isn't dead."

Damon sighed. "Maybe. We'll find out, either way. Somehow."

"Did you get our guest to eat?" The little horticulturist, or whatever she was, wouldn't leave his thoughts. She'd been in Grey's territory for a week, and he'd treated her like he would any trapped guest. But she had made an escape attempt the day before, even knocking out two of his guys before he'd caught her. Now she'd apparently stopped eating.

"No," Damon said, his dark gaze narrowing. "She's a stubborn one."

Damn it. Grey had enough to worry about. He stood and crossed around the heavy oak desk. The former proprietors of the mansion had liked oak, teak, and glass. Pictures of famous golf courses adorned the walls. He moved into the hallway just as the front door opened.

"Grey?" Mason Peterson, one of his top soldiers, poked his head in. "The enemy has breached the gate." The former dentist grinned perfectly white teeth.

Grey paused. "Shadow is here?"

"Yep. And I don't know the guy, but I'd have to say he's *pissed*," Mason said.

Grey shoved the papers into Damon's hand. It was about damn time. "Give Maureen these and tell her to eat if she wants to get any more data to read about the greenhouses." Without waiting for a response, Grey grabbed a walkie-talkie, the red file, and stalked through the entryway and out the door, following Mason to the waiting motorcycles.

"We kept him at the south entrance," Mason said.

Grey nodded. When he had secured the beach area of Santa Barbara, he'd created three entry and exit points. It had taken semis, trailers, barbed wire, glass, and armed guards to secure most of the areas, but even so, the territory was too large. He should've condensed better, but he didn't want to give up any resources. He started the Harley's ignition and swung onto the road, letting the rain batter him on the way.

Finally, he reached the end of a lane heavily fortified and guarded.

Raze Shadow stood in the rain, his arms at his sides, fury crackling across his face. He looked more Native American than his sister did, except for his eyes. They glittered, deep and blue, promising death.

Greyson parked the bike and strode forward, leaving his gun at the back of his waist. There were enough weapons pointed at Raze at the moment. "Thanks for coming." His voice cut through the storm.

"Where the fuck is my sister?" Shadow asked, his voice a low rumble of rage.

Greyson kept his gaze. "She's fine. In a room by herself near the beach guarded by men I trust. Nobody has touched her, and nobody will touch her. If you do what I ask."

"Ask?" Shadow's eyebrows rose. This close, the guy looked every bit as dangerous as his reputation claimed him to be.

The rain increased in force, pinging up from the asphalt. Grey handed over the red file. It'd be a good fight if they went at it, but he needed Raze in good shape to take on the president.

Raze studied him and then took it. "What the hell is this?"

"At least two months ago, President Atherton kidnapped Vivienne Wellington from what was left of the FBI's Behavioral Science Unit and the Scorpius Protocol Infirmary." A euphemism for an Scorpius insane asylum.

"So?" Shadow asked.

"I can't find them. I have intel that you were working for the FBI until very recently," Grey said, sure of his sources.

Shadow didn't open the file. "You heard wrong."

Jesus. The guy kept his gaze on Grey but was scoping the entire area. "You were on point to hunt and take out serial killers, and I know it. So don't fuck me around."

Raze just stared.

"You have better intel than I do about Atherton's location since you were working for him. Also, I've seen your file, man. I know how well you hunt." Greyson kept his voice reasonable.

"Then you should've thought twice about this," Raze said lowly.

Yeah. Grey had known when he came up with the plan that it would end with one of them dying from the other's hand at some point. So long as it was after he fulfilled his promise, he didn't much care. "Find Atherton, retake Wellington, and bring her to me. I'll exchange her for your sister." It was that simple.

Raze's chin lowered. "You can't find your own woman?"

"She's not mine," Grey said quietly. "But I need her. I think Vanguard is also hunting Atherton, so if you need help, go to them. Infiltrate Vanguard. That's the deal."

"I'm going to fucking kill you."

Grey nodded and tossed over the walkie-talkie. "Press the red button."

Raze pressed the button. "What now?"

"Raze?" came clearly over the line. "Fucking kill that dickhead of a moron, would you?" Maureen snapped, her voice clear.

Raze didn't twitch. Not even a bit. "Moe? You okay?"

"Well, I've been kidnapped," she muttered.

Raze kept his gaze on Greyson. "How far are you from where I am?"

Greyson shook his head. "She has no clue." The woman had been sleeping when he drove her in.

"Dunno," Maureen said. "I'm fine, though. But I'd like you to gut that asshole Greyson for my birthday, if you don't mind. Spill his intestines on the pavement so I can jump around on them."

Amusement bubbled through Grey, but he hid it. She truly was something.

"You got it," Raze said evenly, tossing the walkie-talkie back. He eyed the guards on either side.

Greyson caught the device. "Bad idea. If you die, there will be nobody to save her." Turning on his heel, he made his way back to the bike. "Information about our next meeting and the drop are in the file. Don't let it get wet." He started the Harley, swung it around, and rode away, feeling the burn from Raze's glare between his shoulder blades.

Yeah. Dangerous enemy to have. That was life. His front tire skidded on a mud puddle, and he quickly corrected, reaching headquarters in record time.

Drawing in air, he moved to his room and changed his wet clothing for more faded jeans and a black T-shirt. Then he ran his fingers through his hair and made his way toward the back bedroom, where he knocked and then walked in.

Maureen stood and faced him. Her hand was down at her side at an odd angle.

Shit. Did she have a knife?

He sighed. Her hair rioted around her shoulders, so black that it contrasted intriguingly with her light blue eyes. He started talking, barely listening to her responses, his focus on the weapon. When would she make a move?

The conversation didn't interest him, but he kept it up.

Finally, after he didn't say whatever it was she wanted him to say, she stiffened even more. He got tired of waiting. "What are you planning?" he asked quietly, not wanting to hurt her but needing to make a point. If she attacked somebody, she'd better know what she was doing.

She stepped back. "Nothing."

God, she was a terrible liar. "Then I suggest you make a move with that knife in your hand. Let's see where we end up, shall we?" On the last, he lunged.

She fell back and lifted the knife.

He grabbed her hand, which was wrapped around the hilt. Then he let the point rest against his chest.

She blinked, her chest rising and falling rapidly. Her skin was soft, her knuckles small. "Let go."

"Would you really stab me?" he asked quietly, trying to see inside her head. This close, he could smell that wild bluebell scent of hers. Even after using whatever soap and shampoo they had on hand outside in the showers, her natural scent still filtered through. "Moe?"

"Yes." Her jaw firmed.

Her eyes didn't look so convinced.

"Your brother is fine and is going to cooperate." One step forward and Grey would be flush against her. His breath heated, and his body warmed. She was stunning, spitting fire at him. "So how about you do the same?" With an easy twist of his wrist, he secured the knife and then released her.

She pressed her hands against her hips, her lips pursed and looking beyond kissable. "Like I said, I don't think you'd hurt me."

He had been paying attention to the knife and not the conversation. "Baby, if you had any idea what I'd like to do with you, you'd be backing away."

Her eyes flared and heated. Not just with anger, either. There was interest there, not interest she wanted obviously, but there nonetheless. "Greyson, let me make something abundantly clear. I'd rather turn into a nun than do anything with you. A spinster. An old cat lady."

God, she was cute.

"Understood." He barely kept his lips from twitching. Oh, he could kiss her and prove her wrong. But, no. He'd kidnapped her, so that kept her safely off limits from him. From anybody in Merc territory. "If you want to limit your exposure to me, then you're gonna want to eat your food and stop trying to escape."

She frowned. "Or what?"

Man, she really wasn't scared of him. He bit back a laugh. Most people trembled at his name these days, but this little, half-his-size horticulturist had just attacked him with a knife. "Or I'll feed you myself, whether you like it or not." The intimacy of the idea was way too appealing.

She blinked. "I'd rather swallow broken glass than eat out of your hand."

He coughed. That was harsh. "Fair enough. Then behave yourself." Yeah, he liked the temper lighting her pretty face. It really was too bad they'd met by kidnapping. He'd love to explore that kind of passion. "Okay?"

"Sure." Then, completely out of the blue, she kicked up, nailing him in the jaw.

His head jerked back, and he stumbled, stars lighting his vision. Pain radiated through his skull. Shock kept him from reacting.

She punched him in the balls, and only by turning at the last second did he save his boys. She shoved him and ran behind him, heading into the hallway.

He turned, his mouth gaping. What the holy fuck?

The house was currently empty. She ran through the living room, and he set off in pursuit, keeping his strides long but easy.

At the front door, she struggled but finally threw it open.

He continued after her, into the rain, watching her run out onto the once busy street. Rain smashed down, matting her hair to her face within seconds. She turned crazily around, obviously having no idea where to run.

She gulped in and bunched to head north.

"That's the wrong way." He strode down the wide bricked driveway, keeping in control. As always.

She paused and looked at him. The rain plastered her T-shirt to her front, showing full breasts. Erect nipples.

He swallowed and forced his gaze to her face.

Two soldiers wearing the black T-shirts of Merc soldiers paused as they patrolled out of a side lawn to the south. Two more came into sight from the north.

She took in the four soldiers, and her shoulders went back instead of down. Damn, he admired her grit. "You can't get away, Moe," he said, almost gently. "Come back here."

"No." She shook her head, her thick hair spraying even more rain water.

There was nowhere to run, but she wouldn't back down. God, she had the heart of a warrior. His blood beat faster through his veins, and his groin tightened. Maybe someday they could meet up again on even footing when she wasn't his prisoner. When he could make a move. She was something special, and it was a fucking tragedy he'd had to meet her like this. "Now, Moe." Without waiting for her to give in, he moved relentlessly toward her.

She swiveled, looking for some sort of escape.

He grabbed her bicep before she could run, holding firmly but keeping careful not to bruise her. "That was a hell of a kick, lady."

She shoved at him and looked up, rain sliding over her stunning features. "You going to retaliate?"

"Yes." He started walking back toward the mansion, not allowing her to hamper their progress. Oh, she was a fighter, but he was twice her size and had her in strength. Even so, the kick had been impressive. "You are grounded from any books, papers, or magazines for twenty-four hours."

"Grounded?" She snorted, trying unsuccessfully to yank away.

"Yeah." The woman was a thinker, and it'd drive her crazy not to be able to read anything. Television was long gone. "And my earlier threat about feeding you stands. I will."

She shoved him again, this time moving in. "We're not done here, Grey."

He looked down at her pretty eyes, her words diving in and sinking deep. "I think you're right," he murmured quietly. Damn, was she right.

CHAPTER FIVE

If society ends up starving in the aftermath of Scorpius, make sure you blame Greyson Storm. The asshole.
—Maureen Shadow, Notes

MAUREEN PACED HER ROOM, her gaze on the darkened ocean. It had been two fucking weeks since she was kidnapped, and Greyson wouldn't even take her to the greenhouses in the area. Apparently rival gangs had attacked four times, and he was having trouble keeping Merc territory safe.

Rain pattered down. Again. All it did was rain.

She had to get out of there. The more time she stayed with Greyson, the more she actually liked the guy. He was patient and seemed loyal to his men. She'd heard he and Damon talking that morning about some lost women who'd offered their bodies for food. Greyson had taken them personally into Vanguard territory and left them.

During one of her escape attempts, she had run into some teenage girls who'd been trying to barter with their bodies. Greyson had hauled her back before she could discover what happened to them. Now she was thinking he'd taken them to safety, although he wouldn't admit it when she questioned him.

The Mercs were dangerous and tough...but something told her they weren't as evil as advertised.

The man in charge was funny and smart. They'd taken to playing chess once in a while, and the guy was good. And way beyond sexy. She had to stop looking at him with interest.

He was still blackmailing Raze, damn it. How could she be attracted to a guy extorting her brother? Not that Greyson had ever made a move. Not one. Sometimes when he looked at her, those odd eyes heated, but he'd never even made an improper suggestion.

She sniffed. That was good.

A soft knock sounded on her door, and she whirled around. "What?"

A very gray head poked in. "Hi, girly. We got some new bourbon, and the boss won't be back till late. Wanna have a snootful?"

She couldn't help but relax. Atticus Werner was an eighty-year-old soldier and a truly excellent cook. He was one of the few men Greyson allowed in the main mansion. "You're not afraid I'll make a break for it?" She moved toward him.

He grinned, showing a large gap in his front teeth. "Greyson ups the guards around the mansion and beach when he's not around. You wouldn't make it four yards before getting caught. And you don't want to get grounded and not get to read again." His faded blue eyes twinkled as he pushed the door open wide. "Come keep an old man company. We can play gin rummy."

"You already owe me three million dollars," Moe retorted, following the man through the house to the breakfast nook. "Is it just us in here?"

Atticus nodded. "Yep. Damon went with Grey."

"Where are they?" she asked, not that she cared. Yeah. She didn't care at all.

"Somethin' going on up north," Atticus said, shoving his

stocky bulk around the table where rich people once dined. He wore a red shirt with purple pants and green socks.

"Are you color blind?" Moe asked, noting his clothes.

He nodded. "Think so. Why?"

"No reason." Moe reached for the cards already on the table as Atticus poured two generous glasses of Pappy Van Winkle's Family Reserve, a twenty-year-old Kentucky bourbon whiskey. "Whoa. Where did you get the good stuff?"

Atticus raised a glass and sniffed, humming softly. "God, that is good. Boys went raiding the fancier areas in Bakersfield a few days ago. I waited to share this when you could."

Maureen took her glass, drinking slowly. Warmth and deliciousness exploded down her throat. "That was very kind of you."

"Yeah, well, Grey won't let you drink alcohol." Atticus took a healthy swallow.

She frowned. "That's true, but we haven't had any booze in this house anyway. What's up with that?"

Atticus snorted. "I think he wants all his faculties around you. Ditto the other way around."

She paused with the glass almost to her mouth again. "What?"

Atticus nodded at the cards. "Just deal."

Huh. She did so and quickly put her hand together. "Your men are very loyal to Grey."

Atticus nodded, discarding. "Yeah. When all hell broke loose, he found a place for us. With food and water and weapons." He took a card.

"But no women." She shook her head and took another drink.

"Says women cause distractions." Atticus drew from the deck. "He's right, of course."

Yeah, but that was crazy. "You have to form families again." She needed a three of clubs.

"Right now we're still in fight mode," Atticus said, refilling their glasses.

Obviously. Moe kept drinking and playing, hour after hour. Finally, the cards were too blurry to see. "I, ar, think I'm deeerunk."

Atticus chuckled. "Me too. This was fun. Don't tell Grey."

"Bad Grey," she slurred, swaying on the seat. "I can't wait until I leave here."

"I'll miss you. We all will." Atticus stumbled to his feet and reached to help her up.

She stood and fell against the table, slowly righting herself. "Greyson won't miss me."

Atticus gently took her arm like a guy at a ball. "Yessss, he will. Grey is calmer when you're around. Happier. I even heard him laugh once."

She tripped and regained her footing. "Huh. He's a butthead."

Atticus laughed, the sound high. "He's the king of buttheads here."

Humor rippled through her, and she laughed. Why that was so funny, she'd never know. But it really was. She fell against her door and opened it. "Night, A. Thanks for the good booze."

"You got it." Even though he was drunk, he turned the key once she was inside—locking her in as usual.

She paused at the open doors to the deck. Usually somebody shut and locked those before she went to bed. The cool air brushed in, the scent of rain competing with the salty smell of the ocean. She moved to the door, watching it pour.

Where was Greyson? She didn't want to care. Not at all. But was he okay?

* * *

GREYSON PICKED himself off the ground, his head spinning and his gut roiling. Swinging out, he hit the attacker in the temple, and the guy went down. They'd found the nest of Rippers, insane sociopaths, about twenty minutes before, and the fight had been brutal.

A shot echoed, and a guy to his left fell. An enemy.

"Nice shot, Damon," Grey said, stumbling toward two women in the back of the garage. Their bodies were already decaying. Had probably been dead for a week. But one of the Rippers had been fucking a body when they arrived, and Grey had thought he could save at least one of them.

Damon grabbed his arm and yanked him toward the door. "It's too late for them."

It was too late for many people. Grey's gut clenched. One of the women had been a kid. Probably only fourteen. "Fuck."

Damon shoved him into the rain. Pain lanced through his head, and he swayed.

"Shit." Damon turned him and tilted his head, using a flashlight. "You took a hell of a hit to the temple. You okay?"

Fuck no, he wasn't okay. The entire world was spinning around him. "Fine."

"Okay. I'll drive. We're less than an hour out. These guys only had some coke, and I grabbed it for the infirmary. Can't be too picky." Damon jogged for the truck, waiting until Greyson slid into the passenger side. Then they were off. "The other two trucks should be home any minute."

"Home," Greyson muttered, leaning his battered head back on the seat. Headquarters had seemed like home for two weeks now. Ever since Maureen had arrived. "She's gonna be pissed if I don't turn her over once her brother succeeds."

"Yeah." Damon drove faster. "You could ask her to stay."

"Right." Grey shoved old pictures of Zach Barter off the seat. He was starting to doubt he'd find the asshole, and nobody he talked to even knew who the guy was. "She won't stay."

"Probably not," Damon agreed.

Grey reached into the jockey box for some bourbon the

scouts had found a few days before. They'd found five bottles of the good stuff. The really good stuff. "I want her to stay."

"She looks at you like she's intrigued." Damon took a fast turn. "Sometimes she looks at you like she wants to kill you, though."

Grey snorted and opened the bottle. "I've noticed." It wavered in front of his eyes, morphing. Concussions sucked.

Damon cleared his throat. "I ain't a doctor, but I'm sure you shouldn't drink with a bruised brain."

Grey tipped back his head and took a very healthy swallow. "Like you said, you ain't a doctor." He handed over the bottle. "I have two more, and we're drinking them before anybody else gets a chance."

Damon drank it down. "God forbid we share."

Greyson snorted and drank more. "I totally agree."

"So, if you want her to stay, why not make a move?" Damon asked, slowing down for what looked like a pile of bear furs.

Greyson tried to focus, but only one of his eyes was working. His body felt all right, though. "I can't make a move. I kidnapped her, so she has no choice in anything. We're not on equal footing, and she can't make a fair decision." Though man, he had to stop having wet dreams about her. She was all he thought about some days, and that had to end. Right now. "You know?"

Damon took the bottle. "I guess. Just never figured you for an equal partner type."

Greyson turned toward his best friend. Hell. His only friend. "What do you mean?"

"Thought you'd be more of an *I Tarzan, You Jane*, type," Damon said slowly. "No offense."

Huh. Grey took the bottle and downed enough bourbon that the pain in his head finally subsided. "Only one person can be in charge in any situation. That includes personally," he muttered.

Damon glanced his way. "Yeah. That's what I thought." He frowned.

Greyson sighed. "You're right. I mean, about me. But that's after a decision is made. Maureen can't decide to be with me because she doesn't have the freedom to do that." Fuck, all of this talking was making his headache come back. "Enough Dr. Phil bullshit."

"All right," Damon said. "Let's just drink."

Greyson nodded and finished the first bottle. Then he opened a second.

After they'd started the third, his body went numb. Finally.

"We're here," Damon said, pulling into the driveway.

"Going for a walk on the beach to clear my head," Grey said, shoving open the door and falling on his ass. Shit, his brain hurt. Rain pelted down on him, slightly helping to clear his head.

Damon leaned over the console and looked down. "Booze or concussion?"

"Both." Using the tire, he climbed to his feet. "See ya tomorrow." Without waiting for an answer, he stumbled around the side of the house and headed toward the ocean.

Clouds covered the moon and threw rain onto the sand, but the chill was serving to finally focus him. He made it to the deck before he noticed that Moe's outside doors were open. Soft candlelight filtered outside. What the hell?

He paused.

She stood in the doorway, watching the storm pummel the ocean. The candles lit her from behind, making her hair glow. Those blue eyes cut through the darkness somehow.

He moved for her, unable to stop himself. "Your doors should be closed."

She jumped and then pivoted. "Greyson."

Was that relief in her voice? He stepped closer. "Did you hear me?"

She crossed her arms. "I'm not deaf." Her voice slurred a little.

He blinked. Was his hearing fucked up, too? "I know. Sorry."

She shook her head. "Do not be nice to me."

"Okay." He wanted her to smile again like she'd done the other day. Just once. "I'm sorry I had to kidnap you."

She huffed out air. "You didn't *have* to do anything."

Yeah, that was true. "You look like an angel with the candles behind you."

She swayed. "Greyson."

Man, his brain was screwed up. Too much booze and fighting. So he reached for the door. "Go inside, Moe. I'll lock up."

"No." She pushed at him.

No? He didn't move. "Yes."

She stepped into him. "You like me."

The scent of wild bluebells covered him, tempting him. His body went from zero to a hundred in a second flat, and his cock woke up like it had a place to go. "I do like you," he mumbled, wishing she'd stop splitting into two people in front of his eyes.

She ran her hands up his chest. "I don't want to like you."

"Don't blame you." Her hands created too much warmth. Man, he wanted to be warm. Step back. He really needed to step back.

She leaned up and nibbled beneath his chin.

Desire cut through him with a painful sharpness. "We can't. Really."

"I know," she whispered, pressing her full breasts against his chest. "Kiss me, just once."

He couldn't say no. So he lowered his mouth, taking hers. Sweetness. So soft and sweet. She made a sound, one he'd never forget, in the back of her throat. Then she kissed him back.

At that point, he was lost.

Completely.

CHAPTER SIX

I survived being kidnapped first by Greyson and then the president. But I'm...off. Don't know why.
—Maureen Shadow, Notes

Present Day
Vanguard Territory in inner city LA

Maureen Shadow wandered through the Vanguard headquarters' soup kitchen area and into what apparently had once been a free medical clinic. Now it was the health center for the headquarters with the main pseudo-hospital located inner territory. She'd been in Vanguard territory for more than two weeks, and for some reason, she still felt like a visitor.

When Scorpius began killing millions and then billions, Jax Mercury had taken seven square blocks in inner city Los Angeles and created a sanctuary for survivors. He ruled with compassion and an iron fist, and to be included in Vanguard was to be almost safe in a deadly world. Maureen's brother, Raze, was one of Jax's top lieutenants.

She kind of missed the ocean. And Greyson. Maybe.

Three battered chairs remained empty in the waiting area, and she moved past them and the long reception counter to a hallway. "Tace?" she called out, her hands trembling.

Tace Justice, a former Army medic, poked his head out of an examination room. His hair was a light brown and his eyes the sizzling blue of a Texas sky, matching his accent. "Mornin', ma'am."

She forced a smile. "Was your hair really blond before Scorpius?"

He nodded. "Yep. Apparently many a folk has darker hair and even different colored eyes after surviving the bacterium."

She'd heard that some Ebola survivors had different colored eyes afterward. "Um, okay."

He moved all the way out into the hallway, towering over her. "You all right? Any problems?"

She shook her head. A too short time ago, she and Vivienne Wellington had been kidnapped from Greyson and his Merc territory by the psychopathic President Atherton and his equally nutty vice president. That guy seemed even worse, somehow. The rescue had been bloody, but finally her bruises were gone. "No lasting damage." Not physically, anyway. The nightmares were another story.

"All right. What can I do for you, darlin'?" Tace asked quietly.

She drew in air. Could she just offer to help organize the clinic and then find what she wanted? Probably not. Crap. Okay. This was just in her imagination, anyway. "I'm having, well, a possible, well, you know..."

"Female issue?" he asked, his brows drawing down.

If you could call it that. "Um, yeah." She shuffled her feet, parts of her body on fire. The embarrassing parts.

He scrubbed his broad hand through his scruffy chin. "Dr. Penelope?" he called out.

A small woman moved out of a far office. Long, black hair,

pretty Asian features, small hands. "Yes?" She studied them with serious and dark eyes.

"You up to acting like a doctor?" Tace asked, his gaze remaining on Moe.

"I am a doctor," Penelope said quietly. "Hi, ah, Maureen? I think we met a few days ago over unbaked bagels?"

Moe nodded. Penelope hadn't mentioned she was a doctor, but they hadn't really talked much. "Yes. You're a doctor?"

"I am." Penelope looked around the quiet area. "This is my first day."

At the words, another man moved out of the back room. Tall and broad and huge with no expression on his rugged face.

Maureen barely kept from taking a step back.

"This is Marcus Knight," Penelope said quietly. "He's Jax Mercury's half-brother."

Yeah, the guy kind of looked like Jax. Somehow bigger and, well, emptier. "Hi," Moe said.

He just looked at her, his eyes more green than brown, his stance wide.

She swallowed.

Penelope gestured toward an examination room. "How about we chat in here?" She waited for Maureen to nod and walk toward her, entering a sparsely furnished room. Old and torn examination table, old and torn doctor stool, old and torn orange counter.

Penelope followed, pausing to turn and press a hand to Marcus's chest. "You can't come in, M. Maybe go for a walk outside and get some air?"

Next to the hulking Mercury, Penelope looked beyond petite to downright fragile.

Marcus's gaze flicked over her head to Maureen, threat clear in his eyes before he turned and stepped away from the door, putting his back to the other wall and his front facing them.

Penelope sighed and shut the door.

Moe inched toward the table and hopped. "Um, I've heard rumors about him." Apparently the government had experimented on him, and now he wouldn't leave Penelope's side. Ever. "Dr. Penelope? Are you safe?"

"You can drop the doctor part. That's just what folks have taken to calling me. You can call me Penelope if you'd like." The doctor turned and smiled. "I'm perfectly safe." Her face was calm, but turmoil filled her dark eyes. "Now. What can I do for you?"

Heat filled Moe's face. "God. I..."

Penelope set her clipboard on the counter. "It's okay, Maureen. Whatever you tell me is protected. I'm a doctor, and I was one before Scorpius. What's going on?"

"I, ah, think I might've caught something," Moe whispered, a tremble going through her. Nausea filled her stomach. "I mean, sexually."

Penelope's eyebrows raised. "Okay. What about your partner? Did you ask him or her if they have something or are experiencing symptoms?"

Moe shifted on the torn leather. "I don't know. He's not here." She'd kill Greyson. Absolutely kill him if he'd given her something. What the hell had she been thinking?

Penelope's face cleared. "You were captured by the Mercs, right?" Her voice was calm and soothing.

Moe nodded.

"Honey? Were you raped?" Penelope asked gently.

Moe closed her eyes and then reopened them. "No," she said honestly. "I really wasn't." She rubbed her hands down her jeans. "I mean, I was seriously drunk on really good bourbon they'd found earlier that week."

Penelope's lips tightened. "Then it was rape."

Moe winced. "No. He was drunker than I was, and he had a concussion that I found out about the next day. The same day I was kidnapped by the president." She sighed and scrubbed her hands down her face. "Honestly, it was so stupid. I don't know what I was thinking." Except that her body was warm and Greyson Storm was beyond sexy and dangerous. "I've always been drawn to fire," she murmured, shaking her head, shame filling her. "Seriously. It was my first one-night stand, and *he* apologized the next morning."

Penelope winced. "He apologized?"

"Yeah," Moe said, her shoulders slumping. "Said he had no right to take advantage since we were so drunk. But..." Her voice lowered. "I, ah, came on to him. Sure, I was intoxicated, but he actually said no first." God, she deserved whatever happened to her. "I'm a slut."

Penelope coughed. "Honey, you're not a slut. Not at all. You can sleep with whomever you want, and there's no judgment. But now you think you might have an infection?"

Maureen nodded, tears filling her eyes. She'd slept with a guy she barely knew. And he'd taken off a necklace with a ring on it when he'd gotten them both naked. Whose ring was it? Had Greyson lost a woman? If so, why did that hurt? Geez. And now, she had a problem. There weren't any antibiotics. "I'll be the first person to die from the clap post-Scorpius," she muttered.

Penelope snorted and reached for some rubber gloves from a drawer to put on. "Well, let's take a look."

God. Moe shoved off her jeans and lay back on the table. "I don't suppose we have those old cloth cover-ups the OBGYNs used to have?"

"Nope." Penelope sat and rolled closer, a lantern in her hand.

The lamp warmed Moe's tender parts.

"Hmm," Penelope said, prodding her.

Moe hissed. "We used a condom. I just don't get it."

Penelope took a sample and put it on a slide, backing away. "You can get dressed."

Moe jumped down and yanked on her jeans. "Well? Is it crabs or something?"

Penelope set the slide on the table. "I don't think so. I need a urine sample before you go."

Moe tried really hard not to scratch her private parts. It was excruciating. "Okay. Can you even run tests? I mean, what can you do?"

Penelope pulled off the gloves. "We have some tests from the labs and pharmacies Vanguard raided early on. I think you just have a regular old yeast infection, to be honest. But come back in an hour after leaving me the sample."

Moe swayed. "It might not be a venereal disease?"

"Nope. But I'll know for sure in about an hour," Penelope said.

Moe nodded and opened the door to see Marcus waiting right where they'd left him. Heat slashed into her face, but she turned and all but ran for the outside outhouses to pee in a cup. God, please let it be just a yeast infection. Like most women, she'd had more than one through the years.

Bright sun shone down as she quickly did her business and returned to the clinic. This time, Marcus blocked her way.

She blinked. "I have to give this to Penelope."

"I will," he said, his voice gritty.

She was not giving her pee to this guy. "No. It's between my doctor and me. Move, Marcus." There was no way she could get him out of her way if she wanted.

He growled and launched toward her. Panic rushed through her, and she took a step back.

"Marcus!" Penelope snapped, walking out of the examination room.

He stopped cold.

"Let her pass," Penelope ordered.

Without pause, Marcus pivoted, putting his back to the wall and allowing her by. He was at least a foot taller than she, and his very presence was a threat.

Maureen inched by him, holding her breath. The guy was seriously nuts.

"I'm sorry," Penelope said, her eyes soft. "We're trying to work through some issues."

No kidding. Moe handed over the plastic cup. "I'll go, ah, grab something to eat next door." Yeah, she might be running away from the scary guy. She headed into the former soup kitchen to see pretzels and what looked like a slow cooker containing soup along the far counter.

Tables were spread throughout. All sorts of tables. Picnic tables, game tables, card tables...and most were empty.

She made a move for the soup, noting it was still warm. The slow cooker didn't plug into anything, but it was nice that it still held the heat. She ladled some noodles and broth into a chipped toddler bowl with *Star Wars* on it. Making her way over to a picnic table, she moved so her jeans kind of scratched her hoo hoo.

God, how embarrassing.

She ate by herself for a while, mentally counting seconds and minutes in her head. What if it was just a yeast infection? She counted at least forty-five minutes but couldn't relax.

Did they even have medicine for that? If not, how did anybody survive a yeast infection? It itched so damn bad.

The back sliding door opened, and her brother stalked inside. He loped easily, a holstered gun strapped to his thigh.

She leaned back to watch him.

Raze had always been larger than life. Big and strong and fierce. When their father died, he'd become the man of the family at ten years old. And when their mother died only a few years later, he'd taken over in that area, as well. His long, black hair was tied at the nape, and his blue eyes softened with his smile as he caught sight of her. He'd inherited their father's Native American features, while she looked more like their Irish mother.

She smiled back.

Her dad and her brother were soldiers, and she admired them. Loved them. But her romantic type was geeky and next to a computer, and that was fine with her. There was nothing nerdy about Greyson, so he couldn't be right for her. Not a chance. And he'd better not have given her the clap.

Raze reached her, his wide chest blocking out the light from the back doors. "Hey. What are you up to?"

Waiting to find out if she had a sex disease? "Nothing much. Just having soup."

"Good. We sent scouts up north to check out the farming areas you wanted information on. They'll report back in a few days," Raze said.

Excellent. That information was vital. She cleared her throat. "I found out earlier from scouts that Greyson Storm is coming this way from the Bunker later this week. He sent notice so we don't just shoot him."

Raze stretched his neck. "The Bunker is as much ours as Greyson's. If he doesn't let us back in, then we will shoot his ass."

Moe swallowed. The president had recently attacked Vanguard headquarters, and all the Vanguard soldiers had left the Bunker in Century City for the Mercs to protect. Now the Mercs controlled it. The government had created the place before Scorpius, and it had the best medical supplies and labs of anywhere right now. "We'll get back into the Bunker." They had to.

Raze shrugged.

She took a sip of soup, looking for the right words. "We made a deal with Greyson so he'd help us take the Bunker, Raze. If he helped, which he did so we took over the place, we agreed I'd go to Merc territory. Temporarily." She had to see if there were any resources in the greenhouses. And if he'd given her a venereal disease, she had to fucking kill him.

Raze's eyes lost their softness. "No."

Man. God save her from overprotective and stubborn men. "He was kind to me when I was there. Didn't let anybody even so much as give me a mean look. We need allies, brother. You know it."

"I know." He leaned down and pressed a quick peck to her forehead. "But my baby sister ain't leaving Vanguard territory." He glanced at his watch and straightened. "I'll meet you later for dinner." Then he turned and strode away.

She sighed. Apparently she had a few days to get him on board with her plan and remind him that she was an adult. She was going no matter what, but it'd be nice if Raze wasn't all cranky about it.

Movement caught her attention from the clinic doorway, and Marcus strode toward her, graceful and predatory.

Her knees went weak.

He reached her, turning so his gaze was also on the door he'd just left. His fingers curled into fists at his sides. "Penny said to come get you." His body vibrated, and he leaned toward the door as if something pulled him back. "Come."

She pushed away from the table, gut feeling whispering that he'd grab her and run back if she didn't hurry. So she hustled, her body aching, her chest full. What was wrong with her?

Reaching the old clinic, she jogged around the reception area and headed right back into the same examination room.

Penelope was waiting. "Please shut the door, Marcus."

Moe jumped. The guy was right behind her. He closed the door, cutting off his appraising look and hulking threat. "Well?" Moe asked, wringing her hands.

Penelope handed over a square box. "You merely have a very minor yeast infection."

Relief flowed through Moe so quickly, her knees nearly buckled. She reached out and pressed a hand to the wall for balance. "Thank God. So it had nothing to do with drunken sex and Greyson." She definitely owed him a mental apology.

"Eh." Penelope lifted a very slender shoulder. "My guess is that the condom you used was inferior rubber, and you reacted poorly to it. So it got you all irritated, your system ended up out of whack, and you ended up with a slight yeast infection."

Thank God it wasn't more serious. Moe looked down at the box. "We have medicine."

"Yep. Three-day fix," Penelope said, her dark eyes sober. "There haven't been many yeast infections yet."

"Lucky me," Moe said, straightened. "Hey. Thank you for everything."

Penelope swallowed. "Um, there's more."

Maureen blinked. "More? Than a yeast infection?"

Penelope nodded. "Yes. Well, I'm still a doctor, and you know. We do all the tests. We just do."

Maureen stopped breathing. "What else is wrong with me?"

Penelope moved toward her, taking her hand. "Nothing is wrong. But, well...you need to know. With the inferior condom and everything. You're pregnant."

CHAPTER SEVEN

I met a girl, kidnapped her, let her go, and now need her help. I think you'd be greatly amused by this, Miss J.

—Greyson Storm, Letters to Miss Julian

BURNED-OUT car carcasses lined the side of the 405 as the sun beat down on their brand-spanking-new Humvee. They'd taken it from the Bunker. Truth be told, the thing drove like a dream. Greyson slowed down and swerved around what looked like empty bookcases. Must've fallen off a truck or two. "If you see anything worth raiding, let me know."

Damon nodded from the passenger seat, his gaze out the window, looking at hollowed-out buildings flying by on the interstate. "We could hit a business or two, but who the hell knows what's waiting down there."

"We'll come back with a force when we get the chance," Grey said, sliding his necklace to the left beneath his shirt. The ring offered comfort, like always. Miss J had given it to him before he'd left to enter the military, and he always kept it with him. A wolf bayed in the distance. He shook his head, and a chill skittered down his back. "Wolves in LA. Seriously?"

"Keep an eye out for human predators. A gang caught one of our teams last month by blocking off the entire interstate," Damon said.

Gangs would always be a problem. Always had been, and even after the pandemic, always would be. Greyson nodded. "Understood." He ran through the security measures of the Bunker, the place they'd just left. "We need more men, Damon."

"I know. Of course, you could call back the many scouts you have out looking for Zach Barter," Damon said quietly.

"Not an option." Greyson would give up leading the Mercs before he'd give up his hunt.

Damon stiffened and reared up to watch a group of people on the side of the interstate picking through abandoned vehicles. They didn't even look up. "We could recruit more soldiers, or we could consider aligning with Vanguard."

"I guess that depends on what happens next." Grey rolled his shoulders, his hands easy on the steering wheel.

Damon shifted his gun to his other thigh. "They might just shoot us when we arrive in Los Angeles, you know."

"Then they won't get access to the Bunker or any of our resources," Grey said. "And we'll take more than a couple of them out first." He didn't want to kill anybody at Vanguard. Didn't mean he wouldn't.

"The Bunker is worth killing over." The place was one of several underground facilities created by the government in preparation for a pandemic. There was food, water, propane, and actual working computers there. Good generators. Plus, there had to be information leading to the other Bunkers somewhere in there. "I like that we control the place, though."

Grey nodded. His men and the Vanguard soldiers had taken the facility, but then Vanguard had to run home because they were under attack. Now only Greyson and the Mercs controlled the Bunker. "I'll give them access if they adhere to the agreement." He needed to get Maureen back into his territory. It seemed empty and dark without her, and he didn't want to think too deeply about that.

Damon shrugged and drank an entire bottle of water, his dark throat moving. "Well, they're good allies to have. Maybe."

Yeah. That summed up life at the moment. "Jax Mercury would cut off our heads if it meant more resources for Vanguard," Grey mused. "Not that I wouldn't do the same to him."

"Yep." Damon pulled an arm across his chest, stretching powerful biceps.

Grey scratched his chin. "We don't have a computer expert. Not one as good as theirs." Greyson's guys hadn't been able to figure out the computer system like Sami Steel could. The woman was brilliant and some type of former hacker.

Damon nodded. "True. If we're going to find other Bunkers, we need the best. It's amazing the computers are still working."

There had to be other Bunkers out there, and Damon was right. They needed to track them down for resources and information. "The computers are running on generators, and we need to catalog how long we can keep them going," Greyson said. "We don't have the resources to protect the Bunker and Merc territory in case the president attacks again soon."

"If we keep the Bunker for ourselves, Jax Mercury will attack if he doesn't try to kill us today."

Greyson nodded. "Yeah." He hated not having a clear path, but he wasn't sure what to do. There had to be time to make the right decision, but the clock was counting down way too fast. The world was closing in again, damn it.

Damon cleared his throat. "Plus, there's Maureen."

Nerves pricked down Grey's back. The mere mention of her sent his system into overdrive. It was shocking how much he missed the little spitfire. "It would be nice to have her catalog our greenhouses. See if any food can be harvested."

Damon stretched his other arm. "Right."

"Shut up." Grey reached for a bottle of water and drank it down, his throat parched. Summer had blown in with brutality. "The deal with Vanguard was that she'd come to work with us if we helped them take the Bunker."

"Do you think Vanguard will adhere to the deal?" Damon asked quietly.

Grey shook his head. "Not if they can help it. Her brother won't want to let her go again." Couldn't blame the guy. Maureen was special and soft and delicate. Even if she could kick a guy in the chin with no notice. He rubbed his chest. Was she okay? Safe? He needed to talk to her. Had he taken advantage? Fuck, he hoped not. Oh, if they were on even footing, he'd take what she offered and not give it back. Ever. The woman was special. "We also promised you'd help out with their internal problem."

Damon nodded. "I did. Some Pure church at Vanguard only for those who haven't been infected like me. They might be holding kids hostage. Maybe. Who the hell knows."

Grey leaned sideways, studying his friend. "It's not like you to volunteer for other groups."

Did Damon just flush? With his darker skin, it was hard to tell. But that sure seemed like a fucking blush. "We set up the mission after they saved my life last time I got shot. I kinda think I owe them. Just that."

Grey narrowed his gaze, his instincts humming. "Just that? What else could it be?" What was going on?

"Nothing." Damon hunched forward.

"Damon?"

His friend leaned back. "You'll totally take this the wrong way, but part of the undercover op is being run by…"

"A woman. By a woman." Triumph along with interest filtered through Greyson. "Tell me about the woman." Hmmm. Damon hadn't expressed an interest in anybody before, although there had been very few opportunities. "What's her name?"

Damon rolled his eyes. "It's not like that. She looks like the former suburban soccer mom I've heard she was. Pretty and untouchable, you know?" He shook his head. "I just want somebody who knows what they're doing on the inside with her, and none of the Vanguard lieutenants can go in. They've all survived the bacterium, whereas I'm uninfected."

"What makes her untouchable?" Greyson asked, trying to delve more. He and Damon had bonded over the last six months, but they'd never really talked about women. There hadn't been time.

"She's normal," Damon said. "I mean, she was before Scorpius. We never would've crossed paths."

The world had changed. "Because you were a cop?"

Damon nodded. "Yeah. Totally different lifestyles. She's somebody who probably had her own latte machine in her kitchen."

Huh. He'd never met anybody who had their own latte machine. "There aren't any latte machines that still work. Maybe you have more in common than you think." Scorpius had changed everybody.

"No." Damon grinned. "I ain't easy, Grey. That woman needs easy. Nice, flowers, missionary easy." He looked around at the desolate world outside the Humvee. "A guy like me doesn't want nice."

Okay. They'd crossed into chick bonding territory. Greyson nodded. "Fair enough." Grey would have to check the woman out. It was time Damon had some fun, even if he needed a little push. For now, it was back to work. "I think we have to share the Bunker with Vanguard." For the computer expert, if nothing else.

"So what's our plan?" Damon asked, wiping sweat off his brow.

"We walk into Vanguard and make our demands," Greyson said. "We'll deny them entry to the Bunker unless they adhere to the promises we all made."

Damon watched the buildings fly by. "I already miss the hot showers at the Bunker."

No shit. When was the last time Maureen had even seen a hot shower? Grey's blood sped up at the thought of being near her again. Their morning after their drunken sex night had been awkward, and then all hell had broken loose when the president attacked Merc headquarters and had kidnapped her. Grey had saved her, and he'd taken on Vice President Lake to do it. That guy was a stone-cold killer.

Yet another one in a world gone to hell.

Maureen had been taken back to Vanguard territory, and Greyson hadn't had a chance to speak to her about their night together. A night that still haunted him with the feeling of her. Soft and sweet. They'd both been drunk, and he'd been concussed, and the whole thing was a little blurry.

But he had to make sure she was all right.

Then he had to see if she wanted to do it again. This time, he'd be sober and conscious...and remember every second of touching her. But it was her choice to put herself in his hands.

Once she did, he'd take over.

Plus, Vanguard was vulnerable after their recent battle. Maureen would be safer with him, and that mattered.

"Shit," Damon breathed.

Grey looked his way to see a decomposing body mounted to the front of a school bus in the left lane facing them. A man, maybe in his early twenties. The body had been dead for at least a couple of weeks.

Damon lifted his gun to point out the window. "You see any movement?"

"No," Grey said softly, one hand tugging his gun out of the holster at his thigh. "We'll want to remember that's there for when we head back home."

"I wouldn't mind avoiding it," Damon said as they passed the macabre scene. "Maybe take the back roads."

Hell. These days, back roads were twice as dangerous. But if Grey was bringing Maureen out of the shelter of Vanguard, they'd need to assure her safety. "We'll get a map at Vanguard."

"If they don't shoot us on sight," Damon said grimly.

CHAPTER EIGHT

I always figured I'd have kids with some sweet guy I fell for in a lab somewhere. This...I never expected. What now?
—Maureen Shadow, Notes

Three days after finding out she was actually pregnant, really pregnant, preggo with Greyson Storm's kid, Maureen sat on the examination table and barely kept from kicking her feet like she had when she was a child. She turned the bottle of prenatal vitamins around in her hands. Three days. How her life had changed in those three meager days.

"Your yeast infection is completely cleared. You're fine," Penelope said.

She nodded. "I know." Yet she wasn't exactly fine, now was she?

"Have you told anybody about the baby?" Penelope asked, leaning back against the cracked counter, a threadbare white lab coat covering her petite frame.

Moe shook her head. "No," she whispered. "I just, I mean..." Shit.

Penelope nodded. "Listen, Moe. Our medical facilities aren't good, but there are probably still options."

Moe's head jerked up. "Oh. Right. No." She bit her lip. "I want to keep the baby. I already know that." She placed a hand over her still flat stomach. "It's just, there's a lot to consider. The world sucks. The father..."

Penelope nodded. "Yes. I've obviously never met the leader of the Mercs, but his reputation is a bloody one." She lifted a slim shoulder. "You might have an obligation to protect the baby and not tell him." She sighed. "Of course, the entire world is bloody. Vanguard isn't made of angels, either."

Wasn't that the truth. "My brother is going to lose his damn mind," Moe said, taking a deep breath. Raze would never believe she had been willing or had made the first move. He'd always see her as an innocent little girl he needed to protect.

Penelope wrinkled her nose. "You're on your own there." She cleared her throat.

Moe stiffened. The doctor's dark eyes had gone soft. Somber. "What?"

"I have a duty to tell you. There have been no live births for Scorpius survivors." She leaned in, her eyes intense. "We'll change that. Somehow. This baby will live."

Oh God. Moe took a deep breath. The room started spinning. "What? What a minute. What does that mean?"

Penelope moved toward Moe and grasped her free hand. "Women who were pregnant when they contracted Scorpius either died or miscarried. Women who've become pregnant after surviving Scorpius have also miscarried—to the best of my knowledge, which isn't extensive."

Chills tracked through Moe. Fear made her heart seize and then release. "We think. I mean, the world has gone pretty dark. We don't know that for sure." There could be tons of pregnant women out there beyond California. Living their lives and still having healthy pregnancies.

Penelope nodded vigorously. "That's right. There's a lot we don't know."

"What do I do?" Maureen asked, her voice creaking.

"Just be as healthy as you can be," Penelope said, sliding her hands into her pockets. "We'll get back to the Bunker and start going through research. When I was there, I wasn't part of the labs, not really. I just provided medical services to wounded soldiers. So there must be data there about this. Right?"

A sharp rap sounded on the door, and Maureen jumped.

Penelope turned. "Yes?"

Marcus poked his large head in and spoke only to Penelope. "Raze is here. Wants Maureen for a meeting with the guys from up north." The hulking bodyguard didn't move enough for Raze to be visible.

Maureen shoved the bottle of vitamins into her small pack and jumped off the table. Greyson was there. It had to be. Heat flushed into her face and through her entire body. What in the world was she going to do?

She gingerly pushed past Marcus to see her big brother.

His blue eyes narrowed. "You okay? What's wrong?"

"Girl issues," she said primly.

He stepped back, and even Marcus moved a little more to the side. "Oh. Okay," Raze said, pivoting. "Greyson Storm and Damon Winter are here, and they won't talk until you're in the room. You have to know, Jax and I have decided you're not going back into Merc territory this week. Not while we're rebuilding from the president's attack. We have to stay here."

She stumbled and reached for his arm. "I am going. There's a time constraint with any crops that might still be living." She wasn't hopeful. What should she say to Greyson? Her stomach rolled over.

Raze paused and looked behind them. "Dr. Penelope? Would you like to join us? By yourself?"

Marcus pivoted and put his big body between Penelope and them.

"Move aside, Marcus," Penelope said gently, and the soldier turned to put his back against the door. She smiled, her eyes still somber. "No thanks. I have work to do here."

Raze hesitated. "Marcus? Why don't you head outside and patrol? Give Penelope some space."

Marcus turned only his head to face Raze and didn't speak.

Penelope studied him. "That's okay, Raze. Marcus and I need to have a little talk, anyway."

"You sure you're safe?" Raze asked.

She smiled. "I'm sure. Marcus would never hurt me, would you?" she asked him.

Marcus turned back to her as if Raze and Maureen didn't exist. "I'll never let anything hurt you. Ever." His voice was a low growl.

Raze shook his head and grasped Maureen's arm, leading her toward the reception area. "I'm afraid we're just going to have to put him down at some point," he whispered.

Maureen shivered. The poor guy. Many Scorpius survivors developed some sort of obsession, but this was the worst she'd seen or even heard about. "I feel so terrible for him. It's like he's holding on to Penelope like she's a rope in a crashing storm."

"Let's hope he doesn't just hang her with it," Raze said grimly, escorting Moe through the soup kitchen and back into the Vanguard war rooms. "Back to our conversation about Santa Barbara. You're not going without me, and I can't leave Vanguard until we've shored up our defenses and fixed the damage from the last attack." He stepped back to let her inside.

Grey and Damon sat at the far end of a monstrous table. The first sight of Grey after the weeks apart stole her breath. He was every bit as big and deadly-looking as she remembered. And he kissed like a god. A truly talented and hungry god. Her abdomen warmed. She tore her gaze away from his intense stare to look around the quiet room.

Somebody had brought in an executive table with some odd design in the center. It looked like it had been from a law firm at some point.

Jax kicked out a chair next to him in a silent invitation to sit. Or order. Most likely an order. The Vanguard leader had hard brown eyes, black hair, and sharp Hispanic features. The guy had been in a gang and then the military, and there was nothing soft about him. Well, except for the woman he loved. Lynne Harmony was very gentle.

Moe sat with Raze taking the seat on her other side. Talk about being flanked by testosterone.

She tried really hard not to blush.

But her cheeks still heated.

She and Greyson hadn't had time to talk after their one night together, and now what the hell was she supposed to do?

How could she have gotten pregnant? It was still hard to wrap her head around the reality. What about Greyson? Before Scorpius, she would've thought it was the right thing to do to tell a baby's father. But now? Life had changed. She barely knew the guy, and there was a good chance they weren't even allies.

He watched her, ignoring everyone else. "Maureen. How are you?"

Knocked up? Freaked out? Scared to death? "Fine," she murmured, taking a good look at him. In the muted light, his eyes appeared almost all gray without the green or blue hues. His wide shoulder met Damon's, and he'd worn his usual black T-shirt and jeans for the meet. Lines fanned out from his full mouth. "You look tired," she said.

Raze cut her a look.

Grey nodded. "We had a slight rebellion at the Bunker by some of the soldiers left over from the old regime and had to quell the disturbance."

Quell? Something told her that didn't include prison time. "Oh."

Jax drummed his fingers on the table. "Speaking of the Bunker, we're ready to send forces back there to gather more information. We have to find the other Bunker facilities."

Grey lifted an eyebrow. "Vanguard is a mess. I could see the damage the second we approached. You were attacked with superior weapons and even from the air. You'll need weeks to get safeguards back in place. How about you keep your soldiers here to rebuild and just send your computer expert to the Bunker? I'll guarantee her safety."

"That doesn't work for me," Jax drawled. "You've already kidnapped one member of Vanguard, and I'd rather not put any more of my people in your hands."

Maureen watched the interchange. She hadn't exactly been a member of Vanguard when she was kidnapped, but it was nice that Jax considered her one.

Greyson studied her and then turned to Jax. "I understand but don't see how there's much choice. Send Sami Steel to the Bunker, and I'll make sure she's protected. Maureen can come to Merc territory, as promised, and check out our food sources."

His voice, low and throaty, washed over Moe's skin like a caress. What was wrong with her? He was all the way across the room.

Jax sighed. "No."

Greyson spread his hands on the table. Those big, gentle, strong, talented hands. "You're weak here and need to repair. Now."

Raze nodded. "Which is why we have to concentrate here and at the Bunker. We don't have the forces to send into Merc territory to investigate your greenhouses and other facilities right now. Maureen can't go. Maybe in a few weeks."

Moe stiffened. That was too late. "I don't need a force. Just a notebook."

Greyson's lips twitched. "I can guarantee your sister's safety."

Moe's head jerked. The dicks. All of them. "Listen. I'm an adult, and I can make my own decisions. I'm willing to go into Merc territory. Time is of the essence. We have a lot of people to feed, and we're going to be out of canned or boxed goods before we know it." Plus, she needed an opportunity to get to know Greyson. To figure out if she should tell him the truth.

Jax looked at Raze over her head. "No. We'll wait until we can send a force."

Temper swirled through Moe. Just who the hell did any of them think they were?

Greyson didn't appear surprised. If anything, he looked a little bored. "Figured you might say that. Well then, you don't get access to the Bunker."

Heat rolled from either side of Maureen. Shit. This was bad.

CHAPTER NINE

Supplies are getting low, Damon wants to go undercover in an enemy facility because of a woman, and I'm losing focus on my primary objective. I wish you were here to advise.

—Greyson Storm, Letters to Miss Julian

GREYSON fully understood Raze's need to protect his sister. But he didn't give a shit. A deal was a deal, and Maureen needed to check out those greenhouses. He also had to apologize and explain himself to her. Then he'd leave her alone. His wanting her back in his territory had nothing to do with the softness of her skin or the sounds of pleasure she made that still haunted him at night.

Nope. Not at all. Damn it.

Before Jax could react to Grey's declaration about the Bunker, a knock sounded on the door, and a pretty blonde moved partially inside. "You wanted me?"

It took Greyson a moment to recognize Vivienne Wellington. The shrink from the FBI profiling group and prison looked all fresh and shiny—except for the still healing wound across her neck. Last time he'd seen her, she'd been tied up and concussed after the president had kidnapped her and Maureen from Merc territory. "Hi."

She gave him a nod, her eyes narrowing.

Raze partially stood, keeping an even distance between the shrink and his sister. "We told Storm he could ask you a couple of questions, Vinnie."

Vinnie. Cute name. Grey nodded. "I need to find Zach Barter." Barter was the first real carrier of Scorpius, and he'd gone nuts trying to infect everyone else. He'd succeeded, and the government had locked him down. Temporarily.

Vinnie looked around the room, seeming to take mental notes. "Barter was infected, turned into a sociopath, and decided to rape to infect his way through the world. When our infrastructure fell apart, he was let loose."

"Did you meet him?" Grey asked. God, he had to find that bastard and put a bullet between his eyes.

She nodded. "I helped find him in the beginning, and I interviewed him several times. He was nuts."

Were shrinks supposed to say 'nuts?' The woman was obviously not a normal shrink. "Where is he now?" Greyson asked.

"Dunno." She looked him right in the eyes. "He escaped months ago. Rumor has it that Vice President Lake secured his release for some reason. Maybe because of his knowledge about Scorpius."

Man, Grey really hated that guy. Lake was as dangerous as Atherton and needed to be taken out.

Vinnie glared at him like an avenging angel. "Thus there was no need to kidnap Maureen and force Raze to betray his people. You totally wasted your time and could've gotten many of us killed." She stopped speaking but clearly mouthed the word 'dickhead'.

Raze chuckled. "You can call him anything you want, gorgeous."

Gorgeous? Greyson studied the two. Interesting. Raze was with the little shrink.

She rolled her eyes. "I'm trying not to swear so much. It bugs Lucinda."

"Who's Lucinda?" Grey asked.

Vinnie blushed. "Am I done here?"

Raze nodded. "Yeah. *Moe and I* will meet you in an hour for lunch." He waited until she'd exited and shut the door before retaking his seat.

Well. Grey certainly didn't have an ally with the shrink. "Maureen? A couple of the greenhouses have generators, and we've tried to keep them going. But we're almost out of fuel, so we need to know what to save. If anything." God, he needed to talk to her. Just once.

She nodded. "I understand. I can be ready to go in an hour."

"No," Raze said, his strong face showing no give.

Ah, fuck. Grey planted his hands on the table. "It's her decision. Not yours."

Maureen nodded. "That's true. It is my decision, and I'm going."

"You want to go?" Grey asked. He needed the words this time. "Moe?"

"Yes," she said, her gaze narrowing. "But just to get the job done. I don't think I'll need more than a week."

Jax pushed away from the table as if to give himself more room in case of a brawl. "Listen. Here it is. We want to work with you. The president is coming after all of us, and he has better forces. I mean, if he's still alive."

Grey frowned. "Word came back that his helicopter went down after fighting with you here."

"We shot it down," Raze said easily. "But scouts couldn't find bodies. He and the VP might be off licking their wounds somewhere."

Yeah. A bastard like President Atherton would be hard to kill.

Same with Lake. That guy was made of Teflon. "Then we should stick with our promises," Grey said evenly.

Jax sighed. "We want to. Just with a slight time delay. We share access to the Bunker, Damon can go undercover here, and Maureen will visit Merc territory as soon as we have a force to send with her. It's the best I can do."

Maureen's pale face filled with color. "I'm not a soldier, and I'm not under anybody's command. I'm going to Merc territory today. I want to."

That was good enough for Greyson. He gave Damon the signal and barely caught his buddy's sigh before he ducked low and covered his ears. Sucking in air, Grey tossed a stun grenade right behind Jax Mercury before lunging for the floor.

The flashbang exploded, sending out a shockwave.

Greyson's ears rang, but he leaped up and went for Raze just as Damon jumped for Jax. The Vanguard men had been caught off guard and were too slow to react. Seconds too slow. Greyson punched Raze beneath the jaw and followed up with a smash to the floor.

Maureen lurched for him, striking against his back.

He turned in time to see Damon choke out the Vanguard leader. Man, there'd be hell to pay for that one. Greyson grabbed Maureen's arm.

Her eyes were cloudy, and her hair was wild around her shoulders. Confusion blanketed her features.

"You'll be okay. It'll pass in an hour. Or two." Greyson slipped an arm over her shoulders, feeling like shit that she'd been impacted. One of his eyes was a little blurry. "We need to act natural and get out to the truck. There are soldiers in harm's way."

She blinked twice. Then her lips pursed. "You asshole," she slurred. Her right hand came up almost in slow motion, her fingers curling into a fist just in time to glance off his jaw.

He let her hit him, kind of, and then leaned in. "Listen. We're armed, and we'll take out anybody who tries to stop us."

Her eyes narrowed. She opened her mouth to scream.

He tightened his hold and leaned in closer. "Don't make me kill anybody."

She paused. "You are not kidnapping me again," she hissed, looking at her brother with concern.

Raze was already starting to stir, and Jax wouldn't stay down for long. They had to get the hell out of there.

"I'm not. You said yes this time. Stop worrying. Your brother will be fine," Greyson said, opening the door to see nobody waiting. Excellent. All they had to do was walk calmly out to the waiting Humvee before anybody raised an alarm. They'd be on the escape route in less than a minute. They walked by what looked like a mess hall.

A couple of men stood by the far door, across the expanse of tables, arguing about something. Greyson paused, looking for weapons.

"Grey?" Damon asked. "Move. Now."

Grey reached for his gun at spotting a semi-automatic at one guy's waist.

Maureen shoved him. "What are you doing?" She gasped for air.

Damon grabbed him. "Dude. We have to go. Now."

Damn it. He had to act cool. Greyson clasped Moe's arm again and pulled her out into the bright sunlight. "Walk normally to the vehicle so nobody gets shot."

She walked stiffly by him, her gaze darting around.

He shook his head. "There's no escape, baby. And Maureen? This time, it was your choice to come." Yeah. He'd asked her outright, and she'd said yes. "The rules have changed."

* * *

THREE HOURS after being kidnapped *again*, Maureen sat in the back of the Humvee, her head still aching a little bit from the flash grenade. Raze had shielded her, or she'd have a hell of a headache. Grey had been tense and on alert since they'd left Vanguard territory, taking back road after back road on the way to Santa Barbara. Finally, the smell of the ocean wafted through the open windows.

She'd given Grey and Damon the silent treatment as she fought her slight headache, but as the gate for Merc territory came into view, she straightened up. "This is kidnapping."

Grey didn't look her way. "Nope. You said yes this time."

Damon kept point out his window. "For all we knew, you were being held captive there. You did say you wanted to go, and Mercury said no." Amusement darkened Damon's tone.

Moe shoved her unruly hair away from her face. "Don't be obtuse, Damon." She reared up. "Aren't you a cop? You guys just blew up a flashbang in Vanguard territory. You hurt them."

Grey looked over his shoulder finally. "Raze and Jax are fine. I'm sure they got worse injuries in military training exercises before Scorpius." He glanced toward Damon. "I sure as shit did. You, Damon?"

The ex-cop nodded. "They're probably already on the road after us."

Grey slowed down as they approached the first gate. Maureen looked around. She'd been asleep the last time they drove through Merc territory. Barbed wire fencing was wrapped around what looked like a beach community. Tires, trucks, and even semi-trailers were lined around, blocking entry.

Or exit.

"This is similar to Vanguard," she murmured.

Greyson nodded. "There aren't many ways to secure a large section of land." He nodded at two men who quickly rolled the fence away. Once through, he drove down a street lined with mansions. It was definitely the upper end of Santa Barbara.

She studied him. To think. A baby they'd created was now growing inside her. How freaking crazy was that? She didn't even know him. But her kid would have good genes—physically, anyway. Greyson was well over six feet tall with cut muscles and obvious grace. Would their child have his odd eyes?

Would their child even survive to be born?

Would she tell Grey about the kid? Right now, it didn't seem like a protective thing to do. She couldn't stay long-term in Merc territory. Maybe Greyson wouldn't even want a kid. Worse yet. What if he did?

He nodded at different patrols—all men in black T-shirts with big guns.

Her stomach ached. She'd never get out of here if he didn't let her. A shiver overtook her. She had no power, and she hated that. It wasn't fair. "You can't build a society by just kidnapping people," she said. Yet even her brother hadn't been willing to listen to what she wanted. "We've gone back a hundred years."

Greyson stopped the Humvee at new mansion down the road from the one where she'd stayed before. The president had blown that one up. "We've gone back more, sweetheart. Sorry."

No. That absolutely wasn't okay. "Might can't make right. If so, why the hell are we fighting?" she asked.

He jumped out and opened her door, extending his hand. "We're fighting to survive."

There had to be more than that. She let him help her out. At the touch, heat and strength engulfed her entire hand. A spark flew up her arm, and she coughed to cover her reaction. So what. Biology always got in the way. A memory of his kiss crashed into her mind, and her heart rate picked up.

He shut the door. Keeping her hand, he strode toward the front porch. "We need to talk."

Well. That didn't sound ominous.

Damon cleared his throat from behind her. "I'll just grab some fresh clothes and give you guys the house."

She wanted to protest, but curiosity grabbed her. What did Greyson want to talk about? His hold was gentle but firm, his hand warm and strong. Just who was he? Was there a chance he was a decent guy, the kidnapping notwithstanding? She had said she wanted to check out the food resources, and that was crucial. Or did she just want him to be a good guy? Somehow?

They entered the home and walked through the living area. This one was decorated in warm beach tones. Without warning, somebody grabbed her arm and jerked her away. An arm banded around her waist and hauled her against a bony male body.

She cried out and struggled, stopping when a gun barrel pressed against her temple. Her breath stopped. The guy holding her felt tall, and his arm was cutting off her air.

A man dressed in the Mercenary's black T-shirt and jeans outfit stood to the side of Greyson with a gun pointed at Grey's head, and another man had a gun pointed at the back of Damon's head.

Greyson ignored the gun to his face and stared at her. "You'll be okay," he said calmly, his eyes swirling into a deep grayish-green. "I promise." He kept her gaze until she gave a short nod, careful not to nudge the gun at her head.

Grey turned toward the nearest threat. "You sure you want to do this, Lackson?"

Lackson, a shorter guy of around thirty, had slicked-back blond hair and crooked teeth. His body was wiry, and his hand shook around the gun. He swallowed, his Adam's apple visibly moving. "We just want the drugs, man. The clinic is too well guarded. I know there's coke and meth in there. Just get us the drugs, and we'll let her go." He backed away.

"I say we keep her," said the guy holding her. His arm moved up toward her breasts.

Greyson growled. He actually *growled.*

The arm stopped. The body behind her jerked in an odd shiver.

Greyson glared over her head. "You're not steady, and that gun doesn't have a safety, Cromwell. Take the gun away from her head before you accidentally shoot her. Because if you do, I'm going to gut you and make you eat your own intestines before you die."

Damon kept silent, watching the interplay.

Cromwell slowly moved the gun away from her head. She started to breathe again, her hand going instinctively to her abdomen.

Greyson attacked.

CHAPTER TEN

The enemy is all around us.
　—Greyson Storm, Letters to Miss Julian

GREY HAD GONE stone-cold the second he saw the pistol pressed to Moe's head. He kicked Lackson's gun out of the way and lunged for Cromwell, jerking him completely away from Maureen. He chopped down on Cromwell's wrist, sending the weapon to the floor. Then he grabbed the bastard by the neck and threw him into the wall.

The guy hit hard and fell forward, arms windmilling.

A quick glance confirmed that Damon had secured the gun that had been on him and now held it on Lackson and a guy named Smith. The two junkies cringed against the sofa.

Greyson turned back to Cromwell.

The guy was about forty and had been an okay soldier. Not a leader but could handle himself in a fight. Of course, that was before he'd started in on the drugs.

"Damon?" Grey asked. "Did you know we had a drug problem?"

"Don't think we do," Damon said quietly. "Just these guys do."

Cromwell stared at him, his eyes a furious green, his hair salt and pepper. "I don't have a drug problem, dickhead."

Interesting. Lackson definitely did. "Then why do you want drugs?" Grey asked quietly, noting that Maureen had edged around the sofa toward the big fireplace and away from any fight. Smart.

Lackson followed her movements.

Oh. The bastard wanted Maureen. Fury lit down Greyson's spine, and he quelled it. "You shouldn't have touched her," he said quietly.

Damon audibly caught his breath.

Grey ignored him.

"Why?" Cromwell sneered. "We can only have whores here, so you think she's just yours? She's not." He looked at Maureen, contempt in his eyes. "You're not safe. You get that, right? He'll pass you around just like the others."

Greyson partially turned and threw a punch, nailing Cromwell in the nose. Blood spurted, going everywhere.

Cromwell flew back again, cried out, and grabbed his face. "You asshole." His words were slurred, and blood bubbled between his fingers.

Greyson stared at him. He turned toward Maureen. She watched the interaction with wide eyes, a round mark on her temple from where the gun had pressed. The sight of it nearly made Greyson lose what little control he had left. "Sweetheart? I need you to go to your room now. It's past the living room to the right and has a great view of the ocean." He tried to keep his voice gentle.

She only blinked.

Damn it. She was in shock. "Moe." He put snap in his voice.

She jumped but otherwise didn't move.

Cromwell rushed him, going for a tackle. Man, Grey would like to extend this, but Maureen was watching, and he couldn't get her to leave the room. So he partially turned, wrapped his arm around Cromwell's neck, and flipped the asshole. His neck broke with a loud crack.

Grey dropped the body, which let out a death rattle and bounced twice on the ground.

Maureen gasped, falling back against the fireplace, her eyes wide and focused on the dead body. She paled so quickly she swayed.

Grey waited until she lifted her shocked gaze. "He touched you," he said quietly.

The two guys against the sofa started talking long and fast. Begging, really. Greyson silenced them with a wave of his hand. "Damon? Do an all-call. I want to see everyone who isn't patrolling out on the street. Right now."

Damon nodded and reached for a short-range radio on the kitchen counter, sending out the all-call.

Grey turned toward a visibly trembling Maureen. "Go to your new room, honey. I'll talk to you when this is finished." His chest ached at the terror all but rolling off her. He'd caused that fear, but there wasn't anything he could do to reassure her right now. If he was to keep her safe, he had to be the bastard he was rumored to be. So he grabbed Cromwell's body by the hair and dragged it out the front door and down to the street, where his men were already gathering.

Damon kept a gun on the other two, forcing them down the driveway.

Greyson dropped the body in the middle of the street, waiting until nearly forty men stood around. He'd talk to the other thirty when the patrols changed shifts. "I can't be any clearer than this. Cromwell touched Maureen Shadow, who's here under my protection. This is what happens."

The men around him, all soldiers now, whether they'd been before Scorpius or not. Serious eyes, hard stances, they looked at the dead body crumpled in the street with little emotion.

Grey jerked his head at the other two. "They didn't touch her, but they put her in danger." He took his gun from his holster and shot both men so quickly they didn't have time to object. Right between the eyes. A chest shot was better, but he had a point to make.

The bodies fell.

There were a few indrawn breaths, but mostly silence came from his people.

Greyson looked around. "If there's anybody who doesn't want to stay here, who doesn't want to live by my rules, then you can leave right now. Take a week's provisions and go."

Nobody moved.

"If you stay, then I expect you to keep her safe at all costs. Period." He looked at Damon, who'd remained silent the whole time. Oh, disapproval lingered in his dark eyes, but he would back Grey in front of the men. He always did.

Greyson looked around. "Leave the bodies here until tomorrow morning. I want the patrols to see them and know what happens. Then toss them into the ocean for the sharks to eat."

A soldier close to him swallowed audibly, and sweat rolled down his forehead.

Good. Grey was fine with fear if it kept Maureen safe.

He turned to go back to the house, stopping cold at seeing Maureen in the doorway. She had a hand wrapped around the doorframe as if she needed help to stand. Her face had gone stark white, and her lips seemed to be trembling.

Her blue eyes were wide with horror.

God. He took a step toward her.

She jerked and then turned around and ran away.

His chest compressed like he'd been kicked by a horse. An ache settled beneath his breastbone, and his shoulders felt like a thousand pounds had dropped from above. He'd give anything, *anything*, for her not to have seen that. For her not to have seen him. The real him.

He kept his head up and strode evenly toward the house, forcing all expression from his face. If only he could force emotion from his body.

Only silence remained in his wake.

* * *

A BRUISED AND battered Atticus brought Maureen her dinner a few hours later. She sat on the bed, this one another king with blue and yellow linens, staring out at the ocean, not thinking or feeling.

She looked up. "Atticus," she breathed.

He nodded and shuffled inside to place a tray on the end of the bed. His gray hair brushed his collar, and a large bump showed above his right eye. "Bastards tied me up. Greyson found me. I'm fine."

She gulped. "I'm glad you're okay." But she didn't move. She just couldn't.

"Eat up, sweetheart. I made brownies for dessert." His faded eyes twinkled. "We found a bunch of brownie mix last week on a raid."

She looked down at the fried kelp bass. The flaky, white fish had been one of her favorites. But now, her stomach rolled over. She barely kept herself from gagging. "Thanks, Atticus," she murmured.

He nodded and made his way out of the room. "I'm glad you're back, Moe."

She watched the door close behind him. The pictures of old sailboats on the wall failed to provide comfort. Greyson had murdered three men in front of her. Because they'd threatened her. She gagged again.

A sharp rap echoed on the door, and she started, her head going back. Her mouth opened, but nothing came out.

Greyson opened the door and walked inside, having changed

into dark jeans and a plain white T-shirt. Probably to get rid of any blood. He moved to a delicate-looking chair near the sliding glass door and sat, his forearms resting on his knees. "I thought we should talk." Dark and rich, his voice wove through the room, rising above the sound of the rolling sea.

"There's nothing to say," she said, moving back on the bed and farther away from him and the fish.

"There's a lot to say," he countered, his gaze going to her meal. "Eat."

"Not hungry." The mere idea of putting the food in her mouth rose bile in her throat.

He sat back, studying her. "I will feed you."

She shook her head. "I'll eat later. Right now I'm feeling sick. Very sick."

He nodded, no expression crossing his hard face. "I'm sorry you had to see all of that. I wish you would've just come to the room when I asked."

"I didn't know you were going to kill three people," she burst out, disbelief filling her.

He lifted a hand. "I'm not saying it's your fault. It isn't. I just didn't want you to see that."

She didn't understand him. Not at all. "You didn't have to kill them," she whispered.

"I know." He overwhelmed the small chair. "I could've let them go. Just sent them on their way. But then we'd have three more enemies out there. Desperate ones."

She scoffed. "You could handle three more enemies."

"Maybe, maybe not." His eyes were more green than gray in the dusky light. "But I also can't have my men, the ones who stayed, thinking there's any leniency. There can't be any. Not if you're gonna stay safe."

"No. There has to be a better way." Darkness fell over the ocean, lending an intimacy to the candle-lit room. Last time she was in a bedroom with him, they'd ended up naked. She swal-

lowed. Her heart started to thrum. How could she be attracted to
a killer? How could the father of her baby be so cold-hearted? "I
won't be a kidnap victim again, Greyson."

He huffed out air. "You are not a kidnap victim. You said you
wanted to come."

That was before he'd knocked out her brother. Before he'd
killed three men. "If you're not kidnapping me, then I'm free to
go. I don't have to stay here." Under lock and key again.

He studied her, the candlelight throwing the harsh angles of
his face into shadow. "You're right."

She opened her mouth to argue and caught herself.
"Wh-what?"

"You're right. I'm not kidnapping you, so you're free to go. If
you want to go back to Vanguard tomorrow, I'll take you," he said
evenly. "But I'm asking you to at least look at the greenhouses and
let us know our options first."

"You'll take me back?" she asked slowly, her mind spinning
the problem over and over.

He nodded. "Yes. Personally."

Man, Vanguard would probably shoot him on sight. She
looked around, at anything but him. He was just too much. Too
big, too strong, too dangerous. And now he was being reasonable.
She wasn't sure how to handle him being reasonable.

"I, ah, wanted to apologize for my actions the last night you were
here," he said, a very slight Southern accent hinting in his words.

She swung her head back to him, her mouth dropping open.
"You what?" The man who'd just easily killed three men was
apologizing? Like some gentleman from the eighteen hundreds?

He kept her gaze this time. "I took advantage of you, and I'm
sorry."

Confusion blanketed her. He just didn't make any damn
sense. And she couldn't handle gentleness from him right now.
"You didn't, Greyson." No matter what was happening, she'd

made her own decision that night. "We were both drunk, and you were concussed. You even protested."

His eyes lightened. "Not very much, I didn't. Not enough."

Not one part of her wanted to press the advantage he'd just given her. But she couldn't. She was her own person, and she owned up to her mistakes. "We're both responsible."

"That's kind of you to say."

Tears filled her eyes. Damn it. What the hell? She wasn't a crier. Never had been. "I, ah…"

He straightened. "Please. Don't cry."

The world crashed down on her. The loss and the fear and now the indecision. Tears started spilling over, wetting her cheeks, and she couldn't stop them. She coughed, trying to calm herself.

He moved toward her, sitting on the bed. "Moe. I'm so sorry. I would never have taken advantage—"

The tears increased. Shit. Hormones? This was crazy. She planted a hand on his muscled chest. "I'm just a little over-whelmed. This doesn't make sense. *You* don't make sense." Next to him, she felt small and vulnerable. Maybe a little lost. "Whose ring is on your necklace?" she asked. Why the heck had she asked that?

He gentled his touch. "The ring belonged to a lady named Miss Julian. She was my foster mother, and it's my good luck charm."

Foster mother? He had been in foster care. An image of a young and lonely Greyson caught her thoughts, shooting to her heart. More tears gathered. Geez. She needed to be alone. "Just go." *Please, just go.* What the hell was wrong with her?

"I can't." He picked her up and planted her on his lap, cradling her. Heat surrounded her along with ripped muscle. "It's okay. I know. Maybe there's a way I could make sense?" The hope in his voice caught her unaware. "Please don't cry. I'm sorry. I'll take you back first thing tomorrow when it's light. Not in the darkness."

She coughed out a laugh. "I just don't understand how you can go from killing three men to being scared of tears."

He gently wiped off her cheek. "Tears are freaking scary," he murmured.

She wanted to tell him about the baby. Have him shoulder the burden and just take over. He would. She knew it. But...what did that mean for the child? Or for her? This switch from cold-blooded mercenary to sweet guy afraid of tears was overwhelming. Confusing. Her first thought had to be the baby, if it even had a chance to survive. It might be irresponsible to tell him.

He rubbed a massive hand down her back. "Please don't cry. I'll take you back tomorrow."

There was only one chance to get to know him, and she did have a job to do. Not only with the plants but now also for the baby. She was a genetic engineer, and although she'd only worked with crops before, she could use that knowledge to help save the child. "No. I'll stay for one week." The temptation to burrow into his warmth made her stiffen. "We'll talk about it tomorrow, and I'll give you my conditions." She tried to make her voice strong, but the tears clogging her throat didn't help.

He sighed against her hair. "Your conditions. All right. But first, would you mind getting on the HAM radio and letting your brother know you're okay and here of your own volition? If not, Vanguard is going to storm the gates at first light, and I'd rather not have to shoot anybody else."

He wasn't kidding. The words could be taken as light, but the man really wasn't joking. He would shoot if attacked.

She'd already seen that firsthand.

CHAPTER ELEVEN

Somehow, softness and fragility have survived the apocalypse. I'm not sure how to protect that.

— Greyson Storm, Letters to Miss Julian

GREY SWIRLED bourbon in a glass in front of the quietly crackling fire in the main living room with Damon on a matching chair, doing the same. The moon glinted off the ocean outside, but darkness was all around them. "I made her cry," he mused, tipping his head back.

Damon sighed, his gaze on the fire. "She's been working in a lab in the middle of nowhere for most of the Scorpius battle."

"So?"

"So, she hasn't seen the fight to survive up close. It was probably her first triple murder scene," Damon said, his tone grim.

Greyson paused and looked at his buddy. "I'm sorry." The struggle Damon faced every day in this new world hurt to see. "Thank you for backing my play, even if you didn't agree."

Damon sighed. "I always back your play, and I'm not saying I disagree with what you did."

Greyson took a drink. "Okay?"

"I just wish that kind of display wasn't necessary." Damon plunked his boots on the coffee table and settled back in his chair. "I get it, but I don't like it. At some point, we have to go back to living like civilized people, right?"

Grey shrugged. "Yeah, but I'm not sure it'll happen in our lifetime. You saw shit as a cop, D."

Damon nodded, the firelight playing off the dark planes of his face. "I did. But we had a code and the law and a right and a wrong. I'm pretty sure."

"We had that, too," Grey murmured, his gaze going back to the flickering flames. "As a sniper, I trusted that the orders I followed were true. Were right." Now there was just him trying to hold together a band of soldiers shaped by a plague. The enemy was all around him. Many he'd created with his own actions. "You think we could take Jax Mercury and Vanguard in a war?"

Damon tipped back his head and finished his drink. "I think it'd be pretty close to a draw because most soldiers on both sides would end up dead. It's a mistake to engage with them."

"Yeah." Greyson reached over and refilled Damon's glass before topping off his own. "Even so, you've been there several times, and you've had a chance to look around."

Damon took another drink. "I'll diagram weaknesses tomorrow. But if you want to attack, now's the time. You've got Shadow's sister here, and that'll weaken him. They're also damaged from the president's attack, and the repairs will take at least another week."

"I'm not going to attack," Greyson said slowly. "And you know it."

"We both know you like to review your options," Damon countered.

That was true. Very true. "If we align with Vanguard, we have a better chance of taking on the president and his Elite Force." But then who would step up for the government? "Or it might be a better idea to align with the president." The thought made him nauseated, but it could be the smart move.

Damon swirled his drink around. "True. We don't know who'd step into the void if President Atherton is taken out. Could be worse than him, and he seems to be holding the Elite Force together. They have air support, which is more than anybody else has."

"If it's VP Lake, that guy is pure evil. We don't want to deal with him," Grey murmured.

Yet there was one inescapable fact. Bret Atherton had kidnapped Maureen Shadow, threatened her, and bruised her. That alone meant Greyson wanted to gut him. Plus, Grey had been shot during the rescue, and that just pissed him off. His arm still ached. The luxury of vengeance might be out of his reach, however. Difficult times made for odd alliances.

Damon set down his glass. "It might not be a bad idea to reach out to the president. See if he's interested in working together."

Grey rubbed the whiskers on his chin. "If he's alive."

"I've sent scouts up north to Elite headquarters. They should be back sometime tomorrow. If Atherton is alive and back in his place, we'll know it," Damon said.

Atticus poked his head around the kitchen doorway. "There's something wrong with your girl. She's sick."

Grey jumped to his feet, stalking toward the back bedroom. His breath caught in his lungs. "What do you mean?"

"She's outside throwing up," Atticus said. "I went to get her dinner dishes, and she wasn't there. The fish shouldn't have made her ill."

"I've got it," Greyson said, his heart hammering at a frightening speed. He opened her door and moved toward the deck, stopping short.

She rested her head back against the stucco side of the mansion, her eyes closed and her arms wrapped around her midsection. The moonlight shone down, shimmering in her hair and across her pale face.

Tears. Were those more tears?

He moved toward her.

She jerked, her eyes opening and her hand instinctively coming out in protest to stop his momentum.

He paused. "Moe?"

She drew in a shaky breath. The woman looked small and fragile in the darkness. "I'm fine. Just a little sick to my stomach," she said.

Because he'd killed in front of her. A fist dropped into Grey's gut. Damn it. Why hadn't she gone to her room when he'd asked? Maybe he should've forced her and then dealt with the men. "Can I get you anything?" he asked, tempted to wrap her up in his arms. "I think there's ginger ale in the kitchen. We found some last week near Fresno."

"No. I'm fine," she said, her voice shaky.

Maybe it had been the flash grenade. At the thought, he moved for her, tipping up her chin to catch the moonlight. "Look at me," he ordered.

She blinked, her pupils constricting. Good. That was an excellent sign.

"Does your head hurt?" he asked, taking her wrist and counting heart beats.

"No," she said softly. "I'm okay now. Just had an upset stomach."

They didn't have a doctor. Hadn't had one in far too long. "If you're still sick tomorrow, I'm taking you to Vanguard." Vanguard had at least three doctors and an Army medic. One of them would know what to do. Panic tried to take hold of him, but he shoved it away. When she talked to Raze via the HAM radio, her brother hadn't indicated that anything was amiss. "Has anything been going on with you? Any other symptoms?"

She shook her head.

"You've survived Scorpius, right?"

"Yes," she murmured, drawing back, her gaze leveled at his chest. "I'm fine, Greyson."

Why wouldn't she meet his eyes? Had he scared her, or was she just embarrassed? Nobody liked to be caught puking. "How about a hot toddy? We have whiskey around here somewhere, and I'm sure Atticus could find a lemon. It'll help you to sleep."

"No." She sidled past him, eyeing the plush furniture spread across the wide deck, apparently wanting to look anywhere but at him. "This is a nice sitting area."

"Took it from a mansion down the beach," he said, gesturing for her to sit. It seemed like the woman was about to fall down. "We moved it last week." So it'd be there for her in case she wanted to sit outside and watch the ocean.

She finally looked at him and then back at the furniture. "It's all cushiony." Still holding her stomach, she edged closer and sat in one of the chairs, stretching her legs out on the matching ottoman. "This is the high-end stuff. The sets you find in those fancy catalogues with people by Beverly Hills-type pools."

He nodded and strode around to sit in the matching chair. "I thought the same thing."

She gazed out at the rolling ocean with the moon shining down on the waves. "Pretty view."

He made a sound of agreement because *she* was lovely. Even too pale and a little shaky, the smooth planes of her face showed her high cheekbones and full mouth. Those blue eyes cut through the moonlight with a mystical glow. "Your brother looks more Native American than you do," he murmured.

She nodded. "Raze looks like our father, and I look more like our mother."

Maybe he could calm her down with chit-chat. "You were raised in Wyoming?" He'd read that in the dossier he'd had compiled on Raze a while ago.

"Yes. We had a small ranch, and our mom ran a local restaurant in town," Moe said.

"Ah." He chuckled. "You dated cowboys?"

She snorted. "No. Not cowboys, and definitely not soldiers." Like him. "Why not?" he asked softly, curious.

"They're in danger too often and sometimes they don't come back," she said, sounding a little lost. "So I stuck with nice guys. Nerdy and scientific."

So, not even close to a guy like him. "Interesting." Man, she was cute. And no longer crying, thank God. "I'd like you to lock the door to the beach at night, but it's up to you. The bedroom door won't be locked." He wasn't kidnapping her again.

She nodded. "Where are you from?" she asked.

He swallowed. It had been so long since he'd engaged in small talk, he was pretty sure he'd fuck it up. But he could at least answer a question or two. "Atlanta, actually." He kicked back in the chair and faced the ocean. "Was in foster care and then finally got taken in by Miss Julian, whose ring you saw." He smiled at the memory. "She was big on manners and could twist an ear like you wouldn't believe." God, he'd loved her.

"Did Scorpius take her?" Moe asked.

"No. Bee sting and weird allergic reaction took her the day after her eightieth birthday." He'd been overseas, and to this day, he missed writing her letters. He'd never admit it, but he still wrote her notes once in a while—kind of like journaling. There should be a record of life as it was.

Moe reached for his hand. "I bet she was proud of you. Of your going into the service."

He folded his fingers around her delicate hand, his chest warming. Even hurting, she'd offered comfort when she thought he needed it. "You're a sweetheart, Maureen Shadow," he said quietly.

She scoffed. "Only until I'm riled."

He grinned. Yeah, he knew that from past experiences. "Feeling better?"

"Yes." She didn't remove her hand.

"Good." The intimacy of the atmosphere—the ocean, moon, and night—wrapped around them. He should let her get to sleep, but the moment held too much comfort. They'd only had one night together, yet his body started to thrum. What he wouldn't give for a night without alcohol and confusion. A night to explore all of her. For now, he pushed away his desire and concentrated on the ease of the experience. He could worry about tomorrow and everything else later.

She stayed in place, maybe feeling the same thing. "You were a Marine?" she asked.

"Still am," he said quietly. That feeling, that allegiance would never leave him. No matter how screwed up the world became. He had that foundation, and he would hold on to it with everything he had. "Once a Marine...you know."

She chuckled, the sound soft in the quiet night. "Raze said you were a sniper."

"Yeah." He shifted his weight. Talking about his job was something he didn't do. Surely she'd understand that.

"Figures. You seem like a loner," she said, no judgment in the tone.

He blinked. "Actually, that's not true. Snipers work in pairs. Always."

"Really?" she asked, her voice rising a mite.

"Think about it. Everything that goes into lining up a shot. One guy can't do it all. The second guy is called a spotter." Remembering his spotter, Ferris, was a punch to the gut. "My spotter was a guy named Ferris. He was from south Georgia." Grey emphasized a Southern accent. "Guy could shoot like a dream, argue like an old Southern lady, and fight like a boxer. Hell of a dancer, too."

Maureen relaxed into the cushions of the chair with a soft sigh. "Sounds like a character."

"He was," Grey murmured. "Was my best friend and the closest thing I've ever had to a brother." Now he had Damon, but he'd give anything for Ferris to be there, too. Life would be better. The *world* had been better with Ferris in it. Damn Scorpius bacterium.

"Scorpius took him?" Moe asked gently.

Grey nodded. He owed Maureen an explanation that he'd never given her. The reason why he'd kidnapped her in the first place. "Yeah. He died in my arms, and I made him one promise. One vow."

She turned to look at him, the moonlight dancing across her delicate features. "What was that?"

He swallowed and focused back on the mysterious ocean. "That I'd put a bullet between Zach Barter's eyes. No matter what it took."

CHAPTER TWELVE

I know I'm supposed to clinically record the events of the day as a scientist. But for the love of God, I'm knocked up by a man I barely know. The more I learn, the more deadly, dangerous, and intriguing he gets. How screwed up is that?
—Maureen Shadow, Notes

AN EXPLOSION RIPPED Maureen out of sleep. She jumped to her feet and staggered, looking around wildly. Morning light was barely peeking through the windows. Something else blew up in the distance, followed by the scratch of metal and wood cracking. Panic caught her around the neck and squeezed. Barefooted, she yanked open her door and ran into the living room and almost straight into Greyson.

He caught her arms and moved her to the side, his broad torso bare, and his jeans unbuttoned. His dark hair was ruffled, and his steel-gray eyes pissed. "Stay here."

Damon ran down the hallway, jerking on a shirt. "What the hell?" Rough whiskers covered his jaw.

"Dunno." Greyson hustled for the doorway, opening the coat closet at the last second. He reached in and tossed a couple of guns and knives to Damon, taking several for himself. He strode over and placed a small handgun in Moe's hand. "Stay in the house, and if somebody manages to get in the front door, take them out. If you can't, run for the beach. I have patrols out there."

She blinked. The metal in her palm felt heavy and cold. What was happening?

The sound of automatic gunfire pattered through the dawn.

Greyson stiffened and lifted his head to listen. "South entrance. Let's go." He turned and followed Damon out the front door.

Maureen swallowed and turned the gun over in her hand. South entrance. They were being attacked. She'd reassured Raze that she was fine the previous night, but he hadn't sounded convinced. In fact, he'd sounded more than a little bit furious.

Oh God. Had her brother shown up in Merc territory by himself?

She ran out the door and headed straight for the SUV Grey and Damon had jumped into, her feet slapping the already warm bricks.

Grey leaned out the driver's side window, his muscled arm on the sill. "Get back inside. Now."

She turned to see smoke and fire coming from about a mile away. Near the entrance she'd used the other day. "I have to come." Ignoring his frown, she jumped for the back door and opened it, climbing inside. "In case it's my brother." She had to stop them from killing each other.

Grey looked over the seat. "You need to stay here. I'll handle it."

"No." She crossed her arms and met his gaze. Her stomach rolled over, and bile rose in her throat, but she hid the discomfort. "I won't let you or Raze die today."

Grey cut her a harsh look and turned toward the front, started the engine, and shot out in reverse. "If it isn't Vanguard, you're bringing this vehicle back to the mansion. Got it?"

She nodded. "Yes." That seemed fair. It wasn't like she wanted to get into a firefight while pregnant. She pressed a hand to her belly, doubt assailing her. The world had changed for her, and she needed to take a moment. It wasn't only her heading into danger right now, and she had to start putting the babe first.

More automatic gunfire pierced the morning.

"Get down," Greyson ordered, punching the gas and swinging through the high-end subdivision.

Her heart thundering, she crouched farther down on the seat. Her ears rang. A metallic taste filled her mouth. She intellectually knew it was adrenaline, but she couldn't slow her pulse.

In no time, Greyson braked, hard. "Stay here until I call for you." He jumped out and slammed the door.

Moe slowly lifted her head to see that he'd parked behind a stone wall topped with barbed wire and was walking toward a slightly open gate with Damon right behind him. There was only the wall, and she couldn't see a damn thing past it. But more gunshots could be heard.

Nausea attacked her, and she gagged.

Drawing courage, she gingerly stepped from the SUV and moved to the wall, putting her back to the rough stones. They were already warm from the sun, which angled right at them. She took several deep breaths. Quiet suddenly came from the other side of the barrier.

Gulping more air, she edged to the end of the wall and peered through the open gate.

Greyson crouched behind one of the many cars placed strategically between the stone wall and another made-made mountain of tires, trucks, and fencing complete with more barbed wire. Several of his men also squatted behind cars, once in a while levering up to take a shot outside the farthest gate.

A building to the right of the wall, one that had probably held a water system at one time, burned furiously and spilled dark smoke, probably from one of the several explosions she'd heard.

She squinted. Two trucks were angled nose-to-nose outside the tire barrier, with men ducked behind. One levered up to fire, and she caught sight of his hair.

Damn it.

"Raze," she yelled as loudly as she could. "Stop firing, damn it." Waiting a couple of beats to make sure everyone had frozen, she walked past the gate and into the opening.

Within a second, Greyson Storm captured her in a hug, dragging her toward the car. "What the holy fuck are you doing?" he snarled, his arms stronger than steel.

She didn't bother to fight him and just waited until he'd deposited her butt on the ground. In the early hour, the concrete was still cool.

"Moe?" Raze yelled over the crackling fire. "You okay?"

Actually, the world was spinning around her at an alarming rate. She pulled up her knees and pressed her face to them, trying to halt the dizziness. This whole pregnancy thing was messing with her equilibrium, big time. "I survived Scorpius," she reminded herself, her voice muffled by her yoga pants.

Grey flattened his big hand across her upper back. "I know, sweetheart. You okay? What's going on?"

She lifted her head, pathetically grateful when their surroundings stopped swirling around. "Nothing. I may have a bug."

He rubbed a hand down her spine. "Maybe we should get you to a doctor."

A man groaned over to the right, and Moe turned her head to see a guy half-hidden beneath a car with blood pooling on the pavement. She gasped. "Damn it." Turning to the side, she dry-heaved.

Greyson grasped her hair and pulled it away from her face.

She paused and looked at him. He was holding her hair. "Reminds me of prom," she gasped and then dry-heaved again.

He winced. "There's nothing in your stomach. Did you eat the fish last night?"

God. The fish. The idea made her heave again. She shook her head. "No." Swallowing several times, she tried to control herself. "I think your guy over there is bleeding to death," she muttered.

"He has a tourniquet on his arm. You can't see it behind the tire," Grey said, leaning in and studying her eyes again.

Gunfire popped, and she jumped.

"What the fuck?" Greyson straightened and looked over the hood of the black SUV. "Your brother is firing into the air."

"Moe?" Raze bellowed.

She winced. "I'd better let him know I'm all right." Moving toward Greyson, she tried to crawl her way up the car.

He planted a hand on her shoulder. "Stay down."

"No." She tried unsuccessfully to dislodge him. "Let me up."

"Shadow?" Greyson called out. "Your sister is here. Have everyone put down their guns, and I'll let you talk to her."

There was a slight pause. "Guns down," Raze yelled.

Grey waited a minute, looked around, and then released her. "Stand up but stay behind the vehicle."

She rolled her eyes. "My brother won't hurt me."

"I can't see who's with him," Grey returned, his focus absolute on the trucks outside the gate. He partially stood in front of her.

She stood, her knees trembling. Cold and then heat swept along her skin. Maybe she actually did have the flu or something weird. "Raze?" she yelled, waving.

Her brother moved out from behind the trucks, exposing himself.

"Tell your men not to shoot him," she blurted out, her lungs catching.

Grey nodded, but a shot rang out before he could give the order.

Raze dropped to one knee, blood spurting from his thigh.

"Raze," Maureen cried out, bunching to run around the car for him.

Greyson manacled an arm around her waist, halting her cold. "Everyone fucking stand down," he bellowed, his voice low with fury. His body vibrated behind her, one long line of anger. "Who the fuck shot him?" He looked around.

Damon glanced up from behind a green Volkswagen and then jerked his head toward a redheaded guy by a burned-out truck. "Lenny."

"Lenny?" Greyson yelled. "You're on shit duty for the next month. Fucking drop your gun on the ground. Now."

Raze lifted his weapon and pointed it at Greyson's head, right over Moe's. Blood poured from his thigh. "Let my sister go, and I won't scatter your brain right now," he said, his tone beyond furious and bordering on scary.

Moe swallowed. "Raze? Put something on that leg."

Muttering about the fucking Shadow family, Greyson kept his arm around Maureen's waist and drew her around the car, heading for Raze. "If anybody on either side of this disaster fires a shot, I will gut them myself with my favorite knife," he said loud enough for everybody to hear.

Moe struggled against his hold, trying to run for her brother.

He held her tight. "Slow movements. We don't want to spook anybody, darlin'."

Damon suddenly appeared on her other side. "Exactly what's your plan here, boss?" he asked, his gun in his hand but pointed at the ground.

Greyson stopped, partially putting Moe behind him. "Mercury? I promise nobody else will shoot."

Jax Mercury stepped out from behind one of the trucks with Tace Justice on his heels. Both men held guns pointed straight at Greyson's chest. Jax kept his aim true, walking toward them, while Tace jogged to Raze and quickly secured a belt around the injured thigh.

Jax stopped next to Raze, his light eyes revealing nothing. "Send her over, Storm."

Tace helped Raze to his feet.

Damon whistled. "The three top lieutenants of Vanguard. All in one place."

Grey gave a short nod.

Moe's legs wobbled. If he'd decided to take them out, they'd just given him the perfect opportunity. He wouldn't do that, would he?

"She has elected to stay here," Grey said evenly.

"Not a chance," Raze growled, his face pale as he balanced on one leg. "Maureen? You okay?"

"Yes," she said, trying to shove past Greyson. "I'm fine." It'd be easier to push a freaking mountain. "Move, Greyson," she muttered.

He paused, looked around, and then sandwiched her between him and Damon. "If you want to go back with your brother, tell me now. I'll take you right over to him," Grey said low enough that his voice didn't carry. "But I need to know immediately."

She hesitated. "I want to see your greenhouses, the two labs outside your territory, and the Bunker." It was doubtful she could talk her brother into the last two requests, and she had Grey where she wanted him. She could feel it. For the baby, she had to get into the Bunker and find whatever research they had about Scorpius and pregnant women. "Promise you'll take me to all three, and I'll stay here until my work is finished. Then you can escort me back to Vanguard."

"It's a deal," Greyson said, keeping his gaze on the Vanguard soldiers.

By then she'd know him better and have an idea what to do about the baby. Determine whether or not she should tell him. She planted her feet more securely. "I'm staying here until I see the greenhouses," she called out. "Greyson promises to bring me back. I just need a week, Raze."

"He kidnapped you again," Raze thundered, his high cheekbones flushing an angry red.

At least he wasn't so pale. Maureen nodded.

"I did not," Greyson countered. "She said she wanted to come."

"You used flash grenades," Jax snapped, his aim steady. "That's kidnapping."

Before Greyson could argue further, Maureen held up a hand. "Everybody listen. This is my decision. I'm staying a week, and then I'll head back to Vanguard with information. We all need to know what our options are for food since we're running out. Or we *will* run out at some point." Why didn't the testosterone-filled men see that they needed to all work together? God, she hoped she was having a girl. Heck. She hoped the baby lived. Getting to the Bunker and its research data was crucial. "All right?"

"No," Raze said shortly, leaning on Tace.

Concern swept through her. "Tace? How bad is that wound?"

Tace eyed the leg. "Bullet needs to be taken out." His Texas twang deepened. "Within the next few hours would be best."

That was enough time to return to Vanguard. "Go," Maureen said. "Please trust me." She was an adult, damn it.

"Come here and tell me face-to-face," Raze challenged, his jaw set hard.

Greyson snorted. "You go over there, and you're headed back to Vanguard now. You get that, right?"

"Yes." She sighed. "I'm fine, Raze. Sugar cookies."

Raze's eyebrows rose. "I don't care. Come here."

"Sugar cookies?" Damon asked.

"Code for 'everything is fine,'" she said. "From our childhood."

Greyson nodded. "Now we start to back up. Slowly."

Raze said something under his breath to Jax.

Greyson and Damon both tensed, and Grey shoved Moe behind him. She stumbled and grabbed the waist of his jeans to keep from falling. Her fingers brushed bare skin. Figured he'd go commando. She cleared her throat.

"Storm?" Jax snapped. "If she wants to stay here, she can. One condition. I'm staying with her."

Moe peered around Grey to see Raze and Jax arguing furiously beneath their breaths. She couldn't hear the words, but their mouths were moving. *Fast.*

"Apparently your brother wants to stay instead of Jax," Damon muttered.

Not with a bullet hole in his leg. Moe shook his head. "He needs a doctor."

Greyson nodded. "Jax? You and Raze aren't invited. However, if Tace would like to stay and guard Miss Shadow, the medic is welcome if he'll also act as our doctor for the week. We could use him."

Moe opened her mouth to argue and then remembered that Vanguard had several other doctors who could help Raze. "Good plan." If Raze didn't get a move on, he wouldn't get that bullet removed in time. She released Greyson and, pretending a bravado she so did not have, she turned and walked casually back toward the stone wall, pausing at the entrance to turn and wave at her brother. "I'll see you in a week." Then she slid around the barrier, waiting until she was out of sight before wincing at the fury she'd seen on his face.

She took a deep breath. Well. That was probably a huge mistake.

CHAPTER THIRTEEN

We have too many enemies and no friends. Sometimes that makes things easier. Not this time.
　　—Jax Mercury Journal

THREE HOURS after leaving Maureen in Mercenary territory, Jax watched as Dr. Penelope deftly finished sewing up the hole in Raze's leg in the Vanguard headquarters' clinic. The soldier had sat quietly in the small examination room throughout the entire procedure, refusing anesthetic because supplies were so low. Sweat dotted his forehead, and his pupils had expanded into the odd blue of his eyes from the obvious pain.

Marcus lounged by the door, deceptively calm with his arms crossed. Yet he watched every movement made by anybody in the room. He never left Penelope's side after being rescued from the Bunker weeks ago, where the government had experimented horribly on him. Penelope had been a doctor there who saved him, risking her life in the process.

But apparently he didn't remember Jax or anybody else in his life. Only Penelope.

Jax stretched, and Marcus turned, focusing on him.

Geez. Jax wanted to smack him. Did his own brother really think he'd hurt the petite doctor? Jax had been giving Marcus time to get reoriented and calm down before talking to him. But that didn't seem to be working. So they were gonna talk—and soon. After Jax made sure Raze was okay.

"Let me give you an aspirin," Penelope murmured, gently placing a bandage over the wound. Her black hair was piled on her head and out of the way, while her almond-shaped eyes were calm and reassuring. The woman's features were Korean, her coloring dark, her stature petite, and her doctoring extremely competent.

Raze shook his head. "I'm fine, Dr. Penelope."

"Just Penelope," she said, pulling reusable plastic gloves off her hands. "I'm not sure how the nickname started, but I'm fine with people just using my first name."

Raze swung his leg over the end of the examination table and groaned. "The title reassures people. That we have a doctor around." His fingers curled over the edge, and his knuckles turned white.

"We should let Vinnie know about your injury," Jax said again. The shrink and Raze were an item, and she'd be ticked that they hadn't told her about the gunshot wound.

"I'll go find her now. She would've just fretted while Dr. Penelope did the surgery," Raze said, breathing out.

More likely the shrink would've hounded Raze until he took some sort of pain killer, and the soldier hadn't wanted to argue. "Sorry you got shot," Jax said, hurting for his buddy.

Raze cut him a harsh look. "I'm sorry we left my sister in that hell hole."

Hell hole? The Mercs lived on the ocean and had fresh fish to eat. Jax bit back his temper. "She wanted to stay, and she's doing important work to help us all. Plus, we left Tace. He'll protect her." While also exploring what little of Merc territory they didn't know about as of yet. Just in case Vanguard decided to take over the fiefdom at the ocean. Fresh fish would be nice.

"He's there on mission, and you know it." Raze eased to the floor and accepted a crutch held out by Marcus. "Thanks." Careful to give the doctor and Marcus both plenty of room, he hitched toward the door and headed out. "I'm finding my shrink and then taking a nap."

"Meeting tomorrow morning, first thing," Jax said. "We need to strategize about the Mercs, the president, and what's next."

Raze might've growled something.

Jax faced his brother, his chest filling. His lungs didn't seem to be working properly. "It's time you and I talked." Would Marcus even try?

Dr. Penelope gathered up the bloody bandages and tossed them into the garbage can. She straightened and stretched her back. "I'll leave you two alone."

"No," Marcus said, not moving from his position. He'd always been big, but since Scorpius, he was even more tightly muscled and broad across the chest. His eyes were greener than Jax's, his hair a little darker, and his jaw squarer. At six-foot-four, they stood eye-to-eye. "You stay, Penny."

The doctor sighed. "Marcus, we've talked about this. You promised to work on time apart." Her tone was gentle and her eyes concerned. "This is a good opportunity, and Jax is your brother. Family can be everything."

"You're everything," Marcus said.

Penelope blinked.

Jax's formidable temper began to rise. He'd practically raised Marcus, and it was time to stop coddling him. Was the doctor afraid of his brother? He needed to talk with her next without Marcus around. Somehow. But Marcus first. Jax pressed a button on his watch. "Ten minutes. I'll time us."

Penelope nodded, relief in her pretty eyes. "Ten minutes. You can do that, Marcus. I'll be just down the hallway."

Marcus watched Penelope approach the door, his body visibly tightening. She kept her head high, went through, and shut it. He moved to put his back to the examination table, his gaze on the closed door, his arms still crossed.

Jax shook his head. "Dude. You have it bad for her."

"It's not like that," Marcus muttered, not moving an inch.

Jax swallowed, searching for a way to get through to him. "Then what is it?"

Marcus shrugged.

Fine. Different subject. "You don't remember me at all?"

"No," Marcus said shortly, no emotion in the tone.

Fuck. Jax scrubbed his hands down his face, the truth a punch to the solar plexus. His brother had been tortured for months, and part of that had included a drug regimen. The Bunker scientists had experimented on Scorpius survivors because some were stronger and smarter than before. So who the hell knew what Marcus had been through? Penelope knew some of it, but she refused to tell Jax anything without Marcus's permission. "Talk to me, Slam," Jax said, using a childhood nickname.

Marcus blinked and then focused back on the door. "There's nothing to say. How many minutes left?"

"Not tellin' you," Jax snapped.

No reaction.

Jax bit back anger. "Listen. If you want to stay in Vanguard, you have to work on this. You're scaring people." Just how unhinged was his brother? Jax was the Vanguard leader, and he owed the members, all five hundred of them, safety. Or at least the attempt to gain safety. He also owed Penelope a safe haven. "If we kick you out, Dr. Penelope will stay." That was an incentive.

"I go where she goes," Marcus said softly, the tone deadly. "Period."

"You seem to forget that I'm in charge here," Jax said.

Marcus finally turned to meet his gaze. "I don't care."

For a moment, a very brief one, Jax could see the kid deep

down who'd once followed him around. "She does," Jax said. "Are you scaring her?"

Marcus cut him a look. "No."

"Are you sure?"

Marcus lifted a shoulder and turned back toward the innocuous door.

"She seemed pretty happy to get out of here," Jax said slowly.

Marcus's chin lowered, but he didn't reply.

"We're brothers," Jax said.

Marcus lifted an eyebrow. "Why do we have different last names?"

Geez. "Different fathers, same mother. Doesn't matter. We're brothers," Jax said quietly.

Marcus breathed out. No emotion...no reaction.

Fine. Enough. They weren't getting anywhere. "We're done. You can go run after her," Jax muttered. He'd talk to the shrink before trying this again with Marcus.

Surprisingly, Marcus stayed in place. "How many minutes left?"

Jax frowned. "Who cares? I said we're done."

"Penny said ten minutes."

Jax studied this brother who was more like a stranger. A threatening one. "So you just stay here for ten minutes? No matter what?"

"Penny said," Marcus said calmly.

"Aren't you an obedient little bitch?" Jax asked. Could he make Marcus angry? Maybe get some emotion—any emotion— from the guy? "She has you trained like a lapdog."

No anger. No emotion. No...nothing. Marcus just stared at the door.

The alarm went off.

Marcus launched himself at the door and quickly disappeared.

Jax stared at the open doorway, his mind spinning. His chest hurt. What the fuck were they going to do with the guy? How could he get Marcus to remember him? His temples started to pound.

Lynne Harmony poked her head in. "Why was Marcus running?"

"He lost sight of Dr. Penelope," Jax said, trying to unclench the fists he hadn't realized he made. He took a deep breath and studied the love of his life. Of any life. Lynne's blond hair was pulled back in some intricate braid, throwing the sharp angles of her stunning face into pale symmetry.

Her green eyes focused on him. "You okay?"

"No." He moved for her, running his hands down her arms, soothing himself with her scent. She was the former head of the CDC, a kind woman, and one of the smartest people still alive today. She was also the only Scorpius survivor whose heart had turned blue from a failed cure after Zach Barter purposefully infected her. Jax wanted Barter dead as badly as Greyson apparently did.

"Why aren't you okay?" Lynne asked. "Is it Marcus? He has to be getting better."

"He's not." For now, Jax needed her insight. "Do you think Marcus is dangerous? I mean, to Dr. Penelope? To you? To the kids still here?"

Lynne pursed her lips. "I'm not sure about Penelope. He seems to want her safe at all costs. But who knows. Obsession always comes with a breaking point."

That's what Jax feared. The Scorpius bacterium attacked the brain, sometimes robbing the victim of empathy. Of feelings. The plague had left sociopaths in its wake. Some were just cold, some crazy, and some brilliantly insane. Obsession was a problem with all three. "What about everyone but Penelope?" he asked quietly, his gut churning. How could he choose Vanguard over his brother?

Lynne sighed. "I'm not a shrink, Jax."

"I'm well aware of who and what you are, baby. Answer the question," he said.

She bit her lip. "I don't really know. But if anybody is a threat to Penelope, or if Marcus *perceives* anybody being a threat to her, then yes. I believe that person is in danger. Definitely."

Yeah. That's what Jax thought, too.

CHAPTER FOURTEEN

*I got her brother shot. Somehow I don't think this is the beginning of a
beautiful friendship.*
    —Greyson Storm, Letters to Miss Julian

GREYSON PARKED the SUV outside the greenhouse that had once
been a part of the university. Maureen sat in the passenger seat
and reached for the door.

"Wait," Grey said.

She paused and glanced over her shoulder at him. "Why?" In
the strong afternoon light, her eyes looked more like a darkened
sky than their usual lighter tone. Her lips were pink, and color
had finally returned to her face.

Man, she was pretty.

His body reacted, and his jeans became too tight. "We wait
until my scouts have secured the area," he said, his voice lower
than normal. "We don't come out here much, so there could be
problems. Just hold tight."

"Is that where Tace went?" she asked, craning her head
toward the greenhouse.

Grey nodded, unable to stop himself from sliding the hair off her shoulder. "Yes. He wanted to make sure the area was secure before you came out." Of course, Tace was more than likely scouting the territory to report back to Vanguard in case they decided to attack again. But there was no need to tell Moe that. "I hope there's food here."

She looked down at the stack of papers he'd found for her in one of the school offices. A blush covered her cheekbones. "You're always touching me."

He paused. "I'm sorry." Shit.

She looked his way. "I don't mind."

If that wasn't an invitation, he didn't know what was. But he had to be honest with her. "Listen, Moe. I'm trying really hard to be a gentleman, and I never want to scare you."

"I'm not scared," she said, her gaze dropping to his lips.

Hers looked beyond kissable. "Good. But I'm also not a casual date kind of guy." In fact, he never had been. "That doesn't work for me." He'd already tasted her, and he'd already had her. A part of him, one darker than before Scorpius, wanted to bind her to him no matter what.

"I don't know what that means," she said, her gaze lifting.

"It means that if you're mine, you're mine." There were probably better words, smoother words. But he didn't have them. All he had was honesty, and he'd give that to her. "Even before Scorpius, I was a possessive bastard. Probably too much so."

"You didn't hurt women," she said, sounding sure.

That was sweet. "Of course not. But I was way overprotective, and I'm more so now. I take care of what's mine, Maureen. You should know that."

Her mouth opened and then closed. "That's a bit primitive, don't you think?"

He nodded. "Definitely. But it is what it is. And I wanted you to know." He could actually see the pulse in her neck kick into gear.

She swallowed. "Why?"

"Because I want you." Under him, around him, over him. He wanted her in every way there was. "But the decision is yours." If she made it, he wouldn't let her go.

A scout whistled, and he jerked his focus away to see a sign. "We're clear on the right. Waiting for the left." His hands itched with the need to touch her again.

She licked her lips.

He groaned and cupped her chin, rubbing his thumb across her bottom lip. Her skin was so damn soft.

She caught her breath.

Just one kiss. He leaned in, his mouth brushing hers. Fire crashed down his spine, landing in his balls. He hadn't imagined how sweet she tasted. How good she felt. She made a small sound and pressed against him.

The world narrowed, but he stayed alert, still enjoying the moment. They hadn't had nearly enough time that one night.

He deepened the kiss, sweeping his tongue inside her mouth. His instincts bellowed for him to take, to possess, and he quelled them, coaxing a response from her. She kissed him back with surprising force, moving closer to him, her hands pressing into his shoulders. Her fingers curled, and her nails bit through his T-shirt.

The constant noise in his head went silent. Grasping her hips, he plunked her on his lap so she straddled him, deepening the kiss at the same time.

His dick jumped against her core, shoving against his zipper. He flexed his hand and pulled her into his erection, nearly groaning at the contact.

She stiffened and tore her mouth away, turning to the side. "Wait." The breath panted out of her.

He paused and relaxed his hold. Then he quickly surveyed the area outside the vehicle. All clear. For the moment. Gently, he took her chin again and forced her to face him. Her lips were rosy and definitely well kissed. Her eyes had darkened even more, and desire had flushed her cheeks a lovely pink.

He blinked. God, she was perfect.

What were the words? He should say some. But at the moment, his cock was trying to rip through his jeans, and every instinct he had bellowed for him to strip her bare and take everything she had. Everything she was. Oh, he'd keep her safe and protected. But she'd give him everything.

Her eyes widened. "What are you thinking?"

Sometimes the words were better left unsaid. His mouth twitched. "Unless you like an audience, we should probably—"

With a muffled 'eek', she all but rolled off his lap and back into her own seat. "I forgot where we were."

Yeah. His pride might've swelled just a little. "It's okay. We'll finish this discussion later."

She swung toward him, righting her shirt. "Maybe. I mean, whatever." She turned back to the window.

The woman was adorable when riled. Okay. He'd hit her with enough for the moment. Time to back off. "Do you think we'll find food?"

She cleared her throat and smoothed her hands down her jeans. "If there's food, this is the right greenhouse, Greyson. But don't get your hopes up."

He looked around at the empty buildings that had once housed students and faculty who had no idea the end was probably coming. None of them had. "If not, what are our options?" he asked, trying to sound normal and not in need of her body.

"We'll see," she said, her voice a little hoarse. "Where have you been getting fresh water?"

"We had working water for the first two months, and we raided several warehouses for bottled water during that time, so we've had enough. Last month, we started taking the empty industrial jugs to Lake Cachuma and bringing it back," Greyson said. "It's not ideal."

"No," she said. "But Vanguard has been doing something similar, and they collect rain water as well. Water is going to be an issue."

Yeah, that's what he'd figured.

His scouts came around the building and gave him the sign. Tace Justice was with them, no doubt taking tons of mental notes. "All right. You still have the gun I gave to you?"

She jerked and reached for a small pack. "Yes. I put it in here. Atticus gave it to me."

Grey studied her. She'd been off since she arrived, the kiss notwithstanding. Why was she so nervous? "Are you sure you're up to this? We can come back tomorrow."

"I'm fine." Her chin firmed, and she shoved open her door. "Let's see if there's any hope here."

* * *

THE FRONT DOOR of the first greenhouse led to a series of offices with papers strewn all around. Enough light came through the myriad of windows that flashlights were unnecessary in this area. Desk drawers were open and dumped on the floor, and even the books had been ripped off shelves. Maureen glanced down at some papers, picking up a couple. "Graduate student experiments," she mused, reading quickly.

Greyson surveyed the office. "Early looters were just looking for food and medicine. We won't find anything else here."

His voice was a low timber, and it settled right into her belly. Her lips still tingled from his kiss, and her body felt electrified. Ready. Willing and able. Man. She had to get a grip on herself.

Why was life so damn confusing?

She nodded and then moved into the hallway, walking down it to a door that had been left ajar. Opening it, she peered around to see six tables set around the room. The smell of decay hit her, and she took several deep breaths. She couldn't throw up again, damn it. Dead plants and flowers lined the tables, now crumbling to dust. "This was a workroom." Lifting her head, she moved across the room to the next one. "This should be a growth room."

More decay and dead plants. The smell was, well, sad. She surveyed the equipment and where the water should've been supplied. "We're not going to find anything here, Greyson." Moving past the growth room, she made her way to the room that really mattered.

The containment room.

Chances were the university hadn't been working on anything too dangerous. But this would be an indication of what she'd find at the other labs. Probably.

The door to the containment room was only partly closed. Wonderful. Just freaking great. She paused.

"What?" Greyson said from right behind her. This close, she could feel his heat. Feel the strength that was at her back.

"Not good," she muttered. On any level. Professional or personal. She had to get a grip on herself. She started to step inside the room, but he grabbed her arm.

"Wait a minute. Is this dangerous?" he asked.

She shook her head. "Doubtful. Very doubtful. They would've just been experimenting with crops, and possibly fungi. Harmful agents that infect plants." He released her, and she moved inside to see the entire place ripped apart. "Scavengers got here." If they'd taken any food, they might've spread a disease or three. "I was afraid of this."

Greyson looked around at the decay and disaster. "So, no food?

"Not a chance." She turned and looked at him. "We have three more greenhouses to check out on the university campus, but we're not going to find viable food options here. Water is a problem, as is good soil, as are seeds. If we can even find any."

He looked down from his twelve inches of height. "Is it possible, though?"

She tilted her head. "To make these sustain food for about fifty people? Maybe." She shook her head. "But that's limited at some point. You understand that, right? You need land and fresh water to sustain a bigger population. Think long-term."

He scratched his head. "I don't have the luxury of thinking long-term yet."

Ouch. Okay. She kind of knew that already, but she didn't have a choice. "All right."

"Let's check out the other greenhouses, and then you can give me a plan for how to get them up and running again. I just need enough food for the Mercs. Not worried about the rest of the world quite yet."

"That's fine, but you're not seeing the problem. The *bigger* problem," she murmured, surveying the hole in the far wall.

"What's that?" he asked, placing a hand on her shoulder.

Her entire shoulder. The man was so strong and big and capable. Everything in her—especially the pieces she didn't trust—wanted to turn and burrow right into him. To let him shield her—even just for the moment. But she stood taller. "Any bad agents, though there probably weren't many, were let out of here. If we find similar breaches in other labs, particularly one studying the deadlier strands, we're in trouble. Future trouble with all crops and food sources."

He blinked. "What are our options?"

She winced. "We're going to have to view live crops. I'll come up with a plan, but we're sharing it with Vanguard. And we need to visit the Bunker." She couldn't leave her brother out.

Greyson sighed. "Why do you want to go to the Bunker?"

"Resources," she said simply, fully aware she was only telling him half the truth. "As far as I've heard, there are many Bunkers throughout the USA, and one of them, if not several of them, will have the information we need." She wasn't ready to tell him everything—not until Vanguard could be included.

He slid his hold down her arm and took her hand. "So there's nothing here right now?"

"No." She surveyed the equipment rusting in the corner. "If you get fresh water here, which I'm not sure is possible, you might be able to grow vegetables. Maybe." Though it wasn't the best plan.

Although, she didn't have a best plan quite yet. Nausea rolled within her stomach. Suddenly and without question. Must be those stupid pregnancy hormones. She needed to find some crackers. Those were supposed to help, right?

He partially turned her to face him. "You've gone pale again."

Yeah. Morning sickness sucked. But at least that meant her body was still creating the pregnancy hormone, so she was still pregnant. The threat plaguing her wouldn't leave her alone, and she had to banish it. Just because Dr. Penelope didn't know of any live births since Scorpius, didn't mean there hadn't been any. Information was tough to obtain. The room started to spin.

Greyson stepped in. "Moe? You okay?"

She gulped in air and tried to keep the dry cereal she'd eaten earlier in her stomach. Did she owe him the truth? Just in case the baby didn't survive? What would he do? She had to think this through. "Yes. I'm fine. Just that bug. Guess I'm not over it."

He ran a gentle knuckle down the side of her face, swiping across her jawline. His eyes were more green than gray in the oddly lit room. "You sure?"

"Yes." She swept her hand out. "You know I'm not a gardener, right? Not even a farmer."

"I don't understand."

That's what she'd thought. Her stomach started to calm down a little. "I'm a genetic engineer. I work to splice and dice and protect plants and crops. I don't actually garden."

He groaned and looked around.

More nausea rolled. Darn it. She cleared her throat.

"You're even paler," he said quietly.

"I'm honestly fine. Just a bug." She swallowed.

He lifted his chin. "If you're sure, then we need to talk at some point. About what just happened in the car."

Heat bloomed into her face.

"There you go." His lips twitched into a smile. "You're quite the blusher."

That's why she'd never gotten away with anything in high school. "What's there to talk about?" Her voice squeaked.

"I want to kiss you again, and if we're back at headquarters, I don't want to stop with a kiss. Just thought you should know." With that, he took her hand and led her out of the useless greenhouse.

CHAPTER FIFTEEN

There's another attack coming, I can feel it. The question is: from where and from whom?
    —Greyson Storm, Letters to Miss Julian

THE SUN BEAT down and heated the sand all around them as if issuing punishment. After the day of surveying useless greenhouses with Maureen, Greyson finished pointing out weak points to Damon on the northern end of the beach as the still hot sun set over the Pacific Ocean. "Get the patrol boats going more often."

Damon stood in the sand, his tennis shoes covered, his sunglasses reflecting the lingering rays. "You expecting a hit?"

Grey shrugged. "Of course. The president will strike again. If he's still alive." Grey had left Maureen an hour before after they inspected three more greenhouses. The last one, a private one close to the city, had concerned her the most. She'd gathered data and had promised to update him during a late dinner that night. "Or Vanguard will hit again. Or one of the gangs."

"We're vulnerable via the beach," Damon agreed, dusting

sand off his dark jeans. "Patrols on the ocean will help, but that's temporary. Gas is temporary."

Apparently everything was temporary, including food. "I know."

A radio crackled, and Damon drew it from his back pocket. "Status."

"Checking in. Have a report." Bob Murphy's western twang was easily identifiable.

Damon looked in the direction of the nearest mansion. "Meet us in the blue house on the northernmost corner."

"Copy that," Bob said.

Grey eyed the vibrant pinks and yellows across the sky. Was Maureen taking a moment to enjoy the splendor? Somehow, he doubted it. She'd been wrapped up in the paperwork and had barely noticed him leave. He turned and followed Damon into the blue house, which had been outfitted with machine guns to protect the border.

He stopped short in the grand living room when he saw one of his men on a floral sofa with a box of crackers in his hands next to a thin, dark-haired woman in ripped shorts and a tank top.

His guy jumped to his feet. "Hi, boss. Didn't know you'd be coming by."

It took Greyson a minute to remember the guy's name. Then it all clicked. Taylor Jameson. Ex-realtor, thirty-five years old from Alabama, and a hill-billy who was a decent shot and a master with a blade. The guy's blond hair was slicked back, and it looked like he was growing a goatee. "Aren't you on duty?" Grey asked quietly, his body tensing.

"Just got off," Jameson said easily. "Thought I'd sit here and admire the sunset with my lady."

The woman hadn't taken her eyes off the crackers. She had dark hair pulled back in a rubber band, light eyes, and skinny arms. A closer look made her out to be eighteen, tops.

Grey's chest heated. "Did you get any news on Zach Barter?"

Jameson shook his head. "Nope. Checked with two new encampments and used the old pictures. Nobody could even identify him." Taylor winked at the woman, and she swallowed loudly.

Fuck. Greyson stared at her. "Darlin'? What's your name?"

She swung her wide gaze to him and seemed to shrink back into the cushions. "Leslie."

"You hungry, Leslie?" he asked, trying to keep his voice gentle. She swallowed and slowly nodded.

Ah, fuck. He so wasn't liking where this was going. "Did you just meet your buddy here? Maybe while he was on patrol?"

She swallowed but didn't answer, looking like prey caught between hawks.

He sighed. "Did he promise you food?"

She slowly nodded. "After," she whispered.

Fury pounded through Greyson, and it took every ounce of control he had not to grab Jameson by the neck and snap it.

Damon breathed out loudly, his face darkening.

"Clarke?" Greyson bellowed.

The woman cringed and shoved back into the sofa even more.

"Yo, boss." The front door opened, and the assigned guard loped inside. Jay Clarke was an ex-stock broker, a great shot, and a funny guy.

Grey nodded at the woman. "You know anything about this?"

Clarke's brown eyes narrowed. "No. I knew Jameson was off duty and had planned to double check the weapons near the windows facing north. Didn't know there was a kid here."

Good. Greyson nodded. "Take her to Atticus and have him feed her. More protein than anything else." He dropped to his haunches so she'd meet his eyes. "Nobody is going to hurt you, and you can have all the food you want. Atticus is a good guy, and he'll set you up with a private but unfortunately cold shower outside and a nice place to sleep tonight. We'll talk about what you want to do next tomorrow."

She glanced at Jameson and then back. "Do next?"

"There are safe places to go." Greyson straightened and took a couple of steps back. "Stay to the beach on the way to headquarters," he told Clarke. The walk by the ocean with the pretty sunset might reassure her a little. He paused. "How old are you, sweetheart?"

She gulped and looked around before finally meeting his eyes. "Seventeen. I'm pretty sure."

Fuck. He nodded. "Go with Clarke. I promise you'll be safe." For now, anyway. There wasn't a lot of safety if she decided to take off on her own tomorrow. Maybe he could talk her into going to Vanguard.

She nodded and stood, edging toward the back door, her gaze darting from man to man. The poor thing was waiting for somebody to pounce.

Clarke followed her at a safe distance, his face thunderous.

Greyson waited. "How long you been pulling shit like this?"

Jameson leaned against the fireplace. "Shit like what?" He set the box of crackers on the mantle.

"Finding little girls while out scouting and promising them food for sex," Damon snapped. "How long you been a pedophile?"

Jameson swallowed. "I'm not. Hey. That bitch looked eighteen."

Damon snarled. "Things need to change around here, Grey."

Greyson started and looked at his friend. "I don't condone this. Not at all."

"I know, but the situation is ripe for it. It's time to fucking evolve," Damon snapped.

There was truth to that statement, but Greyson didn't want to deal with it right now. "Can we argue later, honey? Right now, I have a moron to kill."

Jameson held up his hands. "Wait a minute. I found her on the upper east side, scavenging through an old card store. I didn't jump on her or make her do anything. She made all the promises if I just brought her here."

Grey might actually throw up. "It didn't occur to you to just feed the kid and make sure she was safe?"

"Dude." Jameson waved his hands. "I haven't had a woman in two months. Come on."

Grey lost it. He punched out, nailing the asshole in the gut.

Jameson doubled over with a pained 'oof.'

Greyson stepped back. "Who exactly did you have two months ago?" He'd made it clear. He'd made it *very* clear that rape was punishable by death.

"A woman living in an old fast food restaurant outside of the city. She was willing, too," Jameson said, his face red. He groaned as he straightened up.

"We have a different definition of 'willing,'" Greyson muttered.

Jameson coughed several times. "Hey. There's no law these days. Prostitution is legal, as far as I'm concerned."

"Can I just kill him?" Damon asked grimly. "Put the body out front? It's our new thing."

The front door opened, and Bob walked in, removing body armor as he moved.

"This shit is hot," he said, shrugging out of the bulletproof vest. He nodded at Grey. "My partner headed down to the infirmary. We got caught by a couple of Rippers on the way, and he needs stitches. The other team is still up north recording the president's actions and will approach him per your directive."

Hopefully they wouldn't get shot on sight. "We have a medic for your partner in the infirmary," Grey said. He turned to Damon. "Make it known that Taylor Jameson was kicked out of the Mercs, and make it fucking clear why. Toss his ass outside the perimeter with nothing but the clothes he's wearing. Tell the guards that if they see him again, anywhere around Merc territory, to shoot on sight."

Bob paused in ditching his armor and setting his pack on the sofa table. "What's going on?"

Damon ignored him and grabbed Jameson by the arm, shoving him around the sofa. "That's a plan." He pushed the sputtering moron down the hallway and out the door.

Grey eyed Bob. "When you're scouting or out on patrol, do you ever trade food for sex?"

Bob was six-feet tall, and broad across the chest, and a former cowboy from Montana. A scar down the side of his neck did nothing to diminish what had to be considered good looks. "Gross. No." He tossed his short-range radio on the back of the sofa. "Do I look like I need to bribe women?"

Grey scrubbed a hand down his face. "It's happening though. Right?"

Bob nodded. "I've heard stories, but Grey, there ain't a lot of women out there. If we find people who are scared and vulnerable, we send them to Vanguard. If they need food, we give it to them first."

Good. "Apparently Jameson had different ideas," Grey said.

Bob reached for his pack and walked around to drop onto the sofa. "Maybe it's time to integrate women into Merc territory." He held up a hand. "I get why you went with male soldiers to secure the territory until things died down, and I agree that women are a distraction. But it's time, man."

"I've never said no to anybody having a relationship," Grey protested.

Damon strode in the front door, obviously catching the end of the sentence. "No, but single women and maybe even kids should be part of the Mercs. Not just chicks attached to soldiers."

Grey breathed out. He'd been mulling over the idea for a while, and it did make sense. How to implement the change, he hadn't yet figured out. "Then we need female soldiers also. If we're to start building a society, we need independent jobs for women. Otherwise it won't work."

"We could just align and combine with Vanguard," Damon said quietly. "Of course, they'd need to move here. They have to get out of inner city LA at some point, anyway. But I'm not sure the infrastructure here would work for that."

Jesus. The last thing Grey wanted to figure out was infrastructure and Vanguard. He jerked his head at Bob. "What did you find out?"

Bob drew polaroids from his pack. "The president is alive."

Yeah. Grey wasn't surprised. He took the pictures and whistled. "You got close to the main house."

Bob nodded. "Climbed a tree. His patrols are systematic, and they have fantastic firepower. They have a good defensible position with the mansion on Lake Tahoe, but entry is easy. The grounds are large, and we got through okay. It's harder to get into the mansion."

Greyson studied the photo of President Bret Atherton. The picture had been taken through a window into looked like an executive office. The president sat at a huge desk, his arm in a sling, bandages across his forehead. He was in his early thirties with brownish hair and blue eyes. Rumor had it once Scorpius spread, Atherton killed the acting president and then eased right into the role. "So he's alive. Any sightings of Vice President Lake?"

"No," Bob said. "We didn't get a visual on him. He might've died when the helicopter went down."

Greyson tossed the pictures on top of the coffee table. "When have we ever gotten that lucky?"

"There's more," Bob said, handing over another set of photos.

Grey looked them over and sat up. "They're installing land mines." Where the hell had they found land mines?

Bob nodded. "We marked locations while we were there, but it looks like they've been doing it for a while. We might've just been lucky on the way in, and we made sure to retrace our steps on the way out. Atherton is preparing for an attack."

Man, what Grey wouldn't do for a few land mines. Or a few hundred. "Anything else?"

"Yes. Atherton met with what looked like several members of the Twenty gang from Las Angeles. I think they're the only gang left, and they're seriously recruiting. Have become a front-line of sorts for the president and his Elite Force," Bob said grimly. "A lot of men are wearing Twenty purple colors these days and taking chances. Bad ones."

"Suicide missions?" Grey asked.

Bob shrugged. "I've heard rumblings but nothing concrete. Something happened at Vanguard not too long ago, but I can't get confirmation."

Grey would have to talk to Tace. Maybe he had info. "Did you see any air support?" he asked, his head starting to pound.

"The president has two helicopters parked near his south gate away from the lake," Bob affirmed. "Have no clue if they're fueled or if Atherton has pilots."

Grey leaned back. The scouts had done an excellent job. He had good people working for him. "You were Navy?"

Bob drummed long fingers on his jeans. "No. Coast Guard. Was on leave at my family ranch when Scorpius hit." His eyes sobered. "Was home in time to say goodbye to everyone I needed to. That's something, I guess." His voice trailed off.

Grey cleared his throat. "So you worked on a boat?"

Bob returned to the present and snorted. "I was an intelligence specialist. So no...no boats."

Grey lifted an eyebrow. "Interesting. Strategy came naturally to you?"

"Why?" Bob asked.

"Besides opening our doors to women and kids, what do you think our next move should be?" Greyson asked, noting that the sun was almost all the way down. It was late. He'd promised Maureen dinner. Yet he leaned forward, curious.

Bob scratched his chin. "We need to make a decision between Vanguard or the Elite Force. They're enemies, and we can only be on one side. I say we pick a side and then move on from there. It's our only way."

"Which side?" Grey asked quietly.

Bob looked out at the darkening night. "The Elite Force has helicopters and land mines. The Vanguard only has seven blocks of inner city LA where they can't stay long term. The EF has former soldiers, as does Vanguard. But if we're following the law, if we're sticking to our vows of service, we go with the president and the EF."

That held a sad truth. Greyson stood. "Thanks. I'll catch up with you later." He made a move for the door.

Bob sighed. "Of course, there might be one problem with that."

Grey paused and looked over his shoulder. "What's that?"

"Rumor has it the president is shit-assed crazy." Bob grimaced. "It's a hell of a dilemma."

Wasn't it, though? And that didn't factor in Maureen Shadow and her allegiance to Vanguard. Grey pushed out into the night, finding himself alone on the wide beach. It was time to figure out if she had any loyalty to him.

CHAPTER SIXTEEN

Our only chance is to head farther north. Of course, more enemies are surrounding us every day. I wonder if there will ever be peace post-Scorpius. At the very least, I hope there will be food. Right now, I have my doubts.

—Maureen Shadow, Notes

MAUREEN LOOKED around a bedroom that had once belonged to a teenage girl. It was on the other side of the house from Moe's bedroom. Posters of movie stars lined the wall, and tons of pictures of a pretty girl with braces adorned the vanity mirror over the dresser. Leslie lay in the plush bed, barely visible beneath the covers. Moe quietly shut the door and moved through the hallway.

Atticus met her in the living room, his faded eyes sober. "She okay?"

Maureen nodded, her heart hurting for the girl. "Yes. Eating dinner put some color in her face, and knowing she's in a safe place should help her sleep."

Atticus shook his head. "I can't believe that moron Jameson."

"Grey really kicked him out?" Maureen asked, her mind spinning. Grey had done some awful things, but at his core, he seemed to be a decent person. This helped prove his decency, and man, she needed him to be a good guy at his core.

"Yes," Atticus said, drawing her through the living room to a table set on the deck complete with two lit candles and wine already poured into glasses. "Have a seat, and I'll bring out your supper. Since you haven't been feeling all that well, I made simple spaghetti with a very light sauce."

She sat and eyed the two plates. With the rising moon, candles, and rolling ocean, the entire scene smacked of romance. "Um, maybe we should eat inside."

"Shh." Atticus patted her shoulder. "It's a nice night. Not too hot, and the ocean is peaceful."

"I agree," Greyson said, striding out of the shadows by the side of the house.

She jumped. The man moved like a wild animal. Quiet, graceful, and sure.

His eyes appeared all gray in the moonlight, his wide chest and strong form somehow emphasized by the darkness around him. He claimed the other seat at the table, his gaze direct. "Are you feeling better?"

It took her a second to find her voice. "Yes," she murmured, taking her napkin. For Pete's sake. Atticus had even found cloth napkins somewhere. The man was definitely trying to set the scene. Why was she so nervous? "I talked to Leslie, and she's sleeping. That was a nice thing you did."

Greyson breathed in. "The people around me, the very few I trust, think it's time to make some changes to the Mercs."

Moe paused. "What kind of changes?"

Atticus brought out a tray with a huge bowl of pasta, sauce in a pitcher, and homemade bread. The smell of the bread nearly knocked Maureen to her knees. "Atticus," she murmured.

He grinned and placed the portions on the table. "We had a little yeast hidden away. Enjoy." Then he was gone.

"Is he matchmaking?" Grey rumbled, his gaze on the bread. He quickly dished them both plates and then cut the loaf.

Maureen chuckled, breathing in and trying not to sigh with happiness. It was amazing what fresh carbs could do for a girl. "If he is matchmaking, he's not very subtle about it." She reached for the pitcher and poured just a small amount of sauce onto the noodles. Her stomach had finally calmed down, and she wasn't going to tempt fate.

Greyson sighed. "Then he's in agreement with everyone else, it seems. The consensus is that we need women Mercs."

"Women in Merc territory?" she mused.

"No. Women Mercs."

That was a good distinction. She took a bite of the warm bread and groaned. She couldn't help it. The delicious taste filled her mouth, and just pure and simple tasted like Heaven. When was the last time she'd had warm, homemade bread? "I love Atticus."

"Lucky man," Greyson said, sampling the fare. He chewed and swallowed. "I think I love him, too."

She grinned. On that note, the Mercs should evolve. "At some point, you do need to let people form bonds. But if you have to move as a group, it'd be less difficult to do now instead of after you've added more members, especially kids." Was this getting easier? To just sit and talk like normal people with him?

"Move?" Grey asked.

She took another bite of bread. "I'll know more when we visit the Bunker. I can't really advise you until I see the place and get into those computers that still somehow work." And she wouldn't give him anything until Vanguard got the same information. More importantly, she had to find out how to save her baby.

He sighed. "We can go tomorrow. I have scouts out clearing the path tonight, and I'll take you to the Bunker at first light."

Sometimes he was so accommodating. Speaking of which,

she looked around. "Where do you have Tace Justice stashed, anyway?"

Greyson grinned and sipped his wine. "We haven't had a medic in weeks, and a lot of folks needed to see him. He'll be busy stitching, checking, and setting for the next few hours, at least. But we made sure he got fresh fish for dinner, so he seemed happy enough."

Tace wouldn't be happy until he was back with his fiancée in Vanguard territory. But he seemed to be safe with Greyson for the moment. Moe drank some of her water, leaving the wine alone. "Are you going to let the Vanguard folks back into the Bunker?"

Grey nodded. "Yeah. It's an easy decision considering they have a computer genius and we don't."

The computer genius was actually Tace Justice's fiancée, Sami Steel. Sami was also one heck of a soldier. Maureen scooped up some of the pasta, enjoying the very light sauce. "When are you planning to give them access again?"

"After we go there tomorrow," Grey said. "I have the place locked down for your visit, and then I'll have to figure out a plan with Jax."

There was something the Mercenary leader wasn't saying, but Moe couldn't get a grasp on it. "So you've decided to ally with Vanguard? If they agree." That would make things a lot easier for her to tell him about the baby.

"I haven't decided," Greyson said. "I just need their help at the Bunker."

"I wish you would align with Vanguard," Maureen said quietly, eating more of her pasta.

Greyson studied her, his deep voice calm and reassuring. "I'll certainly consider it."

She swallowed. "The other night. You said you promised your dying buddy that you'd take out Zach Barter. You didn't tell me why."

Greyson stopped eating and sat back, his wine glass in his

hand. "Ferris's sister was one of Zach's early victims. She was a college student he raped and passed Scorpius on to, and she died shortly thereafter. I promised Ferris I'd end Barter so Ferris could die in peace. He did." His voice remained even, but a thread of emotion wound through the words.

She blinked. "That's a good reason. I'm sorry your friend died."

He took a big drink of the wine. "Everyone's friends died."

Wasn't that the truth? "What if you can't find Zach?"

"Oh, I'll find him. No matter what."

All right. Would that obsession haunt Greyson for the rest of his life? She really didn't know him, but there was something honorable about letting a friend die in peace and then keeping a promise. Man, life had changed when hunting and killing made sense to a scientist like her.

So much for holding out for a nice and peaceful, geeky guy.

Grey's gaze swept her face, leaving tingles somehow. The memory of their night together flashed through her mind. Sure, she'd been drunk, but he'd been thorough. Extremely. Her breath quickened, and she tried to calm herself, but her nerves thrummed. She sat back, her tummy pleasantly full. "So."

"So," he repeated, his gaze darkening in the soft light.

"Grey?" Damon called out, his voice coming from the living room.

Greyson frowned. "You have got to be kidding me."

Moe bit back a nervous laugh.

Damon came into view. "Ah, hi. Sorry about this."

Greyson turned toward him, tension all but shooting from him. "What?"

"We lost contact with the patrol boat." Damon winced. "Can't see or hear them. I figured you'd want to know."

Greyson closed his eyes and breathed out for about five seconds. Then he stood. "Maureen? I enjoyed having dinner with you. Have a pleasant night." Then he turned and followed an apologetic Damon off the deck and down the beach.

That was probably for the best. She'd almost told Grey about the baby after the delicious and comfortable meal. What if Greyson decided not to align with Vanguard? She finished her water just as Atticus came onto the deck.

He sighed at seeing Grey's empty chair. "You go get some sleep, girly. I know you've been sick."

"I'll help you clean up." She reached for a plate.

Atticus waived her off. "No. I like cleaning up, and you need rest. Don't argue with a cranky old man."

She laughed. "Fine. But thank you for dinner. The bread made my entire week."

He beamed. "Good enough. Night."

"Night." She went to her room and shut the outside doors, letting loose a yawn. This whole pregnancy thing during the apocalypse was exhausting. She slipped into a big T-shirt and slid into the bed after using the bathroom.

One of the cool things about the mansion and having the ocean so close was that she could pour a bucket of water into the back of a toilet and still flush it. At some point, the septic system would fail, but not for a while. It was nice to have a somewhat functioning bathroom. At Vanguard, they had to use outhouses.

Life by the ocean wasn't so bad, truth be told.

Could Vanguard move here? She rolled over, her mind spinning. Shouldn't she be falling into a deep, pregnancy-induced sleep? No. Her mind circled around and around what she should do. For hours. Damn it.

Something scraped against the door by the deck.

She sat up. Was it Greyson? She stood and looked around for her yoga pants, the floor warm on her bare feet. Hopefully he'd found the missing patrol boat. Where were those pants?

The outside door blew inward, banging off the wall.

She jumped. "Grey?"

A man stepped inside, a knife in his hand. The moonlight spilled in behind him, keeping his face shrouded but glinting off the sharpened blade. "No."

She froze. Her gun was in the pack across the room, and she was only wearing a T-shirt. She was pregnant and didn't want to fight hand-to-hand if she could avoid it.

The man lunged toward her, and she went with her instincts, screaming Greyson's name.

CHAPTER SEVENTEEN

I think I need to evolve more than the Mercenaries do. I could use your wisdom. Also, there's a girl. Well, a woman who's a scientist. Really smart. You'd like her. But she's safer without me. Really wish you were here.

—Greyson Storm, Letters to Miss Julian

GREY HAD JUST DROPPED his shirt on the floor when he heard Maureen scream. Grabbing his knife off the dresser, he ran out of his room and down the hallway, his feet bare. Panic engulfed him, and he put a shoulder to her door, breaking the lock and throwing it inward.

He stepped inside just in time to see her kick Taylor Jameson beneath the chin. The man fell back, his arms widening, a knife in one hand.

Maureen half turned, her eyes wild. "Greyson."

He grabbed her and shoved her behind him, his chest compressing. Okay. She was okay.

Jameson caught his balance on the deck. "Bitch."

"What's going on?" Damon asked from behind Greyson. He stepped inside. "Shit."

Jameson spit blood onto the deck, the moonlight illuminating him. "You didn't think I'd go away so quietly, did you? I know how to get into this territory. Anytime I want." His mouth filled with more blood, coating his teeth, the sight garish in the night.

"You punch him?" Damon asked.

"Moe kicked him," Grey growled, a red haze covering his vision. He'd only had the woman in his territory for two nights, and she'd been threatened by a gun and now a knife. Vanguard territory was damaged and weakened at the moment, but she'd been safer there. He moved outside toward Jameson, his knife secure in his hand. "Shut the door after me," he ordered Damon as he kept walking.

Jameson backed away, his knife pointed, his gaze alert.

"Make it a fair fight," Damon said. "Remember he's decent with a blade."

"I promise," Greyson said grimly, crossing onto the deck and waiting until Damon had shut the door behind him. "Let's go down to the beach. She doesn't need to hear this."

Jameson smiled and jumped off the deck, moving down the beach a ways, closer to the ocean.

Greyson followed, his bare feet squishing in the sand.

Jameson finally stopped, his boots sinking. "I don't care if she hears me kill you. Then she'll know I'm coming for her." He circled, his movements graceful and practiced. "You took my bitch away. The second you're dead, I'm taking yours. In every way."

"Why the hell did you come back?" Greyson asked, his body heating. He'd given the man a chance to live, and now he had to fight to the death again. If he died, that sucked. If he lived, then Maureen would know he'd killed again. And he fully intended to live. "You could've gone anywhere."

"I like it here, and I want her," Jameson said. "You were a fool to kick me out. Who do you think you are?"

"The guy who's going to gut you," Grey said, moving to his

right. While the asshole was good with a blade, he lacked training and true experience.

Patrols up the beach caught sight of them and headed their way. When they got close enough, he gave them a signal to stand back. They did, watching intently.

"I'm excellent with a blade," Jameson said, moving again.

Greyson nodded. "I've seen you. You are pretty good."

Jameson feinted in and then back. Greyson waited. Jameson moved closer again, turning at the last second and slashing toward Greyson's arm. Grey dodged to the side and twisted, aiming a side-kick into Jameson's gut.

Jameson leaned over with an 'oof,' no doubt already bruised from when Grey had punched him earlier.

Greyson snarled. "Some of us don't need knives." The man would've hurt Maureen if given a chance. "In fact, I believe my woman just kicked your ass. I should've let her finish the job."

"Your woman?" Jameson sneered

"Yeah," Grey said softly, not questioning his response. On the dark beach facing possible death, there could only be the truth.

"I'll make sure she blames you for what I'm going to do to her." Jameson charged him, leading with the knife.

Greyson pivoted and slashed his knife across Jameson's neck. Momentum pushed the man forward until he stopped, both hands going to his jugular. He turned, blood spurting between his fingers. He gurgled.

No triumph rose in Greyson. Imaginary boulders landed on his shoulders, compressing his chest. Another one. He'd just killed another of his own men. What the hell was going on in Merc territory? How had he lost control so quickly?

Jameson dropped to his knees and fell forward, scattering sand.

Greyson looked down at his own chest, which had a spray of blood across it. Fuck. He motioned for the duo who'd been patrolling, and they jogged his way. "Throw the body in the ocean. Thanks." Without waiting for a response, he turned and shucked his jeans, walking out and diving into the salty water.

He washed off the blood, his emotions churning.

The soldiers took the body farther down the beach toward the pier, and he ignored them, focusing on the mansion and Moe's closed door. Was she okay? His temper was still fired hot, and his vision hazy, but he needed to check on her.

He moved against the powerful surf, reaching the beach and his jeans. Shaking them out, he examined them. No blood. It had all hit his chest. Wincing, he slipped into them and left them unbuttoned. He moved toward the deck and washed off his feet in a bucket of water before softly rapping on her door.

She opened it, her face pale, her eyes wide. "Are you all right?" she asked softly, lifting a hand to his chin.

He turned his face into her palm automatically, seeking comfort. The smell of wild bluebells surrounded him, and he breathed in deeply. "You're safe now," he murmured. But was she? Every time he thought he had her secure, something went wrong.

She slid her other hand across his chest. "Greyson?" Her voice was tentative, but her touch sure. "Are you hurt?"

"No." He turned his head to face her, wanting nothing more in the entire world than for her to keep touching him. "It was a fair fight, Moe." He needed her to know that. It was fair.

She nodded, the hand on his jaw sliding down to his chest. "I know." She eased him inside. "The boat you lost earlier. Are your people okay?"

"Yes. Just dropped the walkie-talkie in the ocean," he mumbled.

Her scent filled the space, making it soft and sweet with a hint of wildness. The ocean crashed loudly outside, while peace drew him inside. The woman pulled him in.

"Are you all right?" He should've asked that in the first place.

"Yes." She reached up to tangle her fingers in the hair at his nape. "You're wet." Leaning forward, she kissed his chest. "And salty."

Her mouth on him sent him into overdrive. His vision finally cleared, and all he could see was her. His hands shook, and his blood pounded powerfully through his veins.

He tried to focus and find control, taking her hands in his and removing them from his skin. Then he made the mistake of looking at her.

Her eyes glowed in the candlelight, and the T-shirt left her legs bared down to her small feet. Her hair tumbled in curls down her back, inviting him to run his fingers through it. As she looked up at him, her slender neck elongated, which tempted his mouth more than he could bear. "This isn't a good idea," he whispered.

Hell yeah, it was a good idea. But he'd just been in a fight, and his adrenaline was still pumping. She deserved sweetness and flowers, and he wasn't there right now.

The primitive drumming of his heartbeat was a warning.

She curled her fingers through his. "I'm tired of dancing around this."

Swallowing, he tried one last fucking time to do the right thing. Whatever it was. She looked sexy and sweet, and so damn touchable his body ached. But he wasn't in control. "A lot has happened tonight. We should, ah, talk about this tomorrow." His body didn't agree. At all.

She studied him and then stepped right into him. Her hardened nipples were obvious beneath the cotton. "No."

He blinked and tried to rein in the raw lust pummeling through him. "Maureen."

She leaned up and bit him lightly on the chin. "I like the way you say my name. So sweet and with a hint of a Southern accent that I find intriguing."

Her name? Jesus. The woman had no clue what she was courting. When he saw Jameson come at her with a knife, everything inside him had stilled and then rushed forward, the predator inside him urging him to protect what was his.

"Maureen," he said again, his cock throbbing and his chest burning. "Are you sure?"

She pulled her hands free, and he felt the loss like he'd been kicked in the head.

Then she reached down and pulled the bottom of the shirt up and over her head, leaving her in pale blue panties. Her breasts were high and small with pretty pink nipples.

His blood boiled.

She was so incredibly tempting, his chokehold on his control loosened. A rush of desire hammered into him, and he moved for her, appeasing himself and sliding his hand into her thick hair. He made a fist and tugged her head back, giving him better access to her neck.

She placed her hands on his chest and explored across his pecs with a soft murmur.

It was the sound that finally snapped his control. The sweet, quiet, accepting noises she made as she touched him. He kissed her, holding her in place, seeking her taste like a starving man needed sustenance. Sweetness.

This time, he held nothing back. A shudder of need shook him, and he went deeper, controlling them both as pleasure swamped him.

She levered up on her toes to press against him, her mouth opening, welcoming him in.

Holding her to him, he backed her to the bed, his mouth continuing to take hers. She moved easily, her chest bare against his, trusting him to get them there. Her hand tunneled into his hair, and she pulled, pushing her mouth against his at the same time.

His girl was impatient.

He lay her back and hooked his fingers in her panties,

drawing them off. God, she was beautiful. The moonlight spilled into the room, making her skin almost glow.

He dropped to his knees, his gaze on the prize. Grasping her thighs, he pulled her toward his mouth.

She held up a hand to protest, but he wasn't having any of that. He grabbed her wrists and pinned them to the bed on either side of her hips. She wiggled and then stilled when she realized her position.

He grinned. "You started this." Then he leaned forward and placed a very soft kiss on her clit.

She jumped. "Greyson?" she breathed, need and uncertainty in her voice.

"Yeah," he said, his mouth above her mound again. "You'll be screaming that soon."

* * *

MAUREEN'S LEGS trembled with need. Her entire body was on fire, and she couldn't move. He wouldn't let her move. That thought, that one tiny reality, burned desire through her with harsh flames. But this was too intimate. "Greyson," she murmured again, fighting to free her wrists.

He chuckled, the sound vibrating through her sex.

Their one night together had been fast and explosive. The parts that she could remember, anyway. That bourbon had been strong. But now, he seemed to want to know every inch of her. She opened her mouth to tempt him to move up the bed when he licked her, swirling his tongue around her clit.

Electrical zaps arced through her. She gasped and arched against him, her eyes automatically closing. "Please," she murmured, not sure what she really wanted.

He licked her again, moving his hands from her wrists and onto her thighs, where he could spread her wide.

She wanted to fight the intimacy, to hold her own, but he

licked her again. Not slowly, and not gently. He went at her, mouth heated, tongue talented. It was as if he knew exactly what she needed, and he didn't make her wait for it. The orgasm struck, shocking her system, rolling fast and hard. She cried out, pushing against him, riding the waves one by one until they took everything she had.

He finally released her and stood, slowly shoving down his jeans.

Her breath caught. In the moonlight, nude, Greyson Storm was exquisite. The light from behind turned him into one long, dark line of muscle, ripped and predatory. Only his eyes gleamed in color. He was formed of fierce angles, deadly planes, and hard promise.

Setting a knee on the bed, he moved up her, pausing to kiss her mound, belly, and both breasts before reaching her face.

Then he kissed her again. Not softly with gentleness like before. Not asking a question.

No. This kiss was a raw demand for surrender. His tongue pierced into her mouth, while his hard lips gave no quarter.

Pleasure, hot and dark, wound through her along with a hint of warning, one it was too late to heed. Way too late.

He pressed against her, his hard body pushing her into the bed. He tasted of salt and ocean, intent and man. His chest was harder than granite, and the erection rubbing against her clit felt full and demanding.

She gasped, stunned by the shocking electricity between them. The desperate need she'd never felt before—ever. For him. Only him.

He tugged off his necklace and placed it on the bedside table, quickly returning to kiss her again. Then he released her mouth to nibble along her jawline and up to her ear, his talented hands stroking her breasts. His touch was everywhere, and she wanted more. "Greyson," she murmured, her body on fire and needy. Now. "Explore later. Now, fast." Her body rioted with a sensation that was almost pain. She wanted him so badly. Inside her. *Now.*

He leaned up, his gaze intense. Whatever he saw in her face must've made up his mind. His mouth curved slightly, and he pressed inside her, going slow.

She caught her breath and stiffened, clutching his arms with her hands, her nails digging in, not letting him go. She didn't care if the entire mansion exploded. He wasn't leaving until he was inside her. She widened her legs to take more of him, the emptiness inside her actually scaring her. "Please, Greyson."

He leaned down and nibbled on her lips. "Patience, baby." Then he pushed in another inch.

Her thighs trembled. He was already stretching her, the pain slight but somehow delicious. "Were you this big before Scorpius?" she blurted.

He paused and then barked out a laugh, his hard body moving against hers. "Yeah. I don't think Scorpius changed dick size."

Her face heated. Who the hell knew? She drew in air and relaxed her lower half to ease his entrance. "Have you always had this control?" she asked, curious even though she felt as if her body would die if he didn't get a move on.

"Yes." He lowered his forehead to hers and pushed inside more, caressing nerves inside her she hadn't known she had. "I don't want to hurt you."

The sweetness in Greyson caught her off guard every time. The complexity of the man would take eons to unravel. "You won't. Unless you stop," she murmured. Then she'd have to kill him, and he probably wouldn't like that.

"I won't stop," he promised, moving down her face to kiss her again. Hard and deep. His arms bunching on either side of her, he pressed into her in one long, hard stroke.

The final invasion shot erotic pain through her every nerve, and she arched against him, expelling shocked air. He was inside her completely. All of him. Her body struggled to adjust to his size, even while those nerves inside her implored her to start moving. To feel the friction and the burn.

She caressed down his sides and over his tight ass, squeezing.

"Wait a sec," he ordered, holding perfectly still. He leaned over her, backlit by the bright moon. "Give yourself a minute." His body was rigid as he controlled himself, but the hint of danger, the indication of the edge that lived in Greyson was there on the slight wind.

His caring, his very gentleness when his body was fighting him, wound right into her heart and settled. She caressed up his back to his hair. "I trust you, Greyson."

He tightened somehow, his light gaze on her face. "I'll take care of you, Moe. I promise."

She lifted her thighs and pressed against his hips. "How about now?" she murmured.

He nodded and then pulled out to shove back in. The feelings were delicious. He watched her carefully as if seeing everything, increasing his speed and the strength of his thrusts, until she forgot everything but the exquisite pleasure shooting through her body.

She rose quickly, her body hitching, and exploded with his name on her lips. The orgasm blew through her, forcing her higher, taking her away for the moment. With a mumble, she came down, her body flattening into the bed.

Greyson's mouth found hers again, and he kissed her hard, his body shuddering with his own release.

Finally, he lifted up.

She gave a relaxed sigh and stretched happily. Her eyelids fluttered.

Another hard kiss, and her eyes focused.

"Get ready for round two," he said, his body already moving inside hers.

CHAPTER EIGHTEEN

The woman has turned into my woman, which I wanted to happen from the first time I saw her. In this post-Scorpius world, I don't think either of us realizes what that means. The primitive side of me was there before Scorpius, but it's stronger now. Darker and more absolute.

—Greyson Storm, Letters to Miss Julian

GREYSON DROVE in silence and scanned outside the SUV, having chosen the smaller one for a fast getaway if he needed it. He had a Hummer in front of him on the 405, a truck behind him, and four motorcycles with armed men riding at various locations. He'd give his right arm for air support, but that wasn't gonna happen anytime soon.

Maureen sat beside him in the passenger seat, her gaze troubled and focused out the window.

He swallowed. They'd only gotten about an hour of sleep because he'd been busy memorizing every inch of her body the entire night. He didn't regret a second, but he should've given her more time to rest. They'd been on the road for about thirty minutes. "You up for this?"

"Definitely," she murmured.

He smoothed her hair away from her face. What was going on inside that brilliant head of hers? "There's an organic farm inland in Goleta. My scouts found it a few weeks ago, but I haven't had time to make contact. Want to go there before we drive down to the Bunker?"

She nodded, not looking at him. "That's a good idea. Let's do that."

He eyed her. Having her out of a secure environment made him twitchy, and he didn't like it. "You sure you're okay?"

"I'm fine," she said, not sounding fine. "There's a lot in my brain, and I'm thinking, and I want to share it all with you." She turned, her eyes a sparkling blue in the daylight. "How about when we're safely at the Bunker, we have a talk?"

He frowned, driving around a stack of bricks and down an exit ramp. What looked like windows were stacked on each side, and he stiffened, not relaxing until they'd made it through. "Why not talk now?"

"We're almost there," she said. "Right?"

Was she going to give him the brush-off? Great. He was probably the only guy after the damn apocalypse who got dumped. "Yeah." He followed one of his trucks because Bob, the driver, had been the one to scout out the farm.

The land quickly flattened out on either side, and a large entryway with logs proudly proclaimed *Tall Tree Farm*.

The Merc truck in the lead pulled to the side, and Greyson drove up to the gate.

Armed guards, boys really, flanked the entryway. One had a rifle, and the other a handgun. They both frowned and tried to look tough.

Greyson rolled down his window. "I'm the leader of the Mercs, and we're interested in a trade, if you are. If not, we'll be on our way." He paused and then nodded toward Maureen. "We've brought our own horticulturist with us." With all of her degrees, that had to be close to one of them. "She can take a look."

One kid glanced at the other.

Finally, the first one opened the gate. "Ask for Lou," he said.

This place had terrible security. Greyson nodded. "Got it." He drove down a thin dirt road, his SUV bouncing along, and finally approached a huge, white clapboard house. Rows of trees and gardens stretched out behind it. "This is nice." He'd like to deal if possible.

A rifle poked out of the house.

"Stay in the car," he said grimly, stepping out and keeping his hands up. "I'm from the Merc territory, and we just want to deal. If not, we'll leave."

A round barrel of a woman came out of the house, wiping her hands on a towel. In her early fifties, she had gray hair and sharp blue eyes. She approached. "I'm Lou."

"I'm Maureen." Moe jumped from the car, already moving toward the back of the house. "I'd love to see what you have." She stepped carefully over a huge sleeping tabby and kept walking over the dirt.

Greyson sighed. He'd told her to stay in the car.

Lou hustled after her. "Do you know about farming? We don't know much. Just took over this place because everyone else was dead. There are about thirty of us." She kept rattling, following Maureen, while Greyson watched the rifle. It slowly disappeared.

He moved after Moe, his hand itching for his gun. But that would just spook them.

They turned the corner and ran into a young guy of about twenty holding a baby in one arm and a gun in the other.

The sight made Greyson slightly nauseated. "Jesus. Put down the gun."

Maureen paused. "What a sweet baby." Her face went all soft. "May I hold her?"

Lou paused. "Have you been infected?"

Maureen nodded and stepped back.

"The baby hasn't," Lou confirmed. "We try to clean everything so she doesn't touch the bacteria, but at some point..."

Maureen paled. "I know. Some of the newer studies that came out indicated that the Scorpius bacterium dies out much quicker than we thought without a live host. So only people can transmit it via bodily fluids."

Lou clapped her hands together. "You mean she can't get it by just touching something?"

Maureen slowly shook her head. "That's the latest news I got before everything went dark, so I can't guarantee it. But it's something to hold on to." Then she turned to a row of trees. "Almonds. You have almonds." And she was off.

Lou followed her, wringing her hands. "Yeah, and we don't know what to do with them. I mean, there's so many."

"We'll trade," Greyson said. "How about fresh fish for produce? What else do you have?"

Lou pointed mourned. "We have walnuts, sheep, chickens, wool, oranges, lemons, and some strawberries. There's also basil, carrots, onions, peaches, potatoes, melon, and zucchini. I'm pretty sure."

Maureen dropped to her haunches in front of a tree. "Oh, no. You have Ganoderma here."

Lou paused. "What the hell is that?"

Moe pointed to what looked like mushrooms at the bottom of the trunk. "Conks. It's a genus of fungi. I suggest that unless you have a bunch of phosphates sitting around, you remove trees that have this. Burn them, and especially burn any slash piles." She stood and kept going.

Lou looked at Greyson. "Conks?"

Grey shrugged. Hell if he knew. But it was impressive to watch Maureen in her natural habitat, checking out crops and talking in Latin. She became more likable every damn day, and he wanted her in his life. Every moment. Making it better.

So far, he'd done a crappy job of protecting her. Once he got her to the Bunker, he could get her secured.

Then he'd finally be able to take a full breath again.

"Oh, look at the zucchini," Moe breathed, hustling in the other direction.

Grey grinned. He couldn't help it.

* * *

IT FELT beyond good to be around crops and plants again in the sun. Maureen almost hopped from one crop to the other, giving advice, genuinely liking Lou. As they toured the organic farm, more and more people came out of different parts, listening and learning.

A bunch of people who'd banded together to farm.

Much better than to fight. Maureen laughed at a few little girls who were running through the trees, playing tag. Maybe there was a chance for society to rebuild.

She watched Greyson from beneath lowered eyelids.

He kept on guard, being polite, but still obviously dangerous. The farm people were fun cocker spaniels, and Greyson was a jaguar ready to strike.

Most of the people kept their distance, yet a couple of the younger women sidled closer. One was a cute blonde in Daisy Duke shorts. Every time Greyson asked a question, she giggled like a moron. Maureen wanted to grab him and just kiss him. To stake her claim.

That was so not like her. What happened to her preferring brains over brawn? Or not liking soldiers? The farmers around her, the ones trying to cultivate...*those* were her people. Not this muscled, strategic, graceful man of action. Greyson Storm was the exact opposite of what she'd always dreamed about.

Yet here she was, wanting to scratch the blonde's eyes out.

Greyson nodded toward another set of trees. "Walnuts?"

She moved that direction. "Yes." Darn it. More fungi. "These have Botryosphaeria Cankers. Probably because of the overly wet spring." She turned to Lou. "I'll leave you directions on how to protect the healthy trees the best you can."

Lou nodded and turned to Greyson. "So. We'll trade. We want fresh fish, weapons, and medicine."

Grey smiled. "Fresh fish and weapons. We're out of medicine, or at least close enough."

Lou sighed. "All right. Talk to me about guns."

Maureen glanced over at the guy with the baby again. The child had to be about three months old with a shocking amount of black hair and what looked like brown eyes. Absolutely adorable. She just looked around, keeping track of everything.

Greyson eyed her but kept his distance. Would he even want a baby? He caught Maureen staring and smiled, sending tingles through her entire body.

It was amazing she could still feel anything after the previous night. Well, except sore. She ached in places she hadn't realized existed. Grey was the most attentive lover she'd ever had. There wasn't an inch of her he hadn't kissed, licked, or nipped. Her over-sensitized body flared, wide-awake at the remembrance.

His chin lowered. "You okay? You're getting flushed."

If he had any idea. She choked back a whimper. "Yeah. Just a little warm."

He nodded. "We need to get going, anyway."

Lou frowned. "I'm so sorry you have to leave." She reached out and took Maureen's hands, ignoring Greyson's immediate step toward them. "Please tell me you'll come back. We could use your knowledge, and it'd be fun to get to know you better. We can have dinner next time."

Maureen squeezed the woman's hands. "I'd love to return for dinner." Cultivating relationships with groups was necessary for survival. Plus, she liked this ragtag group just trying to learn how to farm. Everyone had a smile and hope, which was rare after Scorpius. "Grey and I will be back."

Greyson kept silent, eyeing the land around them. "I'll have one of my men hammer out the deal with you later this week. If we did have a little medicine left, what would you need?"

Lou glanced at the baby. "Probably antibiotics."

Grey watched the baby, his expression softening just a little. "I'll find you some. I promise."

Hope smoothed through Maureen. Maybe there was a chance for them.

She really should tell him about the baby. The man had a right to know.

CHAPTER NINETEEN

The woman, my woman, is sweet, smart, and kind. I like that about her. But she's gonna hate it when I lock her down for her own safety. Don't blame her. Doesn't change the reality, though. I know you'd lecture me, but survival is more important than manners right now, Miss J. Sorry.

—Greyson Storm, Letters to Miss Julian

GREYSON BREATHED a sigh of relief when he was back on the road surrounded by his men. Maureen was still silent, and now she was a little pale. Maybe the bug she was fighting was winning.

"Moe? We could go back to headquarters and drive to the Bunker tomorrow," he said, scanning a series of crashed cars on the left shoulder.

She shook her head. "No. I need to check out the Bunker before we come up with any plans."

He liked that she said 'we,' but there was something definitely bothering her. To call her shoulders tight would be an understatement, based on the rigid line of her neck. Had she wanted to stay longer at the farm? Or worse yet, did she regret their night together?

It was too late to go back. He could be a good guy sometimes, and he'd been taught to be a gentleman, but the previous night had nothing to do with manners. She'd given herself to him, and he wasn't letting go. What that meant for them, he hadn't figured out. But it meant something, if not everything. Yet he'd still sent scouts to arrange a meet with the president. He had to look at all angles. For now, it was time to figure out the woman in his life. "Maureen?" he rumbled.

She turned, her gaze direct, her face pale. "Yes?"

He reached out and took her hand, scouting for threats at the same time. "I didn't get a chance to ask earlier. Are you okay? I mean, was the night too much?" He'd forgotten she hadn't been feeling well.

Her eyes softened, but the stress lines fanning out from them didn't smooth. "Last night was wonderful."

All right then. "Something is bothering you, and I can't fix it if I don't know what it is," he said, watching a pile of what looked like shattered plastic canoes on the right side of the interstate.

She sighed, her entire chest moving. "It's not your job to fix what bothers me, but I agree we should definitely talk tonight after we get back from the Bunker. But not until then." She left her hand in his, looking fragile and a little lost in the big seat.

He frowned. "I promised I'd take you to the Bunker no matter what. So I will. Nothing you can say will change that." If she thought she was just going to leave him, she had seriously miscalculated.

"I know," she said, her voice soft.

Irritation clawed up his throat, and he swallowed. "I've tried real hard to be a gentleman with you, but I'm done with the secrets and the fear. I won't hurt you, and you know it. So whatever it is, whatever you're planning to do, or think you're planning to do, it's time you told me."

Her eyes widened and her jaw firmed.

God, she had a cute jaw.

He glanced at the city below the interstate. "We have about fifteen minutes of the drive left, and that's plenty of time to chat. In fact, with the way things have been going lately, it might be our only quiet chance. So tell me what the hell is going on, or we're going to drive around until you do."

She drew her hand away and lifted her knees to her chest, wrapping her arms around them.

"I won't hurt you, Moe," he said quietly, gaze returning to the road.

She sighed. "I kind of imagined this talk on the deck watching the ocean. Peaceful."

This talk? Why the hell did he need peace? Was she dumping him? Things had changed last night. Surely she understood that. He glanced at her. "This is about as peaceful as it's gonna get for a while." That was unfortunately true.

She turned her head on her knees and sighed again. Then she straightened up, put her feet on the floor, and partially moved to face him, even hampered by the seatbelt across her chest. "All right, but try not to freak out too much."

He wasn't a guy who freaked out. "Okay." What the hell was going on?

Her face turned pink.

He watched, fascinated. "Moe?"

She breathed in, her nostrils flaring. "Okay. Here it is. I'm pregnant."

The words didn't compute. He blinked. "Huh?" His mind scrambled. "From last night?" What? Wait a minute. What?

She blinked, and her forehead crinkled. "No, not from last night." She rolled her eyes just a little. He could swear she did. She swallowed. "From last time I was here. The, well...the drunk night."

His brain wouldn't kick back in. "We used a condom," he said slowly, a ringing starting in his ears.

"Yeah, well, it wasn't a good one." She turned back to the front.

His mouth opened, independent of his brain. "Wah, well, uh."

"Nicely said," she snapped, clasping her hands together. "And yes, it's your baby. I broke up with my last boyfriend, a total geek by the way, two years ago."

Whoa. He was totally blowing this. "I, ah, just give me a minute." The ringing turned into a full-on roaring between his ears. He took several deep breaths. This was happening. Holy shit. His mind settled. "Okay. Pregnant." Then he noticed the danger surrounding them on all sides. He had to get her back to headquarters. His hands tightened on the steering wheel.

"Nope," she said, easily reading him. "You promised we'd go to the Bunker. *Promised.*"

Fuck, damn, and double fuck. "You didn't give me all the information I needed to make that promise." But the Bunker had far superior medical facilities than anywhere else, and Tace Justice was in the truck behind them. Maybe she should go there for a checkup or whatever they did for women who were barely pregnant. He kept his speed steady. "I do have the route cleared," he murmured thoughtfully.

"It's important," she murmured. "The Bunker, and the information there."

He looked at her again, seeing her differently. Oh, she'd looked fragile before, but now she looked breakable. Frighteningly so. "I was too rough last night. You should've told me."

Now she full-on rolled her eyes. "Give me a break, Grey. You're good, but pregnant women have been having sex for centuries. Get *over* yourself."

"Hey. I'm new at this," he muttered.

"Ditto," she said softly.

He paused. That was true. He had to be better at this than he was currently being. "No way your brother knows. No fucking way."

She winced. "Yeah. Figured I'd tell him when I was safely back at Vanguard."

The words took a second to penetrate.

He turned and faced her full-on. "That's not gonna happen now. You get that, right?"

* * *

MAUREEN'S MOUTH GAPED OPEN. Oh, she'd expected it a little, but to hear the words uttered in his deep tone brought home the reality. "I think it's a little early to be getting bossy, Greyson."

His eyebrows drew down, and he scouted the area again, his hands loose on the steering wheel, and his body once again relaxed. As much as Greyson relaxed, anyway. "Listen. You didn't really think you could tell me that you're pregnant with my child and expect I'd just let you go. Did you?"

No, but she couldn't let him believe that he called all the shots. "It's my decision."

His chin lifted, but he didn't reply to her statement. "Is that why you've been sick?"

"I think so." She slid her hands down her jeans. "In fact, if we find any crackers scouting or at the Bunker, I'd really like to have them. I've read those help with the morning sickness." It was so damn odd to be talking about crackers with a guy she was just getting to know after he'd knocked her up. She hated that expression. She should probably stop thinking it.

"I'll find you crackers." The soldier still looked a little dazed.

She breathed in, counted to seven, and breathed out slowly before continuing. "There's more."

He slowly turned his head, his eyes darkening to a deep blue-gray with only a hint of the green. "How can there possibly be more?"

Wasn't there always more these days? She owed him the entire truth. "According to one of the Vanguard doctors, there hasn't been a live birth from a Scorpius survivor. All have miscarried as far as we know."

His eyelids lowered to half-mast. "We don't know shit. Everyone is cut off from everyone else, so there is no way to know that a Scorpius survivor can't carry to full term."

She'd needed to hear him say those words. Until that very second, she hadn't realized how badly she needed that from him specifically. The knots in her neck loosened, and the constant band around her chest finally eased. "Yeah," she said softly. "I agree."

"Good." He turned back to the road. "We should probably find a book somewhere on pregnancies," he mused, turning the wheel to drive around a mini-van lacking tires that had been knocked onto its side. "I don't think you're supposed to eat certain kinds of fish."

She swallowed. "I have no clue." Were there fish she shouldn't eat? "Where are we going to find a book?"

"The mansions around headquarters are full of books," he said. "I'll start going through them when we get back tomorrow."

She blinked. "Tomorrow? You want to stay the night at the Bunker?"

"I had a surprise planned for you, but you win that contest." He turned and his lips twitched into almost a smile. "Your surprise trumps them all."

Yeah, that was the truth. She tried to smile back, but her lips trembled. "I'm hoping there's information at the Bunker about pregnancies and Scorpius survivors, you know? There has to be something. I've been scared."

He nodded. "I understand. But everything will be okay."

He couldn't promise that, but she appreciated his attempt anyway.

"I, ah, want this baby," he said quietly. "Thought you should know that."

His soft words wound right through her, settling into her heart with a physical warmth. "Me too," she murmured.

He nodded, his gaze on the damaged concrete on the road.

The truck ahead of them turned off the interstate with two of the motorcycles following suit. Greyson followed, driving down into what used to be Century City. "There's an underground parking area for the Bunker, and we control it. But once we're inside, I want you to wait in the vehicle until the outside doors are closed and I get the right signal by the guard waiting by the elevator."

She looked out at the formerly busy part of town. Business doors gaped open, and window after window was smashed. A clowder of wild cats milled around what looked like a decayed body on the ground in front of a former coffee shop with turned-over outside tables and a couple of ripped umbrellas.

"At some point, the buildings will fall," Greyson said somberly.

"Yes." Nature had already started to retake the area, poking up green in the concrete and climbing the buildings. "The wild cats are new."

"They're everywhere," Greyson said. "Packs of bigger dogs are mixing with wolves, and they're going to be a problem at some point. Most of the house dogs or smaller breeds are dying out already."

She rubbed her chest. "I've heard that wild animals have escaped zoos. There's even a lion named Marvin that lives outside of Vanguard territory. The guards feed him."

"Marvin?" Greyson asked, his focus on a couple of dirt-riddled scavengers, older men, over by a former shoe store.

"Jax named him, I guess." Maureen eyed the men, her heart hurting for them.

Greyson turned another corner and then drove down into a parking garage. Two guards flanked the entrance, and one nodded. Darkness and then cool air suddenly surrounded them. They drove to the far end and parked to the right of an elevator.

A man in black with a huge gun stood by the side. He lifted a hand and gave Greyson some weird signal.

Grey gave a signal back and then looked in the rearview mirror.

Moe turned around to see the other two motorcycles and the truck containing Tace drive in and park.

The outside door closed, and complete darkness descended.

Maureen gasped.

Her hand was instantly enfolded by the strength and heat of his. "Hold on. The generator will kick in temporarily and light the area." Greyson's deep voice rumbled through the darkness, promising of safety.

Something clicked, and then yellow lights illuminated from the ceiling.

"This way." Greyson gently tugged her across the seat and out of the SUV, all but wrapping his body around her as he shut the door.

She coughed. "I see we're going to have to work on this issue."

He moved her toward the elevator, and the guard opened a red door right next to it.

She paused. "Oh. No elevator."

"No. Just stairs." Greyson waited until Tace and Damon jogged up with the other soldiers. Greyson quickly gave orders for lead and tail, putting Maureen in the middle.

Everyone followed suit, and before she knew it, she was in the stairwell headed down concrete steps. Way down. The air cooled, and every landing or so, an armed guard waited. Greyson hadn't been kidding when he said he'd secured the place.

Finally, they reached a landing marked *B*, and Damon went through first. Two more guards waited on the other side, wearing the standard Merc uniform of black T-shirt, jeans, and guns.

Maureen peered at the sparkling white tile and walls with awe. "Wow." The place looked like Scorpius had never happened.

"That's not even the best part," Greyson said, drawing her farther down the hallway. "There are three labs. One was working on Scorpius for sure. The main computer hub is up the stairs over there, and any information you're looking for should be there."

Tace turned around. "We need Sami here. She's the only one who can crack those computers."

Grey paused, looked at Maureen, and then focused back on Tace. "You're right. We'll send word to Vanguard right now that Sami can come here along with a force of two other soldiers at first light tomorrow. We don't have a computer expert and it's time she got to work."

Tace's eyebrows rose. "Aren't you being reasonable all of a sudden?" he drawled.

Greyson kept hold of Maureen's hand. "That's my middle name. Do you want to go and deliver the invitation to Vanguard?"

Tace hesitated. "No. I'll stay on the inside here. But if Sami and her soldiers don't arrive by noon tomorrow, there will be problems."

"I'll let my men know to expect the Vanguard group tomorrow." Greyson looked down at Maureen. "Do you need to rest, or do you want to hit the computer room?"

She paused. "I'm fine. Let's check out what resources we have." Then she wanted to explore the Bunker a little bit. Rumor had it there was still fresh food, including donut mix, somewhere in the cafeteria. "What happened to the people who were living here?"

"Some ran, and some stayed to help us," Tace said quietly. "Most of them were working hard on a cure and didn't know about the human experiments being conducted on Scorpius survivors."

Her stomach hurt for Marcus and the other people who'd been used. "Is there a chance for a cure?"

Greyson shrugged. "If there is, it'll happen in facilities like this. We don't know how many Bunkers exist, but we're going to find out. I think Lynne Harmony is going to continue her research here, right?"

Tace nodded. "Yeah. We've been rebuilding Vanguard, but as soon as we regain access here, Lynne wants to get to work. She might be with Sami when they arrive."

Good. Maureen looked at a staircase at the far end of the pristine hall. Doorways were opened along the way. "Let's go see what we can find." She needed to find a cure to save her baby. And then she needed to be able to feed her baby for years. Hopefully the path to creating a viable food source for humanity was here. Somewhere.

If not, they were screwed.

CHAPTER TWENTY

Access to the Bunker is everything. I took it once by force, and I can do it again. Greyson Storm better see reason before I take off his head.

—Jax Mercury, Journal

HIS DIRTY DINNER dish next to him, Jax looked up from his latest entry in the journal as Raze stalked into the Vanguard war room and plunked down in a seat at the monstrous conference table. He was walking without a crutch and only limping a little.

"Scouts radioed in that there's someone here from the Mercenaries," Raze said, clenching his whiskered jaw. "The messenger won't talk to anybody but you, so we're having him escorted here in just a few minutes."

Jax's eyebrows rose. "Interesting. What do you think Greyson is up to?"

"Dunno and don't care. It's time to end him." Raze jerked his head at the journal. "You still writing in that thing?"

Jax leaned back. "Vinnie says we have to."

"Yeah, but I thought I was the only one who listened to her," Raze said, his lips twitching.

"Your woman is persuasive," Jax admitted, grinning. It was far

164 REBECCA ZANETTI

easier to take notes than to listen to her argue passionately about him taking notes. "Plus, don't ever tell her this, but it does help to organize my thoughts. To plan what's next." Good thing the shrink didn't expect to ever read his journal. She just wanted him to keep one. He shoved over a stack of papers.

Raze twirled a couple around and read quickly. "You've formed a treaty with a farm?" He looked up, surprise in his gaze. "Like we're a country or something."

"It's just a contract," Jax said. "Thought about what your sister said and how we need fresh food. There are a couple of working farms up north, and I've negotiated food in exchange for protection."

Raze winced.

Jax coughed. "Not like that. I'm not the mob, dude. It was a beneficial arrangement. If they don't want to deal, we leave them alone." He shook his head. "But we can't afford to send many soldiers. We need to train and recruit more."

The door opened, and a soldier shoved in a guy wearing the Merc uniform.

"Sit," Jax said easily, shuffling the papers into a manila file. "I'm Jax, and this is Raze."

The Merc was black, about twenty-five with dark hair and even darker eyes. "Greyson Storm says you can bring Sami Steel and two protective soldiers to the Bunker tomorrow anytime after first light."

Jax planted his hands on the table. "Why?"

The kid blinked. "I don't know why. I just have the message."

Made sense. Sami was the only computer expert any of them knew. The Bunker held too much information for Greyson to be stubborn and keep her away from it. Didn't make them all-out allies. "How many soldiers does Grey have at the Bunker now?"

The kid shrugged. "I don't know. My first time there was as an escort earlier today, and then he sent me here. I had to take the long route. The Twenty gang is doing something on the 405. There's a lot of purple."

Great. Why did it have to be his old gang that had survived Scorpius enough to assimilate other people? Jax shook his head. "Where's Maureen Shadow?"

"At the Bunker," the kid said.

Raze stiffened. "Grey took her to the Bunker?"

"Yeah. We had a full force as escort, and he paved the way first," the kid said. "Tace Justice is there, also. I'm supposed to tell you that."

Sounded like Greyson was taking good care of Maureen and Tace. Jax nodded. "What's your name?"

"Sam," the kid said, his gaze darting around the room. The next room was the weapons locker, but he didn't need to know that.

"There's food in the room next to this one. It's not good food, but it's edible. Go get something to eat, and we'll find you a bunk for the night. You'll come with us when we go," Jax said.

Sam's eyes widened, and he pushed away from the table. "That's it?"

Man. Kids and war. Jax nodded. "Did you think we were going to torture you or something?"

Sam lifted a bony shoulder. "I didn't know what to expect. I mean, Grey wouldn't send me in by myself if he thought there was danger, but still. This is new."

Wasn't it, though?

Raze studied the kid. "What did you do before Scorpius?"

Finally, Sam smiled. "I was in college. Studying Eastern philosophy."

Now that came in handy these days. Not. Jax shook his head. "Men's natures are alike. It is their habits that separate them."

Sam's eyes widened. "Confucius," he breathed. "You've studied?"

"I've just read a lot. Go eat something," Jax said.

The kid nodded and reached into his back pocket to pull out and show a folded piece of paper. "He said your name is Raze? You're Maureen's brother?"

Raze nodded.

The kid handed over the note. "It's from your sister." He turned and all but ran from the room, obviously expecting an attack.

"Kids," Jax muttered. There were too many children expecting to be hurt. "Read it."

Raze unfolded the paper and read aloud.

Raze,

I'm fine and at the Bunker getting all the information I can from the data here. I need the intel from the farms you sent scouts up to investigate. We have to come up with a plan for future food sustainability. I'm sure you'll be with the force tomorrow. Please be careful. I miss you. Love, Moe

He refolded the paper. "I don't like this."

Jax nodded. "We'll go tomorrow and get her back. For now, how are repairs coming?"

Raze shook his head. "Not great. We've plastered the bullet holes and tried to repair structural damage, but we lack equipment and supplies. The outside ring of tires and semis is back to full strength."

Jax scrubbed his hand down his face. "Our priority is Vanguard security. Then the Bunker. Finally, the fucking Pure church. Have they made any noise?" It was a church inside Vanguard with folks who hadn't been infected and were becoming an odd cult, if Jax had read them right.

"None," Raze said simply. "But that's because we're focused elsewhere. We need to get in there."

One thing at a time. It was all Jax could do. "Let's get secure first."

"We aren't going to be secure until we take out the brick building outside the barrier and across from headquarters," Raze said grimly. "We have to find explosives somewhere."

They'd used all their explosives in the last few battles, and Jax had always wanted to take down that building. "We'll figure out a way to get some from the Bunker. Somehow."

"Greyson Storm is an excellent sniper. If he becomes an enemy, that's the only building in the vicinity he could use to take us out," Raze reminded him. "We have to demolish it and soon." He drummed his fingers on the table. "Or I could just kill Greyson."

Jax sighed. "I'm not saying no. Let's just look at our options first."

Raze nodded. "I'll get packed for the Bunker."

"We leave in the morning, and fuck the order of only two soldiers. Bring as many as we can afford."

Raze grinned. "Copy that."

If Greyson Storm wanted a fight, he was about to get one. Jax opened his notebook to make a plan.

* * *

GREYSON FINISHED his rounds on the three levels of the Bunker, rechecking the report on firearms. The place had a decent amount of firepower, but not nearly what he would've stocked. There must be a Bunker somewhere primarily devoted to weaponry and defense. He had to find that place.

This one was kind of a hodgepodge, and it seemed like there was one lab here devoted to research on Scorpius, which made sense. It was silly to keep Lynne Harmony out of there. She had been a big-wig at the CDC and was probably the only person alive who'd be able to cure the damn disease if it were possible. Grey was starting to wonder if it'd ever be possible.

One little bacteria, and it had killed most of the human race.

The irony in that wasn't lost on him, but it still sucked.

Maureen was pregnant. With his child. The numbers on the page in front of him morphed, and he shook his head. He'd used a condom, and he'd been careful. Not careful enough.

The medical facilities available were terrible outside of the Bunker. He hadn't had a chance yet to see how they were here. But the risk to Maureen, even without the Scorpius threat to the baby, was far worse than it would've been a year ago before Scorpius. How would he keep her safe? Make sure the baby's birth was safe?

Make sure Moe *made* it to the delivery stage?

His temples ached, and knots formed along his shoulders and neck. She and the baby were his responsibility, and he had to make sure they remained protected. Even if that meant aligning with the president. Or with Vanguard. He needed to make a fucking decision and follow through. He hustled up the stairs to the main computer room, where Maureen was sitting on the floor, sifting through data.

She looked up, her eyes focusing. "Hi."

"Hi." He glanced at the two ergonomically superior office chairs by the three computers on a long table, which had been pushed against the far wall next to a formerly hidden doorway. "Why are you on the floor?"

She gestured toward the spread of papers in front of her. "It's easier to get organized."

He lifted his eyebrows. Maps and diagrams covered the walls, along with what looked like pictures of Vanguard territory.

Behind her was the secret room Vanguard had found weeks ago that held surveillance on the Mercs and Vanguard, as well as reams of papers regarding Scorpius and the government. Damon was back there, going through data. "Damon?"

The ex-cop poked his head out. "Hey. I'm getting hungry. What's in the cafeteria today?"

"I haven't gone by there." Grey had studied schematics for the place and determined how many people were his and how many were originals from the Bunker. "I don't like that we're so outnumbered." Eighty didn't work for him, although most of the Bunker folks were office drones or support staff. The ones who had chosen to remain.

"Vanguard will help with that," Damon said, shoving a manila file onto a cabinet. "Before you ask, I haven't found anything on Zach Barter."

Yeah. That had been his next question. "Keep looking," Grey said.

Damon nodded and moved out of sight.

Maureen blew hair out of her face. "You might have to give up the search for Barter at some point. He's gone."

"I'll never give up," Grey said quietly. It was a fact she should learn and now. He didn't know how to quit, so it'd never happen. Then he studied her. "Hey. When was the last time you ate something?"

She frowned, quite cutely, and then shrugged. "No clue."

He moved toward her and held out a hand. "Then let's get food. Now."

She waved him off. "I'm fine. Don't want to stop working."

Grey shook his head. "Maybe you're fine, but the baby needs food. Now, Moe." Then he caught himself.

Moe started and then looked toward the hidden room.

Damon slowly leaned back into view, facing them sideways, just his torso and head visible. "Baby?"

Greyson swallowed. "Um, yeah. Moe's pregnant."

Damon pivoted and moved into the doorway, his chin dropping. "You're pregnant?"

She gulped and nodded.

Damon looked at Greyson and frowned. "From the concussion night? The bourbon night?"

Grey winced. "Yeah. Condom was faulty."

Damon's eyebrows rose sharply. "Faulty? A condom can't be faulty. Their job is to *not* be faulty."

Maureen sighed and took Grey's hand, letting him help her up. "Even before Scorpius, they were only ninety-seven percent effective. Now, they're getting old and dusty and are probably less so."

Damon somehow paled.

Grey knew exactly how he felt.

Damon cleared his throat. "So. Well. Congratulations."

Moe released Grey and gave Damon a tenuous smile. "Thanks."

"We're, ah, not telling people quite yet," Grey said.

Damon snorted. "No way does Raze Shadow know. No way in hell."

Wasn't that the damn truth? Grey cut him a look. "We're going to keep it that way for a while."

Curiosity glimmered in Damon's dark eyes, but he didn't voice the question. Regarding what would happen to Maureen.

Grey nodded. Yeah. He'd promised to take her back after a week, but how could he do that now? He had to find Zach Barter, and the Mercs needed him to lead them, so he couldn't just go hang out in Vanguard and wait for the baby to be born. But could he force her to stay in Merc territory if she didn't want to stay?

His stomach turned over. There had to be a way to work things out. For now, he had a woman to feed. He took her hand again. "Wait till you see the food they still have here. You're not going to believe it."

She followed him, only gazing with longing once at the tons of research on the floor. "Okay, but I need to get back to work afterward."

That worked for him. She could work for a few more hours, and then she was getting some rest. They were probably due for their first big fight, anyway.

He was more than ready.

CHAPTER TWENTY-ONE

The research in the Bunker isn't making me feel any better about the
sustainability of life on the planet post-Scorpius. The data is sketchy,
and I have to believe there's better information elsewhere. It's time to
find the other Bunkers.
—Maureen Shadow, Notes

MAUREEN GROANED at the pure decadence of the heated shower.
A. Hot. Shower. It was too lovely to think about. Even back at the
lab in Arizona, the showers had been lukewarm and the water
warmed by the sun. But not hot. Not like this. She tipped her
head back and let the heat wash over her already clean body.

A blue light, muted but somehow peaceful, glowed from the
ceiling. Emergency lighting working from generators, but pretty
nonetheless.

Greyson had fed her a very late dinner of truly wonderful
meatloaf, and then he'd brought her to this paradise before
leaving her in peace. This wonderful shower in a suite just for
her. At this point, she never wanted to leave the Bunker. Forget
Vanguard and Merc territory. There was hot water and meatloaf

here. She let the water sluice over her for a few more moments and then reluctantly shut off the stream.

The towels were thick and fluffy. Of course. She dried her hair the best she could and then wrapped a towel around herself, wandering into the bedroom. There she stopped cold.

Greyson sat on the bed, his long legs stretched out on the floor and crossed at the ankles. Next to him, he'd placed a stack of clothing, including what looked like clean yoga pants. "How was the shower?" he asked, his voice a low rumble.

She bit back a shiver that had nothing to do with the cool air. "Amazing. To think we once took such things for granted." Flutters filled her abdomen, and her skin sensitized.

His eyes darkened to a deep gray barely tinged by the bluish-green. "You look scrubbed clean." The rumble turned to a gritty hoarseness.

They'd just spent an entire night in bed doing things that might've been illegal at one point. How could her body be thrumming like this? Her nipples hardened, and her thighs softened. A pulse began between her legs. What was it between them? Why was this so intense? The idea caught her and held on—what was happening? She trusted her brain and always had. But there wasn't an easy answer here.

"You're sure thinking hard," he mused, his erection clearly outlined beneath the faded denim.

"I don't know where we stand," she murmured, her body and her brain fighting for different kinds of release.

He held out a hand. "I do."

She swallowed. Was that ominous? Hesitating for only a moment, she moved forward and accepted his hand.

He tugged, fell back, and planted her on top of him. It was like landing on a solid brick wall. A surprised chuckle bubbled up.

"You move fast," she murmured, her mouth right above his.

His tickled into a smile. "Survival has required speed." Then he flattened his big hand on the small of her back, easily holding her in place.

Only the towel shielded her. "I'm feeling a bit vulnerable," she breathed, losing the humor.

His gaze caught and captured hers as his other arm went up behind his head. "You are vulnerable. In every way possible."

She frowned. "Let's not get carried away. I'm educated, determined, and I know how to fight."

"Show me," he said, almost gently. "Let's see you fight."

What was he trying to prove? He had her pretty much immobilized with one hand, and if she struggled, she'd just lose the towel. From this position, she'd require leverage to even try to knee his groin. "Let me stand up." She had kicked him in the face once, and she could easily do it again.

"No." He lifted and placed a hard kiss on her mouth.

Fire shot through her, liquefying into instant need. How did he do that? "You're making a point, and you'll have to be more direct," she said, her voice way too breathy.

"I'm trying to be subtle," he murmured, stroking up her spine and back down, applying just enough pressure for her to feel his strength.

She shook her head, and her wet hair brushed across his T-shirt. "I don't do subtle. Never have."

"Ah." He reached her lower back and kept going, brushing over her butt to her thighs and back up.

Her eyes wanted desperately to roll back in her head, and only with supreme effort did she keep his gaze. Her blood rushed through her veins, coursing need through her entire body. His hand on her butt nearly made her groan. "Greyson?" She tried to put snap in her voice and totally failed.

He shifted beneath her just enough to move her clit directly above his hard shaft.

She bit back a gasp as tremors shook her legs. Her clit

pounded, and her muscles tensed as she forced herself to remain still and not move against him for relief. Any reprieve.

"I made some decisions today," he said as if they had all the time in the world to chat.

She swallowed. "That doesn't sound good."

"Depends on how you look at it." His hand spread completely across her lower back, and his fingers curled over her rib cage. "I've been struggling to find the safest place for you. Vanguard is contained but has been attacked and is now weakened. Merc territory is widespread with vulnerabilities, but we have trained soldiers."

She tried to lever up and glared when he held her in place. Even desperately aroused, she could find her temper, damn it. "I'll find my own place."

"Then it hit me. It's so obvious." He smiled, looking more like a wolf than a friend. "The Bunker. You're staying here."

She blinked. They were underground surrounded by concrete and metal. Sure, it was pretty in some places, but it was still under the earth. "I'm not agreeing to that."

He didn't so much as twitch. "It's the safest place. I have it locked down, and nobody can get in or out without my say. There's good food, warm water, and decent medicine. It's the perfect place for you—for me to keep you safe."

She lowered her chin. "While you go hunting Zach Barter and fighting gangs."

He nodded. "In a nutshell."

Not a chance in hell. "I won't agree."

He studied her. "I'm not asking you to."

Oh, he did not. He so did not. "You seem to misunderstand your rights here," she snapped.

He flashed his teeth. "I told you what it meant to belong to me. That was your choice."

"Good sex isn't a promise of forever," she said, her body way too warm against his. She wanted to go stiff, but next to him, she was all softness. Her body would not work with her, damn it. When he told her of his possessiveness, of being all in or all out, she'd figured she would handle him later. Was it possible to *handle* Greyson Storm?

"I warned you." His gaze dropped to her lips and then rose. "And that was before I knew you were carrying my child. Even if I didn't before, I have every right to protect you now. Period."

She knew. Yeah, she *knew* he'd turn into an asshole Neanderthal about the baby. Or not care. There were only two ways for him to go, and now she knew which one. On the one hand, she was glad he wanted to be involved. On the other, he so did not get to just take over.

A sharp rap sounded on the door.

"What?" Greyson bellowed.

"We rerouted the scouts here, and they have news," Damon yelled back. "We have to go. Now. I have folks opening the garage door."

Greyson growled and stood in one fluid motion, putting her on her feet. "Damn it. I'm sorry about this. I'll be back in a couple of hours."

Moe blinked. "Where are you going?" How was this making any sense?

"Don't worry about it." He gave her a hard enough look that she almost backed away. "You stay here. Get in that bed, and get some sleep. If I return in a couple of hours and discover you've disobeyed me, *again*, you won't like the result." Without waiting for an answer, he stalked from the room, leaving irritation in his wake.

She watched him leave and then reached for the stack of clothing. Why start following his directions now?

* * *

GREYSON STALKED out of the room, pissed beyond belief that he didn't get to finish his discussion with Maureen. He'd hoped they could agree and then spend the night exploring each other again. He had a raging hard-on and a fully blown temper when he met up with Damon.

Damon held up both hands, even though they were full of two bulletproof vests. "Whoa there, Rambo. Take a deep breath."

Greyson growled.

"You sent scouts to set up a meet with the president, and apparently the guy doesn't sit around."

Greyson stilled. "What the hell does that mean?"

"The meeting is in an hour in Lancaster," Damon said grimly.

Greyson eyed him. "The president came to us. To meet."

"Took a helicopter," Damon affirmed. "Rumor has it, a big one with a lot of troops."

Lancaster was about an hour inland. "They've had time to secure an area, that's for sure. Where do they want to meet?" His mind spun. If this were a trap, he might not make it back.

"Fox Field," Damon said.

The airport? Fuck. Plenty of sniper positions at the small regional airstrip. It was a good choice. "If things go south with the meeting, we can steal a helicopter," he mused.

Damon handed over a vest. "You know how to fly a chopper?"

"No, but I could figure it out if I had to." Probably. Who the hell knew? Grey shrugged into the vest, jogging toward the armory. "We can afford to take teams from here in two Humvees. I'll need automatic weapons and two of the rocket launchers."

Damon nodded. "I'll get the shortwave radios."

Grey paused. "I need you to stay here."

Damon stopped cold. "Not a chance. I have your back."

Ah, hell. "Exactly." Grey turned toward his best and pretty much only friend. "This is a crazy mission, and there's a chance Atherton will just put a bullet in my head and be done with it. If that happens, somebody must lead the Mercs. It has to be you."

Damon snapped the Velcro into place on his vest and started

down the corridor again. "That doesn't work. It's you and me. We've always gotten out of scrapes together. If the president puts a bullet in your head, I want to be there to put one in his."

Grey shook his head, hustling behind his buddy. "What about the Mercs?"

"They're soldiers, not family," Damon said. "If we disappear, somebody will step up and lead. Or they'll align with Vanguard. Or just go on their merry ways. The Mercs are a strong band of soldiers just trying to survive. We created that." He clapped Greyson on the arm. "The Mercs have to change. If we're dead, they change. If we come back, you know we have to shake things up."

Greyson listened, trusting his buddy. "We've built something good."

"Then we'd better survive this so we can make it even better." Damon shoved open the door to the armory. "Let's get suited up."

Grey clapped a hand on Damon's back. "Thanks, man."

"I love you too, buddy." Damon reached for a thigh holster and a handgun. "We have to move." Then he paused. "Maybe you should stay here. Considering the baby and all."

Grey secured his own thigh holster. "No. If I'm going to make the world somewhat safe for that child, then I face some tough choices right now." If he decided to align with the president and go against Vanguard, Maureen might never forgive him.

But at least she and the baby would be safe.

CHAPTER TWENTY-TWO

Sometimes the enemy is the only good choice. I'm sorry about this, Miss J.

—Greyson Storm, Letters to Miss Julian

A DESERTED AIRPORT around midnight was oddly still. The moon was high, the air dry, and the silence threatening. They drove up to the main building and cut off the engines of the two Humvees. The soldiers instantly filed out, taking positions. One went to find the helicopter—and hopefully secure it.

A cacophony of hooting owls started up.

Damon craned his neck, looking around. "Owls? There would never be owls at an airport."

"Not before Scorpius," Greyson returned. "Now animals are retaking the world." Shit, those fuckers were loud. He stepped from the vehicle and lifted his flashlight to peer inside the building. Nothing. Adrenaline flooded his veins, and he settled into the moment, finding his calm.

The door opened.

"Creepy," Damon muttered.

Grey nodded and walked toward the door, acutely aware of

every inch. A flashlight shined in his face, and he paused. "Turn it off, or I shoot you."

The light didn't change.

"Freely? Put down the light," a man called from inside.

Atherton. Grey remembered the guy's voice from when the news still broadcast on televisions. Heat swept through him, and it took a second for Grey to recognize the feeling as fury. The president had kidnapped Maureen and threatened her. Grey had been shot saving her.

He swallowed. This was more important than revenge.

The light faltered and then went out.

Greyson moved forward and reached the door, seeing an armed guard on either side. Beyond them, at a reception area, sat the president, illuminated by several battery-operated lanterns. Two more armed guards flanked him. There were no doubt several guns pointed at Grey that he couldn't see at the moment. He stepped fully inside.

Atherton motioned him over with his good arm. The left one was still in a sling. "Commander Storm. Please join me."

"Commander?" Damon muttered under his breath.

Greyson strode forward, his hands loose at his sides. "You don't know my rank or anything about my term in the service. Let's not pretend you do," he said.

The president lifted an eyebrow. "Oh, I know plenty. Please sit."

Greyson sat on a commercial purple sofa while Damon took up position behind him. He studied the president. Early thirties, brown hair, blue eyes, fighting shape. Even with what appeared to be a fresh scar across his face, Bret Atherton looked like a rich kid who'd inherited the family business. His gaze was cunning and direct. "So, you're the president," Greyson said. "Kidnap any women lately?"

Atherton smiled, flashing a dimple. "No. Have you?"

Greyson didn't react. "Heard you crashed a helicopter."

Atherton leaned back in his muted gray chair. "I did. Damn Vanguard."

"Did the VP make it?" Grey asked.

Atherton shrugged. "Lake is tough to kill."

That wasn't a yes. It also wasn't a no. "Where is he?" Greyson asked.

"Right here." Vice President Lake emerged from an office, looking way too alive. He moved fluidly, his arms and legs obviously intact. But burns marred the flesh of one arm and his neck; wounds that still looked painful.

"Shoot. Thought you'd died," Greyson said, his hands itching to choke the jerk out. He'd frightened Maureen.

"From one little helicopter crash?" Lake stopped at the president's side, a gun in his waistband. "It'll take more than that to end me."

Greyson rocked back on his heels. "A knife would do."

Lake flashed his teeth. "Perhaps. Would have to be the right blade."

"Let's move on to more important matters, gentlemen." Atherton rolled his neck and then winced, his shoulder visibly tightening above the sling. "I suppose Vanguard is trying to rebuild."

"I assume you know they are," Grey said evenly. "You planning on attacking again?"

The president's eyes gleamed. "I truly am. Lynne Harmony and I have some unfinished business."

Oh yeah. Grey had forgotten Atherton and Lynne dated briefly before Scorpius. The scenario came rushing back to him. "I can't remember. First, you wanted her to be your wife. Then you decided she was dangerous and just wanted to kill her. Which is it now?"

Atherton swept his good hand out. "It doesn't matter. But I've found a First Lady much better than Lynne would've ever made. It's funny how life works out, right?"

Wasn't that the fucking truth? Grey counted the guns he could see, calculated probable hidden weapons, and didn't like what he came up with. He'd walked Damon right into a death trap. "You should know. We have weapons pointed at the building, and my soldiers have already rigged the area to explode if necessary."

The men flanking Atherton straightened but he didn't twitch. "It's not necessary to threaten. I wanted to meet you face-to-face and make an offer. I don't expect an answer tonight, and you're free to leave at any time."

That was reasonable. Surprisingly so. "All right." Grey sat back, charting a path between his weapon and the president's heart. He'd be able to get off a shot, but one of the soldiers would hit him and maybe Damon, as well. Though Damon was quick. "What's your offer?"

"You give us access to the Bunker, support us in our next attack against Vanguard, and we'll give you all the weapons, explosives, and air support you need," Atherton said.

Grey lifted an eyebrow. "That's it?"

"No. I'll also send soldiers to help guard Merc territory, and we'll share our farming resources." Atherton leaned forward. "I'm the Commander in Chief. The one you've vowed to follow. I've read your file."

"I doubt that," Greyson said with no arrogance.

"I've seen enough. Your vow covers times of war, and that's where we are. You know it." Atherton's voice was smooth, cultured. Intelligent.

Greyson studied him, and the guy looked back without blinking. Definitely convinced of his path. "Are you crazy?"

"Not any more than you are," Atherton said, somewhat seriously. "I'm stronger and faster than before Scorpius, and I strategize better than I ever have, even though I wasn't bad to start with. I want to put this country back together and need a strong military to do it. It's a goal you should not only understand but also support."

Damon remained deadly silent behind Greyson.

"Why did you kidnap Maureen Shadow and Vivienne Wellington from Merc territory?" Grey asked, his hands relaxed on his legs. The place smelled dusty and stale, and he fought the urge to sneeze.

"Dr. Wellington has information about Scorpius, treatments, and escaped serial killers that I need. Or at least she did before she went insane from Scorpius," Atherton said. "I didn't mean to take Shadow's sister. She was just there at the time."

"How is Miss Shadow, anyway?" Lake asked, his gaze calculating.

Grey focused back on him. "Just fine. Thinks you're a dumbass."

Lake's head lifted. "I sure would like to see her again."

Temper rushed through Greyson's veins, but he hid it, keeping his gaze almost bored as he looked back at Atherton. "I'll let her know."

Triumph filtered across Lake's face. "When we took her from you, you covered her with your body instantly. Tell me, Commander Storm. Is she as good of a fuck as she looks? Those lips alone have kept me up at night. Happily."

Grey let himself smile in warning. Lake was obviously trying to goad him. So he turned to Atherton as if Lake didn't exist. "A president, *the* president, shouldn't kidnap women," Grey said, his chest heating again.

"Neither should a commander in the Navy," Atherton shot back. "Dangerous times and all of that."

There was enough truth in the statement that Greyson's gut churned. "Do you know where the other Bunkers are?" He asked.

Atherton nodded. "I know of two others besides yours, and we're using those to find more."

"Where are they?" Damon asked.

Atherton just smiled.

Greyson breathed in. "What are their specialties?"

Atherton cocked his head to the side. "One specializes in predictions and what could go wrong in the next five, ten, twenty, and a hundred years after a pandemic like Scorpius, as well as medical research. The other holds...weapons and fuel. So much."

God, Greyson wanted his hands on those. No matter whom he aligned with, he needed more weapons, and fuel would be a boon. "I see." He stood, prepared to go for his weapon. "I'll discuss your offer with my men. I don't see why you have to take out Vanguard. They provide needed services for wounded folks."

The president rested his hands on his pressed pants. How the hell were his pants pressed? "I understand. I'd be willing to negotiate for a mere change of leadership at Vanguard."

Greyson's chin lifted. The guy really had a hard-on for Jax Mercury and his lieutenants, didn't he? "We'll be in touch."

"You have a week." The president didn't move, seeming more than relaxed on his chair.

Lake rested his hand on the grip of his gun. "You tell Maureen Shadow I'm looking forward to seeing her again."

Grey smiled, his gaze narrowing on the bastard. "Not sure about the right blade to take you out, but I have a few bullets that could easily find the right path." He kept his gaze on Lake, keeping him in his sights as he made his way to the exit.

Atherton waited until Grey had reached the outside door before speaking again. "I guess I have one more carrot to dangle."

Grey stiffened but kept his expression clear. "Which would be?"

The smile Atherton used this time was all charm. "You align with me, and I'll tell you exactly where Zach Barter is right this second."

Grey's lids half lowered. "Why would I care about Zach Barter?"

"Please, Commander Storm. You've had scouts looking for the

psychopath for months. With pictures, no less." Atherton leaned forward, his gaze intense. "I give you my word that he's alive, quite enjoying his life, and totally unaware that you're looking for him."

Fine. It wasn't like he had hidden his goals. But the topic was now on the table. Greyson looked at VP Lake again. "Did you release Zach Barter from the Scorpius Containment Facility four months ago?"

Atherton sighed. "We're getting off topic."

Grey ignored the president. "Lake? Did you?"

The vice president cocked his head to the side. "Yes." No remorse, no emotion, no...anything.

Heat brushed through Greyson, and he banished the burn. "Why? Why would you do that?"

"He's brilliant, and we needed help with Scorpius." Lake picked invisible lint off his jeans. "That's all you get to know right now."

Greyson turned for the door, his blood heating.

"Do what I ask, adhere to your oath, and I'll give Zach Barter to you on a platter," Atherton said as a parting shot.

CHAPTER TWENTY-THREE

The protection of what meager resources we have left has to be a priority. Enough with the shooting and killing. We need food, damn it.
—Maureen Shadow, Notes

THE UPSTAIRS COMPUTER room was quiet and a little dusty. Maureen's eyes were gritty, and her temples ached, but she kept sifting through data. She hadn't found anything on the Scorpius bacterium and pregnancies. That info was probably in one of the labs a couple of stories down, and Greyson hadn't granted her access yet. A very polite but unrelenting guard had informed her of that fact hours ago.

So she'd turned to doing what she did best. Finding food for the foodless. There had to be plans somewhere for rebuilding after a pandemic that only took out humans, but there was a chance the research was at a different Bunker.

But there should be some information here.

She pulled out a map of the nuclear reactor sites in the United States, and another one with a series of dams. There were so many dams and a surprising lack of nuclear energy in the West. Oh, there were three main reactors to worry about, but the dams were definitely a concern because someday they'd fail. Without people to maintain them, nature would retake her land. Moe was already familiar with crop growth in California, so she bypassed that file.

Hours passed, and soon her head began to nod. Maybe she should get some sleep.

"What the fuck are you doing up?" Greyson snapped from the doorway.

She jumped, scattering papers. "Working." Her voice slurred a little and she cleared her throat. "Just like you were. How did your meeting go, and where were you?" Yeah, she sounded a little demanding.

Greyson's chin lowered in an oddly threatening way. "Did I, or did I not, tell you to get some fucking sleep?"

"I'm not sure you used the f-word," she countered, her temper rising. She pushed to her feet, only stumbling a little. More papers fell off her lap. "We don't have the luxury of sleep right now, and you know it."

"Oh, baby." His voice rumbled low with barely restrained temper and a whole lot of threat. He still had a gun strapped to his thigh, making him look like some deadly SWAT guy. "You do not want to push me right now."

"Why not, Greyson?" she challenged, sauntering toward the door. She was pregnant with his child, and while that seemed to be freaking him out a little, it made her the safest person in the entire facility, at least physically. He might be a scary guy, but she wasn't buying it. Or maybe she was just too tired to care. "I'm not feeling all that vulnerable right now."

"Then you're not as smart as advertised." Barely moving, he somehow secured her arms and lifted her off her feet, cradling her against his impossibly broad chest.

"Hey," she protested, slapping her hands against solid muscle.

"Hey, nothing," he muttered, tucking her close and stomping

from the room. "You're not getting me, and we have to change that."

"Eh." Her eyelids drooped again, and she had to pull every ounce of stubbornness around her to keep from snuggling into him. "You can't just go around giving everyone orders all the time."

"That's kind of my job, darlin'," he said, his breath brushing her hair with warmth. He tightened his hold, all but forcing her to relax against him as he jogged down the stairs to the main hallway below. "If you weren't knocked up, I'd make sure you couldn't sit down comfortably for the next two weeks."

She snorted. Yeah, right. "That's quite a threat." Considering she was pregnant, she couldn't drum up the energy to worry about it.

"Something for future consideration." He loped easily down the long hallway, not hampered by her weight a bit. "For now, you seem to be forgetting I control the Bunker, Merc territory, and you. The doors here lock on the outside just as well as the ones back at the beach."

Her? Oh, no way. Nobody controlled her, not even somebody as dangerous as he. Locking her inside would only serve to tick her off. "It's truly a shame that I have work to do. Work you need," she said flippantly.

He opened the door to her quarters and walked inside, depositing her gently on the bed. "I'm not messing around, Moe. Knock it off."

She studied him. Stress cut lines on each side of his mouth, his eyes had gone gray-dark, and tension all but rippled off him. "Where did you go in the middle of the night, and just who did you meet with?" she asked again, her adrenaline finally starting to pump.

He lifted his head, looking down at her through heavy lids. "I went to Lancaster of all places, and I met with the president."

She blinked. Once and then twice. That was impossible. "You. Did. What?"

"These are difficult times. I'm just weighing my options."

His options. His fucking options. Betrayal chilled down her spine. She jumped to her feet, scattering pillows. How could he? "That maniac kidnapped me less than a month ago."

"So did I," Greyson said reasonably.

Her mouth opened and then snapped shut. She shook her head. The burst of her temper served to awaken her. "Grey. You don't get it. He's nuts. Nuttier than nuts. Wanted to kill either Viv or me and mate the other. You can't trust him."

"Oh, I don't trust him. Not a bit," Greyson said, eyeing the bed. "Now you need to go to sleep."

She held up her hands to ward him off. He could not be serious. This was crazy. He had to listen to her. "We're not done talking about this. If you align with the president, then you can't work with Vanguard."

Grey didn't speak. Just watched her.

Realization slithered through her, colder than a block of ice. She actually shivered. "Oh. You're willing to help the president take out Vanguard. To attack when they're down." How could he even think of doing something like that? She backed away. Here she'd thought she could trust him. Could count on him. "Who are you?"

He sighed. "I haven't made a decision and just wanted to see all my options. Plus, I wanted to meet the president. Get a feel for him."

A feel for him? "He's Freddy Krueger with an army," she spat. Well. At least her questions were answered. "When Vanguard gets here, I'm leaving with them." Her chin lifted. "You attack them, and I'll be there fighting alongside them."

His face gentled. "Ah, sweetheart. That just ain't gonna happen."

Fire swept through her, shocking in its intensity. She snapped wide-awake this time and all but propelled herself right at him. "You can't stop me."

"I already have." A warning glinted in his eyes.

She couldn't help it. Nobody bossed her around. Especially a two-faced jerk who'd met with the nutso president. Greyson needed to learn she wasn't to be messed with. Ever. She kicked up, aiming right for his jaw.

This time he was ready for her. He sidestepped, moved back in, grabbed her calf and lifted, tossing her almost gently back onto the bed. Before she could take a breath, he was on her, holding her down.

She fought him, struggling, but he held her tightly yet gently, not even bruising her. Not even breathing heavily or even bunching a muscle. Finally, she surrendered, planning all the most painful ways she could kill him with enough time and preparation.

"You done?" he asked, his mouth above hers.

"Not even close," she sputtered.

He smiled, some of the tension leaving his jaw as he settled more solidly against her.

Desire mixed with the anger inside her, making her body want and her mind rebel. "Get off me."

"I'd rather say what I have to say without getting kicked in the face." He grasped her wrists and gently tugged them above her head, easily securing them with one hand.

The movement pushed her breasts against his chest, and her nipples hardened. A pulse set up between her legs. How could she be this angry and so turned on at the same time? "You deserve a kick," she muttered.

The color of his eyes darkened to that of an oncoming storm, the warning clear. Deep and dark gray, heavy with intent. He lowered his face to within an inch of hers. "You're with me. Whatever I decide to do, you're on this side of the line. I'll give your brother an out if I take a route against Vanguard, but you're not going anywhere. You're safer here, and that's where you'll stay," he said, his tone rough.

Her mouth opened. Fury tensed her muscles, but she couldn't fight him physically. "I might have to kill you."

His lips twitched, but he wasn't dumb enough to smile at her. "You just might. But to make sure I've said this in the simplest terms, you're mine. I'm keeping you."

His? "I make my own choices, Greyson." She couldn't help but struggle a little, not surprised in the slightest when she didn't dislodge him. It would be helpful if her body worked with her instead of against her. The more she moved, the more her clit brushed against his erection. Heat flowed into her face and sparked electricity into her every nerve. "You can't have me," she whispered.

His chin lifted, giving him an arrogant look that appeared natural on him. "Don't challenge me, baby. Fair warning."

Before she could do just that, somebody knocked on the door. Grey just sighed. "What?" he muttered. "What fucking now?"

"Vanguard is here a few hours early," Damon yelled back. "Right out front with what looks like a rocket launcher."

Greyson growled and stood in one fluid motion, putting her on her feet. "Don't you people ever follow directions?"

Moe blinked. "No."

"Get some sleep. You can meet with your brother at a decent hour like I had planned." He dropped a possessive kiss on her mouth before turning and quickly leaving, muttering about the fucking Shadow family.

Her knees weak, she sat for a moment to gather her strength. Then she planned to go see her brother. This disaster had to be stopped.

Somehow.

CHAPTER TWENTY-FOUR

Sometimes a leader just has to leave emotion out of it. Right, Miss J?
—Greyson Storm, Letters to Miss Julian.

IN THE BUNKER'S main control room, Greyson stared at the display from still-functioning cameras attached to the front of the building. They'd had to engage the backup lights to see the street since it was still dark out there. Jax Mercury had brought a force with him. At least sixteen soldiers, including Raze Shadow and three trucks that Greyson could see.

Damon looked up from the monitor. "We have weapons ready to go if you want. The Bunker has some decent defenses when one is prepared."

Grey couldn't just kill Maureen's brother, especially since he'd just laid down the law with her. He grabbed a wall mic and lifted the damn thing to his mouth. "Mercury. I told you to fucking come after first light."

The Vanguard leader looked up, directly at the camera mounted above the front door, and flipped Greyson off.

Grey released the button. "He is such a dick."

Damon nodded, munching contentedly on some popcorn that smelled heavenly. "We could just shoot one of them."

Grey rolled his eyes. "If you were serious, I'd be concerned and wonder who switched brains with you."

Damon glanced over his shoulder. "My brain is unswitchable."

"Only because nobody would want it," Grey shot back. He eyed the force outside. "Although, is it just me, or are they not taking us seriously?"

Damon chewed some more. "The number of soldiers they brought says they think we're serious."

"Maybe." The fact that he had Maureen Shadow definitely had to tick the Vanguard guys off. "Maybe we should just shoot one or two of them." He could probably guarantee a couple of through and throughs without taking any lives.

Damon set down the bowl. "Listen. I know you. If you let them in, we're aligning with Vanguard. It'd be too messy otherwise."

"I'm not ready to make that decision," Grey said, the sight of Maureen's shocked and disappointed eyes burned into his brain. He studied the soldiers he could see and then engaged the button again. "Mercury? You can bring in Shadow, Sami Steel, and yourself. I guarantee your safety."

Jax frowned. "My forces all come in."

"No. Right now, I'm not interested in having more soldiers in here. I'm well aware of the firepower you have out there, and we all know they could do some damage to the Bunker if you're kept a prisoner. Right now, it's the three of you. Period."

Jax lifted a radio to his ear and listened. He smiled.

Shit. Greyson waited.

"We just took the parking garage," Jax said.

This was giving Grey a fucking headache. "Fine. Keep your forces there, or mine will engage in the stairwells. I guarantee your safety while you're here. Doesn't Shadow want to see his sister?" Yeah, it was a shitty thing to say, but he was rapidly losing any patience he might've had. Sometime in the far distant past.

Damon took another bite of popcorn. "You already know what you're going to do. We both do."

Greyson looked down at his best friend. "Oh, do we?"

"Yep." Damon grinned. "If you weren't going to align with Vanguard, you would've just shot Jax for having taken the garage. Maureen is having your baby. The president kidnapped her, *from you*, and there's no way you can let that go. Not even for air support."

Grey studied him. "He's the president." That had to matter, at least a little.

"Yeah, but the vice president pretty much threatened Maureen when we were there, and I know you're going to put a bullet in his head at some point for that. You can't align with the president and then take out Lake." Damon straightened his shirt. "It's a done deal, and you know it."

"I would've liked a little more time to work things through in my mind," Grey muttered.

"That's the sniper in you. Lining up a shot takes a lot of time and experience. You need to shoot from the hip here, partner." Damon eyed the soldiers outside. "Though this ain't gonna go easy."

Fuck. Fine. "Mercury? Get your ass in the front door with Shadow and Steel. Tace Justice is already waiting on the landing, I'm sure. I guarantee your safety, and we can draw up an agreement for the use of the Bunker and mutual defense."

Raze Shadow shoved by Jax on the street, barely limping, glaring at the screen. "Where the hell is my sister?"

"Your sister should be fucking sleeping since it's four in the morning," Greyson shot back, his temper stirring again.

Shadow grinned. "Giving you trouble, is she?"

"You have no idea," Grey muttered. "I've cleared the front entrance for you three. Nobody else for now until we get an agreement in place. I'm done." He slammed the handheld into place on the wall. "Why can't we just shoot them all?"

"What fun would that be?" Damon dropped his feet to the floor and double-checked his weapon. "Let's go see who's coming to dinner. Er, breakfast."

Grey shook his head and moved out of the control room. There was no way to attack Vanguard and still have any decent relationship with Maureen, so his path was clear. But the president didn't know that yet. Maybe there was a way for Grey to get his hands on that helicopter before the president figured it out.

He reached the entry door in time to see Mercury scuffling with a guard over a gun. His whistle stopped everyone cold. "Let them keep their weapons." At this point, he almost welcomed somebody trying to shoot him. "We have more than they do."

For now.

* * *

JAX MERCURY RELEASED the guard's neck and faced Greyson Storm. "This place is half mine," he growled, more than ready for an all-out war.

Grey rolled his eyes. "Fine. It's half yours." He turned and started to lead the way to one of the bigger conference rooms in the place.

Jax cut a look at Shadow, who just shrugged. Maybe a week with Maureen Shadow had worn the guy down. "I'd like to install troops as soon as possible." No reason not to push the advantage. Especially since Merc soldiers took up residence every few yards. Grey had done a good job of securing the place inside and out. Only prior knowledge of having taken the garage had helped Jax do it again, but he'd lose men if he ordered them inside from there and he knew it.

"Great," Grey grumbled, moving to the head of the table. "Maybe we can have a mixer or two first. A kind of get-to-know-you weekend with three-legged races and balloon animals."

"Man, you're cranky," Jax observed. The Merc leader's odd gray eyes were bloodshot, and his jaw looked like granite. "When was the last time you slept?" He took a seat at the foot of the table as Raze sat to his left, his gaze on the door. Sami hung by the entrance.

"I'd be sleeping now if you'd have arrived at a decent hour," Grey retorted as Damon took a seat to his right.

Well, fair enough. "We thought we might need the element of surprise," Jax said easily.

"I'm not *surprised* you came early," Grey said, leaning back in his chair.

Tace came into view and instantly hugged Sami. "I'm glad you're here."

The woman beamed. The toughest soldier Jax had ever met, one who knew computers like most people knew their own faces, actually sparkled with love. "I missed you," she murmured.

"Tace?" Jax asked before he started puking. "Everything good here?"

Tace nodded. "Yep. Place is solid, and the Mercs have been easy to work with. But I'm exhausted."

Sami yawned wildly.

Jax rolled his eyes while Raze smirked. "Then you should get some sleep. I'll see you guys tomorrow. Or rather, later today." No doubt they wanted a hot shower somewhere. The two instantly took off.

"Did she just hop?" Raze asked, his brows drawing down. "I could swear she just *hopped.*"

Jax shook his head. It didn't help a guy's position when his toughest soldiers looked like morons.

Raze turned back to Grey. "Where's my sister?"

A whisper sounded by the door. "Raze?"

Raze was up in a second, enfolding his sister in his arms. He leaned back to study her. "You okay?"

Jax leaned to the side. Moe's curly hair was all over, she was pale, and she looked exhausted. His temper started to stir.

"I'm fine," Maureen said, patting her brother's chest.

Greyson leaned forward, a fierce frown darkening his features. "She'd be a hell of a lot better if she'd listen to me and get some sleep. Moe, you can't work around the clock. The papers and research and all the data will be in the same place after you rest."

Jax blinked. The Merc leader seemed genuinely concerned. And a little pissy that the scientist was across the room from him. Was there something going on? Shit. That'd be a disaster. No way was Raze gonna be okay with his sister and a Merc. Maybe the best move would be to get Maureen out of there so they could all calm the hell down. "Ah. Do you want to go sleep or stay here for the meeting, Maureen?"

She moved past her brother and took a seat next to Jax while Raze sat next to her, effectively flanking her. But it left Raze's back to the door, and Jax didn't like that. He angled his chair farther over so he could watch the entrance, Raze's back, and Greyson all at once.

Raze dropped his backpack on the floor and drew out several manila file folders. "We doing this or what?"

Jax eyed Greyson. The guy really did seem out of sorts. "You okay, Storm?"

Maureen sniffed. "He's probably just tired from meeting with the president a few hours ago."

Grey didn't twitch. Just looked at her.

"What?" she asked, lifting a shoulder.

Raze narrowed his gaze and looked from one to the other.

Oh, there was definitely something going on. Jax leaned forward. "How's Atherton?"

"Fine. Playing hard on the service to country motto," Grey

said easily. "And he has air support, superior weapons, and deals with farming communities. Also claims he has access to at least two more Bunkers with leads on the others."

Jax surveyed the room. Greyson had two options since he'd let them in the building. One was to try and take them out now, which would cement his partnership with the president. The other was to ally with them. He couldn't tell which way Greyson was going to go. Bastard.

Raze apparently reached the same conclusion because he drew his weapon and pointed it between Greyson's eyes.

Maureen gasped and slapped his arm. "Raze? Stop that. Stop it right now."

In answer, Raze used his free hand to grab her chair and roll her behind him. "She leaves before anything goes down," he said, his gaze fierce.

Greyson, to his credit, didn't blink.

Maureen stood and smacked her brother on the top of the head with the flat of her hand.

Jax winced. "Don't make him shoot, darlin'."

Greyson yawned. "Jesus Christ, I'm tired of this shit. Maureen, sit the hell back down. Raze, drop the gun. Jax, say something interesting." The Merc leader glanced sideways at Damon. "You, I like. You're it. You're the only person I like anywhere right now."

Damon sighed. "That's a heavy burden, Grey. Just sayin'."

Jax bit back a laugh.

Raze growled. "I have a feeling you're not taking me seriously, Storm."

Greyson shot him a hard look. "Yeah. There's a lot of that going on right now."

"Enough," Jax snapped. "We're all tired, and I'd really like to get into one of those showers while we still have hot water. Obviously, you're either going to shoot at us or align with us, so just fuckin' say what the Mercs are doing."

Maureen tugged her chair back into place. "The Mercs are going to align with Vanguard." She sat.

Greyson's eyebrows lifted. "We are, are we?"

She lowered her chin. "Yes. You are."

CHAPTER TWENTY-FIVE

The only way civilization will survive is if the women just take over. Duh.
— Maureen Shadow, Notes

MAUREEN NEARLY BACKED AWAY from the tension suddenly rolling throughout the entire room.

"What the hell is going on here?" Raze asked, his voice dark.

Now probably wasn't a good time to tell him he was going to be an uncle. "I'm tired, and I want this settled," Maureen said. "We need Lynne Harmony here, and we need her now. It's time to find the other Bunkers, and it's time Lynne got back to work curing Scorpius."

The men all looked at her, different degrees of badassery on their faces.

She swallowed. "The only way that happens is if we work together. Greyson has more trained soldiers as well as fresh fish. Vanguard has more people overall as well as the best scientists. The president and vice president pretty much want us all dead. Enough with the posturing." Apparently it was now her job to be the mediator. God.

"Agreed," Greyson said softly, his gaze on her.

Jax nodded. "Good enough."

"Moe? We'll hash this out. Why don't you go get some sleep?" Greyson formed it as a question, but it was clearly an order. "Now."

She blinked. "No. You guys won't get there without a mediator. So the faster we reach an agreement, the faster we all get some much-needed sleep." It was her only chip, and she was using it. There couldn't be that many details to argue about.

"We want equal access to and same number of soldiers at the Bunker," Jax started.

Maureen held up a hand. "We'll get to details in a minute. How long will this Bunker be viable? In other words, how long will the fuel and generators last?"

Grey drummed his fingertips on the table. "From six months to a year. Tops."

Maureen sighed. "So we have a very limited time to figure out how to integrate the two groups in time to move."

"Whoa," Jax said. "Move?"

Maureen shook her head. "You guys don't get it. Water is going to be a problem, and we'll have to move north to fertile land, fresh water, and wild game. We have months to plan, but then we have to go. Your strongholds are temporary."

Okay. So not one of them liked hearing that. She understood.

Raze tossed a manila file folder on the table, and papers slid out. "We have a fresh food source we can access. Vanguard can last a lot longer than a year."

"With rain water, failing structures, and diminishing provisions?" Maureen asked. "Not a chance, brother. You only have a short time before you guys have to move north, even without the clock ticking on the Bunker. Having sixty trained soldiers as part of your crew at that time will only be beneficial."

Greyson tapped his finger on a picture from the file and drew it toward him. Something about his stillness gave her pause. He wasn't happy Vanguard had taken his garage. Not at all.

She cleared her throat. "The Mercs have more space and better food, but the land mass isn't ideal for protection, and you don't have a place for crops or even animals. You'll have to move within a year. Maybe less."

He looked up, his gaze veiled. "I see."

She fought a shiver. "I've been studying maps for the last couple of hours, and I found one of the existing nuclear reactor sites. The ones that have been supplying areas with power."

Raze frowned and leaned back. "We can't use those. They've all shut down."

"Yeah, but they'll fail at some point." She planted her hands on the table. "We have to go somewhere safe where we don't have to worry about that." The map was imprinted on her brain. "The good news is that we just go north. I think to the Willamette Valley in Oregon. There will be game, fresh water, fertile soil, and hopefully some farm animals that are still alive."

Jax's chin dropped. "You want us to move to Oregon? Like the Wild West?"

She frowned. "It's not the Wild West." All right. It might've become the Wild West a little bit now. "Long term, that's our only choice."

Greyson scrubbed a hand through his thick hair. "I appreciate the long-term approach, but for tonight, or rather this morning, let's reach an agreement covering the next month. If we can make it through July without killing each other, then we can talk beyond that."

Jax looked directly at him. "I've already set my terms for the Bunker. I'm fine working together here and keeping our territories separate for now. And I need Damon for a mission."

Grey's eyes darkened. "I want Lynne Harmony here working on Scorpius. Looking for some sort of cure." He twirled the picture around on the table. "The fresh food intrigues me as well.

We've found a couple of organic farms that were once fertile close to our territory."

"What about integrating women and even kids into the Mercenaries?" Maureen asked.

Grey focused on her. "Let's tackle that after the first month. "I'm thinking we should use my new friendship with the president to gain intel on the other Bunkers, VP Lake, and available weapons."

"You want to play double agent?" Raze asked, his voice low.

Greyson shrugged. "Don't see why not."

Jax's eyes narrowed. "Just as long as you remember who you're actually spying for. And against."

Greyson smiled, but the expression didn't remotely reach his eyes. Then he turned, his intense gaze on Moe. "I know exactly where my allegiances lie." He pushed away from the table. "Get some sleep, Maureen." He kept moving. "Now. If you'll excuse me, I have weapons to catalogue." He strode from the room with Damon on his heels.

The atmosphere in the conference room instantly softened. Became more peaceful.

Jax looked at Raze. "Well?"

Raze shrugged. "Dunno. He could be playing us, but part of me doesn't think he'd bother. Though he is a fan of the long game. Snipers are freakishly patient, and his end goal might be something we can't see."

"You think he ever found Zach Barter?" Jax asked.

"He hasn't," Maureen murmured. "But he'll never stop looking."

Raze stretched his legs out. "There's more than Barter going on with Greyson Storm. He's hunting something or someone else. Something bigger. I can feel it."

Maureen swallowed. Right now, the only prey Greyson seemed to be hunting was her.

* * *

MAUREEN SAT IN BED, the battery-operated lantern glowing next to her. She'd found one file on Scorpius in the upstairs control room, and she wanted to be finished reading the research by the time Greyson gave her access to the labs in a few hours.

She rubbed her eyes, having left Raze and Jax in the conference room nearly an hour ago. It had to be about five in the morning.

Her door opened, and Greyson stood there. He still had a gun strapped to his thigh, adding an extra layer of danger to an already deadly predator. Tension rolled from him, and his full mouth curved down as he obviously tried to tame his temper.

She blinked. "Hi."

"I'm certain I told you to get some sleep." Red flushed high across his face, and his nostrils flared. He grabbed the files off the bed and threw them at the far wall, scattering papers across the entire floor in a surprising fit of temper.

Shock shook her, followed rapidly by anger. She pushed from the bed and stomped over to him, shoving a finger in his chest. "You are picking up every single one of those." He was a fucking child having a tantrum.

"Yeah. I'm done," he said absently, as if speaking to himself. With barely a twitch, he moved in her direction, swinging her up into his arms—all raw, easy strength.

He looked around, spotted a chair over by a small desk, and strode over to drop into it.

Her head knocked against his chest. "What are you doing?"

He winced and lifted her—with one arm—and removed his gun, setting it behind him on the desk. Placing her back down, he fisted his hand in her hair, drew her head back, and poised his face right above hers.

She stopped breathing. In her T-shirt and panties, her precarious position became clear.

The dim light caressed the sharp angles of his face, making his eyes glow a relentless greenish-gray. "I've tried explaining nicely. I've tried threats. The only thing I haven't tried is tying you to the headboard." His minty breath brushed her lips.

An image of them in bed, her tied with his magnificent body over her slipped into her mind, clear as a picture. She gave a slight shiver.

His lips pursed. "So, that's the plan."

"No," she whispered.

"Then why, Maureen?" he asked softly, his tone gravelly and his hold implacable. "You're pregnant, you haven't been feeling well, and yet you refuse to sleep. Tell me why."

"I'll sleep now," she said quickly—too quickly.

His gaze narrowed. "No. Now you'll talk. Tell me why."

Saying the words out loud would do more than expose her to Greyson, as if he needed another advantage. It'd make the reality concrete. Her gaze dropped to his lips. Maybe if she just kissed him...

"No," he said softly. "We're not moving until you talk to me."

Her gaze flew up to his. Damn it. He wasn't messing around. Did Greyson ever mess around? She was too tired to fight him. To contest the truth. "I have to save him," she whispered, playing with Greyson's T-shirt.

"Save who?" he asked, his other hand enclosing hers and holding her still.

She exhaled and met his gaze. "The baby. If there's a chance to save him, it's here in the Bunker. Somewhere in the research and the labs. What if I miss it by a day? I don't even know how long the pregnancies lasted. Nobody said. Was it two weeks? Two months? Six months? What about—"

Greyson kissed her gently, stopping her words. He licked the corners of her lips and ran his tongue along the seam.

He tasted of mint and man. Her body went from tense to fully aroused in a nanosecond, every inch of her sensitized. For him.

For this dangerous, mysterious, intriguing, protective man she was just getting to know. One she wasn't sure she should trust.

He lifted just enough to capture her gaze again. His eyes had softened, as did his voice. "Sweetheart. We'll figure it out. With rested brains and refreshed bodies. You're a scientist, and you know that's necessary." He stood and moved to the bed, setting her back on the mattress. Then he lifted his shirt over his head, and the play of muscle, the ripped and predatory planes, caught her full attention. He gently took off his necklace with the ring and set it aside.

His jeans were next, leaving him nude.

Her mouth went dry. He glanced at the gun on the desk, loped over to grab it, obviously unconcerned with his nudity, and put it on the bed table closest to the door. The sound of the locks engaging filled the silence before he pulled back the covers and planted himself in her bed.

"Turn off the lantern," he said.

Her mouth gaped open. Slowly, almost drunkenly, she turned and twisted the light off. "You can't just stay here."

He hooked an arm around her waist and tugged her against him, spooning around her. The heat and strength was decadent. "Looks like it's the only way to get you to rest." His chin rubbed the top of her head, while his arm lay heavy across her waist. "Now go to sleep."

Her body rioted as it started shutting down despite what she wanted. "Tell me something," she murmured, her eyes closing. "Maybe about Ferris."

Grey breathed in as if wanting her scent before he spoke. "Ferris was the best guy I ever met. Friends with everybody, but he became my brother. Was from the south, liked big-breasted blond women with a whole lot of wild hair. Had a thing for babes wearing blue eyeshadow, too." Greyson chuckled. "Forced me to get out of my head and see the world a little bit." He sighed softly. "Saved my life twice. Once in a bar fight and once in the field. I saved his a few times, too. That matters. You would've liked him."

"I think you're right," she said drowsily. "Talk more. Maybe about your childhood. I like your voice."

He kissed her head. "All right. I didn't know my father, and my mother was a teacher who died when I was five. No other family."

Her eyes opened. "Greyson—"

"No. Just listen and fall asleep." He seemed to get bossier each day. "I bounced from home to home, doing okay, learning to survive. Figuring out how to watch and focus and know everybody around me. When I was twelve, I was probably on my way to a great life of crime before I went to live with Miss Julian."

"That's a pretty name," Maureen murmured.

"She was a pretty lady, and I mean lady in the real sense. Pearls, dresses, church, sweet tea, and a good smack with the Bible once in a while," Greyson said, his tone lowering with fondness.

"You loved her," Maureen said.

Greyson kissed her head again. "She loved me first. Showed me that affection and kindness exist for no other reason than because it's right. She was the first woman, the *only* woman, I ever trusted."

"I wish I could've met her," Maureen said.

"Me too." He moved against her, his warmth providing security. "You're the second woman I've trusted. No matter what happens, I trust you with this baby, Maureen. You'll do the right thing, and you'll do your best for him or her. I know that."

Tears pricked her eyes. When he let his guard down, he could be the sweetest man she'd ever met. It was hard to reconcile that with the killer he'd made himself become to survive the pandemic. Or perhaps he'd been like that before in the service— maybe it was just who he was. That might not be a bad thing considering that the world had essentially ended. "I wish I knew you better," she said quietly, her eyelids closing again.

He tucked her closer. "All you need to know is that I'll protect you and this baby with everything I have. Whether you like it or not."

There went the sweetness. Right out the door. She tried to turn over and argue with him, but he held her in place.

Easily.

CHAPTER TWENTY-SIX

As in any war, I've lost a couple of battles. But my resources are vast, and my determination absolute. It's time to bring the enemy to his knees.

—President Bret Atherton, Records

BRET PUSHED battle plans out of the way and stood, stretching his back without causing any pull on his broken arm. Broken, his ass. Shattered. It was only by sheer luck that he had three combat doctors who were still alive and working for him. He looked out the window of the mansion to the stunning lake outside.

The manor had belonged to a wealthy family for decades before they donated it and the surrounding land to the California park service. Weddings used to be performed there...not too long ago.

As if on cue, his fiancée clicked into the room, her high heels announcing her presence. "I brought you a sandwich," she said. "Scouts found ingredients for fresh bread." She set down a china plate.

The smell of freshly baked bread wafted up, and he nearly groaned. Lovely. "Thank you."

She nodded, pressing her hands down her white pants. Her blond hair was pulled back in a braid, highlighting perfect cheekbones and stunning green eyes. If he squinted, she looked like Lynne Harmony. His Lynne. "Can I get you anything else?" she asked, her voice quiet like he required.

He retook his seat, not minding that she remained standing. Her name was Julie, and she'd been a graduate student at one of the UC schools when Scorpius had infected the world. "What were you studying back at school?" he asked, reaching for his sandwich. No doubt she'd already told him, but minor details didn't concern him.

She eyed the chair nearest her but didn't sit. "A bunch of subjects. I was going for a general type of degree."

Yes. Definitely not as smart as Lynne, but she was better than a vacuum at blowjobs. "I see. Do you miss school?"

She shrugged, her low-cut blouse revealing a nice expanse of tit. "Not really. I do miss the parties, though." Apparently gaining courage, she drew out the chair to sit, crossing her legs and letting one of the heels dangle. "How did your meeting down south go?" Her perfectly manicured nails tapped on the arm of the chair.

He chewed thoughtfully and then swallowed. "I don't know yet. I'd like to align with the Mercenaries if they'll follow orders, and I think Greyson Storm still has an allegiance with the military. Plus, I have several things he wants."

Her eyes widened. "The Mercs just want women." Then she drew in air. "I suppose we have a few we could give to him." Her nose wrinkled. "A couple of ugly ones."

He studied her. Evil and mean, he could live with. But just plain dumb? Devoid of depth? She was twenty-four, looked good, and was a great fuck. But that wasn't enough for him. For the country he was trying to rebuild.

The dreams about Lynne had returned. For a short time, he'd considered Vivienne Wellington or even Maureen Shadow as mates, but it always came back to Lynne.

The only time he'd been happy with a woman was when they dated before Scorpius. She'd worked for the CDC, and he'd been in Congress. She was brilliant, and he needed that type of challenge. Of course, she was now with Jax Mercury, and she had to pay for that. Bret might have to break her for such disloyalty and poor judgment, but then he could rebuild her. Into exactly what he wanted.

"Sweetheart?" Julie asked, her neck crooking. "I've lost you."

She'd never had him. He smiled. "Why don't you find one of those non-ugly women and meet me in our bedroom in about thirty minutes?"

Her throat looked delicate as she swallowed. "But we're engaged now. Things are different. The First Lady doesn't have threesomes. You know that."

He imagined that was true. But something told him this bimbo wasn't going to be the First Lady. "We're not married yet." He liked that even though her pupils narrowed, she waited silently for him to finish his directions. "Make that *two* other non-ugly women. Be naked and already started when I get there."

She stood and faltered just a second before turning and gliding gracefully to the door.

He smiled. "Nude except for those heels. Keep those on."

She didn't turn around and was soon out of his sight, heading exactly where he'd told her to go.

Vice President Lake strode in wearing gym shorts and a tank top that emphasized cut muscles and the hideous burn marks down his neck, shoulder, and arm. His white-blond hair had been cut short again, and his eyes seemed an even lighter blue than before. He was one of the few people Bret knew who hadn't contracted Scorpius, and it was starting to look like he never would. "I'll have the Santa Barbara area mapped for you within the hour, and I have the men in place waiting for your order."

Bret finished his sandwich, looking at his number two. "How's the ribcage?" The guy had bruised six ribs in the helicopter crash, which was nothing compared to the burn damage. He'd be scarred for life.

"Fine," Lake said, standing at full attention.

"What was that business with Storm?" Bret asked. "You were messing with him about Maureen Shadow."

Lake didn't so much as shrug. "He has a hard-on for her. The way he covered her on the beach and then jumped to her defense when he rescued her. I was just getting under his skin."

"You sounded as if you were interested in her." It'd be nice for Lake to have some sort of weakness. Any weakness.

Approval tipped Lake's lips. "She's very pretty. But Greyson Storm will make a decision based on training and not a nice pair of tits."

That was Bret's analysis as well. "I appealed to the soldier still inside him. There's a good chance he'll work for us against Vanguard. It's time to wipe that scum from the Earth." His men were still regrouping after the last fight, but there was no doubt they'd damaged Vanguard's holdings. "Structurally, Mercury can't stay in LA for much longer, right?"

Lake shrugged. "Probably not. They're also facing health issues because of the lack of fresh food. Our scouts have confirmed that Mercury has reached an agreement with one of the small co-ops along the coast for poultry, dairy, and vegetables. So has Greyson Storm, by the way. Different farm in Goleta."

"Recommendation?" Bret asked.

Lake eyed the empty plate. "We could take the co-ops by force or just make them disappear. A good attack, and we could move their resources to our farms."

Bret nodded. "Let's plan that after the next mission. I want you to give the men the go order."

Lake's eyebrows rose. "You really want to move forward with this campaign? It could cause more problems than it fixes."

Sometimes it was necessary to just burn it down and start

over. "I'm sure. Give the order right now. It's time to rattle Greyson Storm, and I know just where to hit him."

"Then we should also destroy his organic farm after this attack. Take it out and show him there's nowhere else to turn." Lake smiled, the sight so perfect it was a little scary. "In fact, if you wouldn't mind, I'd like to take care of that myself."

Bret eyed his man. "Of course." He never denied Lake when he got creative. "Have fun with it."

Lake's eyes gleamed. "Always."

Before Bret was done with him, Greyson Storm would beg for an alliance.

* * *

GREYSON JERKED AWAKE, instantly tuning in to his surroundings. It had to be early afternoon. Finally. They'd gotten a little sleep. Quiet day, relaxed body, comfortable bed, and...distressed woman against him.

She moved, a moan escaping her, the sound frightened. She jerked. "Help. Greyson. Please."

He rolled her toward him, sliding a hand down her arm and back up. "Moe? Baby, wake up." He gently tugged her shoulder.

She gasped herself awake, her eyes opening wide. Blinking several times, she slowly breathed out, her eyes focusing on him. "Greyson."

The woman had been scared, and she'd called out for him, just like she had the other night when threatened with a knife. He couldn't believe it. The need to keep her safe, to keep her as his, was frightening in its intensity. He calmed himself, wanting to kiss her. Needing to touch her. "You were having a bad dream, and you needed my help."

She nodded. Her eyes shimmered with a vulnerability that kicked him in the gut. "You saved me last time." Her gaze dropped. "I need you to protect us."

The noise in his head quieted. She was frightened, torn by loyalties, and was still risking him hurting or betraying her by asking for help. By revealing her fear. He'd fought the most dangerous soldiers in the world before, but nobody had ever made him feel this wild rush of hot possessiveness. He cupped her jaw. "I won't let anything hurt you. Either of you."

She moved for him, her mouth settling on his.

His thumb stroked her jaw, and he kissed her back, taking over. She opened for him, showing more trust. Her sweet taste and warm lips almost pushed him over.

His heart thundered into a wild speed. He needed more. Needed all of her. He traced her face, memorizing her pretty features, even as he deepened the kiss and rolled her onto her back. "God, you're beautiful," he said.

She laughed, the sound lighter. "You can't see me."

"I can feel you," he murmured, fighting the primitive urge to drive into her and claim what was his. Gentle. He could feel how much she needed gentleness right now, so he was going to give it to her, even if it killed him. "And you're burned into my brain. Every inch of you."

Her breath caught.

He settled against her, holding his weight on his elbows to keep her safe. Then he licked and nibbled down her jaw and up behind her ear, smiling when her body trembled beneath him. Yeah. He remembered she liked that.

She yielded, moving her head to the side so he could get better access. He licked and tasted, nipped and kissed back to her mouth and down her neck to the delicate pulse point that was already going wild. For him.

Her knees slid up on either side of him, and his dick settled against pure heat. "You feel so good," she murmured, caressing his rigid arms up to his shoulders and then down onto his chest.

He sucked gently on her neck and then wandered up to her mouth and kissed her deep, not holding anything back. She tasted so damn sweet. He could do this forever. But she rubbed against him, urging him on without words.

Yet he wasn't done playing. He tugged up her shirt up and pulled it over her head, humming in appreciation as her nipples rubbed against his chest. Levering down, he nibbled between her breasts, sucking a hard peak into his mouth.

She gasped and arched into him, her nails scraping up his neck to his head. The erotic bite only spurred him on.

He turned and laved the other nipple.

Reaching down, he snapped the side string of her panties in two and shoved them out of the way, finding her wet and hot. So fucking hot. He slipped a finger inside her and groaned against her chest. God, she was amazing.

He needed more. Needed her. Now.

Moving back up her, he grasped her thighs and spread her wide for him. Unhappy with the leverage, he shoved off the bedclothes and stood up, pulling her to the edge of the mattress.

"Greyson," she moaned.

"Hold on. You'll like this." He lifted her ankles to his shoulders, grasped her hips, and tugged her even more to the edge. His dick found her opening with no help necessary. Holding her tight, he pressed inside her, taking his time.

She moaned and pushed against him, trying to get him to hurry.

Wetness slicked along his cock, and he couldn't help the groan. Fire danced down his spine, burning him everywhere. The craving to take her hard and fast shot through him, and he fought himself, pressing all the way inside her and giving her body time to adjust.

Her heat sucked him even deeper. God. He never wanted to be free. Never.

He pulled out and then plowed in again, his fingers curling over her hips. Keeping her open. For him. She writhed against him, her nails digging into the sheet, incoherent murmuring spilling from her.

He increased his speed, going faster, powering into her. Her thighs trembled against him, and he went even faster, the sound of his flesh pounding against hers competing with their ragged breathing.

Her legs tensed. "Greyson," she moaned, her body bowing. She shuddered, her interior muscles clamping hard on his dick, rippling around him, bringing him the closest he'd ever been to heaven. The wild spasms shook her, flinging him into an orgasm so intense he shut his eyes to just feel.

He rode out the waves for both of them, finally stopping, his dick jerking inside her.

She reached out for him, entwining her fingers with his. Claiming him.

He panted and slipped out of her. She rolled over, her body shuddering, her breath still coming quickly. Grabbing the bedclothes, he lay down and cuddled her close. Protecting her.

A knock on the door nearly made his brain blow up. Why did this keep happening? Enough was enough, and he might just gut the person on the other side of the door and be done with it. "Go the fuck away," he snapped loudly.

"Sorry buddy, but we have a problem. A huge fucking problem," Damon said grimly, his voice only slightly muffled. "Get out here. Now."

CHAPTER TWENTY-SEVEN

I have enough enemies. Mother Nature can fuck off. I apologize for the language.

—Greyson Storm, Letters to Miss Julian

"WHAT IS IT?" Greyson snarled, shoving open the door and yanking his shirt over his head so he could glare at Damon. Already dressed in a T-shirt and spandex pants, Maureen followed closely, hopping on one foot and trying to slip on her second sock. "Hold it." He turned and held her arm, giving her balance.

She smiled and finished with the sock. "Thanks."

He pushed her curly hair away from her face. "Why don't you go back to sleep?"

"Damn it," Damon sputtered. "I'm not messing around. You need to come with me and now."

Grey looked down the empty hallway of the sleeping quarters. His body stiffened, and his mind focused. "Are we in danger? Do I need to lock her down?"

Maureen elbowed him in the ribs. "I'm not being locked anywhere."

With her wild hair, mismatched socks, and yoga outfit, it was obvious she'd just gotten out of bed. Grey winced and ran his hands through his thick hair and then along his scruffy jaw. "Where's Shadow?"

Damon grabbed his arm and started walking. "Up on the roof by now, probably."

Maureen stumbled. "We're walking up to the roof?"

Damon nodded vigorously, reaching a doorway at the end of the hall.

She planted a hand on Grey's arm. "Um, how many floors are in this building?"

Grey patted her hand. "I don't know. Thirty-ish?"

She paled. "You know, I think I'll go grab something to eat." A cute frown drew her eyebrows down. "Unless I'm required on the roof? Damon?"

Damon shook his head. "No. Just need Greyson."

Must be something in the distance to see. Grey leaned over and pressed a kiss to Moe's forehead. "Go eat something. I'll be back down in a second." Well, minutes. She nodded and headed off for the stairs to the cafeteria, while he turned and followed Damon into the stairwell. "Tell me what's going on."

Damon started jogging, his steps fluid and graceful. "Oh, not a chance. You're gonna want to see this in full."

Grey increased his speed. Why did Damon have to be so damn dramatic all the time?

"You're lucky I'm the one who knocked on Moe's door," Damon muttered, his breathing still easy, even though they'd just passed the ninth floor. "When Shadow finds out, he's going to try and rip your head off."

"I'm well aware," Grey said, passing the eleventh-floor landing and nodding at one of his guards. Since he had no plans of leaving Maureen at Vanguard ever, then Shadow would just have to get on board at some point. If they had to beat the crap out of each other on a regular basis for that to happen, then so be it.

They passed the twenty-fifth floor and another guard.

"You jog up buildings before?" Damon asked, panting a little now. "As a sniper?"

Grey shook his head. "Most of my work was in the field—not so urban." Most of it. He didn't need to talk about any of it.

Finally, they reached the thirty-second floor, and Damon shoved open the door to the roof.

Greyson walked out into full sun. Jax and Raze stood in the far right corner, which was covered in gravel and bird droppings. Grey made it halfway toward them when the sky in the distance caught his eye. Fuck. "Smoke," he muttered.

Damon nodded. "Yeah. We have a problem."

He hustled to the Vanguard men, and Jax handed over a pair of binoculars while Raze kept looking through his.

"Welcome to fire season," Jax said somberly.

Greyson accepted the binoculars and looked northwest. "Shit." Brownish yellow smoke spiraled high into the sky toward the Santa Barbara area. He looked carefully, calculating. His body stiffened.

"Yeah," Jax said softly. "That."

Grey lowered the binoculars and studied the Vanguard leader. A toxic dose of fury dumped through his veins. This was fucking wrong. So wrong. "I can see five individual fires going."

"I saw four," Jax said.

Damn it. Fear for losing what he'd built, what he'd protected, tasted like acid in his mouth. "You think somebody set those." The president? Or a psychotic Scorpius-surviving firebug?

"Don't you?" Jax asked softly.

"We knew fire season was coming," Grey said, glancing at Damon. "But no. Five individual fires that will soon combine, all set around the same time without a summer storm and lightning? That's not a coincidence." He was going to kill somebody.

"Do you have any contingency plans in place for this?" Jax asked.

Damon threw out his arms. "We planned to have everyone jump into the ocean and hold their breath."

Greyson controlled his breathing to try and mellow the rage building in his body. "We don't have a plan. California always has fires, and we're right on the coast."

Damon shook his head. "There's nobody to stop the spread now. Plus, there haven't been counter measures taken for nearly a year. Nobody has cleaned up brush, dug trenches, or prepared for fire season like before Scorpius."

More importantly, nature had grown wherever it wanted. "We're vulnerable," Grey agreed.

Raze finally lowered his binoculars. "I think the Mercs were targeted, based on where the fires have originated. Just a guess, though."

Sure looked that way. "We have enough enemies that I'm not going to stop and wonder who," Greyson muttered.

"It's the president," Raze said shortly.

"Right now, I don't give a shit," Greyson retorted, turning to face Damon. "Leave ten men here to secure Maureen, and the rest of us need to be ready to go in thirty minutes."

Raze stiffened. "Secure Maureen? Not your job, asshole."

Grey ignored him. "Damon, is there anything here that will help fight the fire?"

"Just shovels," Damon said grimly. "We haven't catalogued anything else here that would remotely help."

"You'll need to consolidate land and protect what's most important," Jax said. "If the fire reaches you."

Grey nodded, already making plans. "Let's move."

"With Vanguard still being repaired, I can't spare anybody to help," Jax said, loping into a jog next to him.

"I know," Greyson said, yanking open the door the stairwell.

Would they make it in time?

* * *

MAUREEN FINISHED MUNCHING on a hard granola bar and
wandered through the cafeteria, which was mainly empty since it
was two in the afternoon. The white plastic tables all matched,
and running refrigerators, still on generators, held goodies below
a long-running counter. The food at the Bunker was pretty good,
but it wouldn't last. Nothing canned would.

She glanced down at her mismatched socks on the pristine
white tiles. Oops. She'd been rather out of it when Damon inter-
rupted them. Greyson sure knew how to wake a girl up. A soft
smile curved her lips.

Why the heck had Damon wanted him on the roof? Hopefully they'd be back soon, but she just hadn't wanted to climb that
many stairs. She yawned and shoved her unruly hair away from
her face.

Man, she'd better get in a shower and wake up before going to
work. Matching socks would help also.

"Maureen?" Her brother asked, coming around the corner
abreast with Jax.

She stumbled and then righted herself.

He lowered his chin, looking her over. His blue eyes lasered
through the fluorescent glow from the lights, and in a faded T-
shirt and jeans with his gun at his thigh, he looked large and
formidable. "Are you okay?"

Gulping the rest of her granola bar down, she nodded. "Just
having trouble waking up." Her face heated, and she felt like she
was sixteen again caught breaking curfew.

Greyson came into view alongside Damon. "I thought you
were going back to sleep," Grey said.

Her eyes widened. He did not.

Raze pivoted. "Excuse me?"

Oh, crap. Seriously. This wasn't going to be good. "Raze—"
she started.

He grasped Greyson by the shirt and hauled him close. "What
do you mean, *back to sleep*?"

Greyson sighed, shoved both arms up, and broke the hold. "We don't have time for this." He pushed Raze lightly to the side and faced her. "Damon and I have to head back to Merc territory to deal with a possible forest fire situation, but I'm leaving guards here so you'll be safe. I'll be back as soon as I can."

Raze shook his head, his brows slashing down and creating hard angles in his face. "She doesn't care when you'll be back."

Man, she was so not ready for this talk. "Raze, why don't you have a seat?"

Her brother looked at her, looked at Greyson, and then looked back at her. "Why?" His voice was a low rumble.

Grey shook his head. "Now isn't the time, darlin'. I have to go. We can talk to him together later."

"Darlin'? Oh, hell no," Raze said. "Not a chance. There is no 'we.'"

Well, this would not go well, but she didn't keep secrets from her brother, and the words had to be said. "Greyson and I, ah, we've been together." She forced a smile, but her lips trembled just a little. "You'd probably like him if you got to know him."

Sometimes she forgot how quickly her brother could move. He barely turned and somehow tackled Greyson onto the nearest table. Although sturdy, it was no match for the size of the two men, and they plunged to the floor, plastic pieces spinning in every direction, the sound deafening. Greyson instantly punched Raze in the face and kicked him away.

Raze came back swinging.

"Hey!" Maureen cried out, moving for them.

Damon and Jax were instantly in her way, all but herding her backward.

"Not a good idea," Jax said grimly, his body unrelenting.

Damon nodded. "Agreed. You need to stay clear. Might get hurt."

All she could hear were furious hits and grunts. Something else shattered. She couldn't even see beyond the duo that was suddenly working against her. Damn it. Backing up, she climbed on a chair and then the table, seeing over their heads.

Greyson and her brother rolled over on shards of plastic, punching each other rapidly.

"Stop it!" She yelled. "For goodness sakes. I'm pregnant, damn it."

Everybody froze. Raze's fist was an inch from Greyson's nose, and Grey's knee was about to make contact with Raze's ribs. Damon and Jax stared at her with similarly shocked gazes. Jax was obviously surprised she was knocked up, while Damon probably thought she was a moron for yelling the news in the cafeteria.

Greyson and Raze rolled in different directions, both coming up on their feet impressively fast.

Raze looked at her, and his chin lowered. "He forced you."

She winced. "I actually came on to him."

"You did not," Greyson countered. "That's not true."

"It's totally true," she said. "You said no. That it was a bad idea." She shrugged. "I thought it was a good idea, but I didn't expect, well, you know. A baby."

Raze staggered back. "There haven't been any live births from Scorpius survivors."

Grey twisted and punched him in the arm. "She's aware of that. God. Don't scare her."

Raze shook his head like a dog with a face full of water. "Wait a minute. Just wait a minute. This happened last time you were in Merc territory? When he *kidnapped* you for the first time?"

She nodded and held up a hand to halt the ensuing violence. "Yes, but it wasn't Stockholm syndrome or anything crazy. I had some bourbon, he had a lot of bourbon and a concussion, and things just happened." The room started to tilt a little, so she locked her legs to keep from falling. "Then it kept happening."

"I'm going to kill you," Raze grunted at Greyson.

Grey sighed. "Fine. Just wait until I take care of the threat to

Santa Barbara." He moved to her, his gaze going alert. "Maureen?"

Darn it. The room tilted more. Before she could explain, her legs gave out completely.

He caught her easily, swinging her up. "Moe?"

She blinked rapidly, her stomach rioting. "It's okay," she muttered. "Just a little morning sickness." Her stomach revolted. She gasped in air and tried to swallow down the bile. But her stomach lurched, and she puked her granola bar and orange juice all over his chest. He twisted his head to keep it from hitting his face.

Raze barked out a laugh. "This might be okay."

She tried to glare at him and then threw up some more, her body heaving.

Greyson sighed. "I'll go get changed. Meet me in the garage in ten, Damon." Ignoring everybody else, he carried a very embarrassed Maureen out of the cafeteria and away from the other men. "We'll get you some ginger ale, sweetheart. It'll be okay."

CHAPTER TWENTY-EIGHT

My best friend is spinning out of control, and he doesn't know it. The guy is driven by multiple motivations, and they're in conflict. There can only be one path. I hope he finds it before he gets himself killed. Guess it's my job to make sure that doesn't happen.

Damon Winter—Journal because everyone says I have to keep one to record history

"THAT WENT BETTER THAN I EXPECTED," Damon said from the passenger side of the Humvee, his gun resting on his knee. "I figured at least one of you would've ended up with something broken. Or maimed for life."

Grey drove carefully out of Century City and onto the interstate, keeping an eye out for any sort of roadblock. His split lip ached, as did his bruised ribs. "There's still time. Shadow was just in shock."

"I don't have a sister, but if I did, I would've gone for blood in that situation."

Grey nodded. "Me too."

"It'd probably help if you had some sort of promise of the future to make, you know?" Damon asked, stiffening at seeing a car burning over on the shoulder of the road. "Somebody around here's building fires. Interesting."

Grey didn't answer. Future? What kind of future could he offer her? Vanguard wasn't safe, Merc territory was facing danger, and the Bunker was temporary. But he had resources, and he'd use them all for her. "We need some time to settle into this." He had to find the other Bunkers, the ones with more research on Scorpius to save the baby. "Figure things out."

"What's there to figure out?" Damon asked. "You want the baby, right?"

"Yeah." More than he had the words to explain. A little boy with Maureen's blue eyes and her curly hair. Or a girl, God help him, with Moe's spirit and intelligence. "I never thought, even before Scorpius, that I'd have a kid. Figured I wouldn't make it back from mission at some point."

Damon nodded. "Yeah, I get that. There were times I was the first in the door, and I expected it'd be my last time. Bringing a woman and a kid into that seemed unfair to them."

Grey cut him a look. "You ever come close to tying yourself down?"

Damon smiled, his eyes softening. "Once. Another cop, crazy as that sounds. Her name was Violet, and she was vice. Tough as nails with a body that could stop traffic. Smart as hell, too. Figured people out within seconds." He sighed. "We tried on again, off again, and the job always got in the way. For both of us."

Grey slowed down to drive around what looked like bear pelts. "That's too bad."

"Yeah, and then she went and married a defense attorney. Slick guy with power suits." Damon shook his head. "Always figured she saw something in him I never did. But I was glad she was happy. Until Scorpius."

The bacteria had ended happiness for everybody. "I would've liked to have met her. She sounds interesting."

"What about you? Any former loves?" Damon asked.

Grey winced. "I dated around quite a bit, but I was always leaving on the next mission. There was a nurse I saw for a while, but she found somebody better for her. Somebody who was there day in and out. I was glad for her." He glanced at his buddy. "I didn't lose anybody else. Not really." Not like Damon. He'd lost his dad and his three brothers to the pandemic. It was amazing the guy could still smile.

Damon nodded and then stiffened.

"What?" Grey asked.

"Not sure."

Something tickled the back of Grey's neck. A trolley bus from San Francisco was next to an army truck on the left shoulder. On the right was a camping trailer. "The trucks have already made it past," he murmured.

Damon lifted his weapon. "I know."

Two SUV's instantly shot from ahead of the others and blocked the road. Three large Fords came out of nowhere behind them, spinning and creating a barrier.

"Well." Greyson slowed down, awareness prickling down his spine. He removed his gun from its holster, preparing for a fight. The odds weren't good, even if each vehicle only had one man. Chances of that were slim.

Damon grasped his shortwave radio and pressed the button. "We need backup, guys. Now."

No answer.

Shit. They knew not to move out of range, but everyone was in a hurry to rush back home to prevent the fire from spreading. "Get the grenades out of the jockey box, would you?" Grey waited until Damon had done so and had passed two over. They had to move, and fast. "I'll take front, you take rear."

"Copy that." Damon tensed to open his door on orders.

The back door of the black SUV opened, and President Atherton stepped out. Two guys instantly jumped from the vehicle, effectively blocking him.

"Are they still called Secret Service, or are they all Elite Force now?" Damon asked, his voice hoarse.

"Great question. Cover me." Grey stepped from the vehicle, his hand on his weapon. He could get off a shot, but then he'd be dead.

The two bodyguards instantly drew guns, pointing them at his chest.

Damon slid his door open and aimed around the metal. "Four guns behind us," he muttered.

"Commander Storm," Atherton called out. "Put the weapon down. You have my word I just want to talk."

It wasn't like he had much choice. Grey slid his weapon back into the holster and moved toward the SUV. "If they shoot me, take them all out and run," he muttered under his breath.

"Don't get shot," Damon returned.

Good plan. When Greyson reached the SUV, one of the guards removed his gun and then stepped aside. He climbed into the vehicle that had seats facing back and took one. "Mr. President," he said, feeling naked without his gun. The knife at his calf provided little reassurance.

Atherton smiled, his teeth a sparkly white. "Commander Storm. I apologize for surprising you like this, but I didn't have another option. Have you considered my offer?"

One of the goons shut the door, leaving them in the quiet interior with the A/C running nicely. "I have," Greyson said, "But, I haven't made a decision."

"I thought that might be the case," Atherton said, handing over a blue file folder with the seal of the presidency on it. "I've been considering the best way to show you my reach, and I think this will help you make up your mind."

Grey flipped open the top to see a picture dated two weeks ago of Zach Barter in a white lab coat surrounded by a myriad of medical equipment. A flash of anger, the raw and dark kind, clamped onto Grey's chest. Bit his spine. Caught his lungs and cinched tight. "Where is he?"

"I can have you there via air," Atherton said. "Or I can bring him to you."

In the photo, an enormous aquarium took up the entire wall behind Barter with what looked like jellyfish and squid, blue and flimsy. Diagrams and charts covered one of the other walls. "What is this?" Grey asked.

Atherton leaned over. "One of the Bunkers I told you about. This one is dedicated solely to curing Scorpius. Oh, it has defenses and some weapons, but it's where the key research is kept."

"And the Century City bunker? The one I control?" Grey asked. In case he still controlled it, considering Mercury now had more soldiers there than the Mercs did. "What is it?"

"As far as I can tell, that one is more of a halfway house. Set in Century City, it's a central local to transfer data, weapons, and food on a temporary basis." Atherton grasped another file folder and handed it over. "I believe it was also one of the Bunkers that conducted human experimentation. To see what Scorpius survivors could do...and take. That was its primary function."

Great. Grey tried to tear his gaze away from the picture of Barter. The man's hair was definitely darker, but it was the same guy. "Why are you letting a psychopath work at a Bunker?"

"I believe that's obvious. He's brilliant, and he's controlled there. We need him on research," Atherton said.

"You want to cure Scorpius?" Greyson asked. That was a rather sane thing to do.

Atherton tapped a manicured nail on the file. "For a while, I didn't really care. Then the reports of pregnancy issues came to light, and I'd like to have children someday. To pass on my legacy. So the research has to continue, yes?"

Pregnancy. Maureen. Greyson kept his gaze stoic and hard.

Showing any weakness to this guy was a mistake. "How is the research coming along?"

"It'd be better if I could get Lynne Harmony to take over. She's much smarter and has a lot more experience than Zach Barter or anybody else still alive," Atherton said, his tone reasonable.

"I thought you wanted her dead," Greyson muttered.

The president sighed. "No. That's untrue. After Scorpius, I became obsessed, as is often the case with survivors. But I've calmed down now, my brain has engaged, and now I just want to cure this disease. I have a fiancée now, and she'd like children as well. We must work together."

"Jax Mercury will never work with you," Greyson said, finally tearing his gaze from Barter's picture.

"I'm aware of that sad fact," Atherton said, his shoulders slumping. "But Lynne and her knowledge are too important. She's worth the war I must wage."

Greyson's eyebrows rose, as did his alert level. "You want to kill Mercury and force Lynne to work for you." He shook his head. "I want a cure, and I don't have any love for Mercury, but even I wouldn't help you coerce her like that." Nor would he kill Jax for the president. But Grey needed that Bunker with its research for his baby. For Maureen and his child.

Atherton leaned in, his gaze sharp and intelligent. "My scouts have reported that fire season has begun in your area. I have two Grumman S-2 Trackers and an S-64 Skycrane with pilots ready to get water and save your territory on my order."

"Did you set the fires?" Greyson asked, flattening his hand on the picture so he didn't form a fist. "Or did the vice president?" Atherton was smart not to bring Lake to this meeting.

Atherton's head jerked back. "Of course, not. A wildfire threatens more than you, you know. Any wildfire could spread and take out many portions of this state, including my head-quarters."

If the guy was lying, he was decent at it. "Somebody set those fires. It's a coincidence otherwise."

Atherton looked cool as could be in his button-down shirt that was somehow perfectly pressed. "I wouldn't take that kind of chance with the land and the existing forest. Many of the homes in the path won't have been scavenged yet. Probably."

Enough with the chit-chat. "What do you want, Atherton?"

"I want you to remember your oath and get back to work, Commander. You might not like me, but I am the Commander in Chief, and it's time to rebuild our military. We have no idea how well other countries fared with Scorpius, and we could face an attack any day. It's possible somebody else even found the cure and is stronger than ever." Atherton's voice roughened with conviction. "You know it's a possibility."

Yeah, it was, but Grey had been working too hard to survive to worry about foreign enemies. He had plenty right here. "You obviously want something else. What is it?"

"Lynne Harmony. I want her delivered to my headquarters." Atherton's face remained perfectly earnest.

Greyson shut the dark blue file folder. There was no way he was kidnapping Harmony and handing her over to Atherton. When he kidnapped a woman, he liked to ensure her safety and then knock her up. He grimaced. His sense of humor needed work, especially right now. "That's a large order, Atherton."

"Yes. I know. How about we start smaller?"

Grey tipped his head. "Go on."

"Retrieve a computer file for me from the computers at the Century City Bunker, and I'll give you Zach Barter." Atherton leaned back, relaxing against the leather. "Then we'll negotiate for fire support and Lynne Harmony."

To have Zach Barter in his sights after all this time sped adrenaline through Grey's veins. "Where is he?"

"I'll tell you exactly how to get to him," Atherton said, the pulse visibly ticking in his clean-shaven jaw.

Greyson pressed his advantage, his eye on the prize. Both of them. "It's the only way. Tell me where he is."

Atherton studied him, his intelligence visible in the calculation in his eyes. "All right. Here's the deal. You get me that file, and I'll give you the location of the second Bunker. I won't warn him or anybody else that you're coming. But you take him out, and you leave the facility alone. If that's possible."

"I'll make it possible," Greyson said. Didn't mean he wouldn't go back and take the facility at first opportunity. "What's in the file?"

"It's a computer file, and it's hidden beneath several layers of security." Atherton handed over a red folder this time. "The directions are there along with a flash drive. Once you copy the file, it automatically destroys any other copies of it on the system."

"Just the record of the file, or all records?" That would be a shitty idea for sure.

"Just copies of this file," Atherton said. "Do we have a deal?"

God, Greyson wanted Barter. Even more, he wanted to find that other Bunker with the superior research. Could his baby be saved? He wished he could give Maureen something hopeful. Something she could rely on. Anything that would save their child. "What's in the computer file?" he asked again.

"Doesn't matter, and it's confidential," Atherton said. "It's also encrypted and unreadable. The directions there tell you how to retrieve it, but not how to read it. In fact, my best guys think it'll take months for them to do it." He smiled again. "And don't try to copy it. As I understand it, that's one shot only." He held out a hand. "Deal?"

Greyson eyed him. "Yeah. Deal." He shook hands, wondering what the hell was on that file.

It couldn't be anything good, but this was Grey's only chance to find the Scorpius research and Zach Barter. He was taking it. Right or wrong.

CHAPTER TWENTY-NINE

Food is important, and I won't quit my research. But finding a cure for this baby, for making sure this child survives, is my primary objective until I succeed. I'm trying to think like a scientist, but I feel like a mother. There's power in the love I have for this little one, and I'm going to use that.

—Maureen Shadow, Notes

MAUREEN BRUSHED BACK her still-damp hair after her gloriously hot shower and made her way up to the control room where Raze sat in a computer chair, his long legs stretched out in front of him. She faltered. Yeah, she should've expected he'd want to chat, but she'd figured on having a bit of a reprieve first.

He rose and moved to her, enfolding her in a protective hug. One of many in her lifetime. "My baby sister."

Tears instantly pricked her eyes. Of course he loved her and wanted what was best for her and the baby. "Raze. I'm sorry to just spring it on you like that." She leaned back. "I should've used finesse."

He grinned, looking so much like their father her heart hurt.

Well, except for the black eye from his fist fight with Greyson. "When, in your entire life, have you ever had finesse?"

She smacked him on the arm, even though it was true.

He drew her over to another chair and set her in it like she was made of fragile china and then sat again, rolling his seat toward hers until their knees almost touched. "I have to know that you weren't forced in any way. Were you scared? Did you think it was the only way to get safe? Were you brainwashed?"

She chuckled, loving him more than ever. "Raze. I started having sex when I was eighteen. Remember Bobby Rollins from the general store? The baseball player for the community college?"

Raze winced and held up a hand in obvious protest. "God, no. We're not doing this. Just answer the question I asked." He exhaled loudly. "No details, no adding to the story, just please answer me."

She leaned forward and took his hands. "I promise you I was willing. More than willing." Heat infused her face. "He's incredible—"

"Now I'm going to puke." Thunderclouds crossed Raze's face.

She sighed. "I was willing and still am. I like him."

Raze scrutinized her, his gaze probing. "Do you love him?"

Her mouth gaped open and then quickly shut. Love? Was there time for love? Could it happen quickly in such crazy circumstances? "Um—"

"Forget it." Raze waved the question away. "I'm sorry I asked that. But about the baby. You do want it?"

She released him to wrap her arms around her abdomen. "With everything I have."

He nodded and patted her knee. "All right. We'll come up with a plan to save him or her. Jax will bring Lynne here to get to work, and you can help with the science stuff. A plant geneticist isn't all that different from a person geneticist, right? It's all genetic engineering."

Not exactly, but close enough. She nodded. "I feel like I have to get on this. Have to start learning about the process. I need more data."

"Then we'll get you more," he said softly. "I'll fix this, Moe. Or I'll make sure you can fix it."

She smiled at her big brother. "Thank you." She was so happy he'd found somebody to love. "Is Vinnie coming to the Bunker anytime soon?" They had been kidnapped together and quickly bonded while trying to survive. Moe could use a friend with all the craziness going on, and while Vinnie was a little eccentric, she was tons of fun.

"We'll see. There are a few things to iron out first." Raze donned his so-serious face. "I know you like Greyson, and I now understand he's the father of your baby, but I don't know if I trust him. He's dangerous, Moe."

"So are you," she whispered.

"Yeah, but my allegiances are clear, and Grey's aren't. He may turn against Vanguard, which is turning against me. I don't ever want you in the crossfire of something like that." He took her hands again. "Promise me you'll consider coming back to Vanguard and doing this with us. We can give this baby all the family he or she needs."

And leave Greyson out of it? He was the father, and he wanted to be a dad. After his childhood of not having anybody for so long, what would losing his own child do to him? She didn't want to hurt him like that, and a baby needed a father. Especially in the dangerous world they now inhabited.

"Maureen? Just say you'll keep your options open. That you'll keep your *eyes* open with Greyson," Raze said.

"My eyes are open," she blurted out, surprised.

He sighed. "Sweetie, you've always fallen hard and with blinders on. From the time you were twelve. It was fine when it was just a moron who was also dating your best friend. But today, in this time, trusting the wrong guy could mean death for a lot of people. You have to use your brain and not your heart this time. You have to."

Was she doing that? Romanticizing Greyson because he'd fathered her baby? Because he was so good in bed and said all the right things? It wouldn't be the first time. Even the act of him killing people had an element of good to it because he'd protected her. Was she blind?

"I love you, Moe. You're good and kind and sweet...and you have a romantic streak a constellation long. But now isn't the time to romanticize. It's the time to be realistic." Raze leaned forward and pecked her on the cheek. "I just decided we'll have Vinnie come here for a while. You two can chat."

Vinnie was a psychologist. "I don't need a shrink, Raze. I just wanted to get to know your lady-love."

"That's a great idea," Raze said, his mind obviously made up. "But first, you have to promise me you'll be rational and watch Greyson with alert eyes. Not only for you but also for your baby. We need to know if we can trust him."

Maureen looked at the man she'd trusted since birth. The one who'd raised her, loved her, and protected her. The one who'd had tea parties with her and had patiently taught her to ride a horse. To dance the two-step. To fight. The very least she could give him was a promise to be alert. "I promise, Raze."

* * *

THERE WASN'T any wind at the moment, which was good news. Greyson stood on the beach, looking west at the smoke hanging over the sky several miles away. The right side of his ribcage still protested from Raze Shadow's punch. He ignored the pain. Right now, his men were busy clearing any brush and foliage between them and the edge of the Los Padres National Forest. "How are we doing?" he asked Damon.

Damon's shoes sank into the sand. "We're trying. It's only

about nine miles from here to the edge of the forest, as the crow flies. Isn't that crazy?"

"Yeah." The forest had seemed much farther away when there was civilization in control of the world. Now nature ruled. Like it or not.

Two men hustled between mansions and jogged down the beach toward them. One was in his mid-fifties with a gray beard and a slim stature. The other had to be around twenty with black hair and bulging muscles.

Damon waited. "This is Tom and Mel. Tom worked for the forest service fighting fires in Oregon for twenty-five years, and Tom was a smokejumper out of Montana."

Grey eyed the kid. "Smokejumper? How old are you?"

"Twenty-four," the kid said, his voice surprisingly deep. "Look young for my age."

Grey nodded. "What do you guys know?"

"It ain't good," Tom said, rubbing his beard. "We're clearing debris as fast as we can, but the territory is too big. We have to consolidate and just concentrate on an area. We're also trying to load up on water and have some pumps ready to go from the ocean, but it ain't gonna be impressive. Sure could use air support."

Mel nodded vigorously. "We need air. Without question."

Fuck. The only way Greyson would get air support was to turn over Lynne Harmony to the president, and even he wasn't a big enough asshole to do that. But if he got his hands on the flash drive, he could drive a harder bargain. Maybe. "We need to save the headquarters area along the beach," he said. "That's the priority."

Tom looked around. "If the fire gets too close, we can talk about a controlled burn with a few of the houses on the far side. But we're a long way from having to worry about that."

Mel winced. "Fire has a way of making its own timetable. If the wind kicks up, we could be in trouble."

Grey sighed. "All right. Start protecting this main strip, and we'll go from there."

The two men nodded and ran off, disappearing between the mansions.

Grey turned to Damon. "Move all of our medical supplies, food, water, and weapons to the subdivision here—concentrate on keeping this mile strip safe." He hated the idea of losing any of the land, especially the college campus, but he had to protect their access to fresh fish and water, even though it was sea water.

"Got it," Damon said, not moving.

"What?" Greyson asked.

Damon just lifted an eyebrow, making it visible above his dark sunglasses. "You're going back to the Bunker. To get that computer file."

"You disagree?"

"Shit, Grey. It could have nuclear launch codes or something on it. Who the hell knows?" Damon asked. "Giving it to the president is dangerous. Too risky."

Dread crept down Grey's arms. "I know it's risky, but what's the alternative? I need that Bunker for the baby, and Zach Barter is there. Forget for a second that I want to kill him, that I promised to do so. He's crazier than crazy. If there's viable research there to cure Scorpius, who the hell knows what he's doing with it. What he will do *to* it." Grey had been thinking of nothing else for the last several hours.

"Why not have Vanguard's computer expert take a look at the file? She's the best, right?" Damon asked.

"You think we can trust Vanguard with this?" Greyson asked, watching the smoke cloud in the distance get bigger. Thicker. "Not a chance." He focused on Damon. "Who's our best computer guy? We have to have somebody."

Damon winced. "Kid named Hector. Sixteen and a great shot from a decade of spending time on video games. It's frightening how well some of these guys can shoot from games like that. Who knew?"

"Get him here," Grey said, moving for the main mansion. He needed to retrieve all of Moe's things from her room in case he couldn't save his territory. There were clothes he'd taken from many of the mansions, and she'd seemed to like some of them. "I'm thinking we'd better get trucks ready to go from here in case we can't contain the fire." Where he'd send his weapons, he didn't know.

Damon nodded and spoke quickly into a shortwave radio. "Bob? Send Hector to headquarters, would you?"

"Affirmative," Bob said, his twang heavy over the radio. "He's just around the corner."

Grey continued into Maureen's room and riffled through the closet to find an old backpack. He moved to the drawers and emptied them, making sure to stuff the pretty lingerie he'd found into the bottom.

Damon moved to the corner and issued orders through the radio. "Keep us informed if the fire does anything. Any change of movement or direction." He clicked off.

A soft knock sounded on the door.

Grey straightened. "What?"

Hector moved inside, dirt across his face and tears in his jeans. He was about five-foot-nine with black hair, blue eyes, and a sparse beard. Very sparse. "Hey, boss. We've been digging trenches behind the farthest row of houses. Big ones."

"Good," Grey said. "Rumor has it you're our computer guy."

Hector winced, looking even younger than seventeen. "I can reboot a system, and I grew up with computers. Mainly played games on them."

"Can you decrypt a file?" Grey asked.

The kid drew his mouth back in an exaggerated wince. "Well, if I have the Internet, I can find a program that can probably decode an encrypted file."

They didn't have the Internet, but they had a hell of a system at the Bunker. Maybe there was a possibility in that setup. In those servers. "Great. Pack a bag, because we're leaving for the Bunker in about an hour. Bring your gun."

The kid gulped and then nodded. He partially turned to show a gun in the back of his waistband. "I never leave home without it."

CHAPTER THIRTY

Scorpius has done enough damage. We can't let it win.
    —Maureen Shadow, Notes

EARLY EVENING, Maureen watched the jellyfish glide gracefully through the small tank, her hands full of papers and her head aching as she sat at a table in the main Bunker lab. "They're kind of weird-looking."

Lynne Harmony glanced up from a stack of graphs spread across the table. The biologist had arrived an hour earlier, flanked by a squad of deadly looking soldiers. "I always thought they were majestic." The former big-wig at the CDC looked about twenty with no makeup and startling green eyes. Her white T-shirt did nothing to conceal her very blue heart.

Moe had met Lynne at Vanguard, but this was the first time they'd sat down to work together. She tried to avert her eyes from the blue glow.

Lynne looked down and sighed. "I should wear darker shirts, but sometimes I just forget."

Maureen winced. "I'm sorry."

"Don't be. It's odd." Lynne's smile was slightly lopsided and pretty endearing. "My heart glows blue." She tugged her shirt aside to show the veins from the heart glowing very faintly. "It's bizarre."

"Does it hurt?" Maureen asked. "I mean, it's blue. Does your blood go slower? Faster?"

Lynne shrugged. "It doesn't hurt. But I don't know long-term effects. Or even short-term. It's not like we have medical equipment here to take a look."

"I've heard rumors, but how did it happen?" Maureen asked quietly.

Lynne sighed. "We were working on cures for Scorpius, and since the bacteria and subsequent infection is impacted by the vitamins in the B family, we were looking closely at squid and jellyfish because of their vitamin B content. We created several experiments, and Zack Barter conducted a few, and he injected me with one that we thought was a deadlier form of the bacterium. It turned my heart...blue."

Man, it was odd. Barter had caused so much pain. It was hard to believe he was still living. "Do people still think you're carrying a more dangerous strain?" Moe asked.

Lynne nodded, her eyes clouding over. "Yes. Bret Atherton and his minions have put out word as a warning from the government. Just to cause me problems and get them more information on my whereabouts."

Maureen shuddered, her body chilling. "I've met the guy. Talk about bonkers."

"Tell me about it." Lynne moved a chart out of her way.

The president had seemed crazy...brilliantly so. "I was so scared when he had us. Vinnie and me."

Lynne's eye softened. "I know. His obsession is with me, so I'm sure he'll make another run at us someday. We just have to be prepared."

"We need to be ready for anything," Moe said, rubbing her still flat belly. "Is there anything in those stacks that might be helpful?" She'd already gone through much of the data on her side of the table.

Lynne flipped the top of a file closed and reached for another. "The research here is preliminary and more of a filing system. Storage, really. There has to be a better lab somewhere."

Yeah, that's what the consensus was. Moe's stomach growled, even though they'd eaten dinner only an hour before. The day had flown by, but she still missed having Greyson near. What the heck did that mean? Shaking herself out of it, she focused back on Lynne. "What do you know about pregnancies and the Scorpius pandemic?"

Lynne sat back, her face pale in the fluorescent lights. "Not much. My focus was initially on preventing the pandemic, and then I became ill, and finally I was on the run and trying to survive. Most of the pregnant women who contracted Scorpius died, as did the vast majority of the population."

Moe listened aptly. "Go on."

"Survivors were limited, as you know. Most of the pregnant survivors lost their babies while battling the initial illness." Lynne tapped her nails on several of the graphs. "There was talk about miscarriages taking place in camps and shelters after the pandemic, but that could be part of the conditions of the time. We really don't know much."

"That's what I've heard."

"In fact, we have another pregnant woman, girl really, at headquarters. We should bring her here," Lynne said.

It'd be nice to be not so alone. "We need to do better outreach and contact other camps. By now, there has to be many formed, right?" Moe asked.

"I think so. Like Vanguard and the Mercs. There are probably groupings all over the country, I think. But there are a lot of scavengers. It's still dangerous out there."

Jax Mercury stepped into the room, movements economical and intense. Moe wasn't sure she'd ever seen the guy relax. But as he neared, his sharp eyes softened to a light bourbon as he focused on Lynne. "Blue? It's after ten, and I thought we'd try one of those hot showers." He grinned, suddenly looking much younger. Much more approachable.

Lynne's cheeks turned a light red. "Mercury. I'm working."

"Yeah, but all that stuff will be there tomorrow." The Vanguard leader rocked back on his heels, charm now oozing from him. "We have the place locked down, and we're safe for the moment. I may have to return to Vanguard tomorrow. We're having problems on the north side. With the renovations."

Lynne's eyebrows rose. "You're leaving tomorrow? Without me?"

He grinned. "I said maybe. I may have to leave." His smile slowly disappeared, replaced with something far more primitive. "Are you coming? Or do I need to come over there and get you?" The tension turned from male to sexual.

Maureen felt like blushing herself. She'd have given the standard line of 'get a room,' but that's exactly what Jax was trying to do. "Why don't you, ah, go on? I'll keep working for a little while."

Sami Steel hustled into the room and drew out a chair. The woman had one speed...fast. Moe had never seen her move at anything slower than a jog. "I'm done for the night. My eyes are seeing triple," she murmured. "You guys want to find the tequila? There has to be some here."

Jax had apparently found his opening because he loped around the table and picked up Lynne, files and all. She laughed, and he tossed the file folders on the table before turning and quickly striding out the door.

Sami rolled her pretty brown eyes. "Geez. Get a room, right?"

Maureen chuckled. "Pretty much. How are you doing on the main computers?" Sami had been working in the upstairs control room all day.

"Well. I'd like to figure out a way to get eyes on the president and his headquarters with the still functional camera system, but I'm not sure we'd be able to broadcast that far."

Maureen frowned. "Without the Internet, how are you getting camera feeds anyway?"

"The Bunker computers are on their own server," Sami started. "See, it's pretty simple—"

Moe raised a hand. "No. It's good. Honest. I trust you." She was already getting tired, and computer talk would put her right into dreamland.

Sami snorted. "If I had a nickel for every time somebody stopped me from talking about very interesting computer issues, I'd be rich. I mean, if we still used money. Maybe we'll use money against someday, right?"

Moe shrugged.

A rustle sounded by the door, and suddenly, Greyson Storm took up the entire space. His thick hair was mussed, and his dark T-shirt looked tattered. A shadow covered his hard jaw, and lines fanned out from his gray eyes. But he looked absolutely delicious.

"When did you get back?" Moe asked, her body flaring wide-awake and ready to go.

"Just now. It's late, and you need sleep," he said, his deep voice a growly rumble.

Sami coughed. "Yep. Get a room," she muttered under her breath.

* * *

GREYSON WAITED as Maureen stacked her papers and then made her way to him, her movements graceful. "Did you eat dinner?" he asked, noting she was still pale.

She nodded. "We did. And I managed not to throw it up." She winced. "I'm sorry about earlier."

"I haven't had a chance to find pregnancy books, but I will."

He took her hand, again struck by how perfectly it fit into his. But even her knuckles felt breakable. Fragile.

"What's happening with the fire?" she asked, covering a yawn with her hand.

The woman needed to get more sleep. If something happened to him on this mission, somebody had to take care of her. The idea of her with another man cut deep, but he needed her protected. Her brother was a decent guy when he wasn't throwing punches. That gave Grey some relief. "The fire is a disaster, but if the wind doesn't pick up, we may be okay. " They needed luck more than skill, and good fortune was hard to come by.

"I hope they save the beach house," she murmured, pushing hair away from her face. "I really like that place."

"Me too." They reached the stairs, and he led the way down to the sleeping quarters, slowing his pace so she wouldn't have to run. "I'm going on a mission tomorrow morning, and I need you to promise to take care of yourself. Eat meals and make sure you get enough sleep."

They reached her door, and he opened it, reaching for the lantern by the bed and twisting it on. Then he surveyed the room to make sure it was empty.

She followed. "Where are you going? I mean, what's the mission?"

He ducked into the bathroom just to make sure it was clear.

"Geez, Greyson. Who the heck do you think is hiding in my bathroom?"

He turned, surveying her disgruntled expression. "How should I know?" They weren't exactly living in secure times, and his people and Vanguard only had a very tenuous truce in place. One he was about to jeopardize big time. "It's better to be cautious."

She rolled her eyes. "What's your mission?"

"Firefighting," he said easily, feeling like a shit for lying to her. They were building something, and she was carrying his kid. So

lying to her made him an asshole. But he couldn't tell her he was
meeting with the president, and he couldn't ask her to keep
secrets from her brother. Plus, he didn't want to get her hopes up.
"I'm trying to protect that beach house."

She blinked, her head tilting. "All right. Then why did you
come back tonight?"

Great question. "There are a couple of pumps here we may be
able to use to pump water from the ocean to spray if the fire gets
too close to headquarters." Somewhat true. "But we need a bigger
generator and more fuel." Also true. Which is why he was
sending Damon back to Santa Barbara with the pumps and fuel
in the morning.

"Oh," she said, hesitating by the bed. "So, um, you're here to
sleep."

He grinned. Man, she was adorable. He moved in and lifted
her chin with his finger, setting the lantern back on the bedside
table. "I'll be here later to sleep." He placed a soft kiss on her
mouth, indulging himself by nibbling on her sweet lips. "I have to
meet with Damon and get the plans in motion. Then I'll be back."

He moved away, pleased with her bemused expression.
Tugging back the covers, he nudged her onto the bed. "Be here
when I get back."

She rolled her eyes and then yawned widely. "Just because I'm
tired."

The temptation to join her in the bed snaked through him
with a heated demand. He swallowed and turned, locking the
door from the inside before pulling it shut, forcing himself back
to work. He'd seen Sami Steel in the lower lab, so hopefully the
main computer room upstairs would be empty.

He found Hector in the cafeteria, chomping on some brownies, pure ecstasy on the kid's face. "Come on," he said, leading the
way through the tables to the stairs on the other side.

The kid followed him, still chewing. "This place is awesome.
Can I stay here?"

"No," Grey said shortly, jogging up the stairs. "After tonight, we're vacating." The idea of leaving the resources available at the Bunker made his gut churn, but he didn't have a choice. If things went wrong, and they probably would, his men would be needed in Santa Barbara to defend the territory. The computer room was empty save for a guard lounging against the door. A Vanguard soldier. "We've got this," Greyson said, moving inside.

The guard eyed him, checked out the brownie Hector was munching on and shrugged. "Jax says we're allies." He moved to the stairs.

Grey barely kept from wincing. He would like to be allied with Jax, and depending on what happened with the president, it might still be a possibility. "Get to work, kid." He waited until Hector sat before handing over the instructions from the president. "Find that file."

Hector started typing on the keyboard. "Man, it's nice to be typing again. How long you think the generators will be working?"

"Less than a year," Greyson said. "Since these are on their own server, is it possible they're somehow connected to other computers within the same network? Other Bunkers?"

"Yep," Hector said. "There are layers upon layers of security here. The hacker has done a good job so far of getting into them, much better than I could do, but there's probably a long way to go. I'm not as good as whoever's been working on this."

"Don't worry about it. Did you find my file?" Grey asked. Damn it. He needed more time to get to those other servers. Or networks. Or whatever it was that would lead him to the other Bunkers.

"Just a sec," Hector said, typing away. "It's right here. Not hidden very well, and definitely not secured."

Grey frowned. "Can you open it?"

"Sure." The kid typed in a series of commands, and code

started scrolling. "Whoa. It's encrypted. I don't suppose you have the key?"

"No. Follow the directions and put the file on here." Grey handed over two flash drives. "Try to put it on both. If you can't, put it on the first one, and put another encrypted file, any one you can find that's about the same size, on the other. Give them the same name."

Hector took the drives. "That wouldn't fool anybody for long."

That's what Grey was afraid of. "Just do it."

CHAPTER THIRTY-ONE

I think I'm falling in love with the father of my baby. That should be
a good thing, right?
　　—Maureen Shadow, Notes

MAUREEN WOKE with Greyson nibbling on her neck. Flames
licked through her, spiraling heat and energy to every nerve. Her
breath quickened. "Greyson."

He kissed her, his tongue thrusting into her mouth, a force to
his kiss that he'd hidden before. His big hands cupped her face,
holding her as he took what he wanted. The feeling of being
devoured was so erotic, her pulse jacked, and her body went from
sleep to full-on ache. She grasped his shoulders and kissed him
back, tasting chocolate and man.

Levering up, he ripped off her shirt. She gasped at his speed,
and her panties dampened even more. What was happening? She
ran her knuckles along his whiskered jaw. "Grey?"

"I want you. All of you." His voice was low, gritty. A hunger
echoed in those words, one of demand.

"Then take all of me," she whispered, meaning every word. A
part of her wanted to comfort him, to ease the rage that seemed

to be possessing him. The other part, the deeply feminine part, needed this primitive side of him. The real Greyson nobody else knew. Or had. She craved that side of him. The scientist in her didn't understand it, but the woman did. "Now," she murmured, sliding her hands across his bare torso. So much muscle and strength. It took her a second to realize he was already nude. Deliciously so.

He stilled and dropped his head. "God, you're perfect." Bracing one hand next to her shoulder, he levered down and licked his rough tongue across her nipple.

She gasped, her legs widening to allow him more room. His erection jumped against her thin panties, shooting sparks through her lower half.

His talented mouth latched on to her left nipple, and he tugged hard, the pull streaking right to her core. She arched against him, her clit swelling. Then he moved to the other nipple, nipping her, causing her to jump and then heat to a fever pitch of burning need.

He moved up, kissing and licking along her collarbone and up to her jawline. "Whatever happens, remember this. Remember me," he said, grinding his cock against her clit.

She grasped his biceps, digging in her nails. What? Remember? "Grey—" His mouth stopped her words as he kissed her hard, playing with her nipples with more than a little bite. The small streak of pain melted into wild pleasure, and she kissed him back, raw need coursing through her body.

Wrenching her face away, she held him, panting. "Now, Grey."

"Not yet." He kissed her again, the demanding press of his firm lips pushing her, tempting her, forcing her to take him, to make him hers. Possession, dark and untamed, ripped into her, shocking in its intensity.

He was hers.

She wanted to be his.

Then he started nibbling again, driving her crazy, his arms undulating next to her as he held himself back. As he controlled himself. For her.

"No," she whispered, raking her nails down his chest enough to bite but not cut. "Don't hold back. Please. Tonight. Don't hold back." She had to have all of him. Whatever was happening, she instinctively felt she needed to leave her mark. To claim him.

His eyes blazed, a light gray in the dim light. His thick hair fell to his shoulders, the dark shadow extending into the harsh planes of his strong visage, his starkly beautiful face. God, he was something.

She played with his ripped abs and caressed feverishly up his sculpted chest. So much power, and right now, it belonged to her.

Yet he still held back. Frustration edged through her along with the challenge. His hard cock pulsed against her, and she reached down, scraping her nail along his impressive length.

He sucked in air, his eyes flaring, his chest stilling.

The calm in the room grew heavy like the air before a lightning strike. The eye of a storm. The hint of the wildness to come. "Maureen," he said. A claiming. A plea. A warning.

It was the warning that did it. She was getting close. Hunger bit into her, and she wrapped her hand around his dick, her fingers against her own mound. Then she stroked him. Top to bottom. And again.

He growled. Low and dark and deep.

She shivered. "Give me everything," she said, stroking him again.

His eyes closed, and his head lifted, elongating his powerful neck. "Whatever happens, you have to know, you're it for me, Maureen Shadow. It's only been you, and it'll only ever be you. I promise."

The words surrounded her, cushioning the world. She let them in, let them be real, and nodded. "Only you," she said back, the words coming from deeper than she thought possible.

He reached between them and captured her hand, tugging her arm up above her head. In less than a second, he secured her other arm and clamped one hand around her wrists. Her back naturally arched, and her nipples rubbed against his chest.

Sparks bit through her. Electricity uncoiled in her abdomen, and all he'd done was take control. His free hand traced her face, her lips, her jaw and then moved on to both breasts. She writhed against him, trying to gain friction, and he held her easily in place. His fingers tapped down her rib cage and belly button, finally zeroing in on her clit.

She cried out, her legs quaking.

He smiled, the look fierce. Then he worked two fingers inside her, twisting and brushing across a flare of nerves that almost pushed her over. Heat rose inside her, filling her, propelling her to a brink that was almost frightening.

She struggled against his hold, trying to free her hands, needing to touch him.

He pressed down on her wrists, immobilizing her. The craving inside her intensified to a dangerous ache, and she rode his fingers, holding nothing back. "Keep your hands up," he ordered, removing his fingers and sliding down her, taking the covers with him.

Before she could think, his mouth settled on her core.

Tension beat inside her, fluttering out. She gasped, so close to exploding she had to shut her eyes.

He licked her, swirling his tongue around, playing. Then he pushed a finger into her, added another one, working deep inside and stretching her.

It was so much, it was everything.

She whimpered, held on to the precipice, catching her breath before she fell.

He chuckled, the sound vibrating through her sex. Then he kissed her gently.

She stopped breathing completely.

He stroked his fingers inside her, going deep, and sucked her clit into his mouth. Her nerves flared, and somehow she built some more before she finally exploded. She cried out his name, cresting wild waves, and her sex clamped down on his fingers.

The orgasm ripped through her, taking everything, forcing her to ride the excruciating pleasure to the very end. She gasped, her body softening into the bed. God.

He moved up and loomed above her. "You kept your hands in place. Good girl," he rumbled, his voice hoarse.

Hands? Who cared about hands?

He grasped her neck and leaned down to her, possession on his lips. "You taste like heaven, and now you're mine. All of you."

She returned his kiss, somehow wanting more. An ache set up inside her, deep down, and she moved against him.

He rose up to his knees on either side of her thighs, grasped her hips, and flipped her over. She landed on her chest, and her head went back. She dug her hands into the mattress, her heart kicking back into gear. "Greyson?" she asked, her body starting to boil again.

"My way," he murmured, pulling her hips up and forcing her to catch herself with her knees. He pressed at her entrance, tightened his grip on her hips, and drove all the way into her body from behind.

She cried out, pain and pleasure swamping her until she could only gasp. "More," she said.

He filled her completely to a point she hadn't known existed. He pulled out and powered into her again, giving her everything he had.

She lowered her head, her nails digging, her body hungering. He was taking her, and she liked it. She craved it. Her body was his to do with as he pleased, and the pleasure that drowned her should give her pause. But right now, all she could do was feel. All of him.

He gave her no quarter, not slowing, not easing. Each

powerful thrust inside her shook her body and the bed, sparking her nerve endings to life. The slap of his muscled body against hers, the sound of flesh meeting flesh, combined with their heavy breathing.

She started to rise again, started to build, her eyelids flew open to barely see the wall. He leaned over her, grasping her neck, one hand remaining on her hip. He pulled her back to meet his thrusts, somehow going deeper inside her, claiming what was already his. His hold was absolute and unbreakable.

The peak was so close. She climbed toward it, her body safe in his hands, her tension rising. With a cry of his name, she broke.

The waves pummeled her this time, shooting out and sparking. She rode them, tossed about, white lightning flashing behind her eyes. The orgasm shook her and wrung her inside out, charging her into mindless oblivion.

Greyson slammed inside her one more time, jerking hard and shuddering as he came. His teeth sank into her shoulder, and she gasped at the unexpected pain.

His hands shook against her.

He released her neck and withdrew, tugging her around to flop down on her, his elbows catching most of his weight. Skin to skin, body to body, panting chest to panting chest.

He lazily swiped his tongue along her lips. "I marked you, baby. You'll keep that for a while."

The man sounded entirely too satisfied. She grinned, her entire body throbbing. Her eyelids shut. Wait a minute. Part of what he'd said...

Had that just been goodbye? She opened her mouth to talk, and he pressed a hard kiss to her lips.

"Sleep. Now," he commanded.

She wanted to argue, but her body was already shutting down. This pregnancy stuff was tiring. She blinked, trying to stay awake, but rest was too appealing. They'd talk in the morning whether he liked it or not.

He shifted her to the side, and the bedding rustled. Cold brushed over her.

She curled into herself until he returned to warm her again.

CHAPTER THIRTY-TWO

I've made a lot of mistakes in my life. This might be the biggest. I hope she can forgive me.
    —Greyson Storm, Letters to Miss Julian

GREY JOGGED down into the underground garage, his combat boots smacking the concrete. The generator lights glowed an eerie yellow across the wide area. "Everything set?" he asked, one flash drive in his pocket and the other in his boot. The good one was in his boot, and he couldn't get them mixed up. That'd be a freaking disaster.

Damon handed over a battered bomber's jacket. "Yeah. Two Humvees are loaded with pumps, a generator, fuel, and as many weapons and explosives as I could get without being too obvious. Our men are on notice to exit the Bunker in exactly five minutes, heading north and not looking back."

Grey breathed in, quieting his voice so it wouldn't echo so much across the chamber. "Good."

"This is a mistake," Damon said, his dark skin flushed. "Giving up the Bunker."

"I know," Grey said. "But Jax has more soldiers than we do

now, and once he's figured out what I've done, they'll attack. We can't spare any more men from headquarters until the fires are out. It's safer for us to vacate." Maybe there would be a chance to align again after he found the second Bunker.

"Jax won't ever let us back in."

Probably not. "But this keeps Maureen safe. If Vanguard has sole control of the facility, she'll be protected. I owe her that, D. You know I do." He'd kidnapped her, impregnated her, and now was leaving her. "I can't think or fight unless she's safe."

"Man, you have it bad." Damon shook his head. "You didn't tell her you were leaving, did you." It wasn't said as a question because Damon knew him.

"No. She'd either have to lie to her brother or betray me and tell him the truth. I won't put her in that position." But his gut swirled as he thought about leaving her. There was a chance he wouldn't make it back, so maybe it'd be better if she hated him. But something told him, deep down, that the thought was a mistake. His body tensed with the need to go back to her. "It's the right thing to do," he said, trying to convince himself.

"Uh huh. Right," Damon said.

Greyson clapped him on the arm and cut the thoughts of Maureen away. This could be his last moment with Damon, and that thought burned. His voice went hoarse. "You're my best friend, and I appreciate everything you've done for the Mercs. Thank you." His heart thumped hard. "After Ferris died, I never thought I'd find another brother, and yet here you are. I'd die for you in a heartbeat, and I'll miss you if I don't make it back. If anything happens to me, I just wanted you to know."

Damon's chest jerked. His gaze softened. "After I lost my brothers, I never thought I'd find another one, either. I'm glad I did, Greyson. Even if you're about to do something colossally stupid."

Grey grinned, his chest warming. God had taken so much

away, it was amazing he'd found this friendship. This brother-
hood. "You have to be long gone from here. Time for you to go."

Damon handed him a gun and then reached for a leather
jacket. "I'm coming with you."

"No," Grey said. "Sorry."

"Wasn't asking." Damon stomped over to two of the seven
Zero XXM electric motorcycles often used by the military. The
body was black, the accents chrome. "These are both charged,
which should give us over thirty-five hundred hours before the
batteries die."

Greyson eyed the bikes. The Bunker had stocked some
intriguing vehicles and weapons. The electric motorcycles were
dark, stealthy, and virtually silent. The president wouldn't know
Grey was there until he wanted to be seen. "You need to go back
and run Merc territory."

"Don't want to," Damon said, swinging his leg over the bike.
"You need backup. Stop being a dick." He gave the sign, and the
Humvees' drivers started their engines, driving out of the garage
and quickly away.

Grey stared at him. It was the first time Damon had ever
refused an actual order. What the hell? He couldn't shoot his
brother, so there wasn't much he could do about it. But Damon
was not meeting with the president. He could take cover
outside the compound in case Greyson had to make a fast
retreat.

Time to go. He jumped on and started the motorcycle. He
waited until Damon had driven out before following, taking one
last long look at the Bunker holdings. The door shut behind him,
effectively making it impossible for him to get to Maureen again.

His chest ached as he opened the throttle and zipped through
the darkened streets. There was no way she'd forgive him for just
leaving her. For lying to her.

He increased his speed, following Damon through the crumbling city, watching out for wild cats and dogs. And people.

Anybody out on the street at this hour was either crazy or up to no good, and he had to focus.

Before he knew it, they were on the US-395 North to Lake Tahoe. The drive should take about seven hours, assuming they didn't run into any trouble.

What were the chances of that?

* * *

MAUREEN WOKE and rolled over to find the other side of the bed empty. Cold. How long had Greyson been gone? She stood and stretched, heading in for a quick shower before getting dressed and leaving the room. The Bunker was quiet.

Maybe he was on patrol outside?

She made her way to the deserted cafeteria. A quick glance at the wall clock confirmed it was four in the morning. Eesh. She should've slept later.

Heavy footsteps sounded, and she turned to see Jax and Raze stalk into the room. Raze had lost the limp from being shot the other day.

"Where's Greyson?" Jax asked, his voice gritty and his eyes gleaming.

She faltered. "I, ah, don't know. I assumed he was in here or maybe doing patrols?" Dread began to pool in her stomach. "What's going on?"

Sami Steel stumbled into the room while tugging a comb through her unruly hair. Her clothes were wrinkled, and her eyes looked drowsy. "Why the hell did you send Clarence to wake me up? I need some damn sleep, Jax."

Jax jerked his head toward the control room at the end. "All of the Mercs are gone, along with two Humvees, some weapons, and pumps to fight the fires. Also two motorcycles. Get up to the computer room and make sure they didn't take anything else. I have Lynne checking the two labs down below."

Sami paused and then launched into a run for the far staircase.

Maureen gaped. "What? The Mercs are all gone?" Where was Greyson?

"Yeah," Jax said, red spiraling across his rugged cheekbones. "When was the last time you saw Grey?"

Heat filled her face. "Um, last night. Around midnight, I think." It might've been closer to one. Who the hell knew.

Raze's eyes turned a hard, deep blue.

Hurt pummeled at Maureen. The bite mark on the back of her shoulder ached a little at the reminder of what he'd done. What he'd said. How could he just leave? "There has to be some sort of mistake," she said lamely.

Sami emerged on the landing. "They've been into the computers, but I'll need a little time to figure out why."

Jax lifted his head, his warrior's body going deadly still. "Any chance we're in danger?"

Tace jogged into the room. "I just checked the sub-level. The fail-safe explosives are still dismantled. The Mercs didn't re-engage them before they left." His words were clipped.

Sami nodded. "If the explosives aren't engaged, then we're fine. Though I have to find out what they took." She disappeared again.

"Maybe they went to fight the forest fire?" Tace asked, shaking out his arms.

"Why not let us know?" Raze asked grimly. "Why leave Vanguard in sole possession of the Bunker?" He aimed his words at Maureen. "You know him better than anybody else still here. What's he doing?"

The questions hurt because she didn't have a damn answer. "I, ah, I don't know." She sounded lost, so she cleared her throat. "He didn't say anything about the computers or about leaving." He'd been too busy fucking her into oblivion to talk. The room started to spin around her.

"Whoa," Raze said, reaching her and settling her into a chair. "Take deep breaths. It's going to be okay, Moe. I promise."

Her brother. The one man in her entire life who hadn't let her down. Ever. "I should've listened to you about Greyson," she murmured, pushing hair away from her face. "Maybe. I mean, I don't know. He might have a good reason for leaving." After the night they'd shared, didn't she somewhat owe him the benefit of the doubt? Why would he just leave?

Raze crouched and patted her shoulder. "Breathe, sweetheart. You have to stay calm."

True. It was time to think and stop feeling. "The only reason he wouldn't have mentioned leaving is because he thought you guys would try and stop him," she murmured, thinking through the problem rationally. "So he has to be heading somewhere you guys wouldn't like." Her stomach rolled over.

"To meet the president?" Jax asked, his voice loud in the quiet morning. "The only reason he'd do that is to align with him and against us."

Raze glanced over his shoulder at Jax. "It'd be easier to do that from the inside here. Lure us in and then attack. Greyson did the opposite. He set us up to be wary of him, and he relinquished any control of this place, the computers, and the weapons. Not a smart move if he's working against us."

Hope drifted through Maureen. That made sense. "He wouldn't put his child in danger," she said quietly. No matter what he thought of her, what he felt for her, he would protect the baby.

Raze frowned. "You sure?"

She nodded. It was the only thing she was sure about at the moment. "Vanguard controls the facility, so we're all safe here." Grey might've left her, but he made sure she was secure. Like he'd promised. Why the hell hadn't he confided in her?

"Why would he meet with the president then?" Jax asked, crossing his muscled arms.

"I don't know," Maureen said—again. It didn't make sense. "We're just guessing that he went to meet with the president. It's possible he's doing something else you wouldn't like." What, she had no clue.

Apparently she didn't know him at all.

CHAPTER THIRTY-THREE

The strategy of this war is the best part.
—President Bret Atherton

THE MORNING SUN sparkled off Lake Tahoe, making the water look carefree and inviting. Greyson left Damon in a secure location yards from the first entry point of the president's compound. The electric motorcycles were excellently quiet.

He flashed his headlight on and slowed down, not surprised when two guards emerged on the road, automatic weapons pointed at his chest.

The first guy held up a hand to stop, and Greyson did as directed.

"Get off," the Elite Force soldier said.

Grey sighed and turned off the motorcycle, parking it to the side and swinging his leg over. The second guard approached him and frisked him, taking all three guns and four knives. Then he spoke into a short-range radio.

Something garbled came back.

The guy grabbed his arm and yanked. "The president is waiting for you."

It was nice to be expected. Greyson walked with his head up, surveying the area, looking for guards. The trees provided decent cover in case of an attack. It was surprising that Atherton hadn't taken most of them down. If the compound were Grey's, he would've removed all trees between the entry point and the house, leaving the lake on one side and the heavy forest on the other.

They reached the house in about ten minutes, and the soldier knocked soundly on the door.

A heavily armed blond man in his twenties opened the door. "Yes?"

"Greyson Storm to see the president," the guard said as if announcing guests at a fancy ball.

Grey cut him a look.

The blond guy stepped back and gestured with his gun. "This way."

Grey took in the spatial relations of the house and then concentrated on the layout inside as he was led through a great room and down a hallway to an executive office complete with golf paintings on the wall.

President Atherton sat behind a massive cherrywood desk, his arm still in a sling. "Commander Storm. I figured we'd meet up again soon."

"Where are Zach Barter and the second Bunker?" Greyson asked without preamble.

Vice President Lake moved into the room, his gun casually in his hand. He covered the door, and Greyson had to fight the urge to turn and tackle him into a wall. Lake lifted his arm to aim the damn gun.

The president smiled, sitting back. "Where's my flash drive?"

Greyson drew the flash drive out of his jacket and tossed it onto the desk. "Here. Now yours."

The president grabbed the drive and twirled it around in his hand. "Please sit down. We need to talk." He leaned to the side and drew out a laptop, inserting the flash drive. "Trevor?" he called.

Grey sat, acutely aware of the psychopath at the door who still had his gun pointed at Grey's head.

A wire-thin man with thick glasses slunk into the room, his brown hair tied at his nape, his beard patchy at best. "Mr. President? You called?"

Atherton turned the laptop around toward the door. "Is this the right computer file?"

Trevor's Adam's apple bobbed as he moved for the laptop, leaning over to type in a series of commands. He hummed, rubbed his beard, and then typed in more commands. "Interesting. I need a couple of minutes."

Atherton nodded and shoved a blue file folder across the desk.

Grey opened it to see the pictures of Zach Barter he'd seen earlier. Barter was in a lab, studying something in a file. "Where is this Bunker?" Grey looked from the file to the president. "How many Bunkers have you found?"

Atherton sighed. "Three, counting the one you hold."

The one he used to hold. Grey nodded. "Where are they?"

"Not telling you yet." Atherton folded his fingers together. "Trevor?" His voice held a clear warning.

Trevor kept typing, muttering something. "Huh. All right." Finally, he straightened.

Atherton's eyebrows rose. "Well?"

"That's a dummy file." Trevor looked over his shoulder at Greyson and shook his head. "It's not even a very good one."

Fuck. Greyson opened his eyes wider. "It's the file you said you wanted. I don't know how to fake a computer file."

Atherton sighed. "How unfortunate. Here I thought we could be friends."

That was so doubtful, it wasn't even funny. Grey tensed, knowing he didn't have time to get to the asshole behind him.

Could he get to Atherton? The desk was a hindrance, and Lake would have plenty of time to shoot.

A ruckus sounded down the hallway.

Atherton smiled, calculation oozing behind his charm. "I do like it when people make things easy for me."

Grey stiffened and partially turned.

Two men dragged in Damon, his hands tied, blood flowing freely down his face. Rips and dirt marred his clothes, and scratches showed down his arm. Blood oozed from his knuckles. "Jesus," Grey breathed. Damon had obviously put up a good fight.

Damon grinned, his lip splitting. "There were four of them."

The two guards forced him to his knees, and he fought them, but Lake planted the barrel of his gun on the top of Damon's head.

Grey's mouth went dry. "Shoot, and I'll rip your head off your neck," he growled, his adrenaline pumping hard and fast.

Atherton sighed. "The flash drive. You have two seconds. One—"

"Here." Grey reached down into his boot and yanked out the correct drive. He tossed it to Trevor. "Let Damon up."

Trevor caught the flash drive, and nobody else moved. He plugged it in and typed rapidly, swearing and typing some more, and finally pausing. "It's the right file, sir."

Grey half turned. "What's in the file?"

Atherton jerked his head for Trevor to go. "I want into that by tonight," he said. "Get to work."

Trevor grasped the laptop and fled the room, his relieved sigh echoing in his wake.

Grey edged toward Damon.

"Stop," Lake ordered, his gun still resting on top of Damon's head, pointing right in the middle.

Atherton cleared his throat and pushed a piece of paper

across the desk. "Here are directions to the Reno Bunker, as well as schematics and the camera positions we've documented."

Grey stilled. "Documented? Wait a minute."

Atherton smiled again. "Yes, well. The pictures are real. We hacked into the systems before they discovered us, and that's what we have. All interior cameras have been shut down, so I can't tell you more about the place."

Heat rolled up Grey's neck to choke him. "I thought Lake sprang him from the nuthouse."

"I did," Lake muttered. "Put him in one of the hospitals to do research, and the scientists there took him to a Bunker. Which we didn't know about."

Jesus. Barter had even gotten away from the president. Greyson eyed Atherton. "Fine. We had a deal. You have the flash drive, and I have Barter's location. Damon and I will be on our way."

Damon started coughing, and blood sprayed. Did he have a broken rib? Grey's chest puffed out.

Atherton shook his head. "You broke the deal by handing over a fake flash drive and also by bringing backup. So, new deal."

Grey's body went cold. He focused. "Let him go."

"Nope. You get into the Reno Bunker, get me the layout, record all weaknesses, entry and exit points, and bring them back to me. If you do that, and if your information is helpful, I'll let you take what's left of your buddy out of here. If not, I kill you both."

The fucking bastard. "You've never had access to this Bunker," Grey snarled.

"Nope," Atherton said cheerfully. "I also don't have a sniper onsite. Not one experienced with infiltration like you are. I've given you enough in the file to get you into the Bunker, probably. It's up to you to get yourself out."

Damon's head lolled on his shoulders. He visibly struggled to remain conscious.

"I won't go without him," Greyson growled. "Every sniper needs a spotter."

Atherton shrugged. "Sorry, but no dice. You had better get moving. And feel free to take out Zach Barter, if he's still alive. I have no problem with that."

Lake lifted up and brought his gun down hard on Damon's head. Damon crashed to the floor, out cold.

Then Lake lifted his weapon and pointed it at Greyson's face. "The president told you to leave."

Grey hesitated, every nerve in his body roaring for him to take out Lake. With great pain. "What about fire support? I'll get you into this Bunker if Damon stays safe and you send air support to fight the fires at Santa Barbara."

Atherton shook his head. "I'll keep Damon alive, and if you make it back with intel, I'll consider putting out your fire. And my men will return your weapons to you once they escort you to the edge of my territory. That's all you get."

Oh, Grey was going to kill that asshole at some point. He moved out of the room, pausing at the door. "I'll be back, Damon." He glared at the president. "If he's not alive, you're going to pay in ways you can't even imagine." His last sight as he left was of his best friend lying with his face in his own blood.

* * *

BRET ATHERTON WATCHED Greyson Storm leave, chills clacking down his spine. The guy was seriously deadly. He didn't know it, but Bret had gotten his hands on Storm's military file. His number of kills was impressive. More interestingly, his ability to infiltrate the enemy camp was legendary. If anybody could get inside the Reno Bunker, it would be Storm.

Lake still stood by the door, a deadly blond bodyguard. "Want me to end this guy?" He kicked Greyson's black buddy.

"No," Bret said. "We might need leverage if Storm comes back.

Take him to the basement cells. Make sure he doesn't die." Yet, anyway.

Lake whistled, and two guards rushed in, picking up the prisoner and quickly disappearing.

Reno was only an hour and a half away, but it would probably take Storm days to calculate how to get inside the Reno Bunker. But he was motivated, so maybe he'd just go in fast. It'd be interesting.

Bret had been trying to take that damn place for two months with no luck. He could go for an all-out assault, but the Bunkers had fail-safes, and some idiot would probably push the button and blow up the entire town of Reno. Especially if Zach Barter was somehow in charge. That scientist was stone-cold crazy.

Vice President Lake stretched his leg and winced. He'd been limping on and off since the helicopter crash but said he was fine. "There's too much blood on the floor."

Bret frowned. "Call somebody to clean it up." He looked up and studied his second in command. "Do you think Storm will get us into the Reno Bunker?"

Lake straightened. "He's good enough. I read his file." Lake rubbed his clean-shaven jaw. "The guy's also an expert in knife fighting and hand-to-hand combat. It'd be interesting to get him in the training field at some point."

Bret nodded. "I agree, but he's not an ally. Tried to trick me with the flash drive."

"Yeah, we figured he'd try something." Lake stood at attention. "Have we decoded it yet?"

"Not yet," Bret said. "But we will. Trevor is on it."

"God, I want to know what's in that file," Lake admitted. "The fact that our techs discovered its location from a different Bunker is significant. Whatever's in it is important."

Bret shrugged. Their techs had been ecstatic to discover the existence of the Scorpius II File. "I agree. Unless it's just a clue to another damn riddle. You'd think the CIA would've had better things to do with their time when designing these Bunkers." He shook his head.

"Agreed." Lake looked down at the blood and grimaced. "I might've hit that guy too hard."

Bret eyed the blood with distaste. "No. He'll be fine, I'm sure. In fact, he should probably be questioned. He's a Merc, and there's a lot we don't know about their territory and organization."

Lake's blue eyes glowed with as much emotion as the guy was probably able to feel. Torturing people made him light up like a Christmas tree, every damn time. He nodded. "I'd love to question a Merc."

CHAPTER THIRTY-FOUR

*Scientific reasoning and data gathering are crucial to our survival.
But sometimes...you just have to go on faith.*
    —Maureen Shadow, Notes

MAUREEN PICKED AT A MUFFIN, sitting at a cafeteria table nearest
the stairs to the computer room. She'd spent most of the morning
working in the downstairs lab with Lynne while trying to desperately convince herself that Greyson hadn't just deserted her.

Now her brother had called her up to the cafeteria and
slapped a muffin in front of her. Tace and Raze sat across from
her, a map of the Merc territory in front of them.

"So headquarters is still here," Raze said, drawing a circle
around the mansion where Grey lived.

Maureen nodded. "Yes."

Tace had his own pen, and he was rapidly diagraming what
he remembered from his time in Merc territory. "The infirmary is
here, and at least one of the weapons depots is in this mansion
right here." He made notations.

Her stomach lurched. "You guys don't really need this right
now, do you?"

Tace looked up, and his gaze cleared. "Oh. Well, yeah."

She frowned. "Raze? I don't understand."

Her brother stared at her, no expression on his hard-cut face.

Dread pooled in her abdomen, and she hugged herself. "What's happening? I mean, the Mercs all left. They're not a threat right now."

"Exactly," Jax said, jogging down the stairs. "The fire is threatening them, so they would've consolidated along the beach and headquarters here." He leaned over her and tapped the location of the mansion. "Weapons, food, medicine...all right here in one location to protect and defend."

Her entire body went cold. "You're going to rob them. Go in while they're busy fighting a fire and take their provisions."

Tace looked at Raze and then back at her. "You don't understand. The wind has shifted. Bad."

She stopped breathing. Fear caught her around the neck. "The wind? The fire is moving west?"

Tace nodded. "Very quickly. Unless a miracle happens, we're going to lose Santa Barbara. Maybe all of it. So we have to get those provisions. Now's our only chance."

Fury boiled through her so quickly she gasped. "Raze? How can you do this?"

"It's me," Jax said, moving around to face her. "I'm the leader of Vanguard, and I've made this decision. It's all on me." His eyes had turned a hard brown, and his jaw looked as if it were cut from stone. "Hate me. Not him."

Her mouth gaped open. Greyson couldn't lose his territory. "You can't do this. They're our allies. They need our help."

Raze sighed. "Honey—"

"Don't fucking 'honey' me," she blurted, shoving to her feet. "I'm not some simple pregnant woman you guys get to brush off. I'm smart, highly educated, and can analyze any damn situation better than the three of you put together."

Jax's chin lifted. "Is that a fact?"

A shiver wound down her spine, but she met his gaze. "Yes, it is." She pointed to the map. "We need the Mercs as allies. If you attack them, they'll have no choice but to align with the president. You're going to make him stronger. It's a mistake."

"The medicine and weapons haul make it a worthwhile endeavor, and the fire makes the timing perfect right now," Jax countered, watching her carefully.

She shook her head. "No." Shoving her hands through her hair, she breathed in and tried to find the right words. "Listen. I know Greyson better than you guys do. Whatever he's doing, it's not to hurt us. I, ah, I trust him." There. She'd said it, and she meant it. She had faith in whatever he was doing. "You need to trust *me*."

Raze rubbed his temple as if his head was killing him. "I do trust you, but I agree with Jax. The medicine alone is worth making the Mercs our enemy. And with Greyson obviously not at headquarters, this is the best chance we'll get."

Jax nodded. "I'm sorry, Moe. But this is the plan, and we leave in an hour." He looked in the direction of the computer room. "And I want to know what was on that file Storm stole by then," he yelled.

"I've been working on it all morning, and I'm still trying," Sami yelled back. "Bugger off."

Jax looked at Tace. "Is she British all of a sudden?"

Tace shrugged. "We might've been role playing a bit last night."

Jax groaned and held up a hand. "Stop. Just stop talking right now."

"This isn't funny," Moe bellowed.

Jax sobered. "Nobody thinks it's funny. But we're at war on every front, and Greyson made his bed when he stole that computer file and so quietly exited the Bunker. He might not be working against us, but he's definitely not working with us. So that means we take advantage of the opportunity *he* gave us."

It was the most words Moe had ever heard Jax string together.

"But—" she started.

Raze stood. "Discussion is over. Sorry, Moe." He gathered up the map and started moving toward the computer room. "Let's finish planning up here."

Maureen watched the three men go, her mouth gaping. Oh, they had not. They were messing with her life, damn it. She took her muffin and stomped through the cafeteria, her mind spinning. If they attacked the Mercs, shots would be fired. Somebody on one or both sides would die. Once that happened, there was no going back.

They'd be enemies until one of them fell.

She couldn't let that happen. When she said she believed in Greyson, she'd meant it. Whatever he was doing might not be good, but it wouldn't hurt her or Vanguard. And he'd be back. If there were any way for him to make it back to her, he'd do it.

She just had to give him a little time.

Walking past a couple of soldiers, she nodded. Okay. This was probably crazy. But she had a plan. Eating her breakfast, acting casually, she made her way to one of the supply closets. A quick search led her to the right tools, which she shoved into a pack she found in the corner. Then, taking a deep breath, she walked with purpose toward the stairs leading into the garage.

A guard smiled. Cute guy. About twenty with brown hair and pretty brown eyes. "Hi," he said.

She returned his smile and tried to preen a little. "Hi. My brother asked me to get something from the garage." She'd have to find the rest of what she needed down there.

The guard frowned. "I can't leave my post, but you shouldn't go down there alone."

She ran her hand down his arm and giggled, trying not to wince at the silly sound. "That's okay. You know Raze. When he needs something, it's right now. He wouldn't send me down there unless it was important."

The kid nodded. "I guess that's true. Okay. There are guards down there, but I'd rather make sure you were safe myself." He winked.

Oh, for Pete's sake. The kid couldn't be older than twenty. She forced herself to giggle again and then started down the stairs. Once she was out of his sight, she quickly tied her hair in a knot and tried to look official.

Sometimes life was made of tough decisions, and she'd just made one.

She'd chosen Greyson.

Right or wrong, it was done.

* * *

GREYSON HID the bike the best he could near the Thoroughbred Casino and Hotel in Reno. After he'd surveyed the neighborhood, he sat in an empty office building and went through the folder the president had given to him. The hotel was the newest in the town, having been built less than five years ago—a front for some CIA offices four or five floors below the casino.

Just how many secret CIA offices were there in the States? How many had become Bunkers after Scorpius infected the world? The damn bacteria had arrived on a meteorite, which apparently, wasn't as crazy as it sounded.

He finished reading the file, which had an impressive diagram of the patrolling soldiers and viewing cameras. The president had done a decent job of watching. Now it was time to infiltrate. Grey would usually take several days to come up with a plan.

But Damon hadn't looked good. At all.

So Grey went with his gut. They wouldn't be expecting an infiltration in the middle of the day. The problem was the guards. The patrols worked in pairs. That would be an issue.

He made his way to ground level and stayed close to the

buildings, moving silently toward where the diagrams showed the guards patrolled. Then he waited.

His mind calm, his body relaxed, he moved right back into his job of hunting, infiltrating, and taking. Boot steps announced the guards, and he edged to the side of a building that had once held a bank and several offices. The guards rounded the corner, and he let them go past before jumping on the closest guy and wrapping an arm around his neck.

With his free hand, Grey drew his weapon and pointed it at the other guard, who'd just whirled around. The guy he held to choke out shook, fighting hard. But Grey didn't relent.

He felt it the moment the guy lost consciousness, and Grey dropped him to the ground. "Cuff him," he ordered the other guard.

The second guy was about forty with toned muscles and hard eyes. "No."

Grey hardened his expression. "I will shoot you in the arm. It'll be a non-lethal hit, but it's gonna hurt. Cuff him. Now." He let the truth of his words show in his gaze.

The soldier swallowed and yanked zip ties from his back pocket to secure his buddy.

"Good. Now push him into the bank," Grey said, following along as the soldier obeyed his command. Money littered the floor inside, a series of one-hundred-dollar bills that crinkled beneath their feet. The guy complied.

Grey stole the unconscious guy's black hat and plunked it on his own head. He motioned toward the door. "Okay. Your time is about up. We're going in like all is good, and you won't die today."

The soldier's mouth tightened, but he nodded. "You won't survive. They'll spot you."

That's why he'd choked out the guy with longer dark hair. "Maybe." He knew how to keep his head down. "Let's go."

They walked around the corner, and he crossed his arms, keeping his gun hidden and pointed at the other guy. Then they moved into the darkened casino. The empty and silent slot machines were eerie, while the mellow yellow lights shone down and showcased the dirt.

Poker chips dotted the carpet in every direction.

Greyson kept his aim true and his head down. The guy didn't know he had no clue where they were going next, so he let him lead. They reached a stairwell behind a series of blackjack tables, and Grey followed the soldier in and down several flights. The soldier finally opened a door, and they moved into a white hallway.

Just like the other Bunker.

Grey shoved the soldier against the wall, face first, and pressed his gun beneath the guy's ear. "Where is Zack Barter?"

"Who?" The soldier grunted.

"Barter. Scientist. Blondish brown hair, blue eyes, looks like a movie star from the fifties," Grey whispered in his ear.

The guy swallowed, sweat rolling down his face. "Oh. Psycho-Doctor. His name is Brad now. He's probably in one of the bigger labs two floors down."

"Good." Grey hit the soldier on the back of the head, and he went down. Grey dragged him to what looked like a closet, opened it, and shoved him behind huge stacks of paper supplies. Then he searched him for zip ties, found some, and made sure the soldier wouldn't be able to move.

Two stories down. All right. Keeping his hat on and his head lowered, Grey hurried back into the stairwell and jogged down, taking a deep breath before entering the sublevel.

The soft humming of equipment broke the quiet. Grey emerged into another long, white hallway, which he followed for several yards until two doorways opened up on opposite sides of the hall. He peeked into one to see a fully functioning lab with several absolutely humungous aquariums on the other side with jellyfish. Lab techs hustled around, all working quietly, all ignoring him. He didn't see Barter.

He moved to the other lab to see about five people working at different stations, some peering into microscopes, and some making notes.

Again, no Barter.

Frustration welled up, but he quashed it, sliding his gun into his holster. A pretty woman of about thirty walked by him with test tubes in her hand. He touched her arm, and she jumped. "I need to see, ah, Brad. Do you know where he is?" Grey kept his voice light and forced a smile.

She blushed and smiled back. "Um, yeah. He's back in his office." She nodded toward another large aquarium. This one held squid and had a door next to it.

"Thanks." Grey kept his voice low and then moved past her as if he had every right to be there. The lab techs largely ignored him. Maybe soldiers often headed down into the lab. He kept going and crossed the threshold, stopping cold.

Zach Barter sat at a wide desk, reams of papers, notes, and pictures in front of him. He looked up. "Yes?"

Everything inside Grey went stone-cold. The noise in his head quieted. Slowly, deliberately, he closed the door.

Zach's blue eyes widened and then narrowed. "What the hell are you doing?"

Grey pulled out his gun. "Keeping a promise." Intent filled him, and he aimed carefully. "For Ferris."

Barter's arms swung out wide. "Wait a minute. You can't kill me."

Grey lowered his chin. "Why not?"

"Because I'm the only one who can cure Scorpius," Barter said, his gaze frantic. "I'm it. It's in my head and in my notes here that only I can decipher."

The need to pull the trigger, to keep his vow, was a physical burn. Grey bit down on his tongue. Hard. "You can't cure Scorpius."

"I'm closer than anybody else," Barter argued, his eyes filling with tears. "I'm the only hope for those who haven't been infected. And for those who survived and want to continue the human race. It's me. Only me."

Damn it. What if he was telling the truth? About continuing the human race? Could he actually save the baby? "You've been studying pregnancies?"

Barter gulped, snot dripping down his nose. "Of course. The focus of this facility is Scorpius research. How could that not be an important part of it?"

Greyson slowly lowered his arm, frustration biting through him with jagged teeth. God. How could this happen? He finally had the bastard in his sights. The crazy, pandemic-spreading, parasite rapist who needed to die. "Looks like you're coming with me." If there was a chance to save Grey's baby, for Moe, for him... he had to make that choice.

Ferris would have understood.

CHAPTER THIRTY-FIVE

It seemed like a good idea at the time. Why is that always the prelude to something disastrous?
    —Maureen Shadow, Notes

HER LATE DINNER sitting like a rock in her stomach, Maureen read through more data on Scorpius experiments while working at a desk in the largest lab downstairs. "So you've combined mostly anti-bacterial agents with different strengths of the various vitamin Bs," she mused.

Lynne looked up from a computer, her eyes taking a moment to focus. "Yes."

"Have you tried any natural remedies?" Moe asked, leaning forward. "Has anybody?"

"Hell, we tried everything we could think of right off the bat, but it all went so wrong so quickly. I can't speak to what the other labs did, or are doing if there are any facilities left." Lynne ground her palm into her right eye. "Why? What are you thinking?"

Maureen chewed on her lip. "Well. Aloe from the aloe vera plant fights bacteria, as does turmeric, which is an herb that might even fight cancer." She flattened her hand on the charts in front of her. "And there's honey. It can help prevent the spread of bacteria. Or lemons or garlic." Substances they might still be able to find on Earth.

Lynne straightened. "We could get those things. When we send the scouts out next week to find co-ops and farms, we could look for those specifically."

"How do the vitamin B injections work, anyway?" Moe asked. "That's outside my purview."

"We don't know how or why, but the concoction of the multiple Bs slows down the bacteria and somehow protects the brain from suffering too much damage. Usually. Not always." Lynne shook her head. "It was a total accident when we discovered it. As usually happens."

"We're going to run out of the injections soon," Moe said. "Right?"

Lynne slowly nodded. "That's true. We've cut back to treatments every other month, and there hasn't been an increase in people going crazy. I'm starting to think B is only needed right after infection and maybe only for the first three months. After that, the brain can protect itself."

Moe frowned. "We hope."

Lynne winced. "Right. We don't know." She lifted a green file folder and tossed it over onto Moe's table. "Research on making B permanent in the body without injections. It's interesting, and I thought we were on to something, but turns out I haven't been able to find a lot of promise in it."

Jax appeared in the doorway, and Moe jumped. The Vanguard leader looked deadly in his faded jeans and worn T-shirt with his gun at this thigh and a knife at his waist. But at least he didn't look as pissed as he had around noontime when he discovered that his garage door wouldn't open.

He lifted an eyebrow. "That was quite the job you did on the garage door today. My techs are still repairing the wires."

Moe swallowed, her back snapping to attention. "I couldn't let you go rob the Mercs."

His chin lowered. "We're leaving the second the door is fixed, and the guards have orders to keep you out of there. No matter what." He looked at Lynne. "Did you eat dinner?"

The scientist shook her head. "No, I missed it."

"Meet me in fifteen minutes in the cafeteria." He gave Moe another hard look. "I'm checking on my garage door first." Silent as death, he turned on his heel and disappeared down the hallway.

Lynne snorted. "I can't believe you stripped the wires and gears for the garage door."

Moe winced. "I honestly didn't think it'd take them so long to fix it." But that was okay. She'd tried to argue with Jax and Raze all day, but they hadn't budged on their plan. But if darkness fell, they'd have to wait until tomorrow because they didn't want to mess with the fire at night. So that gave Greyson more time.

She had to believe in him.

"It's funny that the door is too heavy to lift. I hadn't realized it was fortified to that degree," Lynne mused.

Moe nodded. "We need the generators to lift it. So when we run out of fuel...no more garage." No more Bunker, actually.

Lynne chuckled. "Even so, nicely done. I like how you went around them when they wouldn't listen."

"Yeah, but now Jax hates me," Moe murmured, shuddering. The guy wasn't a good enemy to have.

Lynne scoffed and stood, stretching her neck. "Nah, he doesn't hate you. In fact, while he wasn't amused by any means, I think he respects you even more now. Where'd you learn to be so destructive?"

"My minor was electrical engineering," Moe said, turning back to the files, her heart warming. Lynne was trying to make her feel better, and that was just nice. Plus, maybe Jax didn't hate her. "Have a lovely dinner. I'm sure I'll see you shortly." The woman didn't seem to ever stop working.

Lynne patted Moe's shoulder on her way out of the lab.

Moe returned to reading, looking up at a rustle by the door. "Vinnie," she said, leaning back and smiling. "How are you?"

Her brother's love walked gracefully into the room, a happy hop in her step. "Fantastic." She looked to her side and frowned. "I'm not talking to you. Go away."

Moe swallowed. "Still seeing dead people, huh?"

Vinnie rolled her pretty eyes and sat down, pushing her blond hair over her shoulders. "Just my crazy stepmother, Lucinda. She haunts me on a regular basis."

Moe nodded. Vinnie had survived Scorpius, and then a dangerous drug regimen forced on her by the president when he held her captive for quite a while. She'd had hallucinations since, but she was also the resident shrink. It was an odd reality, to be sure. "Um, okay." Wait a minute. "Did Raze send you to talk to me?"

Vinnie nodded. "Yep."

"I'm fine," Moe said shortly. "I'm glad I did what I did." In fact, she had to think of another way to stop the Vanguard soldiers before they had a chance to leave.

"Yeah, I get it. I'd destroy anything to keep Raze safe," Vinnie said easily.

Moe paused. "Of course. You guys are engaged and everything." The hair stood up on Moe's arms, and she shifted in her chair, her body stiff all of a sudden.

Vinnie snorted. "You're knocked up and creating havoc for your man. Give me a break. You love the guy."

Energy zipped through Moe. "Aren't you supposed to ask me questions until I reach my own conclusions about my life? My motivations?" She crossed her arms and studied the woman Raze loved more than his own life. "What kind of a shrink are you?"

Vinnie grinned. "I'm not a shrink. Never was. I was a behavioral scientist, but I'm the best we've got for this kind of stuff."

Stuff. Her shrink just used the word 'stuff.' Moe groaned and return the smile. "You are so perfect for him." For her rigid, tough, protective, stubborn brother. There was no doubt Vinnie kept him on his toes.

"I truly am," Vinnie said, her eyes sparkling.

An alarm suddenly blared through the facility. Vinnie jumped up, her eyes wide. "Something's wrong."

Moe pushed from the table and hurried behind the blonde, down the hallway and up the stairs to the main control area.

Jax and Raze ran down, guns in their hands, a look of calm on their faces.

"What's happening?" Moe asked.

Jax cut her a look, still jogging toward the stairwell. "Your boyfriend is back."

* * *

GREY SMASHED Zach Barter against the locked door of the office complex, making sure the cameras caught him. He peered inside the darkened reception area for the building. Three silent and pretty much dead elevators with closed sliders were visible beyond where the security guards used to be way back when.

A door opened to the side of the elevator bank, and Jax Mercury bounded out, his gun already pointed at Grey's head.

Grey smiled and stepped back, yanking Barter by his collar.

"Let me go, man," Barter begged, ineffectually trying to pull away.

"Don't make me gag you again," Grey snapped. He'd had to steal a car and had finally just shoved the sniveling moron into the trunk for the last six hours. "There's probably a trunk here somewhere."

Barter stilled. "I don't know when or how, but I am going to kill you."

"Get in line, asshole," Grey said. Having the guy breathing while Ferris was long gone was a physical slice across his chest. He felt it.

The door opened.

Grey shoved Barter in before him and walked in after, his gun safely in his thigh holster.

Jax, Raze, and Sami held defensive positions, each with a gun pointed at his head.

Grey sighed. "Meet Zach Barter."

The air shifted. Tension rolled. Jax instantly switched his aim to Barter's head.

"Wait," Greyson snapped. "If I didn't get to kill him, neither do you."

Jax's lips peeled back. "He infected Lynne. Tried to kill her."

"Yeah. He infected a lot of people," Grey said. "But he's been working in another Bunker, one in Reno, one with a huge-ass lab. A couple of them. If anybody can cure Scorpius, it's him. For now." He looked at Raze. "If anybody can save your sister's baby, *my* baby, it might be this jackass."

Raze slowly lowered his gun.

Maureen and Lynne moved out of the stairwell, both with wide eyes on Barter.

Lynne went pale and stopped right behind Jax.

"Dr. Harmony," Barter said, his voice lifting with what almost sounded like glee. "You're alive. I was so hoping you'd survive." He tried to press forward. "Is your heart still blue?"

Greyson jerked him back before Jax could club him with a gun. "You should stop talking now."

Lynne swallowed. "We have the location of another Bunker?"

"Yes," Barter said, his body straightening. "It's in Reno, and we've done excellent research. All of the data compiled about Scorpius from all over the world is centralized there. Well, the data we had before the Internet went down. I can take you. We can work together again."

Jax growled. A low, odd, animalistic sound.

Grey tensed. He hadn't gone through all of this shit just for Jax to gut the guy.

Maureen tried to step toward him, and her brother pivoted, stopping her. She focused entirely on Grey. "You didn't kill him. For Ferris." Her voice was breathy. Surprised. Hopeful.

Grey shook his head. "Not if he has knowledge that can save the baby. Our baby."

Barter jerked. "You're pregnant? After Scorpius."

Grey clipped him on the back of the head, anger rushing through him. "Shut up. You don't get to speak to her. Ever."

Moe's pretty blue eyes softened. "Greyson."

Yeah, he'd chosen her and the baby over revenge. Over his vow. At her small smile, she knew it. He nodded.

"Thank you," she murmured.

The urge to touch her, to pull her close, almost overwhelmed him. But he turned to Jax. "Here's the deal. You get Barter, and I get another motorcycle."

"You won't make it," Jax said, almost gently. "It's too late."

Grey frowned. "Too late for what?" They didn't know about the president and Damon.

"The fire," Raze said, watching him closely. "The winds shifted this morning. You'll need air support to even have a minuscule chance of saving Merc territory. It's going to be gone by morning otherwise."

Grey blinked. An invisible fist plowed into his solar plexus. His men. He'd given them orders to get to safety if they couldn't protect the homes. They'd listen. They had to. "I'm sorry to hear that." His voice shocked him by remaining steady. "But I still need the motorcycle."

Jax cocked his head to the side. "How'd you find Barter?"

Grey's lips pressed together.

Sami pressed closer. "What the hell did you do to my computer? What file did you take and why?" she asked, her aim level and straight at his chest. "Tell me, or I will shoot you."

Greyson eyed the little hacker. Rumor had it she was a hell of a fighter but a truly shitty shot. "I'm tempted to take the chance, but I'd rather just level with you. There was a secured file, and we took it for the president." He reached into his back pocket and drew out the folded paper holding the instructions. "This is what he said to do, and this is what we did. Don't know what's in the computer file, and neither did he. It was encrypted."

She moved forward, gun steady, and took the paper.

Grey could kick the Glock from her hand, take her down, and pull back up with her blocking him. Then he could force Jax and Raze to drop their weapons if he put his arm around her neck. But Maureen was watching, and he kind of liked Sami Steel. So he took a step back, keeping his hand on Barter's shirt collar. "I'll try and get the computer file back," he offered. "But I have to go now. Motorcycle?"

Jax grinned, the look almost feral. "Even if I wanted to give you one, your baby mama here shredded the wires to the garage door, and they're not repaired yet. I've been promised we'll be able to open the doors within the hour."

Grey swung his gaze to Moe. "You did what?"

She bit her lip.

"Why?" he asked. Why would she sabotage Vanguard? Or the Bunker? He looked at Jax and then at Raze. Wait a minute. "You were coming after the Mercs. When the winds shifted, you decided to go after the medicine and weapons." It's what he would've done. "And she stopped you." He said the last quietly, turning toward her. His lips tickled, and he grinned. God, she was amazing. Fucking amazing. And his. "My girl," he murmured.

A pretty blush covered her high cheekbones.

Raze made a gagging noise.

Grey cut him a look. "Your niece or nephew is gonna be my kid, you know." If it survived.

Raze paled, but his gun hand remained steady. "Not if I blow out your brains," he said conversationally.

"Raze." Maureen turned and punched him in the arm. "Knock it off."

Jax pierced Grey with a look. "So you traded a mysterious, buried computer file from here, one that might've held the secrets of Scorpius—or nuclear codes, or fucking anything—to the crazy-ass president in exchange for Zach Barter and the location of another Bunker." Anger filtered across his face, darkening his skin. Then he visibly calmed. "Though you brought Barter here. To use his knowledge to save Maureen."

Grey nodded. "Yep. I had planned to put a bullet between Barter's eyes to fulfill a buddy's deathbed request. But if he can help us, I can kill him later."

"Not if I kill you now," Jax returned.

CHAPTER THIRTY-SIX

Life was a hell of a lot easier when all I had to do was stand between bullets and people while returning fire. This whole getting to know them, liking them, really makes things difficult. Trust can get you killed.

—Jax Mercury, Journal

JAX'S FINGER actually twitched on the trigger of his gun. Zach Barter. Right in front of him. The man who'd injected Lynne and almost killed her. Who'd made her heart blue. Who had purposefully spread the pandemic that had killed most of humankind. If anybody deserved a bullet to the brain, it was Barter.

Greyson watched Jax carefully, no doubt sharing those dark feelings.

But he was right. Barter might prove useful. If nothing else, then at least with information about the Bunker in Reno. "Can you cure Scorpius?" Jax asked him directly.

Barter swallowed, his throat moving. "We're on to something, but I don't have a cure yet."

Maureen pushed to stand next to her brother. "What about for pregnant women? Do you have anything there?"

Barter looked her up and down. "The application of what we've been doing for Scorpius, with the concoctions of different B vitamins and some natural ingredients would apply to pregnant women." His eyes started to gleam. "In fact, we needed pregnant women to test some of the possible cures on the fetuses, but we ran out."

Jax's gut ached. The guy was all-out freaky and looked like a fucking movie star. "You've run out of pregnant women."

"Yeah," Barter said. "They keep miscarrying."

Moe made a small sound of distress.

Grey smacked Barter on the back of the head again, and the scientist turned and glared. "Not from the tests, you moron. They're just vitamin B mixtures along with healthy alternatives. Of course, I'm available to repregnate our test subjects anytime." Zach smiled as he finished speaking.

Lynne gasped. "Please tell me you haven't forced women to be experiments."

Jax's spine snapped to attention. Had they experimented on women like they had with Marcus? "If you've been raping women as part of your experimentation, I'll kill you right now." The Earth was better without Barter on it. For sure.

Barter sighed and rolled his eyes. "Of course not. My Bunker has researchers in command, and there are rules. Nobody forces any test subjects."

The guy could be lying, but Jax couldn't tell. Sociopaths were gifted at deception. "If I find out differently, you're dead."

Barter paled.

Jax shifted his attention to Greyson, who didn't seem to mind that Sami still had a gun pointed at his head. He wanted to trust the Merc leader, but the guy didn't trust anybody else, so it was just getting harder to try. "How's the security at the Reno Bunker?"

"Good," Greyson said. "I could get in by forcing a guard, but an all-out assault will be met with impressive resistance. The facility is underground, so explosives will be risky. And I assume there's a fail-safe."

Barter nodded. "Yep. One button, and ca-blewy."

What a dick. Jax's lips peeled back. "Then it's a good thing you're going to tell us absolutely everything you can about the Reno Bunker, isn't it?" They'd managed to take this Bunker, and they'd take the next one. Especially if it had better lab equipment and more data than Jax currently had on Scorpius.

Barter's gaze moved to Lynne again. "I'll tell you anything you want to know." He smiled, all charm. "It'll be a pleasure to work with you again, Dr. Harmony. The caliber of other researchers in Reno doesn't compare to either you or Dr. Medina."

Lynne's breath caught. "Have you heard from Nora? Has your Bunker heard from them?"

Barter shook his head. "We had to keep my existence a secret, you know. But our scouts found an ex-member of the Brigade about a month ago, and he said they were going strong and still trying to save parts of the infrastructure."

Jax's eyebrows rose. "Is that a fact?" The Brigade was led by Deke McDougall, and it had been an emergent task force type of unit when Scorpius descended. "Is the Brigade working with the president and his Elite Force?"

Barter shrugged. "It didn't seem like it, but I wasn't privy to the military discussions. The ex-Brigade member is still at my Bunker."

Lynne turned to Jax. "We need to find him. Talk to him. Make sure Deke and Nora are still alive." Hope filled her pretty green eyes.

Jax nodded. "We will, sweetheart. I promise." Nora was Lynne's best friend, and Lynne had been worried since she'd arrived in Vanguard territory during the rainy season.

Grey shoved Barter toward Jax. "So. Zach Barter in exchange for a motorcycle, Jax. That's the deal."

"Why?" Jax asked, sliding his gun into his holster. Raze or

Sami could shoot Greyson if necessary. "You can't make it to Santa Barbara in time to fight the fire. Your men have already gotten your provisions to safety. Hopefully. What are you planning with the bike?"

Greyson studied him, no expression on his rugged face.

Jax waited him out. Either the soldier would decide to trust, or he wouldn't.

"Grey?" Moe asked. "What's going on?"

Greyson's expression didn't change, but his eyes softened to a lighter gray. He faltered and apparently couldn't keep silent with Maureen asking him. "The president has Damon," he said, his voice low and hoarse. "I promised I'd come back for him, but first I had to get Barter here. To save you and the baby."

Maureen breathed out, her eyebrows lifting. "Is Damon okay?"

Grey's mouth tightened. "No. But he will be."

Ah, shit. The president was nuts. Finding Damon still alive was a long shot. But he was leverage, so at least there was hope. Jax thought through the issue. Greyson didn't stand a chance by himself, and all of his men had gone back to Merc territory. "What did the president want?" he asked.

Grey focused back on him. "He wanted the schematics of the interior of this other Bunker in Reno. Weaknesses, strengths, locations of everything."

Jax straightened. "Did you give them to him?"

"No," Grey murmured. "I'm hoping to bargain for Damon."

Jax nodded. No way would the president let either Grey or Damon live. "All right. You can have a bike."

Greyson nodded and pushed Barter toward him. "Any chance I could borrow a sniper rifle also?"

* * *

Maureen found Greyson on the roof, staring out at the huge

cloud of smoke to the northwest. It was orange and dirty and frightening. He stood, legs braced, head up, shoulders stiff. She swallowed and moved across the gravel toward him, giving in to temptation and sliding her arms around his waist.

He shuddered.

She rested her cheek against his broad back, her heart hurting for him. "Jax said the garage door will be fixed in about fifteen minutes," she murmured.

Greyson turned and held her, his chin dropping to the top of her head. "I can't believe you sabotaged the door." Amusement darkened his tone.

She leaned back and looked up, wrinkling her nose. "They didn't give me much choice." There were so many words she wanted to say—*needed* to say—but she couldn't put them in any order that made sense. "They were going to attack your territory, to take your medicine. I had to stop them." Her voice lowered to a hush. "Don't hate them. Please." Especially Raze. She wanted Greyson and Raze to like each other somehow.

Greyson smiled, the curve of his lips somehow gentle. "I don't hate them. It's exactly what I would've done." His grinned widened. "Thank you for protecting the Mercs."

That smile entranced her. She blinked. "I tried, but they're not protected." She looked around him at the terrifying sky. Her chest ached. "The fire. I'm so sorry, Greyson."

He ran his huge hand down her back, his gaze stark. "So long as the men are safe, that's okay. The smoke is bad, but it doesn't mean the fire has reached all the way to the beach homes. There's a chance the guys were able to halt it. Somehow."

It was impossible to tell from Century City. "Do you think Damon is okay?" She whispered.

"Yes." Grey's jaw hardened. "He's tough as they come, and he has to be all right. He'll hold on until I can get back to him."

Yet Grey had brought Zach Barter to the Bunker first. At least a seven-hour drive, and now another long drive north to the pres-

ident's compound. Grey had chosen her and the baby. "Be careful," she said quietly. She couldn't lose him now.

He frowned. "You understand why I have to go, right? Damon
is hurt. Bad. I wouldn't leave you, wouldn't leave the baby, if—"

"I understand," she said softly, pressing her hand against his
heart. "It's Damon, and he's your brother. I'd go if my brother
needed me. In a second."

Grey's brow smoothed out. "Thank you. For getting it. For
getting me."

Fear tasted like acid in her mouth, dread that she'd never see
him again, but she forced a smile. "Of course. When you bring
him back, we'll baby him. Drive him crazy with meddling and
ice-cream." In fact, there were some single techs at the Bunker
who'd probably love a tough guy like Damon. "No matter what
state he's in, we'll heal him."

Grey watched her. "I never even dreamed of you." He ran his
thumb across her lips. "You're too good to be true. Sweet and
smart...spirited. Dangerous."

His touch sensitized her mouth. Her entire body. "Greyson,"
she murmured.

He watched his thumb caress down her jawline. "For so long,
I didn't trust women. After my mom abandoned me," he
murmured as if lost in his own thoughts. "Then the foster homes
weren't great sometimes. Finally, Miss Julian, she helped. But I
thought—"

"What? What did you think?" Maureen asked, breathless.

"That she was an anomaly. Almost not real. I never thought
I'd find...you."

The sweet words nearly took her to her knees. "I'm glad we
found each other," she whispered, her chest expanding. Her eyes
filling. Her father and then her brother were strong men. She'd
thought she wanted something else for herself, but she'd been
wrong. This was what she wanted. Grey. A deadly, strong, protective, wild man just for her.

"Miss Julian gave me a foundation, but I was still damaged. Even when I found brothers in the military." Greyson captured Moe's chin between his thumb and forefinger. "With you, I feel whole. Like there's hope somehow. I forgot that it even existed. In the apocalypse, you gave me hope."

She blinked, emotion swamping her. The clock was counting down. Grey would be leaving in just a few minutes. What if he couldn't get Damon out? He'd give his life trying to save his friend, and that was one of the reasons she cared for him so deeply. She couldn't ask him to be any other way. But they hadn't had enough time together. Not even close. "I have to know. What's your middle name, your favorite color, your favorite ice cream, and your favorite movie?"

He blinked. "Huh?"

Small things, really. But ones she'd know if they had more time together. "Please." Suddenly she wanted to know everything about him.

His jaw finally relaxed. A little. "Henry, black, strawberry, and *Shawshank Redemption*."

"Strawberry?" she said, amusement tickling her.

His brows drew down. "Yeah. What's wrong with strawberry?" he asked in a mock growl.

She chuckled. "It's just so, well, boring."

He twisted a hand in her hair, drawing her head back. "Boring?" Then he kissed her. Slow and sensual, he took her mouth, taking possession. Claiming her.

Her legs went boneless. Pleasure splintered through her, stealing her breath. His scent filled her nose with a combination of aged oak and wild male. She knew his taste, mint and man, and she reveled in it. She wanted more of it.

She caressed him and felt the powerful shift of his muscles through his shirt, needing to memorize every hard inch.

He tilted her head back, stroking her jaw, demanding she open for him.

She opened her mouth, inviting him to take what he wanted. What she needed. He slid his tongue into her mouth, possession in every stroke. His touch filled her, but it wasn't enough. Not even close.

He made a sound in his chest, a sound just for her. She had that power over him. The heady knowledge went to her head, and she kissed him back, pouring every ounce of feeling she had into it. He was going into battle, and he needed to know he had a reason to come back. Motivation to fight with everything he had.

Finally, he drew away with a shudder. "Maureen," he murmured, the sound reverent.

She took a deep breath, trying to get her body under control. Those gray eyes of his would stay in her mind forever. He'd stay in her heart for eternity. "I love you," she said, meeting his gaze. In case he didn't make it back, she had to say the words. "I, ah, know it's fast. Really quick. But I wanted to tell you. So you knew." God, she had to stop talking.

He stared at her, those odd eyes darkening even more. His chest moved. "I've never loved a woman like I do you. Like this. Like you're everything and you're inside me somehow." He brushed her hair back from her face. "I'd do anything for you, Maureen."

"I know," she said, giving her trust. Look what he'd already done by bringing Zach Barter to the Bunker. For her and the baby. His words sank in deep and took hold. Greyson Storm, the deadliest man she'd ever met, the most dangerous, had just said he loved her. Even more, she felt it. Warm and strong and real. His love.

The rooftop door opened, and Raze poked his head out. "The garage door is fixed. Finally."

Greyson released her and stepped back, instantly chilling her. "I have to go, sweetheart."

CHAPTER THIRTY-SEVEN

I've never had so much to lose before, Miss J. Isn't that when you usually lose it all?
— Greyson Storm, Journal after Scorpius

GREYSON CHECKED out the bike in the Bunker garage, making sure it was fully charged. Good. He had three guns and four knives on his body, and he really needed a sniper rifle. Jax had said he could borrow one, but he had to get going.

As if on cue, Jax jogged out of the stairwell with a rifle in his hand and a pack over his shoulder, Raze and Tace on his heels.

Nice rifle. Greyson reached for it. "Thank you for this."

Jax pulled back. "Your plan is to ride a motorcycle for seven hours while carrying a full-on sniper rifle?"

Greyson nodded. "Yeah." It wouldn't be the first time, actually. "You get used to lugging these things around in unfriendly terrain."

"I don't think so." Jax watched as Tace hustled over to a truck and ordered a couple of the guards to load three more motorcycles into the back. Then he packed several vests, a bunch of explosives, and some medical provisions.

Greyson looked toward Tace. "What's happening right now?" His temples started to thrum.

"We're going with you," Raze said easily.

Greyson reared back. "No, you're not. I've got this."

Jax snorted. "Just you, a sniper rifle, and the Elite Force. Do you *not* want to make it back?"

The spit in Greyson's mouth dried up. His throat ached. He cleared it. "You're helping me?" How did that make any sense? Where was the trap? The double cross? "I don't understand."

Jax sighed and spoke slowly as if addressing a moron. "We're allies. Sure, you fucked up by taking that computer file, and I hope you don't fuck up again because then I might have to just shoot you. But I get why you did it, and you need help getting Damon back. Your men are fighting a losing battle with the fire, and you're swinging out there all alone. We've got your back."

Grey couldn't breathe. These men, these soldiers he barely knew, were going to put their lives in peril to help save Damon. He looked toward Raze. "Raze?"

"Maureen loves you, and you're the father of her baby," Raze said, his gaze deadly serious. "If the baby doesn't make it, Moe will need you. If the baby does make it, I hope to God it's a little girl, and I want to be there to see you handle that." His grin was feral.

Jax nodded toward Tace. "Damon might require a medic. Or one of us could end up needing Tace's expertise. Sami would be coming, but I need her on the computer, trying to figure out that file you took."

Grey winced. "Maybe we can get it back."

"That's a good goal," Jax agreed, his eyes glittering.

Greyson's heart warmed. "All right. But, not Raze."

Raze's chin lowered. "Excuse me?"

"Maureen," Grey said softly. "This is a suicide mission, and she can't lose us both. The baby needs one of us around."

"Then we'd better both make it back," Raze returned, moving to help Tace.

Jax shrugged. "His mind is made up. Get on board now."

Raze finished loading the bulletproof vests. "I'll go get the maps and schematics of the president's compound. The materials we have."

Jax nodded. "Everyone go say goodbye. Be back here in ten minutes, and we go."

Greyson moved toward Tace. "I'll help you get medical supplies. Damon looked like he might have a couple of broken ribs, and that was before I left him for twenty hours with the president. We might have to perform a surgery or two on him."

Tace gently eased a few more explosives into the truck bed and turned. "All right. Let's see what we can dig up."

* * *

GREYSON KEPT on high alert as he drove the motorcycle out of Century City, headed north. Within minutes, a caravan on the other side of the interstate caught his eye. One with trucks, bikes, a school bus, and a trailer. They were stopped to fix a tire on the truck. "Wait a minute." He slowed.

Then his heart thumped. He stopped and Raze stopped, too. "Lou?" he called.

The woman had bruises on her face. She turned, her hair wild in the wind. "Greyson?"

He took in the ragtag group. The trailer had fire damage up the side. His heart thumped, and a heavy fist descended in his gut. "What happened?"

Tears filled her eyes, and she limped over to the middle divider. Garbage blew around. "We were attacked. I swear, Greyson. It was the vice president."

Grey's hands clenched into fists. The fucking bastard. "The members?"

Tears slid down her face, leaving dirt tracks. "We lost ten good men in the fight, and the entire farm is destroyed. Burned to the ground. Even the animals were taken or killed."

"I'll get him," Grey vowed. "No matter what. I will."

She sniffed and turned back to her group. "Maureen said, well, she said—"

Raze leaned forward, his bike still going. "Vanguard is a safe place. If Maureen told you that, she was right."

Lou's shoulders shuddered. "Okay. Good. Then we'll be getting there." With one last sad smile, she moved back to her group.

"I'm going to gut him," Grey growled, starting his bike again. It was time to end this.

The rest of the drive was brutal and punctuated by an easily countered attack by a rogue gang and a hit by a lone Ripper, who had succumbed to insanity. Finally, they reached the outskirts of the closest town to the president's compound and stopped at a rundown tavern with the metal sign still swinging in the slight wind but too damaged to read.

Greyson parked and stalked inside, his boots crunching on shards of glass and what looked like silver dollars.

Tace brought the maps, Raze some water, and Jax weapons.

The sun poured through the broken windows, providing plenty of light as well as heat.

Yet the interior of the place wasn't bad. A scarred bar ran the entire length of the space, the shelves behind it broken and empty. Wooden booths against the other wall still remained, but any tables that had been scattered throughout were long gone.

The place was truly deserted.

Jax grasped the map and rolled it out on the bar. "Let's center and get ready to go. Show us what you know, Greyson."

Grey had to banish all thoughts of the fire, all feelings about Maureen and the baby...and go cold. There could be nothing else but Damon and this mission. It was the only way any of them would get out alive.

It was the first time he'd ever struggled to concentrate on a mission, but he dug deep and slid back into training.

He drew large boxes in red on Jax's map. "Here's where the guys saw landmines being planted." Then he drew a line of the path the president's guards had taken him to the main house and back. "Here's a safe route, but it's the only one I know."

Tace studied the area. "If we look at these mines, can't we judge an equal distance to other mines?"

"Maybe," Jax mused quietly. "They'd need a pattern so they could remember where they put mines and not take themselves out. The problem is, we don't know what that is. It could be anything from eight yards apart to three, eight, seven configurations. Who the hell knows?"

That was just fucking great. "We can find the map inside, but getting there is a problem. We'll be exposed on the main trail," Grey said.

Jax nodded. "We go in shooting. Only chance."

Grey pointed to a series of trees to the west of the main house. "I'll set up here first, take out the president, and then provide cover as you take the house."

Raze frowned. "You've shot from trees before?"

"Yeah," Greyson said softly. "It helps when there isn't ice and snow on every damn branch."

"How are you going to get to the tree line without blowing up?" Tace asked, his tone merely curious.

Grey exhaled. "I'm going to travel from the entry point that direction in the most likely route of the patrolling guards. There's enough brush and vegetation that there should be a somewhat discernible path."

"Unless it's the path they used to plant the mines," Jax muttered.

"There is that," Grey agreed, allowing no emotion in. But he didn't have an alternative, so this was the only option. Jax and his men wouldn't get within a yard of the main house if he didn't provide cover. "You need a backup plan in case…"

"You step on a mine?" Raze asked helpfully, gaze serious.

Grey nodded. "Yeah. That."

Jax sighed. "We'll grab the guards at the gate and force them to come with us. They're not gonna want to step on a mine. It's the only thing we've got."

Fuck, that was a shitty plan. All around. Damon had better damn well be alive. Greyson cleared his throat. The Vanguard men didn't owe him anything. Didn't owe Damon. They certainly didn't have to put their lives on the line to help anybody right now. He owed them. "I, ah, just want— "

"Later," Jax said shortly. "For now, let's go." He turned and strode out of the tavern, his boots heavy on the worn, wooden floor.

Tace clapped him on the back as he followed.

Raze rolled up the map and started to move.

"Raze?" Grey said quietly.

The soldier partially turned, his blue eyes somber, his jaw set. "What?"

"If I don't make it, I mean—" Grey took a deep breath.

"I'll take care of my sister. And the baby," Raze said, his gaze softening a minuscule amount. "Don't worry."

That helped. Grey's chest heated. "Tell her, well, something corny. Something good."

"Like the last thought you had before you blew up was of her?" Raze asked.

Grey snorted. "Yeah." Then he sobered. "Because it will be."

Raze studied him. "Yeah, okay."

Greyson started for the door. "You know, if we both survive this, we're gonna be related."

Raze clapped a hand on his shoulder. "One of the small

comforts of the fact that no way will we both survive this is that we won't be related. Ever." He flashed a smartass smile.

Grey chuckled. "Yeah, probably true."

Raze sobered. "Listen. I'm glad she found you. That she had a chance for, well, something real. In a different world, we'd probably be brothers."

The words meant something. Grey nodded. "Yeah. Agreed." But they weren't brothers, not yet anyway, because they were in this world. This shitty, dangerous world. "So I don't have to worry about you forgiving me for this." Quick as a thought, he yanked the syringe from his pocket, slammed the needle into Raze's neck, and plunged.

Raze roared and swung hard, nailing Grey in the cheek with a powerful right cross.

Grey staggered back, taking the syringe with him.

"What did you just do?" Raze bellowed, moving toward him, his stride hitching.

Grey winced just as Jax and Tace ran back inside. "I'm sorry. But she can't lose us both. She just can't."

Fury darkened Raze's eyes, he lunged and fell flat on the floor. Out cold.

Jax's eyes shot darts. "What the fuck did you just do?"

Grey tossed the empty syringe on the bar. "We can't both die today. Moe needs him."

Tace dropped to his haunches and felt Raze's pulse. "What was it?" he asked grimly.

"Methohexital I stole from the infirmary," Grey said.

Tace coughed. "Jesus. You must've nailed a vein for him to go out that fast. You're good."

Grey winced. "It's a gift."

Tace looked up at Jax. "He'll be out for at least thirty minutes —maybe more. Won't be steady for a while after that. Sure as shit shouldn't shoot a gun." The medic focused on Grey. "He's going to kill you when he wakes up."

"He'll probably be too late," Grey said.

"I see your reasoning, but you have got to stop making decisions on your own for everybody else. This is your last shot. And I ain't stopping Raze if he decides to rip off your head." Jax looked around the tavern. "Damn it. All right. Let's get him some cover until he wakes. We can't just leave him in the middle of the floor."

Tace reached for Raze's arms and then paused, looking at Grey. "You have any more surprises in your pockets?"

"No," Grey said. "I can't let him die today." It was the only thing he could do to help protect Maureen and the baby. He didn't have a choice. "Let's put him in the storage room behind the bar. He'll be safe there until he comes to."

Jax cut him another hard look. "We've got him." He and Tace carried the unconscious soldier into the back room and shut the door.

Tace shook his head and moved toward the outside door again. "He's so going to kill you." The Texas twang emerged full force.

Grey sighed and followed them out into the dark. He needed to be in place before dawn completely arrived, and then they could attack as soon as he had a bead on the president. Most of his missions had been more than just taking a person out. The ramifications were broad, but this was the broadest. He didn't know what would happen next, but this had to be the right thing.

He took the rifle out of the back of Jax's truck and started for his motorcycle.

"Happy hunting," Jax said from behind him.

Grey nodded, not turning around.

It was time.

CHAPTER THIRTY-EIGHT

Absolutely nothing is in my control right now. Not the health of this baby and not the safety of Greyson Storm. It isn't safe to travel north yet to check out possible farms and see how crops have fared, and that must become a priority as soon as Grey returns. For now, I feel like I have to do something...but I don't know what. I'm in limbo, and it totally sucks. But there's always Zach Barter. I guess I'll start with him.
—Maureen Shadow, Notes

MAUREEN STOOD outside the pristine prison cell on the Bunker's lower level on the other side of the main lab, the hallway giving her the willies. More white walls, white tiles...and locked cells. Where human beings had been experimented on like rabid animals. No wonder Marcus Knight was nuts.

Lynne Harmony stood next to her, looking into the cell holding Zach Barter. The outside metal door was open to reveal a set of iron bars serving as a secondary barrier that the scientists could look through to study their subjects.

"This is beyond creepy," she muttered underneath her breath.
Lynne nodded. "Tell me about it."

Armed guards took up positions on either side of the hallway, ready to intervene if necessary.

But since the iron bars were engaged and in place, there wasn't much of a threat, now was there? "Is this how they found Marcus?" Moe asked, wondering how Jax's younger brother had survived.

"Yes. I think the outer metal door was locked, but the iron bars weren't engaged that day. We discovered those later. Well, Dr. Penelope told us about them," Lynne said.

The cells each held a cot, sink, and toilet. Zach Barter sat on his thin mattress still wearing his white lab coat, button-down shirt, and slacks, bruises down the side of his face. Greyson had given him a couple of punches, it seemed.

Barter smiled as if delighted to see them. "Dr. Harmony, I've missed you so much."

Chills raced down Moe's back. "What did you discover about Scorpius?"

"I told you earlier," Barter said, his smooth face wrinkling into a frown. "I have several concoctions to test out, and nobody to test them on."

"You do now," Maureen said.

Lynne held up a hand. "I want to see the formulas first, and then we'll talk about experiments. If I remember correctly, you have an eidetic memory, right, Barter?"

He smiled and stood. "You remember things about me. Isn't that sweet?"

Bile rose in Moe's throat. "Do you or do you not remember your different formulas?"

Barter nodded. "Of course."

Her knees trembled, but she kept her face stoic. "But you haven't cured Scorpius in adults, so how can you cure it in a baby?" It didn't make sense.

"I can't cure it in a baby," Barter said reasonably. "Yet, anyway. If you have Scorpius in your blood, in your body, then your fetus has it, too. The goal for pregnant women isn't to cure the bacterium."

Lynne nodded. "The goal is to make sure the baby survives the infection like the few people who've survived it did. There should be a link between mother and child. Since the mother obviously survived, there has to be a way that the child can."

Approval curved Barter's full lips. "That's right, Dr. Harmony. I'd forgotten how quick you are. So smart." He rubbed his hands together.

Lynne crossed her arms over her dark T-shirt. "With the women you tested. How long did the pregnancies last?"

Maureen caught her breath.

Barter looked from one to the other. "The longest we made it was five months. I'm pretty sure."

Maureen swallowed. "What do you mean, you're pretty sure?"

Lynne stepped toward the bars and studied the scientist. "You didn't work on pregnant women."

Barter smiled again, slow and sly this time. "That wasn't my expertise, no. I've been working on Scorpius around the clock, and there was a specific division that dealt with only pregnancies. We shared data, but women and babies aren't my expertise. As you probably know."

Shit, shit, shit. "We have to get control of the Reno bunker," Maureen said quietly, her heart starting to race. There had to be a way to save the baby. She'd do anything. "Then what were you just talking about? That you had a concoction and needed pregnant women to conduct research on? I don't understand."

"The research all goes together," Barter said easily.

Lynne nodded. "That's true." She partially turned so only Maureen could hear her. "But we also let him know right off the bat upstairs that we wanted research for pregnant women. He's a genius. He would've caught on quickly and definitely wants to live."

Maureen's heart sank. "Can you help us or not?"

Barter vigorously nodded. "I can. I'll give you everything I have on Scorpius as well as the Reno Bunker. I wasn't allowed to leave, you know." His teeth sparkled with his newest smile. "Your soldier basically helped me to escape."

Wonderful. That was just great. But maybe he had enough knowledge that Lynne and her team could expand on it.

But Moe had her own expertise. "At the Reno lab, do you have seeds? Is there a collection?"

Barter shrugged. "Not that I know of. But there is a Bunker that's devoted solely to food production and development. It's not the Reno Bunker."

Moe stepped closer to the bars. "What Bunker? Where is it?"

Barter rocked back on his heels. "It seems as if I have a lot to trade here. This cell isn't worthy of me, and I want out."

Moe glanced at Lynne.

Lynne's gaze hardened, and she reached for the steel door and shut it.

Barter rushed the bars and yelled.

Moe stepped back.

Lynne put her arm through Moe's and turned her, walking toward the stairwell. "We have to wait until Jax gets back to let Barter into the lab, and I'd say the nut job needs to stew in a cell for a little while. Let's leave him for now and go see how Sami's doing."

Maureen nodded. "There has to be a link between the Bunkers buried in that system somewhere. If Barter knows about other ones, the information is in there. Sami needs to find it."

"She will," Lynne said, her mouth grim. "There isn't another option."

Moe concentrated on putting one foot in front of the other up the stairs. Where was Greyson? Were he and Raze safe?

They had to be. At least they were working together.

Finally.

* * *

THE FEELING of the sniper rifle in his hands felt like coming home. Most people wouldn't understand, and Greyson was okay with that. But as with any mission, he felt the rightness of the orders. The certainty of what he had to do.

He stepped as lightly as he could, following a barely discernible trail through the thick underbrush. It was almost noon, which meant no shadow.

His favorite time, actually.

He paused, studied the brush, and took three full steps to the north. Then he continued on, making sure the trail continued. Finally, he reached the tree line he wanted.

Footsteps sounded behind him. Shit. Somebody coughed.

He jumped across a couple of yards and ducked behind a huge blue spruce.

"Yeah, well, I don't care what he says. I can date who I want," came a young male voice, maybe about twenty. "What's the point of surviving Scorpius if we don't get women?"

"I know, but just cool your jets," came an older male voice, raspy enough that the guy had probably smoked for decades. "We're still getting organized. Soon we'll start rebuilding civilization."

The duo kept walking past Greyson's position, talking quietly, obviously not expecting to find anybody at the edge of the forest. He shut his eyes and leaned his head back against the tree trunk, mentally tracking their movements.

Once they were out of earshot, he slung the rifle over his shoulder, turned, and scaled the tree.

Branches and needles cut into him, but he kept moving, not feeling anything. Finally, he reached a good position and settled himself. Finding the right prop for the rifle took a few minutes, and then he was looking through the scope at the president's office.

Perfect.

He slowed his heart rate and breathing, stretched out the best he could, and waited.

Waiting was part of the job. Patience was the first thing he'd learned and honed, and it was why so many people couldn't make it in sniper school.

The office was empty. The sun sparkled off the lake to the right, and the wind was coming in slightly from the north. He calculated wind speed and distance, adding in heat. What he wouldn't give for a suit that matched the tree. One time, he'd been in the field and had blended in so well with the brush that Ferris couldn't find him. Of course, it had been during training. During combat, Ferris had known where he was at all times.

Now Greyson had Jax and Tace waiting to move in on his order.

Four months ago, he'd have bet his last breath that this situation would never happen. Mercs and Vanguard working together against the President of the United States. Or that Grey was about to take a kill shot against his Commander in Chief.

Movement caught his eye inside the mansion, and President Atherton escorted a tall blonde into his office. He sat, while she reached over and picked up a pile of dishes. Then she walked gracefully on four-inch heels out of the room.

Atherton sat behind his desk and drew a map in front of him.

"Target acquired," Greyson whispered into his two-way radio, the window giving him a clear shot.

"Copy that," Jax whispered. "I'm at the depot we took out last time. Trucks are missing. Several."

"Affirmative," Tace whispered, his voice a low rasp. "I'm at surveillance point three, ready to go. There are fewer patrols and guards right now."

Holy fuck. Damn it. "They're out on a raid." And who was weak right now? Both the Mercs and Vanguard. Which one was being attacked? Grey's body vibrated, and he took a deep breath. He had to get Damon, and then they'd head south.

"Stay on mission," Jax whispered, obviously thinking along the same lines. "Let's get this done."

The president kept reading, having no idea that a rifle was pointed at his chest. Grey shook his head. He'd vowed to protect the president. But that was different, and those times were over. This guy was a sociopath who'd probably started the fires to remove Merc territory, who'd destroyed an organic farm full of people just trying to survive, and he had Damon held captive somewhere. It was time to move on. Grey's affiliation was to his family, the Mercs, and now Vanguard.

"Shot in ten seconds," he said into the shortwave radio. Then he tucked it away and leaned down to aim after calculating wind, distance, trajectory and everything he used to discuss with Ferris. His aim was for Atherton's upper left quad. *Seven. Eight. Nine.*

Greyson squeezed the trigger.

The bullet impacted the glass and shattered it, spreading damage across the entire window but not getting through.

Atherton jumped up, eyes wide, and ran for the interior door.

"Damn it." Greyson jumped down from the tree, landing and rolling to his feet. "Shot failed, shot failed," he snapped into his radio, running in a zigzag pattern for the mansion.

An alarm blared high and loud in the bright day from the mansion.

"What the hell?" Jax bellowed, the sound of movement coming through.

"Bulletproof glass," Greyson yelled, shoving the radio back into his pocket.

Soldiers poured from the front of the mansion.

Greyson dropped to his knees, pointed, and started firing. One down. Two down. Four ducked for cover.

Jax's truck careened wildly from the road, with him shooting at guards on the way.

Two explosions at the rear of the mansion rocked the ground.

Greyson dropped the sniper rifle, grabbed his handgun, and started running full bore for the front door. He fired as he went.

The guards returned fire, and pain slashed into his arm. His gun flew out of his hand. He dropped to his knees, taking cover. Shit. They had him.

One guy stood from behind a mini-wall, his gun out and pointed at Greyson's head.

Grey went for the gun in his boot just as a motorcycle, quiet and deadly, all but flew over his head. Raze rode it, firing toward the guards and landing inside the vestibule of the house.

Jax's truck reached the side at the same time, and three more explosives detonated around the rear. Tace loved a good explosion, apparently.

Greyson kept low but ran forward, shooting two men and sliding into the house on his knees. His arm hurt, but it wasn't a fatal wound. He'd worry about it later.

Raze picked him up by the lapels. "I'm going to kill you." He clapped a hand over Grey's bleeding arm. "How bad is it?"

"Not bad," Grey said, his arm on fire but nothing really damaged. "Just sliced into me."

Jax ran in behind them. "Hurry. We have no idea where reinforcements are or how close."

Men rushed out of the surrounding land, heading for the house, guns out.

"Fuck." Raze slammed the door and shoved a table in front of it. "Find Damon. I'll hold them off."

Grey nodded and ran through the house and across a kitchen. He shoved open a door to find three women, all crying, looking terrified. "Where would they keep a prisoner?" he shouted, keeping his gun down but very much visible.

The blonde with the stilettos wiped her nose. "Downstairs. There are locked rooms downstairs. On the other side of the laundry room."

"Where's Atherton?" Jax asked.

"I don't know," the blonde said.

Grey nodded. "Get down and stay in here." The women jumped to the floor, and he shut the door. "Where the fuck is Atherton?"

A volley of shots echoed from the rear of the house.

Jax paused.

Grey shoved him. "Go cover Tace. I'll find the downstairs."

Jax nodded and hurried off toward the kitchen.

Grey stalked through the house, ignoring the raging pain in his arm. He checked room after room and finally found the laundry room. A door was on the far side. He inched close and nudged it open, seeing a wooden set of stairs.

The firefight continued all around him, volleys of shots being fired, and more explosives going off. He dodged down the stairs, his senses alert, and reached a wooden cellar. A quick glance around saw only a locked wooden door.

Anybody guarding the area had run upstairs to protect the president.

Grey lunged for the padlock and scrambled around for a key. Nothing. He aimed his gun, turned his head, and fired.

Metal pinged, and a piece sliced across his forearm. He pulled the remainder of the lock off and burned his fingers, dropping it to the dirt floor. His gun out, he yanked open the door and swept the room. "Damon," he breathed.

His friend lay on the floor, a bruised mess, his chest not moving.

Grey rushed forward and yanked him up, shaking him.

Damon's head lolled and blood bubbled from his mouth. His normally dark skin was sallow, and his lips looked blue.

"Wake the fuck up," Grey said, shaking him.

Damon's eyes slowly lifted. "What the hell?"

"Let's go." Grey shoved his shoulder beneath Damon's arm, and his friend sagged, going out again. "Okay, I've got you." He ducked and tugged Damon over his shoulder, gun still out, and ran for the stairs.

Jax met him at the top. "We're going to have to shoot our way out to the truck. Soldiers are coming from every direction. Atherton took off in an armored truck."

Grey nodded just as Tace and Raze rounded the corner. "Let's get him in the back, and then I'll start shooting. You guys provide cover."

"Wait a sec." Tace grasped a detonator. "Um. Everyone run. Now."

They leaped out of the front, everyone firing and running for the truck.

The ground shifted and rumbled. Then the mansion blew up behind them.

Heat flashed, and Grey shoved Damon into the truck. "Go, go, go."

CHAPTER THIRTY-NINE

The president may have ruined one food source, but I'll find another.
He won't win this time.

—Maureen Shadow, Notes

IN THE BUNKER'S upstairs control room, Maureen pored over the maps Sami had given her, outlining organic farms, or former organic farms from Santa Barbara up to Seattle. She incorporated all of Northern California, Oregon, Washington, and Idaho.

Sami worked on one of the two large computers in the hidden room, once in a while swearing loudly enough to make Maureen chuckle.

Vinnie sat down at the table and pushed a cup of tea toward Moe.

Maureen looked up, her gaze focusing. "Thank you."

"You're welcome." Vinnie sipped on her own cup. "I can't stop thinking about the guys taking on the president and the Elite Force, and Lynne told me to bring you tea so I'd stop bugging her."

Maureen took the fragrant blueberry tea and sipped, enjoying the sweet taste. "I've been trying to bury myself in work." She pointed to the map. "Where's Lynne?"

"She's going through all of her data, mumbling to herself, and every once in a while swearing a little bit." Vinnie bit her lip. "She's about to plan an attack on the Reno Bunker, even without Jax. It'd be fun to see his reaction to that."

Moe snorted. "They do always have tension surrounding them."

"Yeah, but now I'm bored." Vinnie nodded. "Sami is still hunting through the computer, Lynne is busy, the soldiers are on high alert, and you're in here diagramming what looks like a Battleship game. I'm a criminal psychologist. I profile people or talk to them. There's nobody to talk to."

Moe sipped some more. "Profile Zach Barter."

"He's shit-assed crazy," Vinnie said slowly.

Moe coughed and nearly spilled her drink. "I didn't know shrinks used that word."

"I'm not really a shrink." Vinnie grinned. "I heard that you asked Barter about seeds. Aren't seeds supposed to be stored all over the world?"

"Yeah, but nobody, at least no one still alive, knows where," Moe said, blowing steam off her cup.

Vinnie pursed her lips and looked through the windows into the cafeteria. "It's crucial, right? I mean, with all the genetically modified crops since they don't reproduce, we're screwed if we don't have more seeds."

Moe shook her head. "No. That's actually a myth."

Vinnie's eyebrows rose. "What's a myth?"

"That GMOs don't reproduce. They do, like any other plants." Maureen sipped thoughtfully. "Now with hybrids, like corn, you get an inferior next crop if you don't use new seeds. But GMOs are fine and do reproduce."

"Then why do farmers, or rather why *did* farmers, always buy new seeds? I saw a news report on it," Vinnie said, her forehead creasing.

"Hybrids outperform inbreds, so it was more economical for many farmers to just buy new seeds, use hybrids, and get more of a crop. It was for financial reasons," Moe said, her mind returning to the walnut problem. She sighed, sadness swamping her.

Vinnie reached out and patted her hand. "I meant to tell you. Congratulations on the pregnancy. I'm happy for you."

"Thanks," Maureen said softly. "I can't believe I fell for a soldier." What he was doing right now was crazy. "It's so weird to think that Greyson is going to shoot the president, but it's the right thing to do. How can *that* be the right thing?" The world they were living in truly sucked right now.

"I don't know, but it is," Vinnie murmured.

Moe nodded. "Have you heard anything about the fires toward Santa Barbara? I haven't been to the roof in hours."

"Bad winds, bad color to the sky," Vinnie said, her blue eyes sober. "I'm sorry, but it doesn't look good."

Something banged in the other room, and Sami stormed in, her eyes a wild brown. "We just had a call over the HAM radio from a group up north that keeps us informed but had trouble getting through all day. Apparently the Elite Force sent a large contingent out about ten hours ago, but I don't know where they went."

Vinnie drew in a breath. "The scouts haven't called in?"

"Nope." Sami took her gun from the back of her waist.

Who would the president attack first? "They're either heading to Merc territory, to Vanguard, or here," Maureen said, her heart beating more rapidly. "All three places are weakened. Vanguard is still rebuilding, Merc territory is under siege by fire, and we're low on personnel because of those two reasons."

Sami headed for the door in a whirlwind. "I'm going to suit up just in case, and I'll call in the patrolling guards. We need everybody here and ready to shoot in case it's us." She disappeared down the stairs, already calling out orders.

Vinnie reached into her boot and brought out a small pistol. "Are you packing?"

Moe slowly shook her head. "I have a gun, but it's in my room right now."

Vinnie pulled her to stand. "Let's go get it. Not being armed is a seriously bad idea."

Moe nodded, her heart racing. Were they about to get in a fight with Elite soldiers without Greyson, Jax, Raze, Tace, and Damon? "Shit. This is a disaster."

"You're not kidding, sister," Vinnie said, hurrying her step. "Let's go by the armory and get more guns. We might need them."

* * *

GREY BENT over Damon in the back of the truck as Jax fishtailed away from Lake Tahoe, shooting over the edge of the truck bed and ducking when possible. Raze shot from the passenger seat, and Tace shot from the opposite side of Grey, covering Damon at the same time.

They reached the edge of the property and kept going.

The men chasing them stopped.

"What are they doing?" Tace snarled.

Grey paused. "Their jobs. The president went the other way. The Elite Force is the new Secret Service. They'll stay to cover him." The damn president had gotten away again. "Who fucking knew there'd be bulletproof glass on the window," he muttered.

"Not me," Tace said, dropping to his butt. "How is he?"

Grey gently pushed Damon onto his back. "Bruised and battered but breathing."

Tace moved closer and opened Damon's shirt, whistling at the bruising. "Let me check him out."

Grey sat back, his mind spinning as the medic examined Damon from head to toe.

Tace finally lifted Damon's closed eyelids to study his pupils. Damon lifted a hand and swiped him away. "Knock it off."

Grey pressed in, his heart thundering. "D? You okay?"

Damon, flat on his back, looked up at the cloudless sky and then turned his head slightly. "Why are the trees flying by me?"

Grey grinned. "Jax is driving. Probably too fast. How are you?"

"Fine." Damon grunted and tried to shove himself up.

Greyson grabbed one arm, Tace the other, and they pulled the ex-cop to a seated position. "Seriously. How are you?"

Damon sighed. "Ask the medic."

Tace studied the injured man. "I'd say three bruised ribs, a concussion, multiple contusions, including a fairly bad knot on your knee, and probably some damaged knuckles from fighting back." Tace shook out his left hand, which looked oddly swollen. "You need stitches in four places, and I think your left shoulder is out of its socket. I'd like to get you back to the infirmary at the Bunker before we try to fix anything."

"Sounds about right," Damon said drunkenly.

Tace leaned in and pressed on his abdomen. "Does this hurt below your ribs?"

"Not enough to worry about," Damon said, shoving Tace's hand away. "Stop pushing on me."

Grey sat back and closed his eyes. "He's fine. Or he will be." Thank God. Then he opened one eye. "What did you learn while there?"

"Just what we already knew. The president knows of at least two Bunkers, Reno and Century City. Hinted at a third one. He doesn't control any yet. As for my knowledge, they don't know what's on the computer program you stole yet." Damon wiped at a cut on his lip. "Oh. And Vice President Lake took great pleasure in burning up some farm a while ago. He couldn't wait until you discovered it."

"I'm going to rip his head off," Grey said, his hands clenching into fists.

"Yeah, well, he took off on a mission," Damon said. "Didn't say where. God, he's nuts."

"He's never been infected," Tace said somberly. "According to most of our intel anyway."

They reached the tavern where they'd left two of the bikes.

Grey faltered. "The winds shifted, Damon. Toward Santa Barbara."

Damon's brown eyes cleared. "Shit, man. We have to get there." He pushed to get up and then fell back, groaning. "Just give me a second."

Grey jumped to the ground on the damaged sidewalk. "No. You're heading to the Bunker with Tace and these guys for medical help. I'll go to Merc territory to see what's happening."

Tace jerked his head. "The president was low in men and trucks. They went somewhere, and Lake is leading them."

Grey nodded. "If they're not in Merc territory, I'll head to Vanguard with as many of my men as I can find to fight there. If the president went to the Bunker, then you need to get back there. But I don't think that was his target."

"I don't either," Jax said through the back window of the truck. "My guess is Vanguard or Merc territory." He nodded at Tace. "The Bunker is on the way. I'll take you and Damon there, grab some soldiers, and then head to Vanguard. We'll get all bases covered."

"Good plan." Raze jumped out of the truck. "Let's go."

Greyson shook his head. "No. I've got my territory."

"No," Raze said, giving Jax a high-sign. "You're not going alone. That's just stupid."

Damon sighed and sagged back in the truck. "I agree with him, Grey. This is a good plan." He passed out again.

Grey looked at Tace. "Take care of him. Please."

"No problem," the Texan said easily, his twang emerging. "We'll see you guys soon."

At that, Jax drove off.

Raze swung his leg over one of the bikes. "How fast do you think we can get there?"

Grey went for the other bike. "Five to six hours if we ignore safety or reasonable speeds."

"Who needs safety?" Raze asked, starting his bike.

Grey eyed him, this brother of Moe's. No wonder she was such a sweetheart. It ran in the family, apparently. "Hey, Raze. Thanks for this."

Shadow's eyebrows rose. "No worries. I want to kick the shit out of you for sedating me earlier. I'm just looking for an opportune time."

Grey grinned. The guy was helping him, but he also wasn't kidding. He'd known when he jabbed that needle into Raze's vein that someday there would be a reckoning, and it was nice that the guy wanted to wait until they could dust it up right. "I'm looking forward to it."

For now, they had to go save his territory. Or Vanguard. Or shit...both.

CHAPTER FORTY

To the death it is, then.
  —Greyson Storm

THEY REACHED Merc territory around eight that night, but it might as well have been midnight. Smoke and debris hung in the air, low to the ground, making visibility impossible. Grey tugged the handkerchief around his mouth down a little. They'd had to stop hours earlier to cover their faces and find glasses to protect their eyes.

The heat was unbearable, and he shrugged out of his leather jacket, even while riding the bike.

Raze rode next to him, his head down, his body hunched low against his bike.

Grey motioned toward the beach, and Raze nodded. At least by the ocean, they wouldn't catch on fire.

They reached sand, and Grey jumped free, letting the bike fall. He'd be back for it.

The mansions down the way were all on fire, blazing wildly. Something exploded down the beach, but all Grey could see was fire and smoke. His entire body ached, and panic swept him hotter than the blaze. He forced down emotion and made himself start moving.

Raze drew out his gun and hugged the shoreline.

Grey followed suit, looking around for his men.

Raze pointed toward the third mansion down that had a small metal outbuilding they'd used to store weapons. Bullet holes marred the entire side.

Anger brewed fast and hot in Grey's gut. He started running for headquarters and nearly tripped over a body.

He halted, dropped to his haunches, and flipped over the body. Bob.

Raze shone a flashlight down to show a perfect bullet hole in the center of Bob's forehead. His eyes were dark and unseeing. Grey swallowed down pain and carefully shut his buddy's eyes. "Rest in peace, my friend." He jumped up and launched into a run, his boots splashing water.

Raze kept pace, the smoke covering them.

A huge hose next to a pump caught Grey's attention. "Jump," he yelled at Raze in time to stop the Vanguard soldier from tripping.

Raze gracefully leaped over the hose and then stopped. He looked down at the pump and then over at the blazing houses.

Grey shook his head. It was too late. Now only his men mattered. Had the president's men killed them all? Were some safe? He pointed farther south, and Raze nodded.

Grey kept an eye out for pumps and bodies as he ran, reaching the headquarters building, which was already a pile of smoldering rubble. The homes on either side burned brighter, still igniting.

A body half in the surf moved in.

He turned and splashed into the ocean, pulling Atticus out. "Atticus?" he yelled, hauling the older man to the sand with Raze's help. Then he dropped and pressed his head to Atticus's chest.

Breath. The man was breathing.

Grey shook him. "A?" His voice cracked.

Atticus shook and then coughed, partially rolling onto his side. He blinked. "Grey?"

"Yeah, it's me." Greyson hugged him, relief relaxing his body to just plain rock.

Atticus pushed him. "The guys. Other side of the mansions. Need help. We still have a truck of medical supplies, and they're fighting for it."

An explosion roared through the smoke and flames. Then gunfire.

Grey jumped to his feet, his boots sliding in the surf. "I'll be back. Just stay here." He turned and ran for the side of the mansion, jumping over burning boards.

The heat slashed into him, hot enough to burn his skin even without actual flames.

The protective glasses he wore helped, and the fire lit his way, but he had to take shallow breaths even with the handkerchief. His lungs burned, hot and painful.

Raze kept to his six.

Grey emerged onto Main Street and almost stopped cold.

All of the homes, every one of them, was on fire. They were spaced far enough apart that smoke came from every direction. In the center was a fully loaded Merc truck. Two men fired rapidly from inside, while two more took cover behind and shot toward a Humvee facing them.

Grey ducked behind a stone wall, his elbow brushing the rock. Pain flared as a burn went deep.

Shit.

He pulled out his gun and pointed it at the Humvee, which had its doors open with the Elite Force soldiers taking cover. They fired a volley of rounds, smashing the windshield of the Merc truck.

Grey levered up and shot, hitting the door.

The EF soldier turned and fired back.

Grey ducked next to Raze, who was struggling to breathe shallowly. Moving in sync, they fired, ducked, covered each other, and then fired again.

The heat was fucking unbearable.

Another Humvee rolled into place. One of the soldiers dodged out and moved behind a stone wall to the south. He had a good bead on them if they moved an inch.

"Fuck," Raze muttered as the fire stormed around them.

"We need that medicine," Grey yelled over the hellacious sounds.

A third Humvee came into view.

"We can't win," Raze bellowed. "Tell your men to abandon the truck. It's our only chance."

Grey's heart plummeted to his feet. Raze was right. They couldn't take on three Humvees. Hopefully the rest of his men had gotten to safety. Maybe they had taken more provisions with them. He nodded and started to stand.

Two trucks careened wildly in after the Humvees, the fire lighting their way.

Jax Mercury fired from the driver's side of one, while Damon drove the other with Tace firing. They hit three of the men in a surprise attack.

"What the hell are they doing here?" Raze growled loud enough that Grey could hear.

Greyson reared up and fired carefully, hitting another Elite soldier. The man went down, dead before impact. The guy behind the other wall half stood and made a run for the beach.

"Let him go," Raze said. "Fight's here." He fired into one of the Humvees, and glass sprayed.

Greyson's arm still hurt, but the bleeding had stemmed. He focused on the soldier on the other side of the first Humvee, aimed, waiting patiently, and pulled the trigger. He hit the EF soldier in the upper left quad, and the asshole dropped hard.

The fight continued. Then the shooting stopped.

Grey tried to see through the smoke. What the hell was Damon doing? The guy had needed stitches, damn it.

Raze stood and looked around. The mansion across the street collapsed, fire whooshing out. "We have to get the hell out of here."

Greyson shoved to his feet, scouting for threats. The Elite soldiers were down, and the fire was getting hotter with the fallen houses. It was going to be close.

An Elite soldier leaped from the back of the third Humvee and ran toward a burning mansion. He partially turned, his face lit by the rioting flames. Vice President Lake had led the mission to take out the Mercs. Greyson went hot and then cold, adrenaline biting through his veins. "He's mine. Secure those Humvees, and we'll fight our way through the fire." Without waiting for a response, he turned and ran between fires to the beach.

He kept low and zigzagged, ducking when a flying board went by his head. Emerging onto the beach, he barely shifted in time to miss a punch to the face.

Lake followed up with a kick to the ribs, and Greyson fell back onto a smoldering lump of what used to be the deck. Burns ripped across his left arm. He bellowed and backflipped onto his feet, scattering more burning boards.

"I've been waiting for this," Lake yelled, circling around.

"Me too," Grey yelled back, ducking his head and charging full bore for the monster. With his momentum, he moved them several yards into the beach and toward the ocean. Cool and calmer air hit him, filling his lungs with something other than painful smoke.

They hit the sand, both rolling in opposing directions.

Grey came up first, but Lake was only a second after him. "You shouldn't have taken out the farm," Grey said, able to stop yelling for the first time. The fires still burned to his left, but they were far enough across the sand that he could talk normally, although his vocal cords felt like he'd swallowed burning charcoal. "Today you'll pay for that."

Lake smiled. A burn slashed across his neck, while soot covered his hard face and blond hair, creating stripes. "I don't think so." His voice was mangled from the fire.

"You're wrong. For the farm and Damon and anybody else you've hurt." Grey reached down and removed his knife.

"Ah. Knives." Lake tugged a serrated blade from a pocket in his cargo pants. "I love the feeling of shoving it into cartilage and muscle."

"You would," Grey said, moving slightly toward the bubbling surf. Wood planks, metal, even plastic washed around them from the explosions where the debris had landed in the ocean. Grey planted his feet in the sand to keep his balance. "You're a sick bastard."

"I've never been infected," Lake said, feinting in and then back out.

So he'd always been an insane fuck. "What's your plan, anyway?" Grey moved a little to the left, seeking an opening.

"To continue the work and make this country great again. Better than before. Stronger without all the issues." Lake charged, and Greyson sidestepped, slashing his knife across Lake's upper arm. Lake growled and turned around.

Grey shook his head. "Issues? Like human rights?"

"Yeah. Those." Lake rolled his injured shoulder as blood slid down his arm.

The moon finally rose enough to shine down on the ocean. Combined with the fire everywhere, the day was almost light again. But with an odd mix of heat and coolness. "What was on the computer file I gave to the president?"

Lake smiled again, blood cracking on his lip. "Wouldn't you like to know?"

Obviously. Greyson edged to the side and then struck, bringing his knife up.

Lake backflipped, landing easily in the sand.

Impressive. Grey cocked his head. "You were Secret Service before Scorpius?"

"Among a couple of other things," Lake said, death in his eyes. "You won't be my first kill. Not by a long shot." He moved away from the ocean a couple of feet. "You're getting very angry. That's a mistake."

Anger would probably be good. At the moment, Grey felt nothing. Not a damn thing. It was training at its best, and he was fucking using it. "Sure. How about I let you live, and you tell us everything you know about the president and his plans?"

Lake snorted. "I think I'd rather just kill you." The vice president dropped into a roll on the sand and came up slashing.

Greyson fell back, swinging and taking the blade across his chest. Pain exploded in his skin. Fuck. He rolled and kicked out, nailing Lake in the knee. The VP went down, pivoted, and came back up.

"Nice move," Grey said, lurching to his feet, his knife out and ready.

"Thanks," Lake said, his eyes gleaming in the darkness. "My next move is a knife to your spine."

Shouts sounded, and the Vanguard men came running around the far mansion.

Grey smiled. "We'd better hurry."

"Grey?" Atticus moved in from the surf, dragging a body, his voice drowsy. "I found Jamie."

Before Greyson could shout a warning, Lake jumped for Atticus, grabbing the older man from behind and pressing the blade against his jugular.

Atticus froze and dropped Jamie. "Greyson?" He asked, blood dripping down his forehead, confusion blanketing his features."

"It's okay, A," Greyson said, stalking toward them. "Let him go, Lake."

The VP looked down at the advancing Vanguard soldiers and

then back at Greyson, his knife drawing blood from Atticus's throat. "Sure." He removed his knife and then plunged it into Atticus from behind.

Atticus screamed, the sound filled with pain. He dropped to his knees in the surf.

Greyson jumped for him, grabbing him beneath the arms. "A? You're okay, A. I promise," he said rapidly, his breath panting out as he dragged the man to solid sand.

Lake turned and disappeared into the ocean, diving right past the reef.

"Tace?" Greyson bellowed, turning Atticus over.

Tace ran for them, dropping to his knees and shooting sand in every direction. He yanked up the elderly man's shirt. Blood flowed across his back. Tace ripped off his shirt and pressed it to Atticus's injury. "Below the kidney, but it's bloody. I'll have to sew him up in the Humvee. Let's go."

Grey paused and looked into the ocean, trying to find Lake. Nothing. Not a sign of him.

"We'll get him next time," Raze said, grunting as he lifted Atticus's lower half. "We have to go. Now."

Greyson growled, his chest filling with a heat to match the fires around them. He stood and grabbed Tace. "Take his front." Then he pivoted and headed into the surf, following where he thought he'd seen Lake go.

The man had ignited Merc territory, killed Grey's men, and destroyed innocent people. He didn't get to live.

Jax grabbed Greyson in a surprise bear hold from the back, yanking him to the shore. "Now isn't the time, man. Lake is gone, and we have to get your people to safety. Maureen is fucking waiting for you."

Grey fought against him, but he couldn't see Lake. The ocean was rolling quietly, filled with debris. Fine. This wasn't over. The first chance he got, he was going hunting. Then he saw Lake's head. To the right, his blond hair glowing in the moonlight. "Let me go. I've got this."

Jax paused and then sighed. "Fine. I hope you can swim."

Jesus. The man had no clue what he could do. Grey set out, going north, diving deep and swimming until he reached his prey. Salt water filled his ears, slowing him. The fire burned to the side, throwing debris above him. But he kept swimming, zeroing in on the enemy. He emerged right in front of Lake.

Lake's mouth gaped open. "What?"

Greyson plunged his knife into Lake's heart, going up and under the ribcage.

Lake's eyes widened, and blood gurgled from his mouth. Greyson leaned in, nose to nose. "That's for Tall Tree Farm." He yanked out his knife, and the water turned red around them. Grey shoved the body out to sea.

He coughed out salt water and watched Lake's body float away.

Greyson swam in and ran for the beach, where his people were waiting. Vanguard counted now, too. Ducking, he lifted Atticus's front as Raze carried the rest of him and started rushing toward the side of the mansion and the transportation on the street.

For the briefest of moments, he paused and watched as headquarters, his mansion, where he'd fallen in love with Maureen...fell.

Merc territory had burned to the ground.

CHAPTER FORTY-ONE

It's amazing to have found love after the apocalypse. All in all, I'm feeling pretty fortunate.

—Maureen Shadow, Notes

EVEN THE AIR above Los Angeles was filled with smoke from the Santa Barbara fire. Two contingents of soldiers had arrived at the Bunker that morning with orders to escort Maureen and Vinnie to Vanguard for a strategy meeting. They sat in the back of a fortified SUV. Sami was coming as well, but she took point with the other soldiers. The petite brunette was fun to watch.

As they drove past downed semis and tires, the first barrier to Vanguard, Maureen's blood started to pump faster. Apparently the president and his Elite Force had attacked Merc territory last night, skipping the Bunker and Vanguard. They'd known somebody was getting attacked. But she hadn't seen Greyson since he left to rescue Damon, and she had to wonder. What now? For them?

The soldiers hadn't told her much. She knew that Greyson

had survived a battle on the beach, but she didn't know any details.

Lynne craned her neck to see out the window. "They've rebuilt the outside perimeters pretty well. Quickly."

Yeah, but if Moe remembered right, the interior buildings were in trouble. She missed the ocean and wanted to go back to Merc headquarters at some point. "How bad do you think Merc territory got hit?" Maureen asked.

Lynne turned, her eyes concerned. "We're about to find out."

The soldier drove them through the interior gate, ending up in a former parking lot in front of a two-story, brick building. Vanguard headquarters. Many of the bricks had been blown off in the last fight with the Elite Force, but most of the windows had been repaired.

Maureen stepped out, her legs shaking. Nausea smashed into her, and she paused, swallowing until it passed. The morning sickness seemed to be getting worse. She tried to take that as a good sign.

"You okay?" Lynne asked, pausing.

Moe nodded and started for the door again. "I'm fine."

The door opened, and Jax strode out, straight at Lynne. He tucked the scientist close, breathing in her hair, his expression the softest Moe had ever seen it. She almost wanted to gape in surprise, but she kept going, wanting to give them privacy.

She'd almost reached the door when it opened, and Greyson stepped out. Going on pure instinct, she jumped for him.

He caught her, his strong arms easily holding her up. Then he let her slide down. Once her feet hit the pavement, he cupped her face, looking deep into her eyes. "Are you all right?" he asked, his voice grittier than normal.

She swallowed and nodded. There was blood on his shirt. Was he shot? "You?"

"Fine. Minor injury not even bleeding any longer." He glanced over her head and surveyed the area, quickly turning her into his side and pulling her inside. Cool air brushed over her. "Your brother is safe. Merc territory was destroyed. If we ever want to get back to the beach, we'll have to rebuild."

In Santa Barbara? Unlikely. The loss washed through her, surprising in its intensity.

He kissed her nose. "I know. I'm with you."

She blinked. "Is Damon okay?"

Grey nodded, his jaw tightening. "Yeah. We lost fifteen men between the fires and the Elite Force." He pulled her into Vanguard's conference room and held out a chair for her. "Atticus is healing up from a knife wound and will be fine in about a week or so. Also, Tall Tree Farm was attacked and burned. The survivors are here at Vanguard."

Thank goodness Damon and Atticus were okay. But pain slid through her for her other friends. "The farm is gone? How many survived?"

"A lot of them, baby." He ran his knuckles across her cheek. "You can talk to them shortly. For now, do you need anything? Hungry or thirsty?"

She numbly shook her head. There was so much to process, but she had to focus on him. He was acting so professional. Casual. Sweet but somehow distant. "What's going on?"

He cleared his throat. "When I left you at the Bunker, both times, you know it was to keep you safe, right?"

It hit her then. Right between the eyes. He'd been abandoned by his mother, and that hurt never went away. Her heart swelled in her chest, plain and simple. He was worried that she'd felt abandoned by him. "I do understand, Greyson," she murmured, meeting his gray gaze. "Honest. I'd do anything for this baby, too. I get it." She did.

His lips curved just as Jax and Lynne moved into the room, followed by Tace, Sami, Raze, Vinnie, Damon, and a pretty brunette with blue eyes.

"This is April," Damon said, wincing as he sat.

"Hi," April and Maureen said at the same time.

Maureen looked at Damon. "Are you all right?" She leaned over and patted his hand, relief flushing through her to see him healthy and talking.

"Yep. Just a few stitches," he said, the bruise above his eye making him look like a pirate.

Everyone took seats, and Jax held Lynne's hand as he started speaking. "Grey and I have reached an agreement regarding our two, ah, entities."

Greyson nodded. "We're going to combine Vanguard and the Mercs, and Damon will head the interaction here at Vanguard while I coordinate the movements at the Century City Bunker and plan an attack and takeover of the Reno Bunker."

Jax tapped his fingers on the table. "We also need Damon and April to infiltrate the Pure group and make sure the women and kids are there voluntarily."

Damon winked at April. "You up to an undercover op, sweet thing?"

April blushed a pretty pink. "I've been undercover for two weeks, sugar lips. Let's hope you can keep up."

Moe coughed to cover a laugh. The woman was a fun one. It'd be interesting to see Damon land on his too-handsome ass over a woman. "I'm assuming I should continue my work to find organic farms in the meantime?"

"From the Century City Bunker," Lynne said. "In case we need to monitor your pregnancy. As soon as we take control of the Reno Bunker, we'll want to check out their data. Zach Barter mentioned using zinc and omega threes with B12 as part of his research, and that makes sense. Those work on brain development, which is where Scorpius localizes."

Moe tried to banish the constant fear for her baby. Greyson reached over and took her hand, enfolding it in his with heat and strength.

The moment caught her and held. Safe. She felt safe with him.

Sami cleared her throat. "I'm close to duplicating the file Greyson took, and I can tell you it's Bunker related. I think it's a map to them all. Maybe even schematics."

"And the president has it," Greyson said grimly. "Damn it."

Sami's eyes gleamed. "Yeah, but the encryption is impressive. We might crack it before he does."

Grey frowned. "I thought when I took the file that it'd all disappear."

Sami snorted, her chin lifting. "Nothing ever completely disappears from a hard drive, Grey. Ever."

Jax cleared his throat. "We also need a long-term plan that includes moving about six to seven hundred people from Los Angeles up north to Willamette, if that's where Moe still thinks we should go." He waited until she nodded before continuing. "I don't think we have a year. We might want to strip the Bunker here and move it all north."

Lynne looked around the room. "I've only been here two months, but it'll be hard to leave."

Had it only been two months since Lynne and her blue heart had reappeared in society again? Maureen couldn't believe what had happened in such a short time.

"We have to find the Brigade," Jax said. "To beat the president and Elite Force, we're gonna need them. It's time to send out scouts specifically for that."

"They could be mounting an attack against the president already," Greyson mused.

Tace grinned. "At least Atherton doesn't have VP Lake with him anymore. That'll throw him."

Maureen looked around, surprise taking her. "Lake is gone?"

Everyone went quiet.

Greyson pushed back from the table. "Good meeting. Damon? Get some sleep before you fall down. I'll show Moe our quarters while we're still here in Vanguard." He drew out her chair, not giving her much choice but to rise.

She stood, butterflies suddenly flapping in her stomach.

Raze cleared his throat. "If it matters, I kind of like the guy. Just saying."

Maureen grinned, amusement warring with tension inside her. "Good to know. Maybe I'll keep him."

Greyson took her hand and led her out of the war room and up a dingy flight of stairs to a landing.

Marcus Knight sat across from a doorway, his legs stretched out, his hawk-like gaze watching them. "Penny's sleeping," he muttered.

Maureen swallowed. If they woke the doctor up, would Marcus attack? Man, the guy needed help.

Greyson nodded. "All right. We're going to catch some sleep, too." He walked all the way down the hall, keeping his body between Marcus and Maureen when they passed the soldier. Finally, he nudged open a door. "I think this is us."

Us.

She followed him inside a small studio apartment that was missing a fridge. Not that they could use one. Instead, a bookcase took up the area where one had been in the corner that had once been a kitchen. Socks were stuffed into the bookcase.

A ripped orange sofa with a short coffee table made up the middle of the room, and a bed was neatly made against the corner. The floor was peeling linoleum without any rugs.

"We should get a rug," Greyson said, watching her gaze.

"We're going back to the Bunker anyway," she said, already wishing for a hot shower, even though it was so warm outside. "But this is, ah, quaint."

He drew her inside to the middle of the space, his gaze a soft gray, his mouth curved. "A couple of things. First, I killed the vice president. He burned down the farm."

She blinked. Murder should be wrong, right? "I'm glad you

did it." Whoa. She really meant it. "He was too dangerous, and now we're safer." She could always count on Greyson to keep them safe.

His eyes darkened. "I also took a shot at the president."

Her chin dropped. "You missed him?"

Grey lifted his head and then barked out a laugh. "That's what surprised you?"

She faltered. "Well, yeah. You're supposed to be this awesome sniper. How did you miss Atherton?"

Greyson shook his head and kissed her, his thumb caressing her jaw. He nibbled a bit and then leaned back. "Bulletproof glass. Or rather, bullet-resistant glass."

"How the heck?" she asked.

He shrugged. "Doesn't matter. I'll get him next time."

Why were her knees knocking together? Her breath sped up for some reason. "Okay," she said, looking around.

"Second," he continued, "it's you and me and this baby. No matter what happens. With the Mercs, with Vanguard, with the Bunker. It's you and me." He pulled his necklace over his head, unclasped it, and slid the ring off.

Then the deadliest man she'd ever met, ever even imagined, dropped to one knee. He barely had to look up to meet her gaze, he was so tall.

"I love you, Maureen Shadow. From the first second I saw you, from the first time we talked, from the moment you stood up to me...I knew it was you. I'll love you forever, and I'll keep you safe. Somehow." He slid Miss Julian's ring onto her finger.

Tears filled her eyes. Maureen couldn't speak. The pretty diamond sparkled in the daylight, promising her the world. Giving her him.

"Will you marry me?" he asked, his voice the low and gritty rumble she loved.

She nodded, tears falling down her cheeks. "Yes," she whispered. "I love you, Greyson." In the uncertain world, with a frightening future, she had this and now. Him. Love and something real.

He stood and kissed her, going deep, promising himself only to her. For eternity in that one kiss. She took it, leaning into him, trusting him to hold her.

Forever.

WINTER IGNITING - COMING EARLY 2018

AN EXCERPT:

This was crazy. Even in a world already gone to insanity, her going under cover was nutballs. April Snyder kept her face stoic even though her body rioted with a tenseness that made her neck ache with knots. "I can do it," she said quietly, lying her ass off.

Jax Mercury, the leader of Vanguard, sat across from her at the executive style conference table, his brown eyes soft. Which was incredibly rare. "You don't know the plan yet."

It didn't matter. Whatever the plan, she was in. "I have nothing to lose," she said quietly. Now that was the truth.

Jax sat back and crossed impressive arms. At the early hour, Vanguard headquarters, and especially his war room, was quiet. After Scorpius had infected and killed most of the world, Jax had created this somewhat safe haven in the middle of Los Angeles for survivors. Vanguard territory took up seven complete blocks of old apartment buildings, a couple of ex-drug houses, and bankrupted businesses. Jax ruled them all. "I'm concerned this will be too much for you."

She blinked and glanced at the empty chairs surrounding a table that must've belonged to a law firm at some point, considering the inlaid design in the middle. This was where Jax and his top lieutenants often planned how to survive. She didn't belong here, and she knew it. "Nothing is too much for me," she said, meaning it. She'd lost everything. Her husband, her daughter, her friends. Scorpius had killed them all. "You need me."

Jax's gaze narrowed as he studied her. "I'm not looking for somebody to go on a suicide mission."

She settled back in her chair. After her teenaged daughter had died, everyone had treated her with a soft touch, including Jax. But he'd never acted like she'd been destroyed. "I'm not looking to die, Jax. I don't want to die. But I don't really care if I do." She owed him that much of a truth. "I might be able to help some folks before I go, so why not?"

He didn't like her answer. By the tightening of his jaw, he definitely wasn't pleased.

The door opened, and Damon Winter strode inside, munching on a Twinkie. The world might've died, but preserved pastries lived on.

Damon winked at her.

April's breath caught. Damon was everything she was not. Big and tough and dangerous. Even before the world had basically ended, he'd been a cop in Los Angeles. Fighting bad guys. And he had that electric charisma she'd only seen in movie stars before now.

He pulled out a seat at the end of the table, finishing his breakfast. "What's the plan?" His voice was a low rumble.

Jax looked his way. "Did Tace release you medically?"

Damon rolled very brown and deep eyes. "Yes. I'm fine. The ribs have already healed, and Tace took stitches out of everywhere he'd slid the needle in. I'm ready for the Op, mom."

Jax grunted. "You've only been here a week, and I'm already regretting aligning with the Mercs."

Damon grinned. "We are a handful."

The Mercs were military soldiers, all men, that had taken over

Santa Barbara before it had burned to the ground. Now they were integrating into Vanguard territory.

April cleared her throat. "How's the integration coming?"

"Not well." Damon lost the smile. "It's a bit rocky."

"Good," Jax said.

April's shoulder's jerked. "Good? Why is that good?"

"We need internal strife for your mission," Jax said. He looked at her and then at Damon. "The Pure church has been courting you for months, trying to get you on board. But Damon's going to be the prize for them."

What? April shook her head.

Damon nodded. "Yep. I'm a prize. It's nice to be appreciated."

Jax rolled his eyes. "They want members and women, and we need to find out why. But they're also low in soldiers, and I'm sure they'd love to gather Damon into the ranks. So you're going to be the key to him, April."

Okay. She was starting to understand the strategy. The Pure church had set up inside Vanguard, and the members had not been infected by Scorpius. Neither had she nor Damon. "They've been slow to recruit me," she murmured.

Damon tapped his fingers on the table. "Catch me up to speed about this church. I don't have any details."

Jax twirled his knife on the table. "We don't know much, which is a problem. They've taken over an apartment complex in the western corner, and they have food and ammunition. No members have contracted Scorpius, thus The Pure."

Damon eyed April and then Jax. "What's the problem? The Scorpius bacteria is deadly, and they should be protected from infection if possible."

Jax lifted a shoulder. "Agreed. But we don't know how many kids are in there or if the members are there willingly. It's too secretive. Creepy, actually. Pastor Zachary King won't let us talk to any of them, and armed guards cover the complex. *In* my territory."

April leaned forward. "Just The Pastor. No name. He said God spoke to him and has decreed him The Pastor."

"Jesus," Damon muttered. "Sounds like a cult."

Jax sighed. "That's what I'm afraid of. Okay. I'd prefer to call him Pastor King so we don't get him confused with a prisoner I have at the Bunker named Zach Barter. So far, the name 'Zach' is causing me problems."

April winced. "We know there are at least five pregnant women in the Pure, and we have to find out if they are voluntary members. I want to do this, Jax."

"You're our best option," Jax said, a muscle ticking in his jaw. "They've been slowly making a move on you for a while."

"Only a few meetings and a lot of chance encounters," she said.

"They'll step it up if they think they can get Damon through you," Jax said, wincing and then pulling a knife from the back of his waist. "Forgot this was there." He plunked it on the table.

April swallowed, her gaze going to the rough hilt. At least it was in a sheath. "Through me? How?"

"Two ways. First, you're going to assist Damon with integrating the Mercs into Vanguard territory, so you have a reason to spend time together," Jax said.

Easy enough. "Okay," she said.

"And second, he's going to romantically pursue you. Big time," Jax finished.

Her body flushed hot. "Huh?"

Damon smiled, and this time a dimple showed in his left cheek. "This might be my favorite mission ever."

Warmth spread into her face, no doubt causing her to look like a tomato. Courage. She had to be brave with these guys. "Why don't *I* pursue *him*?" she retorted with as much spirit as she could drum up.

"Great plan," Damon said instantly, oozing charm.

Jax cut him a hard glare. "Knock it off." He faced April. "The church knows you and has watched you for months. You're not the type to pursue anybody. But they don't know Damon. We can make him into anybody we want right now."

Geez. Okay. So she wasn't a femme fatale. She'd been with one man her entire life, and then he'd died. So she truly had no argument. Except the idea of sexy Damon chasing her, a widow from suburbia, was ridiculous. "So we pretend a romantic, ah, relationship?"

"Why pretend?" Damon asked smoothly.

She gaped. Was he actually flirting with her?

Jax picked up his knife. "I told you to knock it off. I meant it." He glanced at them. "We're going that route, but we might have a problem."

Damon's gaze narrowed instantly. "Why?"

"Because you're black," Jax said bluntly, turning to look at her, "and she's white. Very white."

April's mouth gaped open. "Jax." Had he just said that?

The Vanguard leader met her gaze head on. "I don't have time to be politically correct, April. You're white, he's black, and this church has rules we don't know or understand. They're secretive, and my gut tells me something is wrong there. There's something bad going on, and racism might just be a part of it." He shrugged. "Or not. We just don't know."

"But still," she protested.

"I don't have a racist bone in my body," Jax muttered. "I'm Hispanic, and I have Native American, Korean, Anglo-Saxon, and Texan lieutenants."

She coughed. "Texan isn't a race."

"It should be," Jax returned. "Tace is one of a kind. But my point is, even though we're not racist assholes, the Pure church might be. They might not like interracial couples. Or premarital sex. Or blondes with big boobs. Who the hell knows. I want you to be prepared for that."

Damon looked at her, his gaze warm. "I like that you're offended and surprised by this. By the way."

She shifted in her seat. He was just too much. Dark eyes, rugged jaw, cut cheekbones. His chest was wide and muscled. With a gun strapped to his thigh and a knife to his calf, he oozed deadliness. That shouldn't be sexy...but it was. But she had no business viewing him like that. This was a mission—a job. "I don't know how to be pursued," she blurted out.

His chin lifted, and a different light entered his eyes. A predatory glint. "Then this should be fun."

Panic engulfed her, so she remained quiet.

Jax sighed and shoved away from the table as if bored with the entire conversation. "You two talk and come up with a game plan. April, last time Damon was here, we had him throw a fit about being around people who'd survived Scorpius."

"It wasn't exactly a fit," Damon drawled. "More like a loud objection. A manly one." He winked again.

Was he teasing her now?

Jax grumbled and stood, heading for the door. "Whatever. I'd like to get things in motion tonight. Damon—you're taking point. Figure it out." With the last words, he stomped out the door, shutting it loudly behind him.

Quiet descended.

Her throat clogged. "Um. What does taking point mean?"

Damon studied her, his gaze serious now that Jax had left the room. "I'm in charge of mission parameters."

Considering she'd never been on a mission in her life, she was okay with that fact. "Which are?"

He leaned toward her, wafting the scent of a wild forest her way. "We'll use our real jobs as a cover for this mission. Our first meeting will be today at noon, in the park that's been set up middle territory for the kids, to work on integrating the Merc soldiers into Vanguard."

"So we really do the job while also doing the other job," she said, blinking. This was confusing.

"Yeah. The more natural we are, the better." He reached out and planted his hand over hers.

Heat and electricity zapped through her. She looked at the difference in them. His hand was big enough to completely engulf hers and had scars across the knuckles. From fighting? She lifted wide eyes to him. "I don't know how to act. To pretend." She'd worked at a dentist office before Scorpius had descended, for Pete's sake.

"Just be you, blue eyes," Damon said. "React exactly as you would normally."

She pulled her hand from beneath his and set it in her lap. "Okay." There was no reason for them to hold hands. Why couldn't she breathe? His simple touch had overwhelmed her and forced sensations into her body she had no business feeling. "We don't need to pretend now."

His eyes glittered with a light she couldn't quite read. "Who's pretending?"

ACKNOWLEDGMENTS

I'm thrilled to bring the fourth book of the Scorpius Syndrome to readers, and I have many people to thank.

Thank you to my wonderful family, Big Tone, Karlina, and Gabe. I love you very much.

Thanks to Asha Hossain Design for the fabulous cover, Chelle Olson for the fantastic edits, Michael Pauley for the wonderful audio narrations of the Scorpius Syndrome Books, and The Killion Group for the great publicity plan.

Thank you to my agent, Caitlin Blasdell, who gives fantastic advice across the board, and who has been with me through six series. Thanks also to Liza Dawson and the entire Dawson gang for their hard work and support.

Thanks to Jillian Stein, Minga Portillo, Anissa Hammons, Rebecca's Rebels, Writer Space, and Fresh Fiction for getting the word out about the books.

Thanks to my constant support system: Jim and Gail English, Travis and Debbie Smith, Donald and Stephanie West, Jonah and Jessica Namson, and Herb and Kathy Zanetti.

OTHER BOOKS BY REBECCA ZANETTI (IN ORDER)

The Scorpius Syndrome Series

Prequel: Scorpius Rising

Mercury Striking

Shadow Falling

Justice Ascending

The Dark Protector Series

Fated (Book 1)

Claimed (Book 2)

Tempted (2.5)

Hunted (Book 3)

Consumed (Book 4)

Provoked (Book 5)

Twisted (5.5)

Shadowed (Book 6)

Tamed (6.5)

Marked (Book 7)

Realm Enforcers (Dark Protector spinoff)

Wicked Ride

Wicked Edge

Wicked Burn

Wicked Kiss

Wicked Bite

Dark Protectors: Reese Family

Teased

Tricked

Tangled

The Sin Brothers series

Forgotten Sins

Sweet Revenge

Blind Faith

Total Surrender

The Blood Brother series

Deadly Silence

Lethal Lies

Twisted Truths

The Maverick Montana series

Against the Wall

Under the Covers

Rising Assets

Over the Top

COMING in 2018:

* More Scorpius Syndrome Books

* A return to the Dark Protectors—Spring 2018

* The Requisition Force Series, starting with HIDDEN, Book 1 - Fall of 2018

CPSIA information can be obtained
at www.ICGtesting.com
Printed in the USA
BVHW031753010920
587828BV00001B/123